For the University of Texas at
San Antonio Library, as recommence
for the great tack in promoting
the study in spanish books.

Eduardo Jacqueau

9.27.94.

The Grass Rain

EDUARDO GARRIGUES

THE GRASS RAIN

A TALE OF MODERN AFRICA

TRANSLATED FROM THE SPANISH BY *Helen R. Lane*

MACMILLAN PUBLISHING COMPANY

NEW YORK

COLLIER MACMILLAN PUBLISHERS

LONDON

"You can't imagine how much I miss you, since you left for that land full of rhinoceroses and giraffes. The countryside is very beautiful now, because it has rained so much, and the fields are very green. The sheep are eating a lot of grass and the lambs are playing on the fields, close to their mothers. The wheat and barley are very tall now, so the horses are going to have plenty to eat.

" 'Escogido,' the horse, is also missing you, because the other day he saw a boy like you and he pricked his ears, so that everybody would know that he still remembers you."

—*Letter from* Don Joaquín Garrigues *to my son* Gonzalo

Macmillan Publishing Company
866 Third Avenue, New York, N.Y. 10022
Collier Macmillan Canada, Inc.

Library of Congress Cataloging in Publication Data

Garrigues, Eduardo.
  The grass rain.

    Translation of: Lluvias de hierba.
    I. Title.
PQ6657.A797L5813   1984   863'.64   84–9745
ISBN 0–02–542740–7

10   9   8   7   6   5   4   3   2   1

Printed in the United States of America

Although the scenery and social atmosphere in this book have been taken from direct experience, neither the story nor the characters in it have a direct connection with real facts or people.

Contents

PART TWO

PART THREE

PART FOUR

Acknowledgments

Like a bridge or a road, a novel is not made only by the person who conceives and constructs it, but also by those who travel through it. Among the friends with whom I often met during my stay in Kenya and who helped me know and enter an Africa that does not appear in textbooks, I wish to mention two, who have already been called by that whirlwind of the equatorial sun which turns everything to dust and ashes: René Babault, professional hunter and naturalist, who died in an airplane accident, and Ken Clark, manager of the Galana Ranch, killed in a skirmish with poachers from the coast.

And since it is not often that a novel written in Kenya by a Spanish author is translated into English in France for publication in America, my sincere thanks to those who made it possible.

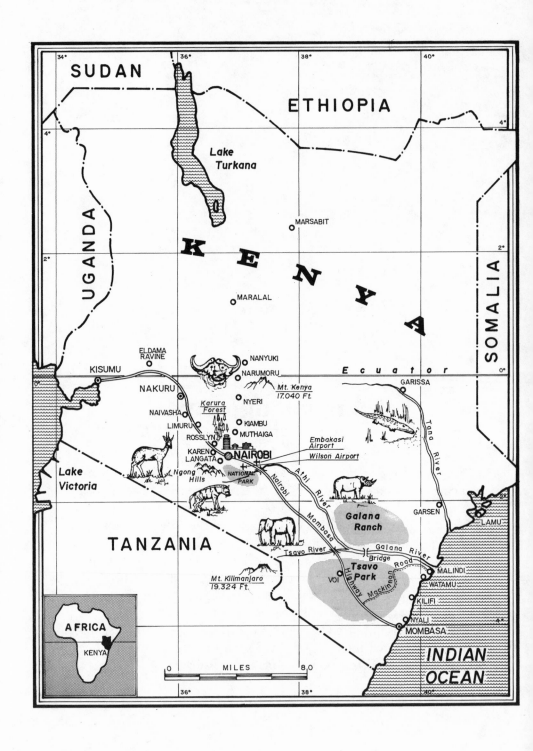

Prologue

THE HIGHWAY from Nairobi to Mombasa ran straight as a die for miles and miles across the plain stretching southward as far as the eye could see. At the halfway point, before reaching Tsavo Park—grayish vegetation and red earth—the road made its way up a high plateau covered with dense brush, with granite boulders and the fat trunks of baobabs standing out above it here and there. The path of the highway had been determined by the contours of the hills, and at times it ran between two cuts of red earth, with stretches of asphalt paving alternating with packed sand.

In the early morning hours of a Friday in August 1977, a white Peugeot bearing a diplomatic license plate was beginning to climb up this grade, and the brake lights flashed red in the morning fog each time the car slowed down to avoid a pothole or negotiate a badly cambered curve. Behind the wheel was John Murphy, Counselor of the American Embassy in Nairobi, described as an environmental expert on the diplomatic list. He had left Nairobi while it was still dark so as not to arrive in Mombasa in the stifling midday heat, driving slowly in the dim light, watching out for the metallic reflections from the eyes of antelopes grazing in the drainage ditches along the edge of the highway and sometimes bounding across it in one leap when startled by the headlights. Every so often he had had to brake after spying the silhouettes of dauntless giraffes impassively ambling along the road, their heads standing out as though outlined in India ink against the faint light dawning on the horizon.

As he left behind the curving section of the road, John lit a cigarette and put his foot to the floor, keeping to the center of the highway since he knew that nobody would be coming toward him from the other direction: Thus far, the only vehicles he had met since leaving Nairobi were a couple of gasoline trucks and one or two *matatus*, small buses full to overflowing with poultry and sleeping Africans.

On reaching the fence closing off the Tsavo Park area, he turned off the main highway and headed down a side road that led to the coast—Mackinnon Road—bypassing the town of Mombasa and the overcrowded Kilifi ferry. He knew this shortcut like the palm of his hand, and despite the fact that it was a dirt road there were not many potholes in it. He kept up his speed, leaving in his wake a cloud of reddish dust. And then, all of a sudden, a truck with all its lights out emerged from behind some bushes and darted out across the road, directly in his path. To avoid a collision, John veered abruptly to the other side of the road. But the wheels of the car skidded on the sand and struck the edge of the embankment, which acted as a trampoline, catapulting the car down the steep slope and sending it rolling over and over into the scrub below. On reaching the bottom, it crashed into the trunk of an enormous baobab, whose bark was dried out and rotten from having been girdled by elephants. And before the astonished eyes of a troop of baboons contemplating the scene from the thick forest cover, the car and the tree both caught fire at the same instant, immediately turning into a giant torch. The body of the driver had been thrown clear of the car and had landed a considerable distance away, amid a clump of thornbush.

The sun had appeared behind the hills, and for several minutes the only sounds to be heard in the valley were the crackling of the fire and the distant echo of the truck that had taken off down the highway toward Nairobi.

PART ONE

African Dawn

THE PLANE PASSED beyond the turbulent air above the desert, the engines resumed their steady throb, and the wings stopped shaking; the Fasten Safety Belts sign blinked off. Bob Fender had spent most of the night curled up in his blanket with his eyes wide open, as though the safety of the entire aircraft depended on his staying awake and sitting tight in his seat, not moving a muscle. He still did not dare get up from his seat, but did venture to slide one hand out from under the blanket and raise the little plastic curtain over the window next to him.

Dawn was now breaking, and a milky light was reflecting off the wings of the plane. They were still flying over desert country, no longer the landscape of sand dunes he had seen in the light of the moon, but rather one of rocks or seared earth, across which the first rays of the sun cast deep shadows. Here and there, nonetheless, the arid plain began to be dotted with grayish scrub growth, and low-lying hills of red earth topped by trees appeared. A meandering river snaked along beneath the fuselage of the plane, bordered by a broad belt of vegetation that in the faint dawn light seemed even denser and more mysterious.

From one of the banks of the river human eyes gazed with fascination at the blinking red and green navigation light of the plane darting above the treetops like a giant dragonfly: the eyes of Abdul Salim the Somali, and three other poachers belonging to the Kamba tribe. For several days now they had been following the track of a huge elephant heading northward along one bank of the Galana River. In a number of places the tracks of the big bull had mingled with those of other elephants that had scented that the rainy season in the mountains of Marsabit was about to begin and were fleeing that desert area. But each time Salim had been able to pick up the trail of the huge elephant again—enormous footprints, with deep wrinkles in the sole and a worn heel—and every so often they had found, alongside the trail of footprints, the marks made by the creature's great tusks as he rested them on the ground.

The night before, a large herd of elephants had come down to drink at a water hole near the spot on the shore of the river where the poachers were camped, and the latter were now waiting for the dawn light to penetrate the dense forest so as to be able to draw closer and see if the huge male was among the herd. Gripping the barrel of his rifle, Salim was muttering prayers in the hope of keeping a treacherous breeze from carrying their scent to the pachyderms and thus causing them to stampede. Hugging the ground like a great feline amid the tall grass, he was closely watching the movements of the great hulking beasts as they entered and left the mudhole, as though they were seeking to become one with the primal ooze once again.

A sudden breath of air rippled the surface of the waterhole, lifting the fog, and the trembling fingers of the poachers pointed to the enormous male ripping up water plants in the middle of the brackish pool: *Ndume, ndume,* the three of them whispered, almost in unison. The big bull shook its head, scenting danger, and flapped its immense ears as it waved its trunk in the air, emitting clouds of water vapor like an enormous censer. It took Salim only a few seconds to aim the sight of his rifle along an imaginary line centered between the elephant's two eyes at the height of the third wrinkle in its trunk. The flash of the rifle shot then tore through the fog hovering above the

4

river, and the thunder of the herd's stampede echoed all along the course of it, putting to flight the flocks of sand grouse that had alighted along its banks to drink. When the cloud of dust that the herd had raised as it thundered off had blown away, the poachers gathered round the body of the dead elephant lying in the mud with its great tusks pointing toward the sky. On the horizon which was just beginning to take on a deep blue tinge, the vapor trail of the plane stood out in sharp outlines, like a fine brushstroke on a painted bowl.

Many miles downstream, where the chocolate-colored waters of the Galana emptied into the harbor of Malindi, another man was contemplating the dawn light filtering through the palm trees along the beach and beginning to flood his window with a golden glow. He knew that when the first rays of the sun stole beneath the venetian blind and across the floor tiles of his bungalow, Guni, his wife, would awaken and his erotic agony would begin. For Alex Townsend-Reeves, life's miracle was repeated each morning as he hastened to make frantic love to his wife in a fit of desperation, never sure that he could stay the course till the end, until suddenly something would stir within him, a strange vital sap that caused him to be reborn from his ashes, to overcome all his indispositions, and to satisfy her again and yet again.

Nonetheless the day would come, some gray dawn as the seagulls along the breakwater were beginning to pierce the air with their shrill cries, when his poor abused body would be unable to respond to the call of his woman. And what would happen then? Guni was almost fifteen years younger than he was, and all her typical Teutonic energies were still intact; whereas in his own case, the decadent blue blood of his glorious British ancestors had been sapped by a telling combination of leisurely colonial life and tropical diseases. His entire body recoiled at the thought that in a few moments hence he would be pinned down by Guni's powerful body and would feel her tongue forcing itself into his mouth, his ears, and any other orifice within her reach. A pointed, rasping tongue that could lengthen and contract at will, like the body of a slug. Though elaborating a metaphysics of coitus was the thought farthest removed from Alex's pragmatic Anglo-Saxon mind, he sometimes wondered whether the daily miracle of his morning erection was not a defense mechanism of his entire body against the onslaughts of that feminine tongue.

Just two weeks before, his wife's lover had been killed in a car

5

accident while driving to the coast. On the first four days following his death, Guni had gone off to weep over his grave and had tossed and turned in bed, moaning like a wounded lioness. She had not even deigned to speak to her husband, as though he didn't exist. But as the fifth day dawned, she had opened her eyes swollen from weeping and fixed her gaze on Alex, sitting in an armchair contemplating her as she slept. She got out of bed and came toward him with such a strange expression on her face that for a moment he thought she was going to rake his flesh with her fingernails; but instead she had taken him by the hand and led him to the bed, making love to him with an unprecedented eagerness and intensity. Many times in the past he had felt a wave of revulsion at the thought of his wife giving herself to another man and had violently wished for the death of his rival. But now he suddenly realized with the painful clearsightedness that the irreparable brings in its wake that the day that his wife's lover had died he had lost his most indispensable ally.

Knowing that Guni might awaken at any moment, he crept out from under the mosquito netting as silently as a spider and stole out of the room on tiptoe. He washed quickly in the bathroom, put on his shorts and a work shirt, and went out onto the veranda. Beyond the row of palm trees lay a beach of gleaming white sand; at this hour the surface of the sea was as smooth as glass, and the only sign of the thrust of the tide was a slight froth of foam along the line of the breakwater. Kneeling at the water's edge, an African fisherman was cleaning crabs with huge shells.

Alex would have liked to take a stroll along the beach, but the presence of the fisherman hunched over the white sand like a black beetle intimidated him. He went back into the bungalow and poured himself a double vodka at the bar. How good this first one of the day tasted: "the hair of the dog . . ." as the old saying went. All the walls of the living room were covered with hunting trophies: heads of impalas, kudus, buffaloes, lions, leopards. He had shot very few—in fact none—of these animals himself; the majority of them had been bought very cheaply from dealers on the black market, or else they had been gifts from hunter friends. Even gambling debts owed him had helped complete his collection. But after making up so many stories for tourists and visitors (who did not know that Alex was gun-shy and had never stepped more than ten paces away from a safari car) he had ended up believing his own lies and now contemplated his trophies with the genuine pride of the hunter gazing at game that

6

he himself has downed. As he looked at the bristling horns of a buffalo or the sharp teeth of a lion, a shiver would run down his spine as he thought of what a close escape he had had on this or that imaginary occasion when he had gone out tracking wild beasts.

There was one trophy missing, however, and unquestionably one of the most important. Despite all the bartering and swapping and dickering that he'd done, he had never managed to include a rhinoceros, one of the five great trophies of African big-game hunting, in his collection. It was becoming more and more difficult to come by one of those monsters with a phallic nasal appendage; poachers had taken so many of them that the species was very nearly extinct, thanks to the astronomical prices that rhinoceros horn brought in Arab countries and the Far East. Could it really be true that powdered rhino horn had aphrodisiac virtues, as Orientals believed?

After breakfast had been served, Bob Fender just managed to drop off to sleep when the loudspeaker began to hiss, announcing that they were flying over Mount Kenya. The sight of the twin peaks piercing the canopy of clouds with the white tongue of the glacier boxed between the two narrow jaws of rock took his breath away. From that point on, the flight seemed very short. The landscape had changed completely. The arid plain had turned into a succession of gentle hills and little valleys, with alternating coffee plantations and cornfields and stretches of luxuriant vegetation. He barely had time to open the novel that he had bought at the airport in Rome when the voice of the stewardess came over the loudspeaker again, informing the passengers that the plane had begun its descent and in a few minutes they would be landing at the Nairobi airport. The city lay sleeping against a background of hills, still wrapped in a blanket of fog; only the cylindrical silhouette of the Kenyatta Conference Center emerged above the haze, reflecting the reddish sun in its steel and glass panels like the eyes of some giant insect.

Before landing, the plane traced a wide circle above the hills, flying over the plain of the National Park at a low altitude and giving the tourists their first glimpse of wildlife: a few herds of antelope that could equally well have been scattered bushes on the parched grazing ground, and two or three vague animal shapes with necks sufficiently long to have been giraffes. Then came the screech of scorched rubber tires as the wheels of the plane touched down on the concrete runway and the roar of engines thrown into reverse. Despite himself Bob felt a shiver of excitement: He was in Africa! And with the same solemnity with which one might remove a chastity belt, he unhooked the buckle of the safety belt.

He peered out through the little window at the people walking out to the plane to meet the passengers, but did not recognize John Murphy's face among them. Perhaps he wouldn't recognize him; people do change a lot in ten years. Nonetheless, all during his long wait in line at the booths where passports and health certificates were being checked, he was quite sure that Murphy would be appearing at any moment. It was only when he arrived in the luggage reclaiming room and didn't see John that he began to feel nervous. It was strange that John wasn't there to meet him, after he'd written in his last letter that he'd come to the airport personally to pick him up. Bob remembered that back in the days when he was a student, Murphy had seldom been on time; he had such a charming way of offering some stupid excuse for having kept you waiting, accompanied by smiles and hugs, that you forgave him.

Bob called him from a phone booth right there in the luggage claim area, but no one at John Murphy's house answered. Through the glass door of the phone booth he could see the baggage carousel going round and round like a trained snake, with frequent jerks and convulsions; it didn't look as though his suitcase had arrived yet. A group of Hindu passengers with snow-white turbans and brilliantined mustaches were milling about the metal snake, picking up all sorts of odd-shaped bundles, as though they had managed to smuggle out the Taj Mahal piece by piece.

He dialed Murphy's number again, in case he'd made a mistake before, but there was no answer this time either; the ringing of the phone at the other end of the line sounded faint and far away. He had the peculiar feeling that it was ringing in an empty house. He then tried the embassy number, and was reassured to hear the sound of a female voice with a distinct American accent.

"Good morning. I'd like to speak to Mr. Murphy please. My name is Fender, Robert Fender."

A few moments of frozen silence went by.

"I'm afraid I can't put Mr. Murphy on the line. . . ."

"In that case I'd like to leave a message for him. Please tell him that I'm waiting at the airport, as we agreed, but that I can take a taxi to the embassy if he'll give me the address."

The quavering voice of the switchboard operator then answered:

"Mr. Murphy died two weeks ago in a car accident." There was a pause, and then she added: "Would you like to speak to somebody else?"

Bob felt as though he'd been hit over the head with a baseball bat.

"But how is that possible? Just last week I received a letter from him telling me that he'd come to the airport to pick me up and that he could put me up at his house. What a terrible thing!"

"A tragedy like that always happens that way—when a person least expects it. Mr. Murphy's car went off the road as he was driving down to the coast."

"I'm really dumbfounded. Could I please speak with the Ambassador, or with somebody else on the embassy staff?"

"Let me remind you, Mr. Fender, that it's only seven A.M. here in Nairobi; the Ambassador and the other diplomats won't be coming in till nine; I'm just the night switchboard operator."

"I see. I think perhaps the best thing would be for me to come to the embassy after I've dropped off my luggage. The thing is that I was scheduled to leave tomorrow for Mombasa and was counting on having certain data and documents that I need for my study. And it was John Murphy who was going to get them for me."

"If your study has anything to do with ecology, Mr. Maguire, the deputy, is taking care of such matters since Mr. Murphy's death. But since Mr. Murphy was a friend of yours, perhaps the Ambassador will see you himself."

"Thanks very much for your help, in any case. I'm going to try to get a hotel room now, and I'll come by the embassy later. What a terrible tragedy!"

After one last shudder, the carousel had meanwhile lain down and died. Not a sign of his suitcases. As he followed a customs officer who dragged his feet as though the soles of his shoes were lined with lead through endless narrow corridors to the claims office, he tried to analyze his feelings with regard to the death of his friend. In fact they hadn't seen each other for some time and they'd gotten in touch with each other again by sheer chance; John Murphy happened to be the person at the embassy in Nairobi in charge of matters connected with the environment, and he had replied when Bob had written to the embassy with certain inquiries concerning his specialty. Even so, he was surprised at his own lack of feeling, on learning the news of his death; all he had felt was a certain uneasiness, a vague malaise, along with annoyance at the loss of his suitcases. He did not even have a clear memory of what John Murphy's face looked like exactly. Everything melted in the halo of fog and humidity hovering over the airport buildings.

The plane had taken off again, heading for Mombasa; the only things visible on the deserted runway were big black birds flying along just above the ground, carrying off in their beaks bits of paper and little scraps of food they'd found in some litter basket.

South of Rome

IT HAD RAINED in Nairobi during the night, and once again Ambassador Poire had suffered from insomnia. Bursts of rain had pecked angrily at his window like flocks of birds trapped on the other side of the glass. On stormy nights, the guards on duty at his residence were in the habit of taking refuge on the porch, which happened to be just below his bedroom window, and as the torrential rain grew heavier and heavier, they would pass from hand to hand a bottle of cheap cane brandy that had been hidden beneath a raincoat; their voices and their laughter would gradually grow louder and louder, ending at times in shouts and fights. It was really a bother that the night watchmen had fallen into the habit of holding their social get-togethers right under his bedroom window, out of all the buildings comprising the residence compound. But the Ambassador had never dared say anything to hurt the feelings of these *askaris*—as they were called in Swahili—who after all stayed awake the whole night through just so he and his family might rest in peace.

William D. Poire was not a career diplomat, but a black lawyer from Savannah, Georgia, who had got his start in politics as a result of the racial concessions of the 1960s. After working for the Democratic campaign of '76, he got his appointment as ambassador—somebody, at the State Department thought it would be a good idea to send a black ambassador to Africa, a representative of a multiracial society. Until then, Poire had scarcely even been outside the States, and had never set foot on the African continent. As he put it, with a note of pride in his voice, "I've never been south of Rome," which was, geographically speaking, incorrect, since his native city of Savannah lay at the same latitude as the port of Alexandria, in Egypt.

Poire had accepted the African post with high hopes, as a sentimental pilgrimage to his ancestral land, and a way of knowing a people who were more natural and simple, less spoiled by civilization. But African politics had turned out to be much more complex and tortuous than it looked from Washington. To begin with, his African colleagues didn't receive him as the long-lost brother from across the Atlantic, but as the representative of a powerful Western nation that maintained relations with the racist regime of South Africa and had supported the last colonial bastions to the bitter end. The fact that he was a black American made his African counterpart all the more suspicious and hostile, as though he were a fraud, a white man hiding under black skin. And then they seemed disappointed by the fact that he could not speak Swahili. In fact, sometimes he had problems in getting understood by his own servants.

Even on the purely sensory level there was something indefinable about Africa that made him uneasy and sapped his energies. Despite the radiant sun and the clear air of the highlands, the Ambassador had a secret presentiment that storm clouds were in the offing, political and social upheavals that would soon darken the horizon of this Eden. If the death of John Murphy, in circumstances that still were not at all clear, had had such a profound effect on him, it was not only because of the esteem and affection that he had had for his colleague, but also because that catastrophe was like the first loud knock at the door by the hand of a tragic fate.

The light was just beginning to filter between the branches of the trees, but the birds were already stirring amid the leaves quivering in the breeze. There was always something disquieting about that silent African dawn reeking of damp earth and decayed leaves, of vegetable detritus. The smell of humus; in a word, of death.

Taking care not to disturb his wife Martha, who was sleeping beside him so peacefully that it almost irritated him, he got out of bed, put on his bathrobe and slippers, and stole out of the bedroom. Fortunately, before setting foot on the top stair, he remembered to turn off the electronic alarm hooked up to the stairway, which he had

11

set off inadvertently more than once during his sleepless nocturnal ramblings. Foreseeing yet another attack of insomnia, he never went to bed without leaving documents requiring his attention at hand in the library next to the dining room; this would not be the first time that the first rays of the sun would find him hard at work next to the fireplace there. On this day, however, he was just finishing arranging some papers on the rug in neat piles when he heard a car turning into the drive. It was a long avenue lined with jacaranda trees, and the flowers that had fallen during the storm crackled beneath the tires with the sound of wood catching fire. Who could be coming to see him at this early hour?

Immediately thereafter he heard the dogs barking in the back patio, and in a few moments the patter of Joseph's bare feet. Joseph was his houseboy; he had spotted the light in the library and was coming at a run to tell him something.

"Excellency," Joseph said, after respectfully bowing his head for the sake of protocol, "there's a man who's just arrived who wants to see you. An American," he added as he finished buttoning his white uniform jacket.

"An American? What's his name? I can't be at the beck and call of every tourist who loses his passport in a park. That's what the services at the Consulate are for!"

"He says his name is Felder, no, Fender, that's it, Robert Fender, and that he's a friend of Mr. Murphy's. He's just come in on the plane from Rome."

On hearing this, the expression on the Ambassador's face changed completely as he removed his reading glasses and immediately rose from his chair.

"Show Mr. Felder—or Fender—in."

Joseph was a bit taken aback by the Ambassador's sudden change of demeanor and stood rooted to the spot for a moment, scrutinizing him from head to foot, taking in the Ambassador's carpet slippers and the red satin bathrobe that he was wearing over his pajamas—the gift of Castor Kingley, the boxer, during the Democratic campaign of '76. The champion's robe had a huge fist edged in black on the back and on the front pocket the words I'LL CREAM YOU in flaming red letters. The houseboy then turned and left the room at a rapid little barefoot trot, thinking to himself that his previous boss, Sir Walter Puntken (F.X., V.C., V.D., Y.M.C.A.), the British High Commissioner, would never have received a visitor in a boxer's bathrobe and with papers scattered all over the rug. The farthest that the distin-

12

guished British diplomat had ever allowed himself to go had been to appear at the official ceremonies celebrating independence dressed as though he were attending a cricket match, taking advantage of the fact that the gala celebration was being held out of doors.

Joseph returned after a moment, preceding the visitor, whom he endeavored to announce in the most formal tone he could muster:

"Mr. Fenler; I mean Fender."

The visitor did not exactly give the appearance of having come straight from an opening performance at the opera; apart from his tired, drawn face and his beard more than twelve hours old, his pants were badly wrinkled, his shirt was missing the top button, and his tie was all crooked. The Ambassador had seen many a traveler who had just arrived from Europe a bit the worse for wear after the long flight, the bad connections, and the exasperating bureaucracy of African airports, but this man looked more like the survivor of a terrible shipwreck.

"So you're Mr. Fender," the Ambassador said, extending a hand with his most affable smile, his words sounding a bit like Stanley's famous "Dr. Livingstone, I presume."

Plainly ill at ease with his sudden intrusion, Bob took heart upon being so warmly welcomed:

"I apologize, Excellency, for bursting in on you at your home like this. I've just arrived on the plane from Rome and I told the taxi driver to take me to the Embassy; it was only after I'd already rung the bell that I noticed that this was your private residence and not the embassy offices."

"You don't need to explain, Mr. Fender. Even though we weren't certain of the exact day that you'd be arriving, we've been expecting you. . . ."

"Oh, so you knew I was coming then!" Bob exclaimed, unable to conceal his surprise.

After casting a sly, knowing look in his direction the Ambassador went on: "And I must say you did precisely the right thing by coming straight here. One can never be too cautious. And it will be easier for us to have a quiet talk together here, don't you think?"

Bob nodded his head, at a loss for words. From that moment on, the two of them carried on a conversation at cross purposes, with an ambiguity as palpable as the sharp outline of their silhouettes cast on the whitewashed wall of the study by the oblique rays of sunlight entering through the windows.

The Ambassador broke off the conversation as Joseph entered to serve them cups of tea and slices of buttered toast. When he had left the room again, the Ambassador went on:

"I hope you didn't have too much trouble getting through customs. With the number of ecologists coming here for the UNICORN Conferences, I don't imagine the arrival of one more scientist is calculated to arouse much curiosity on the part of the authorities."

"No, I must say I had no major problems, except that they lost my baggage."

"Don't worry about it. That's something that happens quite often, especially on flights from Rome. I trust you didn't have any sensitive material in your bags that might compromise you."

"No, of course not, there was nothing of particular value in them —just some biology manuals that I checked out of the archives of the Food and Agricultural Organization in Rome and other documents pertaining to the report on grass that I'm preparing."

"In other words, even if it occurs to them to open your bags, the manuals and the documents would merely confirm your identity. So it's studies on grasses, is it? That's fine, just fine."

The Ambassador beamed a little conspiratorial smile his way as he said this, and although Bob didn't really see what was so amusing about his having lost documents that he'd been working on for several months, he smiled back at him so as not to appear impolite, as he swallowed a mouthful of hot tea.

"What really floored me was the news of John Murphy's death. Even though I hadn't seen him for years, we went through college together."

"We were all very fond of Murphy, both his co-workers and his superiors, and we're all deeply affected by this irreparable loss . . . above all in the present circumstances." The Ambassador paused a moment and then went on, "Nonetheless, as far as your investigation is concerned, I wouldn't leap to conclusions if I were you. You should trust only in what you yourself can verify, with your acute sense of observation and your proven efficiency."

"Naturally, in a study of this type, it's necessary to gather field data. But even so I'd very much like to have some supplementary information, on the characteristics of the region, and all the rest; Murphy himself no doubt had gathered documents that might be of great interest to me."

"Of course. All the background material we've been able to collect is all ready for you."

14

"I can see that you're perfectly organized."

"I'll tell you frankly that I myself usually keep my distance from these operations—let's call them *ecological* studies, just to make ourselves clear, all right?" He gave the word special emphasis.

"Certainly. Ecological or environmental is the proper word."

"In this case however, the matter at hand struck me as sufficiently important . . . to have personally put in a request that an expert be sent."

"I genuinely appreciate your collaboration. It's true that I've been working in this field for a number of years, and I trust I won't disappoint those who, like yourself, are giving me a helping hand."

"On the contrary, I feel very reassured to know that you're here. I suppose that you'll be wanting to leave for the coast as soon as possible?"

"Yes. I was thinking in fact of taking the plane for Mombasa tomorrow; I have to confirm the reservation. The manager of the Galana Ranch, Patterson, is to come to meet me at the Tamarind Restaurant, in Mombasa, and we'll leave from there for the interior. . . ."

"You needn't think it necessary to tell me all the details of the operation. I presume that you already have your own contacts; nevertheless, the Consul in Mombasa is at your service at all times if you should need him for anything."

"I really don't know how to thank you for your extraordinary kindness."

"On the contrary, we're the ones who should be grateful to you for having agreed to undertake this mission. As for the information you need, I think it's better to have it brought to your hotel. In that way you won't need to drop by the embassy; we're under the impression that the Soviets keep a very close watch on everyone who enters and leaves our offices. And the Kenyans have similar intelligence services of their own. So I think it's advisable not to arouse suspicion unnecessarily."

"I quite understand. I thought, however, that our relations with this country were more or less cordial."

"It's a love-hate relation, you know. On the one hand they need us, but on the other hand they hate us . . . as is the case almost everywhere."

"Of course, of course," Bob agreed, surprised at the Ambassador's frankness.

"I'll have the documentation that you need brought to your hotel by Ralph Maguire, my deputy, who's been taking care of 'ecological' matters since Murphy's death. In that way you can consult with him in case you need any additional information."

"Thank you very much, but I don't really believe that that will be necessary. You've done more than enough already."

"Your mission is not an easy one and the least we can do is to give you as much help as possible. Will you be registered at the hotel under the name of Fender?"

"Yes, of course: Robert Fender. The taxi driver recommended the Hotel Norfolk."

"Fine. It's a rather nice hotel, it seems to me, and in an inconspicuous location. Remember that you're entitled to a discount since you're an ecologist. They offer one to all those attending the conferences, and it might seem suspicious if you didn't ask for it."

"Don't worry. I'll ask for a special price. Thanks again for everything, and especially for the breakfast," Bob said, rising to his feet. He was beginning to feel almost embarrassed by this overwhelmingly kind reception.

The Ambassador rose and clasped Fender to the bosom of his boxer's bathrobe with a big friendly hug.

"I wish you all kinds of luck—and above all, take care!"

As he was leaving the Ambassador's residence, comfortably seated in one of the official embassy cars and being driven down the imposing avenue carpeted in jacaranda flowers, Bob thought that the interest that the Ambassador had shown in his study of grass was really extraordinary. He was also certain that there had been something distinctly odd about their conversation, but since he hadn't met many diplomats in his life, he concluded that that manner of talking in circumlocutions and subtle hints, that conspiratorial tone of voice, was the usual way in which ambassadors expressed themselves. Nevertheless, this one surely was a diplomat who was somewhat out of the ordinary, since doubtless they did not all display the same consuming interest in the environment or parade about their residences in the ringside bathrobe of a world middleweight champion. But given the circumstances in which he had arrived in this city nothing that might possibly happen could really surprise him.

The Expert

THE AMERICAN EMBASSY in Nairobi was housed in a modern building on Wabera Street, between the grounds of the Parliament and the
broad esplanade of the Conference Center, whose tubular tower
could be seen from the four points of the compass. That morning, His
Excellency W. D. Poire arrived at the embassy earlier than usual, and
even before taking a look at the telegrams left on his desk every day
for him, he asked the switchboard operator to put in a call to
Mombasa.

"See if you can get me the Minister of State; tell him it's urgent,
and if he tries to give you an excuse, tell him I'm ready to take the
first plane leaving for the coast and come down to talk to the President himself."

The Ambassador paced nervously up and down his office, rehears-
ing the incisive phrases with which he was intending to cut short the
smooth talk of the African Minister, who was as cunning and slippery
as a rattlesnake. From the big picture window, there was a view of the
entire south of the city, the National Park, and farther in the distance,
the Athi plains, bisected by the line of the Nairobi–Mombasa highway, as neat as though it had been marked off with a ruler and chalk.
To the right, where the park area ended, were the Ngong Hills, whose
rugged profile kept changing shape and color with an almost animal-
like undulation as clouds drifted past and the light grew brighter or
dimmer.

Unconsciously, his eyes were drawn to the tower of the Conference
Center standing out haughtily above the other buildings, like a great
burial mound erected in honor of a modern divinity. When Poire
had accepted the post of Ambassador in Nairobi, he had not known
that a United Nations Center for the Conservation of Nature
and Other Resources—UNICORN—even existed; he had never been

17

able to understand why they had decided to locate such an important ecological center in that small city with its colonial atmosphere, surrounded by golf courses and national parks—perhaps precisely because it was a place far enough removed from other conference centers for everyone to realize that a new idea was involved: saving the earth.

Josiah Munyoka, Minister of State for Home Affairs, opened the venetian blinds of his suite at the Nyali Beach Hotel overlooking the tropical gardens and the beach. The tide was beginning to come in over the deserted strand; there was only one man strolling along the water's edge, accentuating the desolation of the gray horizon and the calm ocean. Suddenly a ray of sun filtered beneath the clouds, shedding its light on the naked body of a young Somali girl sleeping in the Minister's bed; her head was shaved bare and her body was almost a child's, except for the round breasts whose erect nipples were pointing upward toward the ceiling. The Minister looked at his watch, closed the venetian blinds halfway, and sat down alongside the young girl. But at that moment the phone rang. The girl gave a start and covered herself with the sheet, looking about her with frightened eyes.

On picking up the receiver, he heard the switchboard operator's agitated voice:

"Mr. Minister, I know you left instructions not to disturb you, but the American Ambassador insists on speaking with you; he says that if he doesn't reach you by phone, he'll come down to speak personally with the President."

On the other end of the line, W. D. Poire tapped his knuckles on his office desk, waiting to be connected with the Minister; finally, he heard Munyoka's mellifluous voice, punctuated by the typical stammer of a British university graduate:

"Munyoka here. Is this Ambassador Poire?"

"My dear Minister, I've been trying to talk with you for several days now, and you haven't answered any of my calls. Two weeks have gone by since our Counselor, John Murphy, was killed on the highway between Mombasa and Malindi, and I still have received no police report or official document of any sort that would allow me to inform Washington as to the circumstances under which the accident occurred."

As the Ambassador was speaking, the door of his office opened a crack, and a middle-aged man with metal-framed glasses, dressed in a light blue suit and a striped shirt, poked his head in. He was about to

18

withdraw it again when the Ambassador caught sight of him and motioned him to come in and sit down. Raph Maguire, Deputy Ambassador, carefully closed the door behind him, crossed the office in two strides, and sat down in an armchair next to the window, lowering his buttocks into it very carefully so that the leather cushion wouldn't make a creaking sound. He sat there as motionless as a paperweight or a stalk of Swiss chard; only an occasional fleeting glint behind the thick lenses of his glasses indicated that he was alive and attentively following the conversation on the phone.

"Yes, yes, I know that the accident occurred on a deserted side road and in the very early hours of the morning, but even so you won't deny that it seems just a bit strange that no one informed the police for over forty-eight hours, by which time the body was decomposed and half devoured by scavengers. To say the least, they are extremely surprised in Washington at this lack of interest on the part of these authorities in an accident that cost the life of a diplomatic representative of a friendly nation such as America . . ."

He finally hung up the phone, visibly irritated, and let off steam with Maguire:

"Nothing, the usual run-around, high-flown phrases, excuses, promises . . . you know these people. He told me he wouldn't leave a single stone unturned, but there's no trusting him. He says he's called upon the services of a very efficient person to investigate the accident."

Maguire swallowed, wet his lips with the tip of his tongue, and wiped his glasses with the back of his tie:

"Ambassador, if you'll allow me to offer you a piece of advice in this case, if I were in your place I wouldn't put the screws on too hard. No matter how many reports and explanations we may eventually get out of these people, we aren't going to bring Murphy back to life. And moreover . . ." He raised his hand, seeing that the Ambassador was becoming impatient.

"Please let me finish. Moreover, we must realize that these people are going through one of their most difficult moments, politically speaking, since the country won its independence. The government in power is losing more and more prestige, while on the other hand the leader of the opposition, Muriuki, is gaining in popularity by the day and growing bolder and bolder, to the point that he might well become downright dangerous."

"I don't believe he'd prove dangerous to us."

19

"I do, in many ways. Any profound change in this country would be bound to affect our interests, especially since Muriuki is of the opinion that we've given too much support to the present government, so that if he comes to power, he'll doubtless react by taking exactly the opposite tack."

"Perhaps the fault is partly ours for having always supported those regimes in Africa which in the end turn out to be the most unpopular."

"In my opinion the question of unpopularity is, in the final analysis, irrelevant to our interests. On the other hand, I think that what is of legitimate concern to us is that we be granted the use of logistic facilities in the port of Mombasa and allowed to refuel our planes in case of an emergency. We have assurances on these two points from the present government, but I don't believe Muriuki would be that cooperative if he came to power."

"In any case," the Ambassador said, "we're straying off the point that we were discussing before. You must realize that we cannot allow a counselor of our embassy, one of my closest collaborators, to vanish in thin air, so to speak, in the Tsavo Desert, in extremely suspect circumstances."

This time it was the Ambassador who cut Maguire short, just as the latter opened his mouth to say something, "Yes, I know you're going to tell me that we don't have any concrete proof that there's been foul play, but you'll also concede that we can't in all conscience affirm the contrary either."

Maguire shot back: "I assure you, as a diplomat and a colleague of Murphy's, that your interest in getting to the bottom of this matter seems to me to be altogether legitimate and does you honor. But I also believe that in certain cases national interests must come before individual concerns, however legitimate the latter may be. And furthermore . . ." Maguire paused and wet his lips with his tongue again, before continuing, ". . . Furthermore, haven't we already requested that the special services send us an agent to investigate Murphy's case?"

The Ambassador smiled enigmatically. He knew that the question would come up sooner or later, and had his answer all ready:

"It's for that very reason that it's in our interest to point out to them how inefficient they are. After this conversation with Munyoka I feel perfectly free to begin our own investigation. If there should be a protest later, we could always remind them that two weeks after the accident, we still had no information whatsoever as to the circumstances under which it occurred."

"Why should we begin to prepare ourselves for a protest, when everything is still up in the air? We haven't even received confirmation from Rome that the 'expert' is being sent."

This time the Ambassador practically burst out laughing.

"In that case, let us suppose," he said, stressing every syllable, "that the man we're waiting for is about to arrive at any moment; or let's even suppose that he's already in Nairobi, and that I've already had a talk with him."

"That's not possible," Maguire said, turning pale. "The UNICORN Conference doesn't begin till the end of next week, and his cover is that he's coming here in order to attend that meeting."

"That may be when the Conference begins, but the expert nonetheless arrived from Rome today. He came to see me at home straightway, which seemed to me exactly what he should have done, in view of the circumstances," the Ambassador crowed.

"That's not possible!" Maguire repeated, with a more and more agitated look on his face.

"It's just as possible as the fact that he's leaving again right away —tomorrow—for Mombasa. A charming man, incidentally, this Fender. Moreover, he makes a very convincing *ecologist*."

"What did you say his name was? Fender?" Maguire stammered, turning deathly pale.

"Yes, Fender, Robert Fender, unless of course he's using an assumed name. What's the matter? Aren't you feeling well?" the Ambassador asked, seeing the look on Maguire's face.

The latter made a visible effort to control his nervousness before answering:

"The name of the expert they're sending isn't Fender, but Sweeny, Charles Sweeny. I met him several years ago on a mission in Turkey, and he's certainly the last person in the world that anybody would ever take for an ecologist, what with his broad shoulders, his bull neck and the huge scar on his cheek. He looks so much like a thug he almost escapes people's notice. They immediately conclude that nobody with a face like that could possibly be a secret agent."

"Well, that's surely not the man I'm talking about." The Ambassador was also beginning to have a worried look on his face. "Fender is tall and thin and gives every appearance of being a real scientist."

"Wait a minute. Now that I remember, there was in fact a man

21

named Fender who was to arrive along about now to make a study on the use of grasslands, or something of the sort, on one of those ranches down on the coast—a report for the Food and Agricultural Organization. Maybe it's the same Fender. . . ."

The Ambassador was dumbfounded.

"Report on grass . . ." he stammered, as though talking to himself. "I fear that there has been a most regrettable confusion," he added, leaning slightly on the edge of his desk for support. "I think you'd best go speak personally with Mr. Fender and try to clear up any misunderstanding we may have given rise to—inadvertently."

Returning to his office, Maguire slammed the door behind him, locked himself in, and collapsed in his armchair. Then he took a bottle of vodka out of a drawer of his desk and took a long swig from it. Next he looked through a file he kept under lock and key, and finally found a telegram from the State Department, on blue paper stamped Top Secret:

TO AMBASSADOR, NAIROBI:

AFTER WEIGHING VARIOUS FACTORS, THIS DEPARTMENT HAS DECIDED NOT, REPEAT, NOT TO SEND "AFRICAN BIRD," IN VIEW OF DELICATE SITUATION CREATED BY MURPHY'S DEATH AND POSSIBLE COMPLICATIONS WITH SECRETARIAT OF UNICORN IF AGENT INCLUDED AS MEMBER US DELEGATION/ AS IN PAST, YOU CAN ACCREDIT EMBASSY STAFF MEMBERS TO ENVIRONMENTAL CONFERENCE BEGINNING NEXT WEEK/

Maguire reread the telegram before setting one corner of the paper on fire with his lighter. The paper curled up and burned away to nothing in the glass ashtray on his desk.

Wastelands

BRUNO TOFFANI'S HOUSE was situated on the outskirts of Garsen, some hundred yards from the Tana River, whose chocolate-colored waters flowed between two gashes of red earth, like a spurt of oil washing over a scar. The building was a former colonial police station: a wooden shack with three rooms and a broad veranda, facing southeast, exposed to the breeze that occasionally blew from the sea. For a garden, there were three or four thornbushes, suckers of a huge acacia whose horizontal branches touched the front of the building itself.

Every morning, even before getting dressed and, on days when he bothered to shave, even before shaving, Bruno armed himself with a feather duster and a flannel cloth and carefully cleaned the relics of his Fascist past, which he kept in the little alcove just outside his bedroom. A Mauser from the Second World War; an infantry helmet; two grenades without fuses; and in one corner, a foot-high bronze statue of the Führer, on a marble pedestal. Pinned to the wall were various photographs of the Ethiopian campaign, torn out of the pages of a calendar, and presiding over the whole, a large portrait of Mussolini in a black shirt, flyblown and slightly faded from the dampness.

Bruno had partitioned off this sanctuary from the rest of the house with tasseled red curtains, and no one was allowed to enter it save on certain very special occasions, and only if personally accompanied by him. As the sun rose, he spent at least half an hour each day cleaning and neatly realigning these precious objects, and then went out to sit on the veranda and contemplate the heat waves rising above the withered grass. It was his habit to recline in the hammock in his undershirt and shorts, enjoying the early morning breeze, till Rose, his wife, brought him a bowl of piping hot coffee, with no sugar. His little girls meanwhile played in the shade of the acacia, not straying too far from the house. At times, he used to wonder why the English had chosen to build the house in such a sweltering, open spot, where the tropical sun beat down, when only a couple of miles downstream the river widened, flowing along amid abundant greenery. But remembering the danger of floods and the frequency with which crocodiles carried off African women who came down to wash clothes in the river, he was happy that the stream was so far away. At least he didn't have to live with the constant worry that the girls might thoughtlessly wander down to the treacherous riverbank.

That morning, as he was swinging back and forth in the hammock with his coffee sitting on the wooden railing of the veranda, Bruno was thinking that it had always been his fate to stagnate in wastelands: from his childhood in the backlands of Sicily to his military service in Somalia during the war in Europe and his confinement by the English in a prison camp on the Northern Frontier. A life full of fantastic projects, in which only the walls of a prison had, now and again, cut off his horizons. He had come here to the coast three years before with a bit of money to set up a fish hatchery on the banks of the Tana. But the caprices of the current—doubtless in collusion with one or another of the evil gnomes that dwell amid the roots of baobabs—had decided to withdraw its waters from the pools where he kept his fish, turning them into gleaming dead bodies lying on top of the mud.

Around that time he had met Rose, the daughter of the KANU (Kenya African National Union) Secretary in Mombasa, and had married her. That political connection, together with his inveterate passion for hunting, had been the reason behind his establishing a network for the trophy racket, with guaranteed protection; half a dozen of the best poachers on the coast worked to bag the trophies, which he then resold at a fat profit to dealers in Mombasa. He also went up to Nairobi every so often, when the contraband was important enough to justify direct sale to the curio shops in the capital. In a few more years—if a single elephant with tusks or a rhino with a horn bigger than the wart on his own nose were still left in the whole region—Bruno would have made enough money to move to Nairobi, where he and Rose could live decently and send their two daughters, Priscilla and Cleopatra, to school. With a bit of luck, they could buy and run a small hotel, or he could set up his own company to conduct very respectable photographic safaris.

It must have been around ten in the morning when Bruno spied the cloud of dust raised by a car approaching, quite fast, along the road from Garsen. For a moment, he confused that swirl of dust being raised with the whirlwinds forming on the horizon. But then he saw that the dust devil was coming closer and closer along the dirt road leading to Garissa. The *matatu* bus had already gone by and Bruno wondered if the vehicle approaching might not be the truck belonging to Patel, the East Indian, who had gone out to pick up Salim the day before. It seemed too early in the morning for it to be coming back, however: Knowing the Somali poacher, he was sure that he wouldn't want to waste the best hours for hunting; unless of course he'd bagged such an exceptional trophy that it would be worth his returning home early in the day to avoid unfortunate incidents along the road.

His doubts vanished when a metallic blue Mercedes emerged from the cloud of dust, turning off the main road into the road leading to Toffani's shack.

"It's good to see you," he greeted his visitor from the veranda, modestly crossing his arms across his hairy chest and bare nipples; all he was wearing—except for his inseparable hat—was a pair of very badly soiled shorts. The presence of this blond, slender Anglo-Saxon had suddenly made him very conscious of his own appearance, his dark complexion and his black, two-day-old beard. He tried to cover up his embarrassment by saying jokingly: "To what do I owe the honor of a visit from Commendatore Townsend-Reeves to this humble dwelling?"

Before returning the greeting, Alex carefully brushed off the dust on his clothes and spat out a bit of dirt that had stuck to his larynx. Not even the best air-conditioning that German factories could provide for their cars could cope with the fine sand that had been accumulating on the trails for centuries, ever since the days of caravans.

"It's quite true that we haven't seen each other for quite a while, you old fox, but you must admit that you've hidden yourself away in the asshole of the world. I thought that now that you've gotten yourself a family connection with the establishment, you'd lose your fear of being clapped in jail!"

"Maybe so, but what better place could there possibly be for bringing up a family decently, far from the temptations and the corruptions of the big city! At the moment, I wouldn't move to Nairobi or Mombasa even if you offered me my weight in gold. They'd have to drag me there . . . at least for the moment. A little coffee? It's delicious—just 'imported' from Uganda."

"My dear Toffani, I think that if you ever ate or drank anything that didn't come from robbing or smuggling, you'd get indigestion or be severely poisoned. Please excuse me if I turn down your offer, but I don't have much time. I have to go back to Watamu; they're waiting for me for lunch in Malindi, and I didn't even tell my wife that I was coming. . . ."

"A surprise, a nice anniversary present, such as a pair of horns for example?"

"Please, you know I detest bad jokes. Look, this time it's something very special. I didn't realize till today that there was something very important missing from my trophy collection: a first-rate rhino horn. I know, don't tell me that there are only a few of the creatures left and that they're very hard to find. That's why I came way out here, swallowing half a ton of dust per mile. Otherwise I would simply have ordered one in a general store in Mombasa."

"Any other trophy, including a pair of fine elephant tusks, and there'd be no problem, but what you're asking me for is just about impossible. Besides, do you know how much they're paying in the Near East for a pound of rhinoceros horn?"

"I know, I know, it's all the fault of the Arabs, as usual. But for once I'm prepared to pay even more than the Bedouins. Only it has to be a first-rate horn; don't give me some piece of shit, because I'd throw it straight in your face. I want that trophy to be the outstanding piece in my collection; it'll be the symbol of my inexhaustible virility in my third marriage!"

"Look, I'm waiting for my boys right now; they'll be back today from a hunting trip on the Galana . . ."

"On the Galana? What does Lawrence Brown have to say about that?"

"We hunt on the other side of the river; Brown's place is on this side of the Galana."

"In other words, you do your hunting in the National Park, naturally."

"Well, are the parks for the people or aren't they?"

"It's better that way. I've known Lawrence for years, long enough to know that he's touchy."

"Bah, Africa's a big place. There's room for everybody."

"That's what I think too, but get me my horn."

"Wait till Salim gets here and talk it over with him. I can't promise you anything."

"Salim the Somali? So that's the sort of people you deal with. I wouldn't even dare open my mouth in his presence for fear he'd steal my tongue."

"Well, you can be certain that if Salim doesn't get you the trophy you want, you can go look for it in the Museum of Natural Sciences, because he's the best hunter in the area. The only thing that matters to me is that they bring me good trophies; how they get them is their business. Won't you come inside?"

"I'll let you offer me a drop or so of that dreadful Italian rotgut you keep under your pillow, but remember that I have to be back in Malindi for lunch."

At approximately the same hour that Alex Townsend-Reeves left Malindi and headed inland, a ramshackle light van with one man and a dog inside had taken the coast highway in the opposite direction, heading south. David McGredy—for that was the driver's name—had an important appointment in Mombasa and had left in plenty of time to arrive punctually. On reaching the Kilifi ferry, he had had to wait for more than an hour, because a *matatu* bus had fallen into the inlet in deep water and they were trying to rescue the survivors, who were splashing about amid whirlpools of floating bundles and drowned chickens.

Despite that delay, at nine-thirty on the dot, the van passed through the gate of the Nyali Beach Hotel and drove down the splendid avenue lined with palm trees leading to the main entrance. Finding no other place in the shade, Judge McGredy parked without a second thought in the space reserved for the hotel manager. He still had time to hurriedly smooth down his unruly shock of hair and shake the dust off his impeccable, crisply starched safari jacket; meanwhile Bush, his dog, peed countless times on the fenders of all the cars parked nearby to mark off the precise limits of his territory.

When McGredy asked the receptionist at the hotel desk to ring the room of the Minister of State, she gave him the answer he had expected: he would have to wait a few minutes because the Minister was in the midst of a long-distance call. As he went out onto the hotel grounds to stretch his legs, McGredy thought to himself that in his thirty years of colonial service, he had fortunately not contracted the typically African vice of never being on time.

Judge McGredy was one of the few pieces of the machinery of colonial administration that had found a place in the new African government. During the Emergency—as the English used to call the era of social upheaval and terrorism that had preceded independence —McGredy had been the magistrate who presided over trials for crimes against the security of the State, at a time when the possession of an empty rifle shell was sufficient reason to send a man to prison. In this capacity, he had signed at least a dozen death sentences against the leaders of the Mau Mau, the rebel movement.

There were some who wondered how it was possible that comrades of those whom the unbending judge had sent to the gallows had kept him in his post when the independence movement triumphed and the hour of freedom rang; there were some who thought that the astute judge had extended his clemency to precisely those ringleaders of the rebellion who had later taken over important posts, and that they were in fact grateful to him for having rid the movement of its most radical elements, men who would no doubt have been an embarrass-

27

ment once it came time to assume the reins of government. In any event, it was to those terrible years that McGredy owed his reputation as the possessor of an inflexible conscience and an indomitable will, and the nickname of Bwana Maximum, which reflected his sinister authority, and perhaps even suggested that he had taken a certain personal pleasure in handing down the maximum penalty—the death sentence.

This was the man who now paced up and down the paths of the hotel grounds in great strides, stooping down now and then to pick up a stone and throw it as far as he could for his dog to retrieve, and who carefully smoothed down the hair on his forehead ruffled by the sea breeze. Despite his advanced age, the Judge still had a thick mane of straw-colored hair that gave him a certain resemblance to an old lion; his small, lean body moved with an agility that did not seem to go with the majestic, hieratic appearance of his great head.

McGredy's dog looked very much like him: a British bullterrier with an enormous head and a long body on short, stringy legs. Seeing the two of them walking together left no doubt that they were made for each other. Even the aggressive set of their lower jaws and their alert, fierce gazes were similar, except that Bush, the dog, had lost the sight in his left eye in a fight with a poisonous snake. The alertness and ferocity were concentrated in a single eye; the other was dull and cloudy.

When a creature stands only ten inches off the ground and possesses a great vulnerable muzzle that drags across the grass, it is not wise for it to go sniffing around in dense underbrush haunted by cobras and green mambas, much less quarrel with one of those reptiles over the possession of a dead rat. Nonetheless, Bush never stopped to consider how large or how dangerous his adversary was, and leaped with the same zest on the testicles of an old buffalo or the neck of a wounded leopard, exploits that he had miraculously survived. The little creature had an instinctive love of hunting and an excellent sense of smell; his greatest pleasure was to leave the well-defined marks of his incisors on the backside of some African "boy." But times had changed; Bush had gotten a good whiff of different political winds since the country had attained its independence, which in canine terms meant that he no longer enjoyed the same opportunities, nor the freedom to bite messenger boys or terrify the African women coming down to the riverbank to do their washing.

Thus, when he heard the footsteps of the chubby, ungainly Minister of State approaching on the gravel walk, the dog did not bark or bare his teeth; he turned his head and growled to warn his master of the presence of this intruder.

"Quiet, quiet, Bush, don't growl at the Minister," McGredy said, stroking his dog's back, secretly pleased that his alter ego was able to express his own irritation at Munyoka's unforgivable lack of punctuality.

"I do beg you to excuse me," the Minister said, waving his hands as though he were bidding the Judge good-bye rather than greeting him. "Knowing how punctual you always are, I'm sure you've been waiting here for some time, but I was held up on the phone by a call from the American Ambassador. He's terribly upset about the death of that diplomat on the highway to Mombasa."

"Or to be more precise, on Mackinnon Road."

"Ah, so you already know about that incident. I forgot that you have eyes everywhere."

"I try my best to keep abreast of events."

"Good enough. That will spare me the trouble of having to go into unnecessary explanations. But it strikes me that we'd be more comfortable if we discussed these matters in my room; and I would take advantage of the opportunity to have some breakfast brought up. Between one thing and another I haven't had a bite to eat yet"—and as he uttered these words, his mind began to hark back to secret pleasures and he ran his tongue over his thick lips, remembering certain delightful little erotic games of the evening before.

As they entered the Minister's room, the Judge glimpsed a half-dressed woman slipping through an inside door, like the shadow of a gazelle disappearing between two bushes, leaving the eye uncertain as to whether the image that had registered on its retina might not have been an illusion. The Minister sat down in a wicker chair on the veranda outside, inviting the Judge to sit down beside him. The dry canes of the Minister's chair creaked painfully beneath the punishing weight of those illustrious buttocks. That corner of the veranda was protected by a red and green striped awning from the sun that was already beating down on the beach and the sea, soaking up the bright red of the clumps of bougainvillea and the cool green of the lawn, washing out all the contrasts, as on a faded postcard.

"The fact of the matter is that, in the present circumstances, the death of that American may turn out to have more serious consequences than might be immediately apparent," the Minister said, plucking a white blossom from the flower bed in the garden bordering the veranda.

As he spoke, he averted his eyes from the Judge's blue ones with their intense pupils beneath his very bushy eyebrows, drilling into the Minister as though the Judge were firing a rifle at him from behind a bush. That penetrating gaze of his had become famous among terrorists and miscreants, and it was said that a number of them had ended up confessing to crimes that they had not in fact committed, merely in order not to have to bear the piercing gaze of those merciless eyes.

"As you know, Mr. Murphy's name was on the diplomatic list as an expert on environment, although in point of fact his activities were much broader in scope. As an ecologist, he had ample freedom to poke about all over the country and satisfy his inexhaustible curiosity with regard to 'environmental' questions," Munyoka went on.

What was Munyoka driving at? Knowing perfectly well how the Minister's mind worked, McGredy was sure that Munyoka hadn't called upon him merely to conduct an investigation of that apparently minor accident. It was no secret that a number of the "experts" on environmental problems were in fact undercover agents of their respective governments, and that the UNICORN Center itself was crawling with informers of various nationalities who were trying to hide their real identity behind their dead-white complexions and their thick-lensed glasses, like fetuses curled up inside glass jars. But McGredy also knew that the death of one of these fake scientists was not sufficient reason to upset the Minister. That was simply the lure, jiggled up and down on a string so as to attract the falcon's attention before loosing it on the real prey. What was it that Munyoka really wanted from the Bwana Maximum?

Lawrence Brown was just finishing the rounds he made every morning along the trails of the ranch when his eye was caught by the movement of vultures circling directly above the river. On the other side of the stream, which narrowed down here and there to get around obstacles such as rocks and fallen trees and then widened out again until it almost disappeared amid the thirsty sand banks, were the Tsavo plains: a vast stretch of ocher earth, covered with a grayish brush that melted into a vague blur at the horizon, without a single hill or promontory that might serve as a reference point.

There was just one dirt trail cutting diagonally through the Park and eventually coming out at the coast highway at Malindi. That was the route used by the people who lived on the ranch, but when the river flooded over in the rainy season, the torrential waters cut off all access to the Park and to the bridge—which was simply an asphalt platform between two rocks—and for all intents and purposes the ranch was then isolated from the outside world.

The hovering vultures took Lawrence Brown several miles upstream to a point where the river narrowed between two banks of dense vegetation; the birds were circling lower and lower above a clearing in the forest where the last flood had formed a little marsh, and some of them had already alighted in the branches of a bare tree towering over the bog. He crossed the river via a ford of smooth rocks, where the van sank into the water only halfway up the hubcaps, and left the vehicle in a place where the grass had been burned by a campfire. The poachers had carefully scattered the ashes of the fire, but they had not been able to conceal the patch of scorched grass alongside the trunk of a baobab. He climbed out of the truck, taking with him the rifle that was suspended from metal supports on the right side of the steering wheel. He followed the poachers' trail along a narrow path that ran parallel to the riverbed: From the signs in the grass and the broken branches, he knew where they had met up with the herd, following the fresh tracks of the elephants, and where they had lain flat on the ground in the underbrush for a long time, waiting for shooting light. And he knew, long before he stepped into the clearing, what he was going to find in the grass.

The only question in his mind was whether he would find the carcass of a rhino or of an elephant. But it was much more likely to be the latter, since in recent years poachers had wiped out so many of the rhinos in the Park—sometimes right in front of tourists' cameras—that the few that had remained in the area had crossed the river, taking refuge in the thicker vegetation of the Galana Ranch.

Before entering the clearing, Brown cocked the rifle after inserting a cartridge in the chamber; the bolt of the rifle slid home with the thud of well-lubricated metal, disturbing for a few seconds the peaceful murmur of the current and the warm stir of life in the thicket. By this time the poachers were undoubtedly far away, but Brown knew that if they were caught red-handed they would not hesitate for a moment to use their weapons against him, and even though he would not be the one to fire the first shot, he was not inclined to allow himself to be hunted down like a rabbit.

In the forty long years that Lawrence Brown had lived in Africa, he had witnessed that scene perhaps thousands of times: a shapeless mass of flesh with the belly ripped open, and hyenas fighting with the vultures over the feast of bloody entrails. Even so, the sight still turned his stomach, and he was overcome by uncontrollable nausea. On detecting his presence, the hyenas disappeared at a run into the underbrush, screaming hysterically, and the vultures wheeled above the swamp, hiding the sun's rays for a few seconds with the sinister flapping of their wings. The body then lay there, indecently exposing to view its jaws with the tusks missing, its trunk hacked off with machetes, and its abdomen gaping open, swollen from the sun's heat and stained with bird droppings. There was something horribly grotesque and unaesthetic about such a death, one that robbed that mastodon of all the majestic presence that was his in life, when he strode silently amid the forest, with his back brushing against the lofty vault of lianas, delicately gathering small fruits and tender shoots with his trunk, or polishing his gleaming ivory tusks against the bark of the acacias.

It had been a good while since Brown had abandoned his activities as a professional hunter, but he still continued to allow safaris on the ranch, since the payment of hunting licenses and the camping fees helped him defray the expense of the antipoaching team that continually patrolled the ranch property. He merely supplied the food and camping facilities and supervised the activities of the professional hunters who, paying him a stiff fee, brought their own clients to hunt on the ranch.

Suddenly, he remembered to his annoyance that he was going to have to go to Mombasa the next day to pick up the American. It should really have been Patterson's job to go, but he was down in bed with an attack of malaria; on the ranch Lewis Patterson was in charge of the cattle and the Oryx Project, and had agreed to go pick up an American ecologist who was coming to make a study of vegetation and varieties of pasture grass in semiarid regions: That was the name scientists gave to wastelands.

Muthaiga

THE HOTEL NORFOLK had a certain romantic flavor about it, with its clay roof tiles and its ramshackle terrace with ancient wooden benches, and it was not hard to believe that the building had once upon a time been the train station on the Uganda railway line. The rooms overlooked a central courtyard with an old automobile and a cart, both of them relics of the colonial period. In the middle of the patio there were also two immense wire birdcages, whose occupants were capable of producing the entire gamut of exotic cries and cackles.

After reserving a room and leaving his camera and his traveling bag—the sole survivors of his mislaid luggage—in the hotel check-room, Bob Fender caught a taxi and headed for the downtown area. He needed to buy at least a few items of clothing, till his suitcases turned up. But after going into several shops, he realized that it was not easy to find lightweight men's clothes of the sort that in American department stores are sold in the "Tropical Adventure" section. The one thing available in a wide variety of models and at reasonable prices was safari outfits. He finally ended up buying a pair of green pants with a great many pockets and a safari jacket with loops on the breast pockets for large-caliber bullets. As he tried it on in front of the mirror, Bob smiled at the thought of what his students at Columbia would have said if they could have seen him in that professional hunter's getup. . . . But what else could he do?

On returning to the hotel, he found a message from Maguire inviting him to have lunch with him at his club, where he would hand over the documentation Bob needed. At twelve-thirty on the dot the embassy car pulled up in front of the hotel to fetch him. The driver took the same avenue lined with bougainvillea that the taxi driver had taken to bring him from the airport to the Ambassador's residence.

33

On a broad expanse of sparse grass a number of Africans were taking a siesta, in full sunlight, not even seeking out the shade of the eucalyptus trees. Beyond a cluster of trees he could clearly see the bluish outline of the hills that in the morning had been veiled in clouds but now stood out sharply against a bright sky.

The Muthaiga Club was an old colonial mansion, painted pink on the outside; inside it had spacious salons with sofas upholstered in flower-print fabrics, and elegant curtains. Circulating through these rooms were venerable ladies with withered features and gentlemen who looked as though they had just stepped out of the pages of a Victorian almanac. On the walls were prints of foxhunt scenes, with huntsmen in pink coats and thoroughbred horses with bulging eyes, jumping over towering hedges.

In one of the ancient salons Ralph Maguire was waiting; he was as out of place amid that colonial fauna as a Yankee in King Arthur's court. With his metal-framed glasses and his blue gabardine suit just a bit tight in the sleeves and the legs, he couldn't be anything but the American diplomat. Bob walked over to him.

"You must be Maguire; my name is Fender."

"Pleased to meet you, Mr. Fender," Maguire said, looking him over from head to foot.

Bob thought he perceived a gleam of surprise in Maguire's eyes, and the diplomat rose from his chair so abruptly that all the papers in his hand fell to the floor. Maguire clumsily picked them up and handed them to Bob, still staring at him intently.

"The Ambassador gave me this for you," he said, thrusting the envelope at him rather brusquely.

"Thanks very much, and please excuse me if for some reason I startled you."

"No, on the contrary, I'm delighted that you were able to accept my invitation; John often talked about you. It's just that he used to go about Nairobi dressed in exactly that same sort of outfit," he said, pointing to Bob's safari suit. "And since you have dark hair too and practically the same build, when I saw you come in it gave me a turn."

"It's true that when we were at college together people used to say that John and I looked a lot alike; though the fact that I'm wearing the same sort of outfit is just a coincidence. They lost all my baggage somewhere, in Rome perhaps, and I bought myself these clothes so as to have something to wear till my suitcases turn up."

34

The lunch dragged on endlessly. Maguire asked him a number of questions about what exactly he would be studying in the Galana area, but Bob noted that he wasn't really interested in anything having to do with ecology. Why, then, had he invited him to lunch? The way the diplomat had of wetting his lips with his tongue before he spoke, as though he were a snake about to strike, began to make Bob nervous. He had the impression that Maguire would have liked to tell him something, but that—for some reason or other—he couldn't manage to get the words out. Every so often, he would break off in the middle of a sentence, while his fingers toyed with the bread crumbs on the table, pushing them together into a little pile, exactly as a battalion of diligent ants would have done.

After the last sip of coffee, the two of them got up from the table together at precisely the same moment, as though a recess bell had rung. They walked outside, strolling along a gravel path bordered with clumps of oleander and jacarandas, full of small birds of different colors and horseflies that buzzed continually.

"I can imagine what it must have been like for you to find out what had happened to Murphy, especially in those particular circumstances."

"It was a blow, I admit, even though we hadn't seen each other for a long time. But he was the one who organized all of this. I'm quite sure that if he hadn't been here, I would never have come to Kenya."

"I wonder how it happened that the people in the embassy in Rome never told you about the accident, so you could decide if you wanted to cancel your trip here."

"I almost prefer it that way, because this study of grass is important to me, and my encounter with Africa was already long overdue."

"I realize that for an ecologist such a profusion of animals and plants must be a sort of paradise," Maguire said as he began to sneeze violently.

"Have you caught a cold?"

"No, not really, it's my wretched allergy. In a civilized country, it would be called hay fever; but in the middle of the jungle, with all the infinite variety of pollens and exotic seeds, the term is quite inadequate."

"Have you tried immunization shots?"

"With very little success. The proper time to have that sort of vaccination is just before the change of seasons. As you know, the climate here is divided into the dry season and the rainy season, but in the time that I've been assigned to this post, I've had more than sufficient occasion to note that the seasons here are as unpredictable as everything else in this country."

"The short rains should be beginning about now, and the long ones around the month of April—following the monsoons."

"Yes, all that is quite true in theory, but in practice it doesn't work out that way at all. The short rains overlap with the long ones; or else, quite to the contrary, more than six months go by without a drop of rain. I've finally come to the conclusion that in Africa there's no such thing as a climate; it's merely something that Europeans have invented. Here in Nairobi it's cold in the shade and hot in the sun, and that's it."

Bob wondered if it was because the wine had gone to Maguire's head that he was talking so much. On the other hand, he realized that beneath that burning sun, with the horseflies' incessant buzzing in the background, nothing that anybody said had the least importance. The moment that words came out of a person's mouth, they fell apart into separate syllables that were immediately absorbed by the sunlight filtering through the branches of the trees and drowned out by the intense odor of pollen given off by the plants and the grass.

Maguire began to sneeze violently again, and then the sneezes gradually subsided.

"Anyway, to return to the subject of Murphy, I just wanted to tell you again that I understand perfectly what you must be feeling. It's not easy to arrive in a foreign country and be told that your best friend has just died."

"As I said before, John and I had hardly seen each other over these last ten years; as a matter of fact, it seems to me that if it hadn't been for my report on grass and the fact that I began to write to the embassy to obtain the UNICORN material, our paths might never have crossed again. But even so, a friend from a person's youth always means a lot."

Again the same sensation of a stuck phonograph record. The powerful reverberation of the light on the parched grass created a sort of barrier off which words rebounded, resounding in Bob's ears in precisely the same rhythm as that of the horseflies circling round and round the flowers.

Once he had overcome his third attack of violent sneezing, Maguire finally brought up the subject that was uppermost in his mind.

"The one who's very deeply affected by all of this is poor Ambassador Poire; he was very fond of John, and it's my opinion that this unfortunate occurrence has unhinged him just a bit. I hope that his concern about this whole affair didn't disturb you unduly."

"As a matter of fact, he did seem quite upset, but as I recall, he didn't say anything really odd. What exactly do you mean?"

"I'm referring to the accident. As you know, Murphy's car went off the road as he was driving down a side road to the coast—a little local dirt road that hardly anyone uses, or more precisely, one perhaps used by quite undesirable sorts: poachers, charcoal smugglers, and people of that kind. The thing is, the accident happened very early in the morning, at dawn, and therefore there were no eyewitnesses. . . . But perhaps you already know all of this."

"No, I didn't know all these details. How would I have known?"

"Well, the thing is that since nobody alerted the police, the dead body lay in the open, amid the brush, for nearly two days, and as you can well imagine, the scavengers did their work. So it was impossible even to perform an autopsy."

"To tell you the truth, I prefer not even to imagine it. It's making me sick."

"I apologize for being too explicit, but I think this information will help you avoid certain misunderstandings; as a result of all these circumstances, a number of vicious people have begun to spread the story that perhaps somebody deliberately caused that accident, or hid the body temporarily."

"How awful!"

"You shouldn't be surprised. In Nairobi there are unfortunately a great many people with time on their hands, and on account of the sort of life he led—he was rather independent and something of a womanizer, if you know what I mean—your friend Murphy couldn't help but cause talk. So don't be surprised if they tell you the most fantastic stories about how and why he died. I merely wanted to put you on your guard. It seems to me that even the Ambassador has allowed himself to be influenced at one time or another by these wild theories."

"Be that as it may, he didn't make any sort of comment to me on the subject. The only thing he was interested in during our entire conversation was my research in the Galana region, and he urged me to try to check the facts as carefully as possible, which is only as it should be; he didn't make the slightest reference to Murphy's accident. What you've just told me is the first news I've had of what happened."

"Ambassador Poire was greatly affected by the death of his collaborator, and at certain times he too allowed certain dark thoughts to get the better of him. But if he didn't say a word to you about the whole affair, I'm glad."

"Now that you mention it, it seems to me that at a certain point our conversation was taking a rather odd turn, but I didn't attach any particular importance to it."

"I can see that you're a steady, well-balanced sort. And that's a good thing, because after you've been here a couple of weeks you'll find that between the merciless sun that pierces your brain and this air full of strong odors and heavy fragrances, a person begins to go out of his mind; it's a mild but insidious form of madness."

"By the way, is the place where Murphy had his fatal accident near the Galana Ranch by any chance?"

"Well, as a matter of fact, yes. Mackinnon Road runs practically parallel to the Galana River. Both of them end up at Malindi, where, incidentally, Murphy is buried."

"That's what I wanted to ask you. I hope it'll be possible for me to go place some flowers on his grave."

The Fishbowl

THEY WENT BACK INSIDE the club and since Maguire had an appointment on the other side of the city, he offered to drop Bob off at his hotel on the way. After taking the documents up to his room, Bob went out again to take a stroll through the city. On his walk earlier that morning, the distinctly European appearance of the streets and buildings had surprised him. The only picturesque touch was the traffic policemen, impeccably uniformed in the style of the old British colonial police; a few African youngsters were running about the sidewalks, offering to watch cars in return for a few coins. There was nonetheless a special quality in the air; a soft breeze rippled the flags on the buildings and a subtle smell of dust and humanity that he found exciting hovered above the crowds in the streets.

As he rounded a corner, he surprised himself contemplating the beautiful proportions of a mulatto girl lying on the white sand of a beach at the edge of transparent waters. It was an advertisement for an excursion to Mombasa, in the window of a travel agency. Would it be possible to escape for a few days from the Galana Ranch and visit those marvelous beaches? He suddenly recalled Murphy and all that Maguire had told him, and felt an ache in the pit of his stomach, but he immediately found himself enveloped by the crowds and the heat, and forgot almost instantly that he was supposed to be feeling sad.

He ventured on into the district that lay behind the market, where the streets were narrower and the houses, painted different colors, had more of an African flavor. There were street peddlers sitting on the sidewalks and stands with tropical fruits that seemed to be ripening before his very eyes in the equatorial sun and giving off an intense perfume.

All of a sudden he was drawn to a strange-looking shop, whose show window reflected the light in such a way that one could hardly see, behind the glass, the display of little ivory figures amid a jumble of other mysterious baubles giving off a bright gleam from the half-shadow inside. The shop was so dark that when he entered, it took a few minutes for his eyes to adjust to the dim light. He felt a little as though he were inside a fishbowl, in that atmosphere that was cool and slightly humid in contrast to the burning heat outside. When he could finally see again, he suddenly felt as though he were immersed in a strange world of stuffed animals: heads of lions with bared fangs and buffalo heads focusing their glass eyes on him. All the walls seemed to be covered with such spoils, and on the floor were big piles of zebra, antelope, leopard, and other animal hides.

Bob was so dumbfounded by the terrible slaughter that collection represented that he very nearly found himself incapable of feeling indignation. In show cases protected by thick glass panes there were also enormous pieces of carved ivory, elephant tusks of various sizes in silver and gold settings, alongside semiprecious stones and other handiwork of dubious Middle Eastern taste. There was a smoked glass panel separating the main salesroom from the back room, and Bob had the vague feeling of being observed, as if the customers were

39

rare specimens in a tropical aquarium, whose reactions were carefully studied from the other side of the glass. To lend one last touch of secrecy to that cave of Ali Baba, there was a hustle and bustle of customers and clerks going in and out the back room, through a passage protected with heavy red curtains, which each time were carefully closed.

On seeing him wandering all about, a solicitous African clerk, whose broad smile revealed a huge gap in his upper teeth, approached him.

"If one of these zebra hides interests you, I can make you a special price on it of a hundred and fifty shillings, or a hundred and thirty each if you take two of them"—the man seemed disconcerted by Bob's blank gaze—"or perhaps you prefer a leopard skin; we can wrap it very carefully so you won't be bothered by customs when you go back to your country. It's true that the ones you see here have a few holes in them; they're bullet holes; but if you want a really perfect one, I can show you something interesting in the storeroom we have in the basement. We also have some magnificent ivory pieces down-stairs; we've had to be a bit discreet about where we keep them, you understand, ever since they declared the ban on elephant hunting."

Bob was so amazed by this whole situation—having been an active conservationist for the last fifteen years—that he didn't know whether to laugh or insult this man. Obviously the clerk felt a bit disappointed at the lack of interest in the face of his tempting offers. Finally, thinking that he had stumbled onto the cause of this indifference, he said:

"Perhaps you've come to see the boss, is that right? To exchange money, naturally." The man took Bob's silence as assent and felt less uneasy. "Don't worry, he'll take care of you right away, as soon as he's finished with Mr. Ogutu." He lowered his voice slightly on utter-ing that name, and added: "He's a big shot in the Ministry of Commerce. Every so often it's necessary to butter him up a little, if you get what I mean"—and he rubbed his thumb against the tips of his other fingers—"to make certain that Mr. Patel's name won't appear on the list of licenses that they withdraw every year—the Africanization policy, do you follow me?"

Bob couldn't get over his astonishment. How could this man be making all these confidential remarks to a complete stranger? How could this clerk be sure that he wouldn't go tell all that to the police? There could only be one possible explanation: Such corruption must be something taken entirely for granted, something accepted by the authorities themselves. The clerk disappeared for a moment behind the red drapes, and then reappeared, with the same smile that revealed the big gap in his teeth:

"Mr. Patel will look after you in just a moment; if in the meantime any of the merchandise here interests you, I'll wait on you myself."

Bob found himself fascinated, altogether in spite of himself, by the dizzying atmosphere of complicity and mystery. The only similar sensation he remembered dated back to his trip to the Far East, when he had visited an opium den: After that experience, he had been ill for almost all the rest of the trip, but no doubt it had been worth it. When the curtains opened again, allowing Mr. Ogutu to pass through with an attaché case tucked tightly under his arm, Bob was ushered in turn into the sanctum sanctorum of the back room, the walls of which were also hung with red velvet.

"So you want to change some dollars, Mr. . . . ?"

"Fender, Robert Fender."

"Delighted to be of service to you, Mr. Fender."

From behind a Victorian mahogany desk the Indian held out a plump, slippery hand; the only thing that felt solid was an immense bluish stone mounted in a ring that gave off a watery gleam beneath the neon light. The man had hair plastered down with brilliantine, a chubby little face with smallpox scars, and a forced smile, as though it hurt him to stretch the corners of his mouth. For a few seconds Bob raptly contemplated a huge carved ivory piece that occupied the place of honor on the desk: a scale model of a Victorian locomotive, with the engineer's head peeking out of the little window as the fireman stoked the boilers with shovelfuls of gleaming white coal. It had required an enormous chunk of ivory to carve that monstrous gewgaw, a unique masterpiece of universal bad taste. Patel's voice, speaking English with a heavy Hindu accent, finally broke through to him.

"The exchange rate is fairly low, Mr. Fender. As you doubtless already know, with all this tourism it is easier to secure foreign currency than it was. Nonetheless, we always have a special price for our friends from the American Embassy. You do work for the embassy, isn't that so?"

"Not exactly. I'm an ecologist."

"In that case, you must have come here to attend the UNICORN Conference."

"No, my trip here has to do with research that I must do in the Galana area." Bob noted that Patel had frozen like a pointer on hearing that, and he felt it necessary to add: "As a matter of fact, however, I am in touch with the personnel of the embassy; I've just had lunch with Mr. Maguire, who had to give me certain documentation I need for my study."

"I understand. You need say no more; your credentials are more than sufficient. Tell me, how much money do you want to change?"

"I really don't know exactly. It depends. . . ."

"I understand, and will tell you immediately what the exchange rate is. Twelve points per dollar."

"You mean twelve shillings to the dollar?"

"Yes, I'm sorry I can't offer you more, but as I say, the exchange rates are low."

Bob calculated that that was an excellent deal for him, since the rate Patel was offering him was thirty percent more than the official exchange rate. He did his best to conceal his surprise.

"All right, I'll accept that rate, but I warn you that I don't have much money on me. Would three hundred dollars be all right?"

The hand with the ring moved abruptly, again filling the small room with bluish reflections, which momentarily flashed across the red velvet hangings and the thick glass window.

"Don't worry about having cash. I'll accept a check for whatever amount you say. All you need do is put your address on the back of the check and write in the sum you need on the front."

Mr. Patel slipped out through the drapes for a few seconds and came back with big packets of Kenyan bills. Bob thought he detected a glimmer of disappointment in the Indian's eyes when he saw that the check handed to him was for only five hundred dollars. Nonetheless, Patel's plump fingers moved with incredible speed over the keys of a calculating machine and his lacquered fingernails separated the bills with the expertise and precision of a professional gambler shuffling cards.

"Here you are," he said, putting the packet of bills held together with a rubber band inside an old envelope. "This is the safest possible strongbox," he said, pointing to the wrinkled envelope. "Nevertheless, I don't recommend that you walk around the streets with this money. There are unscrupulous people wandering about loose in the streets, you know."

"In any case I'm only a few blocks from the Hotel Norfolk."

42

"So much the better. That way you don't risk running into trouble."

As he left the shop, with the greasy touch of Patel's hand still fresh on his fingers, it occurred to him to wonder whether the money-changer might not be in cahoots with some stickup man who saw to it that Patel's own clients were robbed. He felt relieved, however, when he felt the burning sun on his shoulders again and mingled once more with the lively crowds on the streets after that prolonged immersion in the fishbowl.

Meanwhile, within the sanctuary draped in red velvet, Patel the East Indian had picked up the telephone and was dialing a number with swift movements of his chubby fingers: "Operator, I'd like to put in a call to Mombasa; yes, that's right, to the Nyali Beach Hotel. I'd like them to ring Minister Munyoka in his room. Try to get the call through with as little delay as possible; it's important."

Bwana Maximum

THE TIDE HAD RISEN over the sands in front of the Nyali Beach Hotel, and the waves breaking against the coral reef nearly covered the masts of the boat that had gone aground there several years before. McGredy and the Minister went on talking, in the shade of the awning through which a transparent green light filtered down onto Munyoka's bald head. The latter had ordered some seafood to round out his copious breakfast, which was gradually turning into lunch, before the half-amused and half-revolted gaze of McGredy, who had refused to share the feast. The fact that he had been willing to collaborate with the African government did not in any way imply that it was necessary for him to fraternize with these people, whom he continued to regard as fundamentally uncivilized and depraved.

"My dear McGredy," the Minister was saying at that moment, at the same time using the sharp-pointed pincer of a crab to dislodge a piece of crabmeat that had gotten stuck in a cavity, "you know that frankness is a luxury that we politicians can scarcely permit ourselves. Nonetheless," he added, as he slowly swallowed a bit of crab, "nonetheless, in your case, it is my opinion that telling you anything but the truth is a waste of time."

Munyoka smiled, pursing his slightly greasy lips. It was obvious, McGredy felt, that he was trying to ingratiate himself with the Judge, but McGredy continued to look straight at him with his piercing eyes, not moving a muscle of his face. Feeling that coldness, Munyoka turned off his smile and sat up straighter in his chair, as though he were still sitting in the dock on trial during the Emergency.

"Look, in order not to waste words, I'm going to tell you something straight out: It wasn't us. If I thought that the police, or even the Special Branch had anything to do with this affair, I wouldn't have called on you to investigate the accident in which the American was killed. I'm not so stupid that I don't know that you always pursue your investigation to the very end, regardless of the consequences."

"From what you've just said, it would appear that you harbor certain suspicions that the accident was deliberately provoked."

"I have no way of being certain, naturally. But there are unquestionably certain suspicious circumstances. I suggest that you yourself go out and have a look at the place where the accident happened, and you'll see. It's a perfectly straight stretch of road, along the old Mackinnon trail; Murphy knew those side roads well and it's difficult to understand why he went off the road. As far as we've been able to find out, he was neither drunk nor high on drugs."

"Could it have been a mechanical failure?"

"I'm no expert on the subject, of course, but it's hard for me to think of any sort of mechanical failure that would make a car jump the ditch and crash a hundred yards down below in the bottom of a ravine. Moreover, I think Murphy was a good driver. To be quite frank, it looks as though there was foul play."

"Do you have any idea who might have wanted to do him in?"

"I'm not certain on that score either. All I can say is that in recent days John Murphy had often been seen in the company of certain undesirable elements. His insatiable curiosity concerning the environment had led him to establish contacts with certain members of the opposition; he had been seen several times recently with that charlatan who likes to call himself the friend of the people, though this doesn't prevent him from running up debts in the most expensive restaurants in Nairobi and maintaining his own stable of race horses."

44

"J. M.?"

"Himself in person; it's a crying shame that the President hasn't already expelled him from the KANU, though naturally, what with all his tricks he's managed to put one over on certain imbeciles, and with every day that goes by, it's going to be more difficult for us to get rid of him. But to return to the subject of Murphy, I fear that in this case his curiosity may have cost him dearly; if Muriuki's friends suddenly got wind of the fact that he was something other than a mere ecologist, and that he was trying to stick his nose into their affairs, I think they'd be more than capable of laying a trap for him. Furthermore, it's only to be expected that he who plays with fire ends up getting burned. . . ."

So that was what the Minister was up to; he doubtless wanted to accuse Muriuki, his hated political rival since the days of independence, of plotting the death of the American. Had he already cooked up the "evidence" that would irrefutably prove the relationship between J. M.'s activities and the accident on Mackinnon Road? The Judge imagined the scenario: that deserted stretch of parched ground where the accident had occurred, where Munyoka's men would have left a trail of false clues that would lead him to accuse Munyoka's enemy—like a garden carefully prepared in advance so that a band of children hunting for Easter eggs will be sure to find them.

The Judge smiled enigmatically, reaching down at the same time to pat Bush's sleek back as the dog lay stretched out on the tiles with a good inch of his tongue hanging out, panting from the heat.

"If it turned out that there was dirty work involved in this whole affair, isn't it more likely to have had something to do with Murphy's private life? You're doubtless aware of what I'm referring to."

"Yes, I am. I know that Murphy's love life was quite complicated, but I don't think he would have been done in for that reason. We all have our little weaknesses, but after all we're in Happy Valley here and I don't believe that anybody takes certain peccadilloes too seriously."

"I'm not referring to some unimportant little love-adventure, but to a long-term relationship far more liable to cause trouble. If what certain gossips claim is true, Murphy had been having an amorous liaison with a married woman for some time. . . ."

"Are you by chance referring to Townsend-Reeves's wife?" Munyoka interrupted him, trying to restrain his laughter. "My dear sir, you must be joking."

"I don't see why you should say that. The rumor's been going round that when the accident happened, Murphy was in fact heading down to the coast for a rendezvous with his mistress."

The Minister went on laughing, and coughing at the same time, since when he had burst out laughing he had choked on a bit of crab.

"We all naturally saw Murphy with his mistress, and with his mistress's husband as well. What is it you Europeans call that—a *ménage à trois?*"

"Do you mean to say it was a relationship that the husband himself more or less accepted?"

"Accepted is a euphemism; encouraged would perhaps be the more accurate word in this case. Alex is one of those men who can't live without a woman—I believe that this is his third marriage—and who nonetheless have great difficulty satisfying females, at least on a very elementary, but nevertheless important, level of their love lives."

"The fact that Townsend-Reeves may not be particularly virile— something quite difficult to verify, certainly—doesn't eliminate the possibility that in a moment of spite he might have made an attempt on the life of his rival; quite to the contrary."

"In theory, I wouldn't argue with you. But knowing Alex as all of us do, I would tend to reject this possibility absolutely. I think he'd lack the courage to do such a thing; he doesn't have enough guts. He's a decadent sort, a holdover from the past, the tag end of a race."

"I confess I don't like to hear you speak that way of a British subject who as it happens comes from a distinguished line distantly related to the royal family. The fact, however, that he comes from a civilized background doesn't make him any the less suspect in this case. On the contrary: We may be confronted with a carefully planned act of vengeance, carried out through a third party. . . ."

He paused, looking at the Minister with the eyes of a python hypnotizing its victim, and went on: "I know that Alex Townsend-Reeves has dealings with ivory dealers and other undesirables on the coast; it's common knowledge. Nothing could be easier than to buy off one of the thugs who operate in that area and obtain the necessary information, through his own wife, as to the American's plans, to lay a trap for him."

"All this sounds quite incredible, and not at all in keeping with Townsend-Reeves's character," Munyoka answered. "He's never been able to face up to a problem—remember how he behaved during the

Emergency, when he fled from his house, letting all the weapons in it fall into the hands of our freedom fighters?"

"That's quite true. And who knows how many atrocities that wild bunch committed with those arms!"

That observation on McGredy's part brought on a moment of tense silence. Even the cicadas had suddenly stopped chirring; the palm trees had also ceased stirring in the breeze; it seemed as though even the seagull soaring above their heads in full flight now hovered motionless, its outspread wings outlined against the incandescent disk of the sun.

"In any event," the Minister doggedly went on so as to break the silence, "the other theory appears much more likely. It's quite certain that if Muriuki's people discovered that Murphy may have known too much about their machinations, their organization, they wouldn't have hesitated for a moment to wipe him out."

His words hung for a moment in the dead-still air, as though the syllables lacked the force necessary to penetrate the suffocating heat. At that very moment, the telephone in the bedroom rang, breaking the spell. Bush awakened with a start and growled, and the Minister got up to answer it. He remained on the phone for some time, but because of the breeze that had risen once again and was making the palm fronds rustle, the Judge was not able to make out what he was saying; the only thing that he could gather was that he was speaking with a certain Patel. When the Minister came back out, the Judge noticed that his lips were set in a tense grimace.

"It would appear that the situation is becoming more complicated. The Americans have come up with the idea of sending an agent, again under the disguise of an ecologist, to investigate the Murphy affair. I should have guessed as much when the Ambassador was so insistent this morning; I ought to have suspected he was up to something."

"If it helps to clarify matters, his investigation may turn out to be helpful to us."

"Knowing how the Yankees go about things, it's my opinion that this is merely going to complicate matters; not to mention the fact that since I've found out what's going on, other people undoubtedly have too. I don't think Muriuki is going to be exactly pleased that there's a new agent on Murphy's trail; and the worst of it is that this is going to put them on the alert."

"On the other hand, it occurs to me that this detective may serve us as a decoy; if we followed his path at a prudent distance, we'd be able to observe the reactions of the persons involved in this whole affair, if your suspicions turn out to be correct. . . ."

"It's not a bad idea to let the American serve as a decoy, but on the other hand his safety worries me. I don't want to have another spy whose bones are bleaching in the sun in the Tsavo desert."

"I don't think that Muriuki would be stupid enough, if he was really responsible for the other accident, to try to do the same thing all over again."

"Nonetheless, it wouldn't be a bad idea for you to keep an eye on this fake ecologist, for his own safety, naturally. I think he intends to come down to the coast, on the pretext of making a study of grass. . . ."

"A study of grass? What a clumsy cover!"

"Well, as you already know, the Americans have never been noted for their brilliant imagination. Or maybe they just think we're idiots."

"There's no doubt about it—they've lost a great deal of the traditional British subtlety. Meanwhile, I see myself being transformed, step by step, from a judge into a bloodhound and then into the guard dog of a fake ecologist. Do you think I should buy myself a butterfly net so as to escape everybody's notice?

"What do *you* think of all of this?" he said, addressing Bush.

The dog, who had awakened when the phone rang, followed the conversation attentively, looking at each of the two men as they spoke and turning his muzzle, so as to be able to observe their expressions with the keen pupil of his one remaining eye, as though his canine intelligence were capable of understanding this complicated situation. When his master addressed him, he began joyously wagging his tail.

Langata

AFTER DROPPING BOB OFF at the Norfolk, Maguire ordered the chauffeur to drive across the city again in the opposite direction. They then headed up the highway to Langata, taking the road that led to the National Park; the parched plains of the Park and the road to the airport lay on their left. Following the road to Langata a few miles farther, one reached the little village of Ngong, located on the very crest of the hills. But the car turned off the main highway onto another road running along the edge of the Park. On the other side of the barbed wire fence giraffes could be seen stretching their long necks over the fence to reach the plants growing in the ditch along the roadside.

Because they were so close to the Park, the gardens of the outlying area of Langata were regularly visited by antelopes and warthogs that wriggled through holes in the fence. And every once in a while a pair of lions made their appearance in Langata, terrifying the African gardeners, who had no aesthetic appreciation for the beauty of a feline lying amid a bed of roses. For the old-time colonials who lived in Langata—former ranchers or white hunters, for the most part—that dangerous proximity was a reason for pride and rejoicing. Although they knew that at some time or other they might be bothered by antelopes eating up their geraniums or even by some wild beast getting into their stables, this was a price they gladly paid for sharing with those animals the open spaces of Langata which bordered on the foothills of the mountains, covered with underbrush and dense forests, haunted until recently by leopards and rhinos. They wouldn't have lived on the other side of the city for all the money in the world, and they used to joke about the people who lived in the Muthaiga section, which they regarded as an excessively residential and overly civilized quarter of the city that little by little had been infiltrated by a contemptible fauna of diplomats and businessmen, and even—these were the ones who aroused the most scorn—a number of ecologists from the Center.

Walter Seago's house was located in this outlying area, a few yards from a ravine covered with dense, wild vegetation. At the bottom of the little valley that the terrace of the house overlooked, the forest of Langata stretched out in the distance, and above the treetops, the first foothills were visible. At that hour in the afternoon they were a grayish color with dark spots here and there, like the hide of an old buffalo. The midday evaporation had spread a thick layer of fog over the forest, which was taking on a reddish tinge in the afternoon sun. Above the expanse of straw-colored prairie grass the sky was blue and transparent, without a single wisp of cloud.

Walter Seago had just fed his animals and had put water on to boil for tea, a ritual he had followed since the very first day he had arrived in Kenya, in 1930. Apart from his preference for open spaces and the splendid view that he enjoyed from his house, living in Langata was a necessity for him, since only there could he have enough land to maintain corrals for the zebras, antelopes, and giraffes that he captured, with the proper legal permit, in different locations in Kenya, before shipping them off to zoos with which he was continually in touch. Most of the zoos required a period of quarantine and health surveillance which Seago complied with by keeping the animals in special enclosures that he had had built in his garden, until the time came to ship them off to their destination. In addition to this occupation, which frequently took him away from the city on long safaris, Seago had a job in the Museum of Natural Sciences and was an active partner in a business run by Zimmerman, the famous taxidermist.

Whatever time he did not devote to capturing, studying, or stuffing animals he spent gathering information for the British intelligence services, whose operations in all of East Africa he had supervised and acted as an adviser for since the Second World War. That was why Ralph Maguire was visiting him; inasmuch as Kenya had traditionally been part of the English sphere of influence, even the Americans accepted a certain leadership on the part of British intelligence and were in the habit of consulting with Seago on nearly all of their operations, especially when a problem arose. His profound knowledge of African politics and the fact that he was a close friend and adviser to the President himself were substantial reasons for seeking his aid.

Seago received Maguire on the veranda of his house, dressed in

50

his invariable shorts, long wool socks whose tops were neatly folded over just below the knee, and an old and faded but at the same time spotlessly clean blue shirt. His bare elbows and knees, as bony as a skeleton's, looked a bit like the joints of a wooden doll; his face and his hands were very dark and deeply furrowed with wrinkles and scars. His snow-white hair, his slightly sunken chest, and his gentle gestures might lead one to believe that he was a frail and vulnerable little old man; but any appearance of fragility was completely deceptive.

Despite his seventy-odd years, he had the strength and endurance of a much younger man, and he was capable of walking and running for hours at a time amid the most tangled stretches of jungle at a pace that would have left any athlete panting for breath; his deep-set blue eyes beneath wrinkled eyelids reflected an indomitable courage and great steadfastness of character. His long experience of life in the jungle had caused him to develop extraordinary faculties, quite like those of the wild animals he captured, and despite the fact that he sometimes liked to give the impression of being a bit clumsy or absent-minded, the truth of the matter was that he was instantly aware—thanks to his keen sense of sight, hearing, and smell—of whatever was happening around him, at any hour of the day or night.

Seago had a quintessentially British sense of humor, and as he knew perfectly well that this gift was almost completely lacking in Ralph Maguire, he pulled the latter's leg continually, leaving the American constantly confused and perplexed.

"So the agent that you've been waiting for has finally arrived, has he?" Seago asked as he poured Maguire a cup of tea.

"Through a series of odd coincidences, there was every indication that the man who arrived was the agent that they were sending from Rome; hence it doesn't surprise me that the Ambassador should have taken him for somebody he really isn't at all. Fortunately, I've just had lunch with the ecologist, on the pretext to give some documents to him, and I was able to verify that Poire hasn't said anything that might alarm Mr. Fender."

"I presume you've already given Mr. Fender the necessary instructions so that he can fulfill his mission."

"What mission?"

"Investigating the circumstances surrounding the accident that cost Murphy his life."

"But I've told you that Fender is *not* the agent," Maguire repeated

51

emphatically, vigorously wiping his glasses with the back of his tie. "I thought I'd explained all that to you over the phone."

"Yes, I understood what you said. But it seems to me that in view of the present state of affairs, we should act as though Fender *were* the agent."

"Now I'm the one who doesn't understand then," the American said, half choking on his tea.

"It's very simple. This Fender person went to talk to the Ambassador this morning, isn't that right?"

"As it happened, the taxi took him to the Ambassador's residence by mistake."

"In any event, after that you invite him to have lunch with you in the most crowded club in Nairobi."

"For the precise purpose of removing any possible suspicion that he might be an undercover agent."

"Exactly. And then you hand him an envelope full of documents, right?"

"Right, a series of documents from UNICORN. I could have left them at his hotel for him, but I preferred to speak to him in person so as to correct any mistaken impression that the Ambassador might have created in his mind."

"If you want my opinion, knowing that Fender had a personal talk with Poire first of all, and then later with you, he surely must be the agent. I don't believe that the two highest ranking officials of the U.S. Embassy in Nairobi would waste their time with any of the ecologists coming here to carry out a study on the behavior of the female bustard in heat.

"Moreover," Seago added, "we must grant the fact that your scientist has a special gift for not letting his presence pass unnoticed. After causing a great to-do at the airport, because his baggage had been lost, the first thing he did after you dropped him off at his hotel this afternoon was to turn up at Patel's shop."

"Patel the moneychanger? How do you know that?"

"Never mind how, the fact is that if I know that, Munyoka will soon know too, and it won't take Muriuki long to find out either, since the opposition has excellent secret sources of information within the government itself. And so, as I was saying, Fender is the agent."

"But you know very well that that's a mistaken impression," Maguire said, on the point of bursting into a series of nasal explosions.

"Forget what you and I know. What really matters is what other people think—what the Kenyan authorities believe, and the Soviet intelligence service. By now they're convinced that Fender is a spy, and therefore the best thing for us to do is to go along with them."

"But that would be tantamount to perpetuating this unfortunate misunderstanding."

"Don't be so dramatic; it's not worth getting worked up over. If all of them have made up their minds as to Fender's *real* identity, why should we disappoint them?"

"This strikes me as a very dangerous game to be playing."

"I don't agree. I think that at this point it would be more difficult to try to convince everyone that Fender is *not* the agent. What would you like us to do—send a public announcement to the *Daily Nation*: 'To whom it may concern: I have the honor of informing you that contrary to all appearances, Mr. Fender is not a spy. His *real* purpose in coming to Kenya is to carry out a study of grass.'?"

"I think that something could be done to clear up this mis-understanding."

"Look, it's my opinion that we shouldn't try to make things more complicated than they are already. Let's simply act as though Fender were in fact the agent. I think that sometimes it's necessary to go along with appearances; I'm one of those who believe that the first impression is extremely important. In the long run, it sometimes turns out to be the right one."

"I don't know whether you're saying this in all seriousness or not, but I repeat that it strikes me as a dangerous game, an extremely dangerous one. As I see it, the situation is *already* quite complicated enough."

"On the contrary, as *I* see it going about things in this way would help simplify the situation, at least for us. Our rivals are going to be so confused they won't know which way is up. In any event, while Fender is in the Galana area, that will attract the attention of those hawks, and keep them far away from the real prey."

"I must admit that the idea is intriguing. I hope that Muriuki's henchmen won't take it into their heads to play any dirty tricks on him."

"Not this soon after Murphy's accident; I think they're smart enough not to resort to outright violence too often. Even though they don't share the same ideology, they can't allow themselves to forget that America is a very powerful country."

"That was what I thought too, at least before I arrived in Africa. Ever since I've been here, however, I realize that the importance of different countries is a very relative thing, when you think of how certain states that are so small, comparatively, are capable of creating such enormous problems."

"That's altogether true; everything is quite relative. Be that as it may, I'm glad to see that you're beginning to adopt a sufficiently realistic point of view, since that's the only one that allows one to survive in these emerging countries."

"That's exactly the right word. One tends to forget that just a little over ten years ago, they were not yet independent nations. The American eagle is more or less losing its way—not to mention its feathers —on these impressive plains seared by the equatorial sun."

Maguire smiled, with a certain expression of childish impishness, proud of having uttered an intelligent, almost poetic phrase. A breeze from the plain had suddenly come up, driving the last wisps of fog over the crest of the hills. Only the slow, rhythmic flight of a bird of prey cleaved the transparent blue twilight sky.

PART TWO

The Nairobi Airport

His ROOM directly overlooked the main courtyard of the hotel, where the large metal birdcages were, and Bob had been awakened by the murmur of the birds as they sensed that day was about to break. In those few fractions of a second in which conscious awareness forces its way through the cotton wool of dreams, Bob intuited—rather than heard—a rustling sound different from that of the birds, inside his own room. It could have been feathers rustling, but in fact it was papers fluttering on the rug. Someone had left the window open, open wider than it had been the night before, and the dawn breeze filtering in through the opening had scattered the documents all over the rug. He had sat up in bed, quickly turned on the light, and had lain there for a few seconds contemplating the documents lying all over the floor, not believing his eyes. Who the devil could have been interested in poking about in those dull papers on ecology?

The taxi was waiting for him in front of the hotel entrance, with its motor running, its defective headlights illuminating a very fine rain. He had made a point of leaving for the airport with time to spare, so as to be able to try once more to recover his lost baggage. The flight that would take him to Mombasa was the same one he had taken the day before in Rome, one that stopped in Nairobi before depositing its load of tourists headed for the beaches on the coast.

It was still dark but the outline of the hills was beginning to emerge from the heavy blanket of fog that covered part of the plain and the trees in the Park. But Bob knew now that the impasto of clouds would soon be pierced by the dizzying wheeling of the sun, whose heat would suck up the ephemeral humidity like the nozzle of a vacuum cleaner, dispelling the illusion that this was an African Switzerland. As Maguire had said of Nairobi: cold in the shade and hot in the sun.

The taxi driver headed down the highway to the airport very slowly, since the gazelles that had jumped over the fences of the Park during the night had not yet made up their minds to abandon the succulent patches of grass growing in the roadside ditches and stood for a few moments with their eyes riveted on the headlights of the taxi before beginning to trot erratically along the wet asphalt. "Step on it, will you please, I still have to inquire about my lost baggage," Bob barked at the driver, who barely understood English, much less his passenger's impatient tone of voice.

The moment Bob set foot in the airport, however, he realized that there was no point in his having gotten up so early: The counters and the offices were more deserted than an abandoned temple. A few functionaries drowsing in the customs booths turned surly when he roused them. Irritated by this general somnolence and emboldened by the guards' indolence, Bob headed off to investigate on his own, walking down to the far end of the corridors, opening doors and storerooms in search of his baggage. He finally ended up lost in a veritable labyrinth of passageways that led to repair hangars full of antediluvian rusting planes, with their iron backbones in the air. He realized he wasn't going to find his suitcases out there and tried to return to the main lobby, but managed only to wander even farther inside the labyrinth of hangars.

After going through the umpteenth door, he found himself in a dark hangar, at the end of which he made out the scorched entrails of a wrecked plane; at the other end of it, some porters were transferring odd-shaped bundles from a Land Rover to an air freight container.

They were great, long objects, wrapped in burlap, which the porters were obviously handling very carefully, and in total silence. On either side of the van stood two policemen with their machine guns ready. A squat, tubby man in shorts and half-boots and an unusual ranger's hat was supervising.

Bob stood there as though hypnotized, realizing that he mustn't be seen, but on the other hand eager to find out what was going on; at that moment, a white object slid out of one of the burlap wrappings and hit the ground with a great hollow thump. It was a huge elephant tusk! The freebooter in the broad-brimmed hat then pounced on the porter who had dropped it, swearing at him in Swahili. Involuntarily, Bob also let out an exclamation, and suddenly found all eyes turned upon him, not to mention the sinister eyes of the submachine guns.

"*Porco Dio!*"—the freebooter cursed—"Catch him!"

His loud shout had the virtue of breaking the spell, and Bob turned on his heels and began to run through the passageways like a soul being carried off by the devil; he knew that if he could manage to find his way, they wouldn't be able to catch him, since he'd won a number of cross-country races in his university days and still went jogging regularly on the shores of the Tiber. The murderous look on the faces of those individuals made him even more fleet-footed, and he soon found his way through the labyrinth of the airport, with a sudden sense of direction born of the most spontaneous and genuine terror.

He came out at the other end of the building, in a deserted courtyard, knowing that he had given that band of smugglers the slip. He leaned against the brick wall with his heart in his mouth, and tried not to think of what might have happened to him if he'd been caught.

The sun hadn't come up yet, but a reddish glow was spreading across the horizon; the looming mass of the hills, by contrast, was still dark, covered with a thick blanket of fog. Inhaling deeply to catch his breath, he swallowed a great mouthful of humid air that smelled of rotting earth. All at once, he felt an instinctive fear and his skin turned to goose flesh all over; he felt suddenly that this country possessed a dark, visceral power. All his childhood apprehensions about Africa—a mixture of stories about cannibals and movies with explorers immured in underground temples—came back to him in a rush, without his being able to do anything to stop the stampede of phantoms. Behind the papier-mâché decor of the Muthaiga Club, beyond the modernistic silhouette of the UNICORN Center, the depths of Africa were still out there, vast plains and jungles where poachers continued to kill elephants with poisoned arrows, and the lion lay in wait in the shadow ready to leap upon the antelope's throat.

At precisely seven A.M., Tony Allen had finished cleaning and adjusting his weapons. He had timed to the minute exactly how long it took him to drive out to the airport, so that if he left his house in Langata when the plane flying in from Rome was just beginning its first turn above the hills, he would usually be in time to receive the passengers practically as they stepped off the plane.

That morning, however, he could not trust his calculations; the hills were shrouded in such a thick cloud cover that he wouldn't be able to see the plane until it was on the second leg of its approach, coming in over the Park and already preparing to touch down. He began to put the weapons away quickly; he had to pick up three new Italian clients and then take them out to the Galana Ranch the following day. Before leaving his house, he locked the weapons in the reinforced metal cabinet that he kept in his room; there had been special security measures decreed during the Emergency, and the new African government had kept them in force: Anyone who was robbed of a weapon was responsible for the loss of it, and could end up in prison.

As he drove at fairly high speed along the highway from Langata, he kept looking out of the corner of his eye at the monkeys perched on the wooden fence posts of the National Park. Ever since he'd been a child, he had always had mixed feelings about monkeys, baboons especially; they half repelled and half fascinated him. In the jungle he had sometimes come across one that was wounded or sick, and the pathetic expression in its eyes had always disturbed him; he would have fired on certain men—and in fact had had shootouts with poachers and cattle rustlers when his father had the ranch in Rumuruti—with fewer scruples than he would have on those hominids, whose sad eyes were capable of expressing all the perplexity and anxiety characteristic of a species higher up on the evolutionary scale.

He soon left the Park behind and turned onto the highway leading to the airport. Perfect timing, he thought; catching sight of the nose of the Jumbo emerging from the layer of clouds with all its flaps down, about to land. As it lined itself up with the end of the runway, it seemed as though the great metallic bird was hovering motionless in the air, supported by the blanket of fog, tinged red by the sun.

"*Ndege Kubua*, great bird," he murmured in Swahili.

As he waited just outside the customs office for the travelers to go through the passport check, he wondered, for the hundredth time in his life as a professional hunter, what these new clients would be like. A new safari was always a new adventure, not so much because of the dangerous situations he might get into—they had gradually grown fewer and fewer as he acquired greater experience and knowledge of possible tight spots—as because the individuals that he would be living side by side with, practically beneath the same tent, were an unknown quantity.

People who had never been on a safari and who had only a stereotyped image of a hunting expedition could never imagine the group therapy involved in sharing the most complete solitude of jungles or deserts, for weeks or months at a stretch sometimes, with perfect strangers. Sleepless nights, mosquitoes, interminable silent waits in hunting blinds, exhausting marathons in jeeps—all that in the company of individuals whose character, education, and psychology one could begin to guess as they got off the plane. If Tony had had to make a list of his most prized trophies, first place would not have gone to his collection of animals but to the mixed bag of human types that he had known and had to contend with amid the oppressive intimacy of a safari camp. Alongside real gentlemen, and ladies with a fantastic appreciation of true sport as well as an impeccable upbringing, there was also a fair-sized gallery of vulgar nobodies, *nouveaux riches*, and cowards.

Tony knew that he was criticized for having allowed himself on occasion to get up the skirts of one or another of the young ladies who had come on safari with their men; this was of course absolutely contrary to the professional code of the "white hunter." What those who judge him so severely perhaps did not know was how difficult it was at times, after many days of abstinence in the jungle, not to return the caresses of a woman who slides her soft fingertips along the crotch of your pants, while the pupil of her husband's eye is glued to the telescopic sight of his rifle.

Besides, he thought, were those well-heeled travelers, each and every one of them without exception, all that worthy of consideration and esteem? Who was the one who had to track down the difficult animals, to put them under the very nose of a nearsighted dentist from Minnesota who'd made himself a pile of money? "That's the elephant." "What elephant?" "The one with the big long tusks, the

61

only one that's looking at us, you dumbhead!" "Ah, yes, now I see it!" "It's too late now, because it's charging, and I'm the one who'll have to shoot it down; for the love of Christ, you might at least step aside!"

And the meticulous preparation of the bait, the endless lists of impedimenta, the continual repairs of vehicles that broke down. . . . Not to mention how *pleasant* it was to enter dense jungle at nightfall on the trail of a raging leopard wounded in the belly by one of those squirrel hunters who took himself to be Trader Horn! Tony tried to think of something else, since he was working himself up into a bad mood before he'd even laid eyes on the new clients.

For different reasons, Bob too was watching, from behind the glass panel of the customs area, the arrival of the passengers and the conveyor belt bringing the baggage in from the plane, hoping at any moment to see his suitcases appear thanks to some stupendous magic trick on the part of the airline company. As he was looking through the glass, a group of three passengers who couldn't possibly have been anything but Italian—two men and a woman—attracted his attention; they had already picked up their baggage, with the help of several porters, and were walking over to the customs counter with several long leather cases resembling those used by gangsters in movies to pass off their machine guns as musical instruments. The silver-haired man, who was in his fifties and well preserved (despite a dangerously receding hairline and an incipient rigid pouter-pigeon chest), and the boy in jeans bore an unmistakable family resemblance, though the youngster was slimmer and better looking. The woman, whoever she was—friend? wife? mistress?—was attractive and elegant enough not to pass unnoticed: very dark eyes, an olive complexion, chestnut brown hair tied back with a scarf that matched the shirtwaist dress which she wore with a wide black leather belt.

At that moment one of the customs officers opened one of the leather cases and a large-caliber rifle appeared, its double barrels gleaming. In other words, that group had come to hunt. He noted that another robust-looking man, dressed in colonial style—short pants and knee socks—was coming over to greet them after showing a paper to the customs official. With his deeply tanned skin and his straw-colored hair, he was the very picture of the professional white hunter.

On seeing that his bags still hadn't appeared, Bob began to be aware of a mounting feeling of indignation, especially when he saw all the party's hunting equipment being carried out past him to the exit. It wasn't fair that those responsible had mislaid all the suitcases belonging to him, a scientist who had come to study nature armed only with harmless biology and botany manuals, while on the other hand they had safely delivered and let through the whole arsenal belonging to these people who had come prepared to wipe out every last trace of African fauna.

Once aboard the plane to Mombasa, Bob relaxed. The flight seemed very short. After miles of flying over a great tableland of red earth dotted here and there with grayish shrubs—Tsavo Park—he could see, to the right of the plane, the snow-covered summit of Mount Kilimanjaro, floating on a pedestal of clouds that made it look even more unreal, more aloof from the arid plains all around it. Immediately thereafter the voice of the stewardess came over the loudspeaker, announcing that they were about to land. For a few minutes they flew over the ocean, separated by a ribbon of sand from the turquoise-colored waters of a lagoon framed by the dense vegetation of a mangrove swamp, with the roots of the trees reaching down to the very edge of the ocean. Near shore, the water was so clear that the sharp contrast between the sandy bottom and the transparent coral reefs was readily visible.

After a tricky landing, with the belly of the plane brushing the tops of the last palm trees (owing to certain financial irregularities the money necessary to add a few hundred yards of concrete to the runway of the new airport was missing), the European tourists clapped their hands with excitement at finding themselves on the shores of the Indian Ocean. As he poked his head through the door of the plane, Bob found himself face to face with a solid wall of hot, humid air that reminded him of the New York City subway in summer. There wasn't so much as a puff of breeze blowing at the moment; the wind sock hung limply from its pole. The palm trees surrounding the airport building looked as though they were painted on the grayish sky. Even though the haze was filtering the sun's rays, Bob noted that the ground was burning hot beneath his feet, and he followed the crowd of passengers fleeing from the disembarkation area as though they were afraid they would remain stuck in the tar. He crossed a glass-enclosed waiting room where travelers of different races, dressed in different tunics and garments ambled about with indolence, like rare species in a tropical aquarium. Through the dirty windows of the waiting room, the plane seemed to disappear at times in a halo of humid

63

haze, as though the outlines of the fuselage, so clear and sharp a moment before, were also beginning to dissolve in that universal decal.

It was only nine in the morning, and he wouldn't be meeting the manager of the Galana Ranch at the Tamarind Restaurant till twelve. So Bob leaped into one of the ramshackle taxis waiting in line in front of the exit, opened the window so that a bit of air would blow in, and shouted at the top of his lungs:

"Take me to the ocean!"

He had suddenly been seized with an irresistible, irrational impulse to get to the beach, to touch that expanse of transparent blue water that he had seen from overhead.

The Wildlife Situation

IN ONE OF THE MEETING ROOMS of the presidential palace of Mombasa—the former residence of the British governor—the Council of Ministers was having a quiet session chaired by the President himself. Comfortably sprawled out in a Victorian armchair, Mzee—The Old Man, as the Africans called him, with a mixture of familiarity and veneration—was distractedly listening to the ministers' discussions, as his mind wandered in secret drowsiness and his eyes followed the movement of the sailboats heading out to sea from the port of Kilindini.

At that moment the Minister of Health and Social Welfare, whose deep, monotonous voice always made his hearers feel uncomfortable, was reeling off endless statistics concerning the number of hospital beds in the country. It was already almost eleven A.M., and the sound of the locusts gnawing the leaves of the bushes was gradually growing louder and louder; the breeze stirring the palm trees in the park was already bringing puffs of heat with it, mingling with the smell of fish from the docks and brine. The hospital bed count appeared to be having an even more soporific effect on the ministers, whose mouths were beginning to gape open as though they were inhaling whiffs of chloroform.

The ivory and ebony handle of the fly whisk that the President always carried in his left hand began to jiggle slightly, an unmistakable sign of boredom or impatience.

"Before this session adjourns," the Minister of Tourism and Wildlife said, taking advantage of a pause as his colleague caught his breath, "I believe I ought to call the attention of the members of the Council to the articles that have recently appeared in an English newspaper on the hunting situation in our country and the illegal trafficking in trophies."

The mention of that subject had the virtue of rousing those present from their torpor. For a few seconds, meaningful looks and grimaces were exchanged, though no one dared speak up. The subject was in fact a touchy one for two reasons: not only because some of those seated around the table were implicated—either directly or indirectly —in the trophy racket, but above all because some of the members of the President's family—known as the "royal family"—had earned very healthy sums as a result of their dealings in contraband ivory.

"As a matter of fact," the Minister of Foreign Affairs remarked, finding himself obliged to say something, "I'm hoping to meet with the British High Commissioner to express my surprise and my indignation."

"The point is," the Minister of Tourism went on, "that this is not the first time such items have appeared in the English press, and I believe that, aside from the repercussions that this may have on the prestige of our country, it may also have a direct effect on the number of tourists who visit Kenya."

The Minister of Health and Welfare unexpectedly took the floor again, irritated perhaps because his soliloquy on hospitals had been interrupted.

"The first thing we ought to do, if we don't want them to attack us, is to examine the wildlife situation and that of the national parks and see if they can be improved."

"The only way of effectively controlling illegal hunting and the sale of contraband trophies is to prohibit all hunting and close the so-called curio shops," the Minister of Tourism said. "And such a measure is impossible, for many reasons."

"Naturally," the Minister of the Treasury, a man with greedy little eyes, said, "we cannot dispense with the important source of revenue that the sale of hunting licenses represents, or with the stimulus to trade provided by the curio shops."

"That is true, absolutely true," the Minister of Labor and Unemployment seconded him. "If a total hunting ban is decreed, we must ask ourselves what would happen to all the workers whose livelihood depends on hunting, from the safari boys and trackers, down through the skinners and tanners, to the highly specialized craftsmen who work in the taxidermists' shops."

"Not forgetting the poor *wananchis* who live in remote places and whose only means of subsistence comes from bagging an occasional antelope," the Minister of Trade—one of those who were getting the biggest take from the trafficking—declared. "For those unfortunates, forbidding all hunting would be to condemn them to death," he added, suddenly overcome with emotion.

"Let's not exaggerate," the Minister of Tourism put in, taking the floor again. "Those who are so concerned about what might be lost in the way of revenue from hunting licenses and the fees for hunting blocks will be reassured to learn that nowadays the revenue derived from these sources is not even a tenth of that brought in by tourism, photographic safaris, and so forth."

"If you think it necessary to declare the ban," the President interrupted at that point in a threatening tone of voice, "why don't you do so? In the final analysis, it's entirely up to you."

The Minister of Tourism turned deathly pale, and was unable even to stammer a few words in reply. No one dared open his mouth, for fear that his speaking up would be the drop that would make the President's wrath spill over, for the giraffe tail in his hand was jerking back and forth with worrisome swiftness. Even the cicadas fell silent for a moment, and the ministers could have heard a fly buzzing in the room.

In fact, an audacious fly flew in through the open window whose Impressionist chiaroscuro might have inspired Matisse and landed squarely on top of the President's bald head. But the President was immediately aware of the tingling sensation caused by the little hairy feet traveling over his bald pate, and his powerful broad hand delivered a blow with all the precision and force of a drop hammer.

"Your Excellency, my dear colleagues," Munyoka, who had been conspicuously silent until now, said, taking advantage of the momentary confusion caused by the presidential slap—a number of the ministers were rubbing their heads as though they had received the

66

blow—"up until this point I haven't cared to take part in the discussion, not so much because the subject of hunting doesn't interest me, but simply because there are other subjects that interest me more."

Munyoka spoke in a soft, deliberate tone, in just slightly affected, perfect English, knowing that this impressed a number of his colleagues who had not had the good fortune to receive a university education in the seat of empire itself. Even the President kept respectfully silent and the only sound to be heard in the room was that of the blades of the enormous fan cleaving the slightly humid air, casting bluish reflections in the corners of the room that lay in shadow.

"What interests me more than forbidding the activities of a poor hunter who ropes a gazelle is rounding up the poachers in the world of politics, who are digging a trap beneath our very feet. And I will not be scandalized by the fact that a few elephant hides or ivory horns are smuggled out of the country along the trails of the Tsavo when it is clear to me that those same trails are being used by our enemies to bring arms and explosives into the country that will blow us all sky high."

Munyoka paused to drink a glass of water and wipe the sweat from his forehead and his double chin, noting as he did so that he had electrified his hearers.

Then the President spoke up.

"I believe that these grave accusations and threats deserve a detailed explanation. What do you mean when you talk of traps and explosives? From whom is this danger of subversion coming?"

"I believe that it is no secret to anyone that in the last few months the leader of the opposition has managed, by means of idle promises and demagogic tirades, to lure a fair number of followers from our ranks, thereby making him feel more secure and arrogant than ever. But since Muriuki knows that the reins of government are still held with a firm hand by our President, he is conspiring to take power by other means."

"What proof do you have of this?" the President asked cuttingly.

"Convincing proof is very difficult to obtain, but I have followed J. M.'s movements for some time now and I know that he has recently been in contact with various embassies of Socialist countries. He has also visited a number of African countries lately, most notably Tanzania and Zambia, where guerrillas fighting against racist regimes are being trained."

"Support for African liberation movements has been a basic policy

67

of ours since we ourselves were the first freedom fighters in Africa,"
Mzee answered. "And don't forget that J. M. was one of the most
daring of all the guerrillas during the struggle for independence."

"Whatever J. M.'s merits during the Emergency may have been,
and I do not deny them, he is dragging his name in the mud these
days, what with his arrogant and subversive attitude. We believe, for
instance, that on another of his trips, he contacted in either Belgium
or Amsterdam the arms dealers who operate there. Probably at this
very moment, Muriuki is awaiting an important shipment of arms."

"Probably . . . we think . . . we believe . . . Are these the only proofs
you have against J. M.—I assure you that with accusations as flimsy as
that, you're not going to braid the rope to hang J. M."

Although his voice was trembling with repressed indignation,
Munyoka pulled himself together enough to go on:

"There is another piece of information, which also has to do with
Muriuki's activities. I am referring to the accident in which a diplomat attached to the American Embassy lost his life; there is every
indication that this accident was deliberately caused by Muriuki's
men, who feared that the American—who frequented opposition
circles—might have contrived to learn too much about their plans,
their organization. The diplomat in question happened to be one of
the closest collaborators of the American Ambassador, who keeps
calling me to protest the fact that thus far we have been unable to
shed any light on the circumstances surrounding his Counselor's
death. As Your Excellency and my colleagues may know, we need
the Yankees' friendship today more than ever, to keep us supplied
with military matériel and technical equipment for our army."

"And how come that no one has been able to provide the Ambassador with the information he requires? I thought that an exhaustive
investigation of the accident had been ordered."

"In point of fact, I have just put one of our best bloodhounds on
the case, but it is nonetheless not easy to determine the precise circumstances in which the accident occurred, as it happened on a
deserted road, with no eyewitnesses, and the dead body was soon
ravaged by scavengers that scattered the remains over a wide area of
the Tsavo desert."

"I see that you don't have very convincing proof in this case either.
It's not possible to bring charges against a man merely because a
foreigner lost his life in the Tsavo desert and then his bones were
scattered far and wide by scavengers. Do you think the vultures and

the hyenas are going to tell you how the accident happened? Do you think the stones and the dry riverbeds are going to testify against Muriuki?"

"As the minister responsible for the security of the state, I have given instructions to the person in charge of the case to leave no stone unturned, regardless of who the guilty party may turn out to be. But is not an easy task to investigate the activities of a man who enjoys parliamentary immunity, who occupies a high post in our party and who, I will even venture to say, still enjoys to some degree the trust of our respected and beloved President."

"You may rest assured that if we should some day discover that any of the suspicions that you have voiced prove to be well-founded —either about him or about any of you sitting here around this table —I myself would tear him from my bosom and crush him with my own hands, like a poisonous snake," and as he spoke these words, the President's powerful fingers tightened their grip on the stiff hairs of the giraffe tail. "But before taking any action, it is necessary to have something more than a string of suppositions and slanderous charges. The net of accusations cannot be so loosely woven that it unravels in our very hands."

The President paused, having run out of breath; a few giraffe hairs that had come loose from the fly whisk slid like an ill omen across the white sheets of paper before him.

"Listen to me carefully," the President said, once he had caught his breath. "Listen to me, all of you, not just you, Munyoka. Though the days and the years slip by, and my hair grows whiter and whiter, like the snows crowning the mountain that can sometimes be seen from that very terrace just outside, I have not yet completely lost either my reason or my memory. . . . Mzee hasn't yet become a hopeless idiot!"

A murmur of approval ran through the room, and fingertips tapped on the ebony table in a muffled gesture of applause.

"I am therefore well aware, and have observed for some time, that a number of the members of the opposition, including my friend and comrade J. Muriuki, have strayed from the path that we traced together for building this nation." Once again, there was an approving murmur. "And I will tell you straight out that if they continue to carry their arrogance to extremes I myself will assume the responsibility of putting an end to this situation!"

A gleam of diabolical wrath suddenly appeared in the President's eyes, and with an abrupt gesture that took them all by surprise, he brought the lashlike fly whisk down on the Council table with all the strength of his outstretched arm, causing the papers on top of it to fly up into the very noses of the ministers.

"However," he went on, "as long as it is within my power, I would rather that this didn't happen, especially as regards J. M., who was my friend and my ally during the difficult years of the Emergency, and gave ample proof of his love of independence and freedom, first as he fought in the forest, and then again later in the English concentration camp. That man came to visit me when I was in prison and when I was in exile, as many times as was necessary, risking his political future, and perhaps his neck as well! And I am not going to be the one to throw his body to the hyenas, on the basis of a flimsy string of suspicions and conjectures!"

The President's eyes swept over the members of the Council as he prepared to bring the meeting to a close, but Guichuli, the Minister of Defense, raised his hand; perhaps because he was advanced in years and he did not fear the President's wrath as much as the others.

"I merely wanted to add, in connection with the subject we were previously discussing, that I have for some time been concerned about the activities of certain armed malefactors who pass themselves off as poachers and who may very well be no such thing. I'm referring to the Somali agents, who cross over into our country all along the northern border, and represent a real danger. If the information that the Minister of State has put before us regarding the acquisition of arms by the rebels is true, my blood runs cold at the thought of an internal conspiracy, aided by these agents who have infiltrated our country."

"Another one who sees ghosts moving about when it's simply the bushes rustling. Would you care to explain to me old Guichuli, what possible relation there might be between the imaginary conspiracy of the opposition in the capital and the bands of bandits or brigands know as *shiftas* marauding about hundred of miles away along the Northern Frontier. Or for that matter, a bunch of Somali poachers coming down to the coast to sell a pair of elephant tusks or a leopard skin riddled with bullet holes? It seems to me I've heard enough nonsense for one day, and it's too hot. The meeting is adjourned."

The President got up from the table so abruptly that his huge Victorian armchair fell over backwards, and the pitchers of water in the center of the table tottered on their trays. As several aides came hurrying into the room, fearing that the President had fallen out of his chair, the latter left the room, his massive figure swaying energetically back and forth and his hand still waving the fly whisk up and down as though he were keeping time to a military march.

The ministers respectfully remained on their feet as he filed out of the room, and as several of them talked in hushed tones or gathered together the papers scattered all over the tabletop, the Minister of State and Wanayaki, the Minister of Foreign Affairs, stepped aside to one corner of the room.

"Congratulations," Wanayaki murmured slyly. "You've managed yet again to infuriate the Old Man. You've seen that whenever the subject of J. M. comes up, the Old Man goes out of his mind."

"If I wait for Muriuki to get the upper hand and clap us all in jail, I don't imagine my advice from Muteba Prison is going to prove very useful to anyone!"

"You haven't been a great admirer of J. M. for quite some time, I know, but despite the fact that he's ambitious and arrogant, I believe that in the final analysis, he's probably still loyal to the Old Man."

"You're wrong there. As I see it, the American's accident was the handwriting on the wall. They wouldn't have bumped him off if they hadn't thought he was on to something very serious."

"Do you really believe that Muriuki was behind that?"

"I'm convinced of it, and I'll soon have proof, because I have Judge McGredy himself working on the case. And I didn't want to say a word about the latest thing I've found out, because I know that it would have really sent the Old Man into a fury."

"What is it you've learned?"

"The Americans have just sent a new agent, a second Murphy, disguised as an ecologist. He came down to the coast just today, to snoop around and find out what he can about Murphy's accident, and all the rest. Fortunately, my men detected him immediately, and we'll be keeping him under surveillance. I have Bwana Maximum on his trail."

The Hunter

MEANWHILE, the suspected agent was taking his first swim in the Indian Ocean. Bob took his pants off behind a bush and ran across the gleaming white sand already warm. The water was just as clear and transparent as it had appeared to be from the plane: It was as though he were looking at the sandy bottom through a sheet of glass. Bob flailed his arms frantically and dove under, feeling the sting of the salt water in his eyes. He swam till he was exhausted and then ran up onto the beach to collapse in the shade of a coconut palm. He felt relaxed and happy all of a sudden, as though he had been born again in that baptism of transparent tropical waters.

At exactly eleven o'clock, he picked his clothes up, dried himself off as best he could, dressed, and returned to the place where the taxi was supposed to be waiting for him. He froze—the taxi was gone! All he needed was for the taxi—and the last traces of his baggage, including the manuscript of the study on grass—to disappear! But soon he spied the silhouette of the ramshackle vehicle around a bend in the road, in the shade of some palm trees; one of the taxi driver's feet was sticking reassuringly out of the front window, as he lay sprawled out in the back seat sound asleep.

To reach the Tamarind for his meeting with the manager of the Galana Ranch, they crossed the old section of Mombasa, along narrow little streets jammed with vehicles, a miscellaneous collection of rickety jalopies, carts drawn by oxen with a strange hump, and buses painted in gaudy colors and chock-full of passengers. Bob was surprised above all at the prodigious numbers of people packed together like sardines inside those vehicles: Behind the windows he could see arms, legs, hands and faces pressed flat against the window-panes, looking as though they were about to shatter them at any moment. In the back of a light truck was a youngster with curly hair and a flowing djellaba, doing incredible acrobatic tricks with just one foot resting on the tailboard; it seemed as though he was about to come sailing out at the first pothole or stone in the road, but by some miracle he kept his balance.

Nonetheless, there was something about that human crush, that dense atmosphere compounded of damp salt air and animal effluvia, the adobe houses painted in rain-streaked colors, that seemed familiar to Bob. Perhaps it reminded him of the cities in the south of Italy, where he had recently traveled in the scorching heat of midsummer.

The restaurant was on the other side of a bridge—the Nyali Bridge —a swaying metal structure on which a phenomenal traffic jam had built up at the point where traffic coming from the island and heading north merged with that moving toward the city. The daring cyclists, trying to dodge in and out unharmed between trailer trucks and vans, and the wildly extravagant gestures of the uniformed traffic police-men, blowing their whistles and waving their arms as though they were conducting an orchestra, made a notable contribution to the general chaos.

When he finally made it to the Tamarind, he was relieved to find the lobby pleasantly cool and quiet, thanks to the thick walls and the gleaming tiles. In a corner of the lobby was an aquarium full of continually bubbling water, in which most unfriendly looking lobsters were contending with each other with pincers and antennae. Mr. Pat-terson had not yet arrived. Bob sat down to wait at one of the marble-topped tables, with a view of the dockside area of the old port, with its little sailboats and its tiny houses of whitewashed adobe, their minute windows open onto the bay.

Lawrence Brown arrived at the Tamarind at eleven forty-five, a quarter of an hour before the appointed time, and in rather a bad mood. It wasn't so much the fact that he disliked going into the city and having to put up with the exhaust fumes and the traffic jams at the entrance to Mombasa as it was the thought that he would be obliged to go to Malindi—a much shorter trip, to be sure—the very next day, to pick up Tony Allen's clients. Quite simply, he hated to leave the ranch, which despite being arid and isolated, nonetheless seemed to him to be one of the few remaining spots in Africa that could still be regarded as being livable.

Bob was waiting for him, drinking beer at a table near the fish tank where the lobsters were thrashing about, interweaving their pincers and antennae so violently that one didn't know if their movements were the thrusts and parries of a duel to the death or clumsy lovemaking. There were so few people in the restaurant that it wasn't at all difficult for him to recognize Bob as a stranger.

"The more you drink, the more you sweat," said Lawrence Brown, pointing to the beer, without even taking the trouble to introduce himself. "I've come to take you to the Galana Ranch, Professor Fender."

"You must be Patterson," Bob said as they started to walk out.

"My name is Brown, Lawrence Brown; Patterson's sick in bed with an attack of malaria."

"I'm sorry to hear that. I thought that Anopheles mosquitoes were practically wiped out in this part of Africa."

"In this coastal area, lots of people take quinine. I myself never take any sort of junk like that; I must have long since become immune, after all these years of knocking about around here. . . ."

From the way Brown flung Bob's travel bag into the back of the Toyota, the latter realized that the man was not in a particularly good mood, though there was something about his brusque gestures and the stern expression in his blue eyes that made one trust him instantly. The Toyota was a typical safari vehicle, with spare tanks mounted above the fenders, the headlights and the radiator protected by metal grillwork, and two sliding panels in the roof, like the hatches of a submarine. As they took off, all of its innards rumbled; Bob could feel the heat of the engine through the floorboards.

"Do you live at the ranch too?" he asked.

"Yes, I'm the one in charge of hunting at Galana." Bob looked at him with such a surprised expression on his face that Brown felt obliged to add, "As you know, the activities at the ranch fall under two heads: cattle raising, including the Oryx Project, which is Patterson's department, and hunting and game control, for which I'm responsible."

"I didn't know that any hunting at all went on at Galana Ranch," Bob said, in a disappointed tone he did not attempt to conceal. "I was under the impression that it was a game sanctuary."

"Indeed it is, but it's hunting that supports all the rest; not only through the money taken in from hunting licenses and the daily fees that clients are charged for camping at the ranch, but above all because it allows us to maintain antipoaching units, without which Africans would invade the ranch and not even leave us the trophies hanging on the veranda."

"I'd heard talk of the activities of poachers, but I had no idea that the situation was that bad."

"It's worse than bad. The only reason that the African government allows us to retain possession of a large land grant north of the Galana River, run by Europeans, is that we serve as a barrier against the incursions of Somali bandits, who infiltrate the country along the banks of the Tana and then spread out all along the coast. If we weren't there to hold them back, the *shiftas* would one day drop in to have breakfast at the Nyali Beach Hotel."

At that point Bob noted a series of little scratches and scars on the hunter's powerful forearms and chest, doubtless—he thought—the result of continually pursuing wild animals, or perhaps men, through dense brush.

"And what is the government doing about all that—the problem of poachers, I mean?" Bob shouted, trying to make his voice heard above the roar of the pistons.

"The government is too busy dividing up the fat profits from the illegal trafficking in trophies, in which a great many high-ranking officials are involved up to their necks, to be bothered with them."

"And couldn't a stop be put to this whole situation by forbidding all hunting?"

"Since the law prohibiting elephant hunting was passed in 1974, it is estimated that some five hundred tons of ivory have left the country each year, either by way of the Port of Mombasa or the Nairobi Airport. Of that total, less than five percent can be attributed to the natural death of elephants and legal hunting for purposes of game control. All the rest came from illegal hunting, and was exported from the country with fake permits."

"From what I've seen in the curio shops and at the airport this very morning, namely a shipment of ivory leaving the country right under the noses of the police, there's no doubt in my mind that the authorities are looking the other way. But if there were a total ban on hunting, it would be far easier to detect violations."

"Imposing a total ban has been considered many times before, and even been put into effect in other countries, with quite unsatisfactory results. In the end, the only thing it accomplishes is to drive out those who hunt for sport and respect the game laws, and leave the reserves at the mercy of poachers."

"I find it hard to believe that with an effective system of inspection and control, a prohibition of all hunting activities could not be enforced."

Lawrence Brown raised his eyes from the road for a moment and looked Bob up and down; Bob realized that an expression of profound scorn, tinged with the merest hint of irony, had appeared in his pale blue eyes.

"Professor Fender, how many times have you been in Africa?"

"Not once. This is the very first time that I've ever set foot in this part of the world."

"You see—and yet you're trying to preach to those of us who cut our baby teeth here. You scientists and ecologists, you American ones in particular, live in an absolutely unreal world. The first thing you ought to learn is that for Africans wildlife has no value, except for what can be gotten from it in terms of meat or money, through the sale of trophies. In Swahili, for instance, the word *nyama* is the one used both for meat and for game, for wild animals. They're all *nyama*, with no distinctions made."

"It's too bad they don't include a few lessons on African dialects in courses on biology," Bob said, trying to be clever. But Brown went on as though he hadn't heard him. In fact, what with the roar of the engine, he may very well not have.

"You'll understand then that to them the value of even the most exotic and interesting species is measured in pounds, like ordinary beef. The aesthetic difference between a magnificent kudu with horns curving in a spiral, and one of those scrawny *ngombe*—cows—that they prod along dusty roads, is something to which they're totally insensitive. You may or may not believe it, but in Africa we legal hunters are the only real conservationists. I'm referring to those who hunt for sport, not to the gang of Italian butchers who settled in East Africa after the war. They're not able to tell an impala from a giraffe, and all they do is wander around killing females and leaving wounded animals behind...."

"Of course, there must be good and bad hunters, as with everything else. To my mind, however, the simplest solution would be to close hunting to everyone, without exception."

"Look, Fender, it's not a question of good guys and bad guys, like in Westerns; it's that some respect the laws and others don't. The British authorities left very strict hunting rules behind. If they're observed, there's no need to worry: Game not only will have a very good chance of surviving, but will doubtless even increase. When I began to work in the Galana area, around ten years ago, you couldn't take one step anywhere in the region that extends to the Tana River without running across a rhino lying underneath a bush. Today, there are a couple of dozen at most left outside the Galana Ranch, and what's worse, behind the trail left by each animal, you'll see the footprints of a poacher. The way things are going, in just a few more years —and maybe I'm being too optimistic—between the animals that are being killed and the trees being cut down to make charcoal, the entire country is going to be left as bare as the palm of my hand. This is what the Africans call *the building of a nation.* You've no doubt read that in the papers."

At the end of this long tirade Brown seemed so worked up that Bob was afraid he'd run into one of the *matatus* full to overflowing with Africans and careening from one side of the road to the other. They crossed another narrow bridge, a wooden one, this time.

"I don't doubt that you know what you're talking about, and I assure you I meant no offense by what I said. I'm making a study of the importance of grass in the ecological cycle, and the hunting situation is not my principal interest."

"You don't owe me any explanations. All I want is to have another talk with you after you've been in Africa for a few weeks."

On the other side of the bridge, the traffic flowed more freely; the road ran between sugar-cane fields, and in the distance were hills of dark earth with waving fields of sisal, whose straight, geometrically planted stalks gave the landscape a civilized, harmonious look. Only the occasional bole of a baobab, with its fat trunk and its twisted branches reaching toward the sky, reminded Bob that he was in Africa. Although it was still hot, as the Toyota picked up speed, a refreshing breeze blew in through the window.

A Pair of Leeches

EVERY TIME Bruno Toffani went to Nairobi with a load of ivory and trophies he followed the same route, leaving behind him a trail of tips and bribes, like Tom Thumb marking the path leading him to the giant's lair by dropping little pebbles all along the way. He would

77

leave Garsen by night, driving along the trails of Tsavo Park, whose gates opened for him after hours once he had prudently greased the palms of the watchmen, and then come out at Voi onto the main Nairobi-Mombasa highway. Just in case he happened to have the misfortune of running into a game ranger wandering about loose, he always carried several hundred-shilling bills inside the folder containing his driver's license, and—as a last resort—a sawed-off shotgun underneath the seat.

He would ordinarily arrive at dawn at the Embakasi Airport, on the way into the city, and there unload part of the merchandise in a dark hangar with the help of his agent at the airport, who received a substantial commission for securing the necessary export documents and keeping a close eye on the goods being shipped out by air freight.

After that, he would go off to have a shower and breakfast at the Mansarde Hotel, a comfortable *pension*, a place where he was not likely to be seen coming or going, which at the same time happened to be very close to the main office of the Game Department, where he also had the necessary *rafikis* or friends to provide him with fake certificates for the sale of trophies on the local market. Although Bruno had more than enough money to pay for a room at one of the best hotels in Nairobi—the Norfolk or the New Stanley—ever since the days when he had been an emigrant thug, he had clung to the habit of making himself as inconspicuous as possible. He instinctively crossed over to the opposite sidewalk when he saw a policeman coming.

After washing down the dust from the back roads with a good slug of *sambuca*—which in hunting circles would have been known as "having a wee early morning nip"—he put on a fresh safari suit, set his ranger's hat at just the right angle, and headed out into the street toward Patel's. He preferred to make his way there on foot, for even though the tusks that Salim had gotten the day before and other valuable trophies were safely hidden in the false bottom of his Land Rover, duly watched over by one of his men, he didn't want to drive around the city in broad daylight with a load like that.

It must have been about eleven when he arrived in front of the moneychanger's shop. He knew that he had about an hour to discuss matters with his associate and agree on prices before the photographic safari vans coming back from the parks would vomit their loads of tourists out onto the streets of Nairobi, all of them eagerly buying up motheaten zebra hides and fake lions' teeth. Meanwhile the clerks of the curio shops were busy cleaning and polishing trophies and silver souvenirs with kerosene-moistened rags, leaving the shops reeking of an acrid, penetrating odor mindful of a pharmacy.

On the other occasions, Bruno had tried to pass himself off as a tourist, casually asking the clerks the price of this or that article so as to see how much of a profit Patel was reaping on the trophies that he resold, but this little game soon came to an end the minute the money-changer recognized Bruno's unmistakable figure from behind the glass panels of the shop's back room. This time Bruno walked straight inside the moneychanger's sanctuary, parting the red drapes with one sweep of his hand and tossing his hat covered with dirt on top of the immaculate ivory carving representing a Victorian locomotive. Patel, who was leaning over his office desk counting currency, gave a start on seeing that sudden apparition, and turned as pale as alabaster beneath his ashen complexion, instinctively stretching out his hairy forearms to protect his banknotes, like a broody hen spreading her wings to shield her chicks from danger.

"Damn it all, Toffani, you gave me a start. Can't you let me know you're in the shop before you come barging in here?"

"When I've come other times, you've gotten mad because I hang around talking with your employees, so what is it exactly you want me to do?"

"What I don't want is for you to go around asking stupid questions about the prices of the merchandise and getting the sales staff all upset. You know very well that I'm obliged to sell the trophies at a higher price than the one I pay you for them. If you only knew how much it costs me to keep this shop going. You don't know what I have to pay in commissions alone to the bigwigs in various ministries! Otherwise, my shop license wouldn't be good for even one year."

"I trust you realize that I too put out a whole lot of dough in tips and commissions."

"I know. But I don't ask you how much you pay for the trophies you buy in the jungle, so you shouldn't ask me questions about how much I sell them for."

"You're right there," Toffani granted, in a sudden burst of sincerity. "When you come right down to it, the prices you ask are your business. But it seems that all of us are more and more inclined to stick our noses into other people's business. Just this morning, as I was in the process of shipping off some ivory at Embakasi, I had to scare off a nosy sort who, if I hadn't been watching, would have started poking around right inside my van. I think he was just a tourist, but you never know. He might very well be one of those ecologists whose very next step would be to write a four-page article in all the newspapers about ivory contraband."

Patel opened his eyes a bit wider on hearing that, and immediately connected it with Bob Fender's visit to his shop the day before.

"Describe to me what that nosy sort looked like, because I think I may have met up with him myself. Was he wearing a pair of green pants and a safari jacket with big loops on his pockets for bullets?"

"I only saw him for a second in very dim light; he took to his heels like a fallow deer buck, with my men chasing after him, but I do seem to remember that he was wearing some sort of explorer's outfit. I never managed to see his face but if my boys had caught up with him, I guarantee you they'd have taught him a good lesson. Do you know who that man is?"

"It may be, it may very well be, the very same one I'm telling you about. An American has arrived in town, half a spy and half an ecologist, who's been snooping around all over. . . . He was here at the shop too, and I changed some money for him, though as a matter of fact I don't think that's what he came here for at all. Do you remember that other American ecologist, the one whose name was Murphy?"

"No, I have no idea who you're talking about," Toffani said, so emphatically that it sounded just a bit suspicious.

"Yes, of course you do, my good man. The one who was killed a few days ago on Mackinnon Road."

"An American?"

"I'm surprised you don't know anything about it, because the thought occurred to me that that was about the same area in which your men operate. As a matter of fact, people said that the American who died in a car accident as he was crossing the Tsavo was also an agent, and it's my opinion that this other one has arrived on the scene to investigate his death. He left just today for the coast. In other words, he might very well be the man you ran into at the airport. But don't worry, I think this guy is interested in sniffing out bigger trophies than a few mere elephant tusks."

"I hope so. As long as he doesn't stick his nose in our affairs, he can go poking around the tomb of the Duke of Aosta as far as I'm concerned. But to get back to the business at hand, this time I've brought you a pair of tusks worthy of being placed at the entrance of the National Museum."

"A pair?"

80

"A fantastic pair; perfectly matched, large and beautifully curved, and weighing over ninety pounds apiece. A collector's item, and it would be a shame to sell that pair by weight, to be sawed up and turned into stupid carved pieces, like that ridiculous piece of trash," Bruno said, pointing to the ivory locomotive.

"I won't have any more of your derogatory remarks about this masterpiece. Your sensitivities are too crude to appreciate it. And where, may I ask, is this trophy of yours?"

"I haven't brought it here yet. I'm thinking of asking seventy-five thousand shillings for it, but I won't even get it out of the van for less than fifty thousand on the table."

"Fifty thousand shillings! Are you out of your mind?"

"Fifty thousand just to start talking prices; we'll go on with the discussion once I've seen how much you're willing to pay me for the rest of the trophies I've brought. There are other interesting items, but you're going to fall in love with the tusks. They'd be worthy of occupying the place of honor in a sultan's palace!"

"Speaking of sultans, how are things going between you and Bwana Game?"

"Lawrence Brown, you mean? May the devil take him!"

"I've been told your men have to watch their step so as not to impinge on his territory. I imagine that's quite difficult, isn't it, seeing as how there are no one-way traffic signs in the jungle?"

"Damned Britishers! We should never have allowed them to win the war! If it were left up to my men, especially to Salim the Somali, they'd long since have run Brown out with a shower of arrows. But that's exactly what I'm trying to avoid—a serious incident in that area—because of my political connections. Do you follow me?"

"I understand you perfectly, but I presume that some day there's bound to be a clash, since the two of you operate in practically the same area, and interesting trophies are getting harder and harder to come by all the time."

"You're absolutely right there. The entire Tsavo area and the shores of the Galana are very nearly hunted out."

"It's your fault, since you've killed off everything that moved in that whole region."

"The thing is that the animals are not stupid, and they seek refuge on the Galana Ranch, where there's more cover and they know they're better protected. Just yesterday I had a very tempting offer for a good rhino horn, but I'm afraid that if I want to get a really decent trophy, I'll have to send my men to the other side of the Galana River, and I'm going to try to avoid that as long as I can."

"It's incredible that after Africanization and all that business, it's the old-time white colonials who continue to run the country. I wish we Asiatics had been able to hold onto a few small privileges!"

"Don't complain. You're set up like a pasha here in this precious shop, and making a bundle on the black market in currency exchange —do you think I don't know that trading in trophies is only peanuts for you? Whereas some of us you call whites"—and as he said this he rolled up his sleeves to show the color of his forearms, which between his deep tan and the dirt on them was obviously quite a bit darker than that of the Hindu's skin—"have to wander all over the place, from sunup to sundown, over god-awful roads, sweating for every penny. You at least don't have to risk your neck!"

"Yes, but if I make just one wrong move, I risk having my license taken away and getting myself thrown out of the country."

"And what do you think will happen to me the day my father-in-law loses his post in the KANU, or I get an irresistible urge to boot my wife right out on her ass! The two of us are in the same boat, believe me."

"As a matter of fact, I wanted to talk to you about that very thing, the future. Do you know J. Muriuki?"

"The Marxist politician?"

"Yes, the leader of the opposition—who, incidentally, is about as Marxist as you or I are. The thing is that for some time he's been trying to establish closer relations with me, and according to all indications his stock is going up in the world of politics. He might very well become the next President, in the not very distant future. But by then it would be too late to become a bosom buddy of his; I'd have to make my move now. . . ."

"And you want me to be the one to contact him for you?"

"I'm watched very closely, but you're not. You could take advantage of the fact that you're here in town to go see him. They say he receives anybody and everybody, so as to gain followers. You could tell him what the situation is like down on the coast, tell him that people are hungry and dissatisfied, that'll please him, and the problems that you're having with an Englishman whose ranch occupies a huge stretch of land between the Tana and the Galana. Lay it on a bit thick and tell him that the foreigner has any African who sets foot on his ranch beaten up, even if he's only a honey hunter.

82

Muriuki's a passionate defender of the poor *wananchi*, as you know."

"That's what he says in his speeches, but then it turns out that he doesn't exactly live like a pariah, according to what my father-in-law has told me. He said he keeps race horses and owns fine coffee plantations."

"That's all quite true, but the important thing is to get on the good side of him. Tell Muriuki that whole business about the new agent too. I'm certain that'll interest him. Fender, the American's name is, I'll write it down for you; but above all don't let on that I was the one who told you."

"What's the point then?"

"It's how things are done; he'll know where the information is coming from even though you don't tell him. But given my relations with the present government, I couldn't go to him openly myself."

"And so you're sending me, is that it? And what about my family connections with the KANU? If my father-in-law finds out I've gone to see Muriuki, I'll lose his confidence, and I'll be lying dead in the water with all my sails struck again."

"Don't be stupid. How's he going to find out if he's in Mombasa, and you're here in Nairobi, where you're practically unknown? Nobody will ever know. And I asure you that it's a contact that's of interest for your future. If we want to survive, our only way out is to behave like leeches, that change mount when the lead mule gets sick or old."

"Yes, but for the moment I don't think that things are going all that badly for us with the old mount. I don't like games like this!"

"They're not games. Get it through your head once and for all that in Africa the endangered species aren't elephants or rhinos, but people like you and me, Asiatics or Europeans who don't have cushy jobs or loads of money, people that these savages are eager to bump off so as to grab the few pennies we earn by the sweat of our brow. Pay attention to me for once, and don't be pigheaded. Go and see Muriuki; you won't regret it!"

The Kilifi Ferry

As THEY ROUNDED A CURVE, Bob had the impression that the road was going to plunge directly into the sea. It was the Kilifi inlet, a broad arm of the sea that extended several miles inland, with the bright blue water forcing its way through rocky gorges and thick vegetation. Bob thought the spot must have been a perfect shelter once upon a time for slave traders. In several places along the shore, the half-moon of a beach could be seen where the waves died gently away—a landing stage. Some canoes were tied to wooden mooring stakes, and a few small sailboats were heading out to sea, taking advantage of the afternoon breeze.

They had to wait for a while until the ferry boat that plied back and forth across the harbor returned from the other shore, and when the gate went up, a swarm of pedestrians, cyclists, and vehicles rushed onto the floating platform like a plague of locusts. The crossing seemed endless, though it lasted no more than a few minutes. Bob had closed the car window in order to keep out the nauseating smell of diesel exhaust, and under the rays of sun coming through the windshield, every inch of metal was incandescent. A crowd of Africans was filling the narrow deck, jammed against the railing, with flies clinging to the corners of their mouths and eyes, looking with curiosity at the occupants of the vehicles. Some of the women, with lighter complexions, long loose-fitting robes of black cloth, and black veils over their faces, gave evidence of the profound trace left by the Arab slave traders along that coast.

Bob had never had such a feeling of claustrophobia as on that ferry boat, which seemed about to capsize at any moment, overloaded as it was with vehicles, animals, and human beings. The idea crossed his mind that all those people on the deck could stage a sudden rebellion and occupy the interior of the vehicles and the roofs of the buses. Great seabirds flew over their heads, emitting strident cries, as though to incite the passengers to mutiny.

84

However, as the ferry boat touched the other shore, the crowd silently drifted away, with a seeming air of resignation.

Suddenly there came back to Bob's mind the memory of the last time that he had gone out to Long Island with John Murphy on a hunting trip. John's parents had a small house on the outskirts of a little town called Wading River, where John spent the weekends and organized his hunting trips. Usually he hunted wild geese and duck, and occasionally even bagged a buck or a wild turkey. Sometimes he would take the ferry across to Shelter Island, where the keeper of a private hunting club would allow him to enter the grounds provided he didn't interfere with the activities of the club members, who were rich and powerful people. One morning, before dawn, the two of them had started out together for the club, and the rising sun found them aboard the ferry that went across North Bay to Shelter Island. He remembered the scenery, with shocking clarity.

It was a freezing cold morning, and the ferry boat literally broke through the layer of ice on top of the still waters as it made its way across the bay. Along the shores of the island the layer of ice was thicker and covered with a thin mantle of snow that had fallen during the night and covered the sand on the beach as well. A thick blanket of fog was still hovering above the dense woods on the island, and the open sea that we could just barely make out at the far end of the bay cast strange glints in the reddish light of the rising sun. The entire scene seemed totally unreal; in order to have a good look at it, John and I got out of the car, and we stood there as though hypnotized, clinging to the railing, with our hands numb from the cold and letting out steamy puffs of breath through our mouths, reluctant nonetheless to return to the shelter of the car.

Once we reached the other side, after the prow of the ferry had broken a path through the solid crust of ice along the shore—it seems to me I can hear the splash of the icy water against the metal hull at this very moment—John drove at top speed along the muddy roads of the island, since obviously we were missing the best time of day for shooting geese, which took flight at first light. Coming out of the trees, we arrived at a snow-covered beach where the water formed a deep pool, collecting the waters of a little stream flowing out of the woods. We settled down there, after putting up rudimentary hunting blinds we made from dead leaves and reeds we gathered from the shore.

As usual, John took the best spot, one where the visibility was good and the geese could be seen as they came flying past from the other side of the bay; and I was left with a far less advantageous spot, at the far end of the little stream, where you were hard put to see the birds until they were directly overhead, and you had to take aim between the tops of the trees. When John took me hunting, he always put me in the worst spot, since that way, knowing that I was a poor shot, "at least I wouldn't scare the game off," as he put it.

After we'd been there a few minutes, I began to hear the far-off cackling of geese and in the distance I spied the little dark dots of geese coming our way up the bay and about to fly past us above our heads. My heart began to beat faster, and I held on tight to the stock of my shotgun as I saw the flock approaching, flying past the beaches, about to choose a quiet spot to land. But as they flew directly overhead, they were borne upward by the wind and passed so high above us that John didn't even bother to shoot. Following his example, I didn't shoot either. But curiously enough, a pair of geese from that same flock separated from the rest, flew in a low circle over the beach where we were, and finally landed at the very edge of the little stream where I'd set up my blind.

John couldn't get off any shots at them because they had come flying in from the other direction, but I suddenly found myself with a pair of magnificent Canadian geese just a few yards from my hiding place. I lay there as though petrified by the beauty and the majesty of those creatures that had sought out the middle of the little stream where there was more running water, and were swimming about very slowly, stretching their necks out every so often to poke about in the transparent bottom or smooth their feathers against the reeds. I must have made some sort of clumsy move, however, for the geese, who were only a few yards away, remained motionless for a few seconds, looking toward my blind in alarm, and then took flight. I remember that the sun's rays were now shining down diagonally on the little stream, illuminating each little detail of their wings and their snow-white breasts as they took flight; if I had had a camera I would have been able to capture on film every last little drop of water dripping off their feathers, and the way they retracted their feet as they took off again.

But at that moment John, who had been watching the whole scene from his blind, no doubt biting his nails in frustration because the geese were out of range of his shotgun, could contain himself no longer and shouted at the top of his lungs: "Shoot, you idiot, they're taking off! Shoot!" His voice echoed curiously across the bed of the *frozen stream and through the woods. The echo mingled with the loud report of my shotgun and the thud of one of the geese as it landed, in a flurry of feathers and blood, on the snow of the beach.*

John then emerged from his blind, shouting for all he was worth, a mixture of congratulations and insults for my not having fired at the geese sooner: "You could easily have gotten both of them!" He was so excited as he came running across the snow that he didn't even see the frozen surface of the little stream, slipped on the ice, and went sprawling, ending up with his nose buried in the mud right in front of where I was standing with my smoking shotgun. "What are you complaining about?" I said to him. "I downed two geese: the one lying there on the beach . . . and you!"

Bob had relived each one of the gestures and words of that scene as though it had happened only yesterday. For some incomprehensible reason, the atmosphere saturated with heat, humidity, and flies, the blinding-bright blue sky and the intense green of the palm trees had brought back the memory of the lead-colored waters of the Atlantic, the icy air of the bay, the whiteness of the snow and the feathers of the goose. It had been a long time since he had remembered his student days with such immediacy. For the very first time since he had learned of John Murphy's accident, he suddenly realized that his friend was dead; he would never again see his smile or hear that hearty laugh that came from the bottom of his heart. John would never again latch onto the best spots on a hunting trip, or the prettiest girl at a party, explaining to Bob that she really wasn't his type anyway.

He felt an intense sort of cold, despite the heat, and an emotion that gave him cramps in the pit of his stomach. The silhouettes of the seagulls reminded him of the majestic flight of the geese; he had taken the Kilifi ferry and landed on Shelter Island.

Contraband

"Too EASY! *Porco Dio!* Too easy!" Bruno Toffani kept muttering to himself in the back seat of the car that was taking him, as dusk fell, along the highway to Langata. Seated on either side of him was one of J. Muriuki's bodyguards, and he had to thrust his arms well forward so as not to brush up against the butts of the pistols poking out from under the suit coats of the two men accompanying him. Why had he listened to the advice of that East Indian, Patel, and got himself mixed up in politics? If he had had the moneychanger within reach at that moment, he would have boxed his ears.

That morning, following Patel's advice, he had dropped in at the Hotel Hilton, the bar of which was known to be a favorite haunt of J. M.'s. The leader of the opposition met regularly with his cronies, did his drinking, and even settled political matters there, boldly and openly criticizing government policies and telling jokes ridiculing those running the country. Toffani sat down at one of the tables with menus encased in plastic like those at a run-of-the-mill American lunch counter, and playing the role of the ingenuous fool, he asked one of the men at a neighboring table if J. M. had been around there lately. He was merely trying to feel out the terrain, perhaps for later, knowing that because he could easily pass for a coffee dealer or an agent from a travel bureau he would pass unnoticed in that crowd. To his great surprise, the person he spoke to, a young, slim, flashily dressed black wearing a Panama hat, picked up his glass of beer and came over to sit at his table. Toffani wondered for a few seconds whether he hadn't ended up in the wrong pew since that bar was frequented by gay hustlers who competed with the Somali whores for tourist pickups. But he soon realized that, on the contrary, his question had hit closer to the mark than he had counted on.

The dandy in the Panama hat winked at him, and touching the

brim of his hat with his index finger he murmured, "If you want to talk with Ndume, today's your lucky day. For two bills I'll arrange for you to see the boss this very afternoon." Toffani shivered on hearing that name: Ndume—the bull—one used by J. M.'s followers, because of the politician's massive bulk, the defiant tilt of his head on his broad neck, always held as erect as that of a young fighting bull.

Too late to backpedal; the young man was no doubt one of Muriuki's henchmen whose suspicions would be aroused if his offer were not accepted. Although he was taken somewhat by surprise, Toffani was such an old hand at bribery that he tried to strike a bargain: "A hundred shillings now, and the rest when I've gotten to meet him." The man's only answer was to hold out his hand, taking the bill that Toffani held out to him between two fingers, and it was only when he stashed it away in the inside pocket of his suit coat that Toffani saw the dull gleam of a gun beneath his armpit.

The henchman told him not to budge from his hotel during the afternoon, and Toffani had locked himself in his room with a bottle of *sambuca* to calm his nerves. Why in hell was he sticking his nose into trouble like this? At exactly five o'clock he heard a car engine, and through the window he saw the young man with the Panama hat and a couple more thugs who had come to pick him up. They stuffed him into the back seat of the car, the way the police haul off a dangerous criminal, and drove through the city along the highway that led to the hills.

As the car drove up the Langata grade, all sorts of doubts and apprehensions nonetheless crossed Bruno's mind. Might this be a trap laid by the Special Branch in order to capture a possible supporter of Muriuki's? Though he might indeed have run into one of the politician's inner circle of supporters, he might just as easily be talking to a police informer, or a member of the much-feared secret services. In fact those toughs who made up the ranks of the espionage and domestic counter-espionage services all looked alike, frequented the same places, and sometimes even switched over from working for the government to working for the opposition with the greatest of ease.

As the setting sun began to turn the crest of the Ngong Hills a deep gold, Toffani remembered that it was along the deserted trails across the tops of these hills that the police were in the habit of taking the most dangerous criminals and terrorists abandoning them after having put a few bullets through them; so that the hyenas and other scavengers prowling about devoured the corpses, spreading the remains so far and wide that it was impossible to identify such victims of state terror.

Hence, even though he had not yet gotten out of the tight spot he was in, Bruno breathed a sigh of relief on seeing the car turn off the Ngong highway onto a gravel road that led to one of the first houses on the outskirts of Langata—J. M.'s house.

On more than one occasion Bruno had visited the home of an African politician—beginning with that of his own father-in-law in Mombasa—and hence was not surprised at the rather untidy appearance of the garden or the filthy looking dwelling. In the parking area, brand new Mercedeses sat side by side with broken-bottomed *matutus* with dented fenders and doors tied shut with lengths of wire. From the back yard came puffs of thick smoke, redolent of aromatic spices and other cooking ingredients; chickens had wandered into the entry hall of the house and were pecking about underneath the chairs in the anteroom where a large group of followers and favor-seekers were waiting to be received by Muriuki.

The bodyguards, however, led him through the garden, thus avoiding the crowded entry hall, and took him round back to Muriuki's private office. In the middle of a half-wild garden full of clumps of unpruned eucalyptus, several old women dressed in African tunics were fanning the coals of a fire on which an immense pot was boiling. Before entering the house, Toffani had to dodge a bunch of children in rags who were chasing a big red and black chicken that was running about and cackling as though they were about to cut its neck off; and in fact that was precisely what the youngsters had in mind, since one of them was wielding a razor-sharp machete. Toffani endeavored to erase that fateful omen from his superstitious mind, furtively crossing himself several times. They made him wait for a few minutes on a little glass-enclosed veranda from which he could see the back of Muriuki's bulky frame bent over his desk, surrounded by his toughs and collaborators. Bruno noticed that one of the men who had brought him there—not the one with the hat—said something in J. M.'s ear, and that the head man then turned to one of his aides, holding out some papers to him. The aide—whose face looked vaguely familiar to Bruno, no doubt because he had seen his picture in some newspaper—left the office and walked over to Bruno, holding out his hand to him. "You're Patel's associate, right?"

"Yes," Toffani murmured, a bit taken aback. How the devil had they known?

"The chief can't see you right now, but he gave me a message for you," he said, waving an envelope full of documents. "Come outside with me for a minute, if you will; we'll have more peace and quiet in the garden to talk."

Outside, a cool breeze had come up that was making the eucalyptus leaves quiver, and the last rays of sunlight played over the bottoms of the hills. Muriuki's aide walked Bruno to the far end of the garden, taking him by the arm and shifting to the familiar form of address. Finally, with an air of mystery, he took the documents out of the envelope; they fluttered in the breeze.

"At the end of this week a Dutch freighter is arriving in Mombasa, which will dock at Pier 23 in Kilindini Harbor. It will be carrying a shipment of coal and building materials, and also several bundles of merchandise consigned to Muriuki, although his name does not figure on any of the bills of lading or shipping documents. The captain knows that this is a very special consignment and will take the necessary steps to see that the port authorities don't ask too many questions about the contents of these bundles."

He looked at Toffani intently to see if the latter was following his explanation, but Bruno remained silent. His face was deathly pale, and the wart on his nose, which had suddenly turned a bright red, betrayed his nervousness.

"All you have to do is present yourself to the captain with these papers, and have the bundles taken away in a truck at an hour when no one will notice. If it's necessary to pay any further tips, we'll cover the costs. Once you've left the port, you know the trails along the coast better than anybody else and you'll know how to get the merchandise to a spot in the interior where it will be safe from all eyes. You may even bury the bundles, since they're wrapped in plastic, but don't jolt them too much—don't start jumping up and down with them—in other words, as the English say, Handle with Care. Do you get what I mean?"

Toffani nodded, among other reasons because he had been left speechless; his years of brushes with the law had wised him up enough to know that that was not a proposal but a demand, with the same peremptory force as a court verdict. If he had shown the slightest sign of doubt or vacillation at that moment, the road back to Nairobi would pass, for him, by way of the crest of the Ngong Hills.

"How will I know the name of the ship and of the captain?" he said finally, swallowing hard.

"They're in these papers; but be careful not to lose them. The merchandise will be handed over to anyone possessing these documents, and I don't like to think what might happen to us if it fell into the hands of the police. And I don't need to tell you that Ndume's reaction to any sort of slip would be extremely severe."

"Don't worry, I have a fair amount of experience in handling delicate cargo. I'm quite used to getting shipments of trophies and ivory out of the country right under the authorities' very noses."

"I know. That's why we've chosen you. But don't forget that this is a much more important matter. Some of the bundles are heavy matériel. Do you follow me?"

"I understand, I understand perfectly." Even though the light was fading fast as dusk fell it was not difficult to make out the letterhead of an arms factory. "I'll try to hide the shipment in the best possible place."

"We'll get in touch with you again, through Patel, though we'll be laying low for a while just in case. It isn't necessary, of course, to let your associate in on all the details of the operation, or let him know where you've cached the arms. Just tell the Indian that the boss will soon be needing a sum of money changed to pay for certain merchandise that will be coming from Europe, and that you'll take charge of transporting it."

"All right. You can count on my being discreet." Toffani's eyes had a wicked gleam in them; he had just remembered what Patel had told him about the secret agent, something that would surely interest Muriuki, and might even serve him as more or less of an out if the operation should fail for any reason. "We mustn't be overconfident, however, since the whole coastal area is in a state of unrest these days on account of the accident that happened to that American. You know—the diplomat who got killed on Mackinnon Road."

"Why wouldn't I know, since they're blaming his death on us now? As though we were responsible for every drunk who crashes into a tree at some ungodly hour of the morning."

"The thing is that the police have been sniffing around there, and now, according to what Patel tells me, they're going to send another American agent, who'll be using the cover of an explorer, to go on with the investigation of the accident."

"What terrible pests these imperialist agents are! They're like flies— you kill one and a thousand others come zooming in."

"The worst of it is that the area where the accident occurred happens to be dangerously close to our center of operations: in the eastern sector of the Tsavo, bordering on Mackinnon Road. In fact, the agent is going to be staying at Galana Ranch, whose manager, Lawrence Brown, is another big shot. One of those old-time English colonials, stiffer and tougher than a truncheon, who has tyrannized all the Africans in the area. I hope that those people won't coming poking around while I'm transporting the merchandise."

"Well, if any of them tries to stick his nose in our business, don't hesitate to teach him a lesson. You should try to avoid violence as long as it isn't absolutely necessary. Don't forget that we're in a delicate situation at the moment. What I'd like is for you to keep a sharp eye on the American, without trying to get rid of him. And as for the Englishman, guys like that are going to run into a stray bullet when they least expect it. The minute Muriuki takes over, it'll be open season on British *muzungus*. Whites may be lording it over everybody now, but you're going to see them running like rabbits one of these days. In the meantime, we have to wait. . . ."

"It's been hard for me to keep my men from shooting it out with Brown, because he sometimes hunts down poor poachers as though they were vermin."

"You know that the chief will be grateful for your help, and will back you up if you have any kind of problem. But first make sure that the merchandise gets hidden in a safe place."

"Of course; leave it to me. I'll see to it that there's no trouble. I do think it's necessary, though, to send some of my men over to the other side of the river to keep an eye on the agent's movements."

"Do whatever you think best. What I'd like you to do is to throw a good scare into him, so he learns not to get involved in things that aren't any of his business, but without rubbing him out. That would only lead to complications for us."

"Don't worry."

"That's how it'll be then. Until we pick up the arms. After that, the entire area will be all yours. I assure you that you won't regret having done Ndume this favor. He knows how to pay his friends back."

The man abruptly broke off the conversation because by now they had walked back to the house and could be overheard. Before bidding Toffani good-bye, he said to him:

"And don't forget to tell Patel that we'll be visiting him one of these days for that money-changing operation."

Too easy. As he was climbing back into the car that would take

93

him back to the city, Bruno realized that he was trapped. The documents that he was carrying in the pocket of his safari jacket seemed as heavy as lead. He would gladly have thrown them out the car window, whereupon the Park monkeys prowling about in the ditch along the road would have torn them to little bits with their teeth and their sharp claws. But he couldn't even allow such a thought to cross his mind. From that moment on, his very life depended on those filthy papers, as though they had sewn them to his heart. The very fact that they had sent only one of the bodyguards with him on this return trip was disturbing proof of how sure they were of him: He was involved up to his neck.

The only positive thing about the whole business was that he now had Muriuki's backing to enter Galana Ranch property. This might be worth some two thousand pounds to him, the sum that Townsend-Reeves would pay him for a good rhino horn, not to mention what he might get for a pair or two of good elephant tusks. That wasn't a bad deal. But the rest of the business smelled to high heaven. Alongside this contraband shipment of arms, his own trafficking in contraband ivory and charcoal seemed like child's play. Why had he had to run across that man of Muriuki's so soon? If it had taken him a couple of days longer to find him, he himself might already have left the city. He'd been just too damned lucky!

As they drove down the grade from Langata, the lights of Nairobi began to dot the dusk, and towering above them all was the brightly lit Conference Center, already half-shrouded in the evening fog. Seen against the light from the valley, the city had a magical, mysterious halo, with a promise of luxurious brothels and splendid feasts. Bruno was so distraught, however, that he'd lost all desire to eat and fornicate.

Too easy. *Porco Dio!* Too easy.

94

Akkokantera Bark

THEY REACHED THE GALANA AREA in the late afternoon. They had left the main road, taking the shortcut called Mackinnon Road, and entered the National Park via the Sala gate. Bob felt as though he were enveloped in that mantle of red dust full of bushes stretching out their bare branches like hands of a starving man. The burning hot sun had beat down all day long in that clay bowl, so that it mattered little whether the window of the Toyota was open or closed: The dust filtered into his body through every pore, and the heat turned into a solid, palpable substance, like a second skin. Lawrence Brown didn't seem at all affected by the suffocating heat; on the contrary, he seemed to come to life again from the moment they passed through the iron grille barring the entrance to the Park:

"This is Commiphora forest—or *nyka* as they call it around here; in certain places, the branches of the trees intertwine, and tall grasses and thornbushes grow between them, turning it into an impenetrable tangle. Although the Tsavo seems a bit more civilized now, what with its trails of beaten sand and a couple of lodges for tourists, in reality it's still a wild, desolate area. In the old days, the slave caravans left behind them a macabre trail of those who died on the way, of exhaustion or sickness. Even today there are people who get lost and die of dehydration hereabouts. If you don't know the terrain and wander off one of the trails, it's nearly impossible to get your bearings because of these damned bushes that all look alike, and the shimmering reddish light that's exactly the same color as the ground."

The Park guards had dug ponds in certain places so that the animals could drink, hollows that had filled up with stagnant muddy water so that they looked more like shell holes, giving the landscape an even greater air of desolation. It was only when they crossed *luggas*—dry riverbeds—that there were any signs of green vegetation, and in the shade of a thorny acacia one glimpsed from time to time the silhouette of an antelope, so motionless, its coloring blending so perfectly with the background of dead leaves and ocher ground on which it was lying that one had to look back to convince oneself that it had not been a mirage. There was not the slightest sign of the largest animals, elephants, buffaloes, or rhinos, only the traces of great havoc wrought on the vegetation, branches of bushes broken off and trunks of large trees with every last bit of their bark stripped off.

"That's the work of elephants," Lawrence Brown said, pointing to the bare trunks. "They're looking for water. Every so often there's a tremendous drought, and the animals die by the thousands—all by themselves, for a change, without the help of man. That strip of greenery you see down there lies along the banks of the Galana, which marks the borderline of the Park; on the other side is the ranch."

The vegetation in fact began to turn green once again as they approached the river, and a breath of humid air came in through the car window. Bob was able to record in his field notebook another variety of vegetation different from the monotonous Commiphora: different species of acacia, *Cassia, Delonix, Melia volkensi.* Beneath the stunted crown of a *tortililis* acacia a herd of splendid impalas was grazing, scattering as the car approached with such long, clean leaps that their legs seemed to be equipped with resilient springs. He also recorded in his notebook the existence of *Sarse vivaria,* wild bowstring hemp.

"Look at that antelope camouflaged underneath the branches of that bush," Brown said. "It's a gerenuk, or giraffe antelope, with a long neck."

Bob could see nothing, no matter how hard he stared. He realized that the intense pupils of Lawrence Brown's eyes, accustomed to the shimmering light and the slight variation in tone of that reddish crust of earth, acted like the photoelectric cells of a computer, giving him all the information he needed, never missing the slightest trace left by an antelope or the least bit of dried elephant dung, even though beetles had already scattered it. For the manager of the Galana Ranch, those sandy trails, covered with tracks of every size and description, revealed clear signs of the movements of herds and the patterns of life in the wilds, as flashing traffic signals did to a citizen of the world of paved freeways. Nonetheless, Bob felt sure that Lawrence Brown was trying to detect the trace of naked feet—or the print of sandals—that would betray the presence of poachers in the area.

At that moment, Bob saw that the hunter's face had changed expression: Down by the Galana River, a whirlwind of dust raised by another vehicle had just appeared, on one of the side roads leading off from the main road through the Park. As though propelled by a secret spring, Lawrence Brown pushed the brake pedal to the floor, stopped the Toyota short in its tracks, and headed it across country in the direction of the trail where an off-white canvas-top van with Africans inside had suddenly appeared.

"What's happening?" Bob said, his head having hit the roof of the safari car the moment that Brown had applied the brakes.

"Can't you see? That van there!"

"Yes, I see it, but what's up?"

"They're obviously poachers," the hunter growled, flooring the accelerator.

Bob found himself unable to ask even one more question, since the car was bumping about so as it crossed that terrain full of anthills and fallen tree trunks that he was obliged to clutch the panic bar for all he was worth. The occupants of the other car soon realized that Lawrence Brown intended to cut them off, and tried their best to shake him, taking off at top speed in the direction of the main road through the Park. The two cars raised great clouds of dust and the *nyka* forest soon turned into a roiling sea of red grit.

Despite the fact that Brown was driving with his foot to the floor, the other car had had a head start and reached the exit of the Park a few minutes before they did, whereupon the iron grille opened as if by magic, and the vehicle immediately disappeared down Mackinnon Road. When Brown's car reached the gate, however, the iron grille was closed and the gatekeeper did not appear, even though Brown drove up honking his horn like a man possessed. The gatekeeper wasn't in his booth or anywhere nearby: It was as though he had been swept away in the wake of reddish dust left by the other car. The hunter leaped out of the car and found that the guard had taken refuge in an outhouse some twenty yards from his booth. He knocked in vain on the door of the latrine, which resounded like a tin drum; the only reply was a series of muffled grunts, accompanied by other indescribable noises. After considerable time, the gatekeeper came out of his shell with an embarrassed smile, still buttoning up his pants. Brown, his face red with rage, ordered him to open the iron grille.

Although the discussion took place in Swahili, Bob gathered that the gatekeeper was refusing to open up, and was asking to see the car papers again. Brown refused to show them to him, saying that he'd already seen them when they'd gone through the gate just a few minutes before. But the gatekeeper stuck to his guns and walked round and round the car, contemplating the license plate and staring wide-eyed at this or that detail as though he'd never seen an automobile before in his life. The hunter was so overwrought that Bob feared he might leap on the rascal's neck. But after a few minutes of violent verbal interchange in African dialect, Brown climbed back into the car, turned it around, and drove back over the same road they had come by.

"There's no point in chasing after them any longer," he said, once he'd calmed down enough to be able to speak. "They've doubtless taken one or another of the trails leading off Mackinnon Road or lit out along the highway to Malindi, and it'll be impossible to catch up with them now."

"I may be terribly stupid," Bob stammered, trying to clear his throat of the dust that was sticking to his glottis and rubbing the knee that had hit the dashboard as the car lurched back and forth, "but I don't understand what that whole chase was all about."

"This area of the Park is too remote to be visited by tourists, and seeing that there are very few big department stores and movie theaters round about here, anybody who's driving along these trails, especially at this hour, is more than likely to be a poacher or a smuggler of some sort. Mackinnon Road is their favorite route for taking their merchandise down to the Port of Mombasa to sell."

"Couldn't we simply have taken down the license number of that car and notified the police?"

Lawrence Brown smiled scornfully.

"Any of the cars using the trails around here are well known to the police and the Park rangers who, as you've seen, give them complete protection. In this instance, I think that Land Rover we saw belongs to an Indian who works for an Italian crook named Toffani. He controls a large part of the illegal trafficking in this area along the coast, and he's bought off more than half the Park guards and the local police."

"Isn't there any way of putting pressure on the authorities to make those venal guards follow the straight and narrow?"

"To be frank with you, I understand why they allow themselves to

98

be bribed; the commission they're paid for a rhino horn is perhaps the equivalent of several months' salary for them. Moreover, we can't expect all of them to be heroes, and some of those poachers can be pretty tough customers to deal with. They're always armed, and they're the sort who shoot first and ask questions afterward."

"Where do they get their arms? Do the police provide them with weapons as well?"

"No, they obtain them themselves. The traditional hunting weapons are bows and poisoned arrows; the poison most often used is made by boiling the bark of a species of Akkokantera. It's a primitive but effective system; if the arrowhead reaches a vital spot, it can kill an elephant in two hours. Unfortunately, what usually happens is that the elephant wanders off badly wounded and it may be several days or sometimes weeks before it dies."

"It sounds pretty horrible."

"It is. It's an extremely corrosive poison; once, years ago, I saw a ranger who'd been wounded in one arm by a poisoned arrow after a run-in with poachers. The skin of his arm literally fell off in great shreds. I don't know if the poor fellow survived or not."

"How awful!"

"This, however, as I was saying, is the traditional method, used mostly by the local tribes, the Wakamba and the Waliangulu. But lately, many of the poachers who operate in this area have gone modern; and the Somalis even have automatic rifles. . . . I don't know where they get them."

"Supposing they were poachers and had used their arms against us, what would have happened if we'd managed to catch up with that van?" Bob glanced around him; it didn't look as though there was any sort of weapon at hand in the Toyota.

There was no answer to his question; the hunter merely looked at him out of the corner of his eye and smiled again. Meanwhile they had arrived at the same point where the chase had begun, near the road leading to the Ranch.

"I'd be willing to bet my right arm that if we'd managed to catch up with those guys, we'd have found that they had a fair-sized load of trophies under the canvas of their van. The other day I found the carcass of a huge bull elephant in the very area they were coming from, right on the borderline of the Ranch. You can have a look for yourself—I'm going to drive down and show you the place."

Lawrence Brown left the main trail and took off down one of the smaller ones running parallel to the river. As they went farther and father along, the brush became thicker and thicker, till the grass touched the bumpers of the car and the canvas roof began to rip leaves off the low branches. Bob had the sensation that the jungle was closing in behind him. The late afternoon light grew dimmer and dimmer as they went farther into the dense forest with only a few openings overhead through which the rays of the setting sun filtered, vividly backlighting the dark vegetation giving off moisture and an odor of vegetable decay. Bob suddenly had the feeling that instead of entering the jungle he was sinking to the bottom of the sea in an amphibious vehicle: The colors of the plants made them look like coral formations, and the tall grass swayed slowly back and forth as the car passed, like seaweed rippling in an underwater current.

Moreover, the trail now ran along the bed of a narrow little stream, where the vehicle had to make its way around fallen, half-rotted tree trunks and rocks covered with moss, and heightening the impression of an underwater excursion. Brown had to turn on the car lights to see where he was going. They finally came out in a clearing covered with tall grass, in the center of which was a small water hole.

"Napier grass?" Bob asked, pointing.

"Yes. They call it elephant grass here. But look over there."

The first thing Bob noted as he got out of the car was a strong smell of carrion coming from the marsh, and then he saw, in the center of it, an immense animal carcass; in the dim light he was just able to make out, because of the color of the skin and the size of the ribcage, that it was the dead body of an elephant, already half eaten by scavengers. All that was left were a few strips of dried skin stuck to the abdomen and the spine; the head too seemed to be intact, being half submerged in the mud. A whitish crust, a mixture of decomposing flesh and bird droppings, was floating on the surface all around the animal.

Several vultures were still mounting guard on the bare branches of the nearby trees, and their sinister silhouettes were sharply outlined against the mauve sky, looming like giants in the last incandescent glow of the sun as it set. Brown noted a strange stirring in the elephant's abdomen, and threw a rock that fell a few inches short of the swollen belly. The head of a hyena, with its eyes wide open and its back completely smeared with blood, immediately appeared. Sensing the presence of humans, the animal let out a howl and ran off, leaping awkwardly across the mud and the aquatic plants. On reaching the other side of the water hole, before hiding itself in the jungle, it turned around for a moment to look at them, its paws and belly covered with mud and its head smeared with blood. Reflecting the headlights, its yellowish eyes gleamed satanically. Then it disappeared, filling the silence of the thicket with the echo of hysterical laughter.

"That elephant was killed by poachers just a couple of days ago, but the scavengers have taken it upon themselves to do away with it quickly. Nothing is lost in the jungle: As you see, the ecological cycle works perfectly."

Bob climbed back into the car without a word. All of a sudden, darkness had fallen.

The Red Bull

MASSIMO SAN MINIATO had decided that he wanted to see Nairobi by night no matter what. Normally, the people who came from Europe on safari, affected by the altitude of Nairobi and tired after the long flight, scarcely left the hotel on their first day, but these Italians seemed indefatigable. After being taken shopping all morning, they insisted on visiting the Museum of Natural Sciences and the Snake and Reptile Park in the afternoon.

So Tony Allen had taken advantage of the first day to analyze the characters of his most heterogeneous group: the Italian aristocrat in his fifties, Julia the raving beauty, and the Count's son, slim, svelte Paolo. Tony was one of those who believed that a person's first impression is almost always the most reliable one, but in the case of young Paolo, he felt that outward appearances were likely to be deceptive. The young man spoke in a soft, gentle voice, and the gestures of his graceful arms and hands might appear to be precious. But this impression of fragility was much more a reflection of his physique than of his character, for the gaze in his deep black eyes was steady and direct.

Of the three, the most representative human type was Count San

Miniato. Self-assured and authoritarian, he belonged to a caste of European aristocrats that had learned through centuries of history to hone its instinct for survival. Their selfishness increased, but not their ability to analyze their errors. The coffered ceiling of his ancestral dwelling may have been shaken and cracked by wars and revolutions, but the Count's coat of arms affixed to the facade was undoubtedly still intact. Tony knew that a clash of personalities between himself and the Count was very nearly inevitable, but for his part he would try to avoid a showdown as long as possible.

Julia, on the other hand, was hard to pigeonhole. Though she was extremely beautiful, he had the feeling that she had more than a gorgeous body going for her. She was certainly not one of those adventuresses who board a plane the minute they're offered an exotic vacation and the chance to be photographed in a safari costume standing on the back of a dead elephant! Tony, however, had vowed to himself that he would never again get involved with the wife or mistress of a client. As an old white hunter's saying had it, "Never try to sleep with the wife of the man who's paying for the whisky you're drinking." At least, not while on safari.

Tony took his clients to a restaurant, run by a *pied noir* Frenchman driven out of Algeria, that was usually a lively spot at night. The Red Bull was frequented by a motley clientele, a mixture of former landowners expropriated by Africanization, famous white hunters, Greek and Italian businessmen involved in the coffee racket, East Indians who'd made piles of money, and the few—very few—Africans who felt at ease among that select post-colonial mafia. Nonetheless, in the place of honor—directly below the huge buffalo head painted red that gave the place its name—the owner always kept a table reserved for members of the government.

Every so often some big fish in politics would turn up there accompanied by his fingerlings and sharks, and after they'd had a big blowout, they would go off without paying, merely shaking the hand of the owner, who would then see them to the door, bowing and scraping, delighted to have been able to please such illustrious spongers. And even though at this season most of the Ministers were on the coast, trailing along after the President, the table was left vacant as a symbol of respect for those in power.

When Tony and his clients entered the restaurant and Julia had made her way regally across the dining room, her dark hair pulled back with a simple tortoise-shell comb, a murmur of approval ran through the room and even the glass eyes of the old red buffalo seemed to have a gleam in them. The owner, Jean-François, immediately hurried over to them, making multiple salaams and explaining to them with a multitude of precise, precious gestures, the composition of the various dishes. Tony was sitting opposite Julia, and despite his vows, his eyes wandered now and again—admiring the curve of her breasts beneath her low-cut silk blouse—and then meeting the Italian woman's deep black eyes that shone intriguingly in the candlelight.

It was past nine and the place was full of life; the pleasant aroma of the candles mingled with the ladies' perfume and the appetizing smell of Parisian dishes seasoned with African spices. But suddenly in the midst of the general hubbub and the clinking of glasses and dishes, there was a hushed silence followed by a wave of rustling and murmurs, as when a fox suddenly slips through the door of the henhouse. An African with a distinguished air and an athletic build had just appeared in the doorway of the restaurant and—without waiting for anyone to come greet him—strode straight across the room, followed by his retinue of aides and bodyguards (one of them was wearing a broad-brimmed Panama hat)—and sat down at the empty table underneath the red buffalo head. His bright eyes defiantly swept the room, and his broad neck and head, held proudly erect, were mindful of the insolent bearing of a young fighting bull. It was J. Muriuki, in person.

The waiters were standing about as though rooted to the spot, and in the midst of the impressive silence one of them dropped a trayful of dishes. The din momentarily broke the tension and voices all over the room exclaimed in a half-whisper: "Ndume! Ndume!" Throughout all this the owner, Jean-François, who had been preparing some *crêpes flambées*, stood there not knowing what to do, his trembling hands not even feeling the heat of the skillet that was burning his fingers. Should he go greet Muriuki or should he tell him he was sorry, the table was reserved? Finally he opted for the first course of action, and several waiters followed him, offering drinks and appetizers, with a great deal of bowing and scraping. The fox had taken possession of the henhouse.

"Who is that guy?" San Miniato asked Tony Allen.

"You see before you the next President of Kenya," Tony answered, adding in a low murmur, "if he knows how to play his cards right and doesn't act rashly."

"And if he does act rashly?"

"His dead body will appear on the crest of the Ngong Hills, to be devoured by hyenas, in less time than it takes to do this"—and Tony snapped between his strong fingers the plastic swizzle stick. "For the moment, he is only the leader of the opposition, but many people think that he may get to be President, even before "Mzee" dies. I personally think that the Old Man still has enough guts to strip the hide off that young bull—to the very tip of his tail!"

"What are his political views?" young Paolo asked.

"As far as I'm concerned, all African politicians are trash. This one boasts of being a friend of the people, and he talks of redistributing land and of social justice. But that doesn't prevent him from flying to London to have his suits tailor-made and going to the racetrack on Sundays, where he bets his last shilling on his own horses. The only thing that this politician has in common with the members of the government is his greed for money, and the privilege of not paying his debts. Apart from the fact that he belongs to the same "Kikuyu" mafia, that makes him more dangerous."

"I agree with that kind of Marxism!" San Miniato put in.

"The very thing he's done tonight, coming to have dinner at the ministers' favorite restaurant, knowing that they're all in Mombasa, is a gesture of defiance. Politics in this country continues to be based on a few primitive rules, and the different factions scrupulously respect each others' territories, as lions do, or bands of hyenas. If the Old Man gets wind of this, he won't like it."

"What could happen to him?" Paolo asked, very impressed.

"It's my opinion that for the moment both of them are avoiding a direct confrontation, but the Old Man is not going to allow this young upstart to cut the ground out from under him. Coming here is a more serious act than it appears to be; that's the sort of attitude that the government will not tolerate: He wouldn't be the first member of the opposition to have an accident on a lonely stretch of road."

"Well, it'd be a shame if they killed him," Julia put in, "because he's one of the handsomest blacks I've ever seen in my life. Moreover, from his noble and distinguished manner, I'm quite certain that he's basically an idealist."

"You might possibly change your mind if Muriuki actually seizes power and you should happen to be living in this country," Tony replied. "The worst thing about these countries when they decide to wage a revolution is that the new regimes are just as corrupt and inefficient as the old ones, but you get a few more dead in the road-side ditches and a few more buildings burned to the ground. The only thing that changes is the hammer and sickle that they put on the flag, and the source of the arms that they use to kill each other."

El Sombrero

ONCE DINNER WAS OVER, they accompanied Julia back to the hotel, but Massimo San Miniato seemed to be all wound up. He had seen a bright sign blinking in the blue African night: El Sombrero. Disco-Night Club. Strip-Tease. All this in neon letters on something resembling a glowing heart.

"It looks like an amusing place. Can we go back there?" San Miniato asked, like a child bent on mischief.

Paolo was tired and would have preferred to stay behind in the hotel, but his father insisted on dragging him along to that den of iniquity.

El Sombrero was really a brothel disguised as a discotheque; upstairs there were rooms where the customers could satisfy the needs aroused by the erotic dancers. The downstairs was divided into two quite distinct areas: the dance floor, which was a grotesque caricature of European discotheques, with its deafening music and its lights blinking like the rooflight of an ambulance; and the deep shadow around the edge of it, where a sweaty, overexcited crowd elbowed and shoved each other aside, and where the prostitutes had to seek out potential customers by literally groping about. Perhaps they had a radar system like that of bats to detect their prey in the darkness.

Bruno Toffani was seated at one of the tables at the back, mulling over his troubles with the aid of a bottle of Kenya Cane, and shooing away the girls who had come over to his table to offer to keep him company. El Sombrero was one of his favorite haunts, and he dropped in every time he visited the city. Coming as he did from the

105

burning hot stretches of desert along the coast, he enjoyed both the unbreathable atmosphere of the joint and the ear-splitting music, and was in the habit of bargaining for the services of one or another of the unfortunate girls in the place with the same savvy and perseverance with which he haggled over the price of the most valuable pieces of ivory. But that night he was in no mood for carousing; he was simply waiting for the show to begin, to try to relax for a while and forget the damned job that had been foisted on him by that bastard Muriuki.

Meanwhile, the Italians, led by Tony Allen, had come in, and were slowly working their way through the motley crowd, as though entering the heart of the densest jungle.

"Where shall we sit?" Paolo had asked, overwhelmed by the crush of people and the strong odors that filled the place. Two huge African whores, whose teeth had a sinister gleam beneath the fluorescent light, had pounced on him already. But seeing the horrified expression on the youngster's face, Tony had chased them away with two cutting words in Swahili.

"Let the kid shift for himself," San Miniato had then said to Tony in a low voice. "He's a big boy now."

"You were lucky this place was still left," the waiter said, seating them at a table near the dance floor. "And the show is just about to begin. There's a fantastic erotic dancer: the Queen of Sheba."

In fact, preceded by a furious roll of drums, there appeared from behind a bamboo curtain a white woman long past her prime, blinking in the glare of a spotlight which cruelly revealed her wrinkles and flabby flesh. To the rhythm of a semi-Mideastern melody, the dancer began to strip off her finery, which, from the struggle she was having, seemed to have been nailed to her body with tacks. Finally a pair of breasts appeared that, from the sickly white look of them, seemed to have been wrapped in fig leaves to preserve them, like goat cheese; two tiny electric bulbs hung from the tips of her powdered nipples. And after another drumroll, the matron rid herself of her spangled panties, and the murderous spotlight focused on a pubes studded with rhinestones that flooded the entire stage with multicolored reflections.

"Not bad, not bad," San Miniato said, applauding enthusiastically.

"Where's the toilet?" Paolo asked, the dancer's contortions having brought on a sympathetic reaction in his intestines.

"The trouble with that kid," the father said to Tony when Paolo left the table, "is that ever since I separated from his mother, he's

106

been raised in cotton wool. You know what women are like; out of fear of losing them, they keep their sons tied to their apron strings, and won't let 'em knock around the world a bit. That's why I've brought him here to Africa, so that he'll learn what life's all about."

"I think the experience of the safari, and life in camp may be a very good thing for him," Tony commented, not knowing quite what to say in reply to such confidential remarks.

"Look, just last year Paolo was on the point of entering a seminary and taking vows as a priest, not because he had any real vocation, but because of the sort of life he was leading in Palermo, in an old mansion on the outskirts of the city, where his mother kept him practically locked in. Thank God, that crisis seems to be a thing of the past, but now that he's come to Rome to study, he's gone to the opposite extreme and fallen in with a group of undesirable friends, the sort that hang out around Trinità del Monte, with a cigarette that stinks like the devil dangling out of the corner of their mouths. As we say in my country, the kid's fallen out of the frying pan into the fire."

At that moment, seeing an empty seat, one of the Somali girls prowling about the place came and sat down at their table. She was a young whore, with thin legs and small breasts like little daggers that barely showed beneath her dress, and a pleasant smile. And so when Paolo came back to the table he found his place occupied. He stood there for a few moments not knowing what to do.

"Come on, my boy, sit down with her, she's not going to bite you," Paolo's father said to him.

Paolo sat down warily on one corner of the chair, doing his best to create an invisible barrier between their bodies, but the girl, who couldn't have been much over fifteen, promptly moved her thigh so that it was touching his, and with great self-assurance, laughing and drinking the while, began to slide her thin fingers down the inside seam of his pants. Paolo immediately realized, to his horror, that his father must have hired the Somali girl to seduce him.

"I see she's taken a shine to you and is getting affectionate," San Miniato said to him, and then, turning to Tony: "These two turtle doves need a little nest where they can be alone. Could you show them the way to one of those reserved rooms upstairs?"

Tony thought to himself that he'd been hired as a professional hunter, not as a pimp for his client's son, but he decided he'd better go with Paolo, because the youngster looked so pale and drawn that he might tumble down the stairs and crack his head open. When they reached the upstairs landing, seeing the desperate expression on the boy's face, Tony took him aside and said to him: "Don't worry, I'll take her on. Since your father's already paid for the girl, we won't let her off scot-free. Wait for me here and don't move."

And taking the girl by the hand, he went into one of the rooms with walls upholstered in red velvet, a dim little fringed lamp on a table on one side of the bed and a washstand on the other. Paolo stayed there on the landing, leaning against the wall in a cold sweat that left the nape of his neck soaking wet and made his lips tremble feverishly. The sounds from the adjoining rooms came to him through his body as he slumped against the thin partition: laughter and muffled murmurs, bedsprings creaking, and soon thereafter, strange groans that as far as he could tell might be either moans of pleasure or of pain.

Tony then came out of the room, tucking in his shirt, a vague expression of satisfaction on his tanned face; out of the corner of his eye, Paolo saw the naked body of the girl lying on the cot, with her head buried in the pillow, still writhing in strange contortions. As they were about to start down the steep flight of stairs, Paolo was overcome with a sort of vertigo and was about to lose his footing, but Tony, who had noticed his deathly pale face, grabbed his arm in his iron grip.

"We're going to have a drink in the bar," he said, still gripping his arm firmly as they went down the stairs. "Looking the way you do, I don't think your father's going to believe you've just had a good roll in the hay."

They met another customer coming up the stairs accompanied by a Kenyan whore of huge proportions: her breasts and hips were so outsized that they had to turn sideways to get past, the way a boat slips between two dangerous reefs. The man, too, was rather odd looking: he was wearing a big broad-brimmed hat, a filthy, threadbare safari jacket, and his skin was so deeply tanned and so dirty that it was hard to tell what color it was. The man was, of course, Bruno Toffani, who had managed to forget his troubles with the aid of his bottle of aromatic cane alcohol.

On reaching one of the rooms, Toffani carefully closed the door. He was still carrying on him the papers that Muriuki's aide had handed over to him; as he stripped off his clothes in one corner of the room, he thought that it would be a good idea to leave only the copies of the documents in the pocket of his jacket and stash the folded originals inside the lining of his hat. By doing so, he would be running less of a risk of losing the compromising documents: Those pieces of onionskin paper, already a bit greasy and sweaty from contact with his body, might be either a blank check to be presented to Muriuki, if everything went well, or his death sentence if the contraband shipment were discovered or intercepted.

As the well-stacked whore was making her ablutions in the washbasin, Bruno put his clothes on the back of a chair and then tumbled into bed. The sight of his companion's huge buttocks and her breasts as turgid as zeppelins throwing their shadow on the red velvet of the wall excited him and put everything except the details of fornicating out of his mind. If Paolo had stayed in the hallway, listening to the sounds coming from that room, he would have been surprised at the expressions uttered in a voice hoarse from cane brandy, directing the whore's maneuvers with the same precision with which a captain would conn his ship from the wheelroom.

"More to the right, my little pilot; let out a bit more sail but be careful you don't break the mainmast; come climb up the yard, that's it, move more to port, farther to port; trim a bit of ballast, we're about to founder. . . ."

Unfortunately he had drunk too much, and the minute the act was consummated, he fell fast asleep, like a baby, between the breasts of that outsized nurse. When he woke up an hour later with a bad headache and looked around, the whore had disappeared: And his clothes, which he had left so carefully folded on the chair, had also vanished.

Despite the fuzzyheadedness from his hangover, he realized that the loss of his jacket, with his wallet and the copies of the documents in the inside pocket, could get him into serious trouble. His hat, his inseparable companion, was still hanging on the bedpost, thank God, with the original documents stuck under its lining. His first reaction was to get the hell out of there, but how could he run around the streets naked? He felt helpless, tricked.

Suddenly overcome with cold shivers and fear, his teeth began to chatter. And Bruno Toffani—who hadn't cried since the end of the campaign in Ethiopia when the British officers had ripped the Fascist insignia off his lapels—collapsed on the bed, and burying his face in the pillow, burst into deep, desperate sobs.

PART THREE

The Galana River

THE GALANA CAMP had been set up on the top of a little hill that sloped gently down to the river. Permanent cabins had been built for the safari clients, with thatched roofs of wild cane, and on the same level stretch of ground a number of supplementary tents had been erected, one of which Bob was occupying.

Stretched out underneath his canvas field tent, with his eyes wide open in the darkness, Bob was awaiting the dawn of a new day. The breeze coming from the other side of the river brought odors of aquatic plants and mud and sounds of the last animals that had come down to the water holes and were now retreating again to the dense jungle. The light was little by little filtering through the canvas, illuminating the inside of the tent with a pale greenish light that surrounded objects with a ghostly halo.

They had arrived there the night before, long after dark, and the camp had been dark and deserted. But soon lanterns that moved back and forth in the dark like fireflies had been lit, and before the car had even stopped, hands had reached out to open the doors and unload the equipment, as words of welcome in Swahili rang out in the night. In just a few minutes the entire camp was lit up and everything made ready, and supper was served in an open-air dining room made of tree trunks with a straw roof overhead and heads of buffaloes and antelopes hanging on the walls. After dinner, Lawrence Brown and Bob sat around the glowing coals of a bonfire that had been lit near the veranda to counteract the dampness coming up from the river.

Bob noted that the hunter seemed more communicative and relaxed now, as though setting foot on his own territory had calmed him down. He had broken out a pipe and was taking deep puffs on it and every so often taking sips of a glass of whiskey he was holding between his knees. Meanwhile the camp had fallen silent once more, and the stirring of the animals in the nearby jungle could be heard. The wind had driven the great black thunderclouds from the sky, and suddenly a round red moon appeared on the other side of the river, making every object in sight appear enormous and giving the trees of the forest grove an eerie look.

As though they had been waiting for that very moment, two huge rhinos burst out of the bush and trotted slowly down to the riverbank. They must have been wallowing in a water hole, because their backs were covered with mud, making their thick rough hides look especially impressive and antediluvian. The rhinos remained at the water's edge for some time, drinking and snorting and brandishing their spectacular horns, which shone in the moonlight like scimitars. Then they turned on their heels and went trotting up the riverbank again, and finally their shining backs disappeared in the night.

"I've never seen anything like that in my life," Bob mumbled. "It's as though we'd been able to look through a hole in time and see a scene from the remote past of this earth."

"You'll understand now why I intend to preserve this sanctuary," Lawrence said, exhaling a puff of pipe smoke. "There aren't many places like this left in the world."

"It's so impressive it seems almost unreal," Bob said with a smile. "I know you'll think this is ridiculous, but do you know what it reminded me of? When I was still in college, I went with some friends to Disney World, in Florida—it's a sort of enormous amusement park. One of the attractions, in fact, was called A Jungle Cruise and consisted of floating in a small boat down a simulated tropical river, from the shores of which wild animals with gaping jaws leaped out threateningly. They were naturally made of papier-mâché, but alarmingly lifelike, I assure you.

Lawrence let out a booming laugh: "Well, I assure you that the animals here are not made of papier-mâché; and if I were you, I wouldn't try to pull their tails."

At that moment, a loud splash came from the river. No animal came into view, however.

"It's only a crocodile, doubtless catching himself some fish."

"I didn't know that there were crocodiles in the Galana."

"More than we'd like."

"How big are they?"

"There are bigger ones in Lake Rudolf, and in the Tana River, which isn't far from here. But the ones in the Galana can be just as dangerous—or even more so. In Lake Rudolf, for example, there are so many fish that there are few known cases in which crocodiles have attacked human beings. There are very few fish in the Galana, however, and the crocodiles attack antelope and sometimes even carry off Africans if they wander down too close to the river. Crocodiles are as unpredictable as sharks, in their behavior: A boy can cross the same ford in the river with his herd a thousand times, and then the thousand-and-first time . . . wham! A huge tail lashes out at him and he's never seen again." He finished the phrase by banging one palm down on the other, imitating a pair of jaws snapping shut.

Later on, when Bob was alone in his tent, he again heard that sharp snapping sound above the water, and felt a cold shiver run down his spine. That was no big bass leaping on a moonlit night on the calm surface of a lake in Connecticut, but a reptile with scaly skin and powerful jaws, capable of devouring an antelope and even a human being. Despite being very tired, he found it difficult to fall asleep. His eyes kept opening, contemplating the shadows of the branches on the roof of his tent, and his ears pricked up at every little sound in the African night: the rustle of the leaves, animals stirring in the bush, the distant call of a night bird.

Through his overexcited mind there passed, as in a movie, the scenes he'd been witness to since his arrival in Nairobi. The most recent images in particular were vividly engraved on his memory: the scene of the ivory smugglers, at the airport, the wild chase after the poachers across the dusty Tsavo plains, for instance, and the swamp with the rotting body of the dead elephant, lit up by the bright headlights.

What would have happened if Lawrence Brown had managed to catch up with the poachers and the latter had begun to shoot at them with their automatic rifles or their poisoned arrows?

As the images flashed on and off through his mind, he eventually dozed off. Two or three times during the night, he awakened with a start. But as the soft light of dawn poured in through the canvas as though through a color filter, flooding the tent with a pale greenish light he was quite sure that he was going to be able to drop off to sleep again, when a strange hand suddenly unzipped the flap of his tent with a sinister noise that struck terror in his heart.

This time he sat bolt upright in the bed, and was even more frightened when the dark face leaning toward him in the semidarkness reminded him of the faces of the black malefactors of his dreams.

"Good morning, Bwana Fender, *chai tiari, chai*—tea is ready," the boy bringing him breakfast said softly.

"Thanks, leave it on the night table next to the bed," Bob mumbled, trying to regain his composure.

As soon as the boy had gone, he got out of bed and peeked out of the flap of the tent so as to contemplate once again the spectacle of the Galana that had so impressed him the night before. It was still not yet fully light, and a thick, clammy layer of fog was hovering above the river. In any event, the panorama was not as strikingly beautiful as it had been the night before. The river was deserted—there was not a single animal to be seen on the shores, only countless animal tracks that had opened bloody gashes in the red earth embankment. Even the river seemed to have diminished in size, baring little islands of sand in midstream resembling big beached fish, and the color of the water, which had gleamed like a lava flow in the bright moonlight, was now a dull chocolate in the light of the sultry, murky dawn.

Bob felt somewhat let down, as though he had been taken in by a mirage the night before. But he was not about to lose heart entirely; the first thing he had to do in order to shake off the spiderwebs of the night and get the circulation going in his legs which were numb from the cold, was to go for a good fast run. After that, if Patterson had recovered, he'd have a talk with him so as to begin to gather data for his study on grass. That was what he had come for and he was not going to allow either John's unfortunate death, Lawrence's obsessions, or the loss of the research documents that had been in his suitcases to discourage him.

116

Fortunately, in the travel bag which carried his camera and certain documents, he also had his running shoes and a jogging T-shirt which read New York Marathon. He got his shoes out of the bag and eagerly began lacing them up.

A Jungle Cruise

CROUCHING BENEATH A THORNBUSH close to the path that ran down to the river, Mkubua Shana nibbled on an acacia branch, licking from time to time the bitter sap oozing from the bark, and thought to himself that life is not always easy for a young lion.

Mkubua Shana was the third, and smallest, of a litter of lion cubs that followed their mother, Mziwa Moto (Warm Milk) in her forays along the shores of the Galana. Although he was very nearly two years old, the age at which a lion can start to fend for himself, Mkubua Shana was still relatively underdeveloped, and his mother, who continued to feed him and care for him as though he were a cub, had teasingly given him that nickname, which meant "The Biggest" in Swahili. All was well until the day that an old, ill-tempered lion fleeing from the desert fastnesses of the north had made his appearance in that area, after heaven knows how many misadventures and misdeeds. Old Sahib, for that was his name, had a front paw that had once been fractured by a bullet, and a back furrowed with deep scratches and scars from his having so often crept through *bomas*, thornbush, to steal cattle from humans. From the moment that Mkubua Shana's mother had incomprehensibly decided to have a love-affair with that selfish, ill-humored old male, the cub's life became unbearable, and soon Mkubua Shana made up his mind to strike out on his own.

But it was not all that simple. It had been easy enough to leap upon a zebra and begin to bite its hindquarters and belly when his mother —Mziwa Moto—had chased it and cornered it and held it by the

117

neck as it was dying, but it was quite a different matter for Mkubua Shana to lie in wait, surprise his prey, and overpower it with no help at all. The first time that he had managed to ambush one of those quadrupeds, hiding in the dense brush growing around a waterhole and then suddenly leaping out from behind the bushes onto the back of a zebra, his intended prey had vigorously shaken itself, laid its ears back, and letting fly with a couple of good hard kicks, sent him sailing through the air.

After that dismal failure, the young lion had decided to bag smaller trophies. But which animal should it be? Gazelles ran too fast; impalas excelled at prodigious leaps; oryxes had long sharp horns and knew how to use them to defend themselves; monkeys scratched and bit and rained down heavy objects from the trees; the offspring of rhinos and hippos were jealously guarded by their mothers—and how!

The night before, after hours of waiting in silence amid the canebrake along the river, he had succeeded in creeping up on a young male kudu with stripes on its back that gleamed like chalk marks in the moonlight. Taking advantage of the moment when the kudu had lowered its neck to drink, Mkubua Shana had managed to knock it down in one leap, and was still struggling with his prey on the shore, having very nearly overpowered it, when a huge crocodile suddenly emerged from the water, grabbed the hindquarters of the antelope between its powerful jaws, and began to drag it into the river. The lion fought back for a few moments, burying his paws in the sand, trying to recover the kudu, but almost immediately he was obliged to let go or meet his own end in the deep waters of the river.

The young lion had gone on prowling about the canebrake, reflecting on his failures and licking a paw that had been wounded in the struggle with the reptile, when he spied a silhouette in the distance, running toward him along the path at the river's edge. He was not immediately able to identify what species of animal it was, though his first impression, from the way in which the creature was running in great strides and raising great clouds of dust with its heels, was that it was an ostrich. But then, straining his eyes to get a better look, he decided that it looked more like a human being. After his night of prolonged waiting and fasting, he prayed to the gods that it was really an ostrich, a bird large enough to satisfy his appetite, and at the same time not too agile or dangerous.

He knew that, in the final analysis, a man might also prove to be edible, though only in certain circumstances. His mother had taught him that humans could be divided into three categories: those who came down to the river to get water, carrying a jug on their heads and almost invariably surrounded by a group of lively cubs that ran about on the sand and threw stones into the stream (these water-carriers were the female of the species, whose meat could be sweet and tender, providing they weren't one of the older ones, who were tough and leathery). Then there were those who drove cattle along the dusty trails; these usually wore red tunics falling from their shoulders, carried long spears, and took shelter at night in dens made of cane-stalks and cow dung that gave off a pestilential smell (this type too might be edible, but only if one took advantage of a moment of carelessness on their part, since that sharp lance they carried might cause deep, painful wounds). And finally, the category that was undoubtedly the most dangerous: that of white men, who traversed the jungle in metal vehicles, shooting with their weapons at everything that came within their range, and gathering together at night in a camp, where they sat round a fire telling each other of their heinous deeds, with great shouts and roars of laughter, as they downed enormous quantities of very strong spirits.

Unfortunately, the closer he came to the creature that was running along the path at the river's edge, the more remote the possibility became that it was an ostrich, since it had neither showy plumes on its body, nor a great beak, nor thighs whose upper portion had a bluish tinge, as was the case with ostriches. Yet at the same time, the creature admittedly did not quite fit any of the categories of human beings thus far known to him: It did not have a jug on its head; it was not wearing a red tunic falling from its shoulders and it definitely was not carrying a lance; it might have been a white man, yet its skin was of an indeterminate color, as though it had been sunburned, and it had a colored handkerchief around its head, fluttering in the wind, and peculiar slippers of a flashy color, with broad flexible soles. However, famished as he was, perhaps it was better not to be too choosy about this easy prey that Providence had sent his way. A shiver of excitement ran down his spine, and his tail began to lash from side to side as he crouched in the grass, tensing his muscles, ready to leap upon the runner at precisely the right moment.

Bob Fender, who had tied the handkerchief around his forehead to keep the sweat from streaming down, had already run a good three miles and was beginning to get his usual rhythm back. What with getting ready for the trip and his arrival in Kenya he hadn't been able to go jogging for more than a week, whereas in Rome he managed to run at least a couple of times a week, along an avenue bordering the Tiber, in which the bright blue of the Mediterranean sky was reflected on clear mornings, along with the contrasting rust-red of the old buildings. That dusty path along the bank of the Galana bore almost no resemblance to the course he was accustomed to run in Rome, though it too was along a river; it did remind him, however, of the habitual circuit he used to make in Central Park, from the West Side to the edge of the reservoir and back, when he lived in New York.

As he ran along, the Galana widened, eventually dividing into rivulets that trickled across great sand banks, where flocks of white birds had alighted—herons or perhaps small cranes—and watched him pass with that absent look of birds, who always seem to have flown in from distant worlds. The blinding bright sunlight had begun devouring the landscape little by little, sucking up colors and forms like an immense cloud of locusts hovering above the trees in the thicket. During the summer heat in New York, a dense layer of moisture also hovered above the trees in the park, stretching their skinny branches toward the sky as though begging the sun for respite; running very early in the morning along the deserted paths, he had the same sensation that he was now experiencing of slipping, like a hypodermic needle, between the epidermis of haze and the thick skin of warm earth. And on arriving at the edge of the Municipal Reservoir, he was surprised to see each day that the water level had gone down even farther till finally it revealed the very backbone of the basin, a wall, normally submerged, made of concrete and stone, on which large flocks of seagulls were perched, watching the incandescent ball of the sun climbing higher and higher behind the skyscrapers, and contemplating the reservoir exposed in all its nakedness.

Bob had just rounded a bend in the path when he noticed a muscle pulling, and a bad cramp ran up his right leg. It had been ages since a thing like that had happened to him. Fortunately, there was a tree near the path which he could lean on to do the necessary knee-bends to work the cramp out of his leg.

The lion, hidden in the bush only a few paces away, was disconcerted when the runner stopped and began to go through a series of strange movements and acrobatic exercises as he clung to the lower part of a tree trunk. Was this creature a monkey after all, and not a human being? He first leaned on the trunk with his hands out-

120

stretched, and bent his knees with all his strength as though he were trying to uproot the tree; then he placed his foot on a low branch and bent his torso down over his leg till his hands touched his instep; and finally, he hung with his entire weight from the branch, flexing his knees in spasmodic jerks.

Nonetheless, the fact that the runner had suddenly turned into a monkey did not lessen Mkubua Shana's desire to sink his teeth into the creature; as a matter of fact, those curious exercises had stimulated the flow of the young lion's gastric juices.

Taking care lest a single branch creak, the lion emerged from the bush and stole silently toward his prey.

But at that precise moment, the roar of an engine was heard, and Lawrence Brown's car rounded the bend in the path at top speed, sending stones and pebbles flying to either side. When the car reached Bob, it braked to an abrupt stop and the hunter, who seemed quite nervous, poked his head out the window: "Hurry, clear out of here. Get in the car."

"Don't worry," Bob said, limping slightly as he walked over toward the car. "It's only a muscle spasm. I can get back to the camp on foot."

"Get in, I said, and don't stand there like an idiot!" Lawrence shouted.

"Even though you may be the manager of the Galana Ranch," Bob said to him, raising his voice in turn, "I'll have you know that I don't take orders from anybody. Are you also going to forbid me to walk around the camp? What harm is there in . . ."

"There's a lion five paces away from you, about to leap on you at any moment," Lawrence murmured, his eyes focused on a spot behind Bob.

On hearing those words, Bob covered the distance separating him from the car in nothing flat—his limp seemed to have disappeared as if by magic—and leaped inside with astonishing agility.

"What was that you said about a lion?" he asked, once he'd slammed the door shut behind him.

"See for yourself," Lawrence replied, heading the car straight toward the bush.

Branches could be heard hitting the underside of the car, followed all at once by an incredible roar, so loud it seemed to be coming from inside the vehicle. Then Bob saw a tawny shape running off at top speed through the bush, though he couldn't make out what it was.

"Is that a lion?" he asked, very excited.

"Of course, and a good-sized one at that; it's still young, and couldn't overpower a buffalo or a large antelope yet, but it's big enough to have been able to give you a pretty bad time of it."

"For heaven's sake! In other words, you saved my life, right? I apologize for not being more careful."

"I came this way at this time of day by sheer chance. Normally I make a tour of the ranch before the heat of the day sets in, but today I amused myself following the tracks of this lion; it's one that's been prowling about the riverbank at night. When I saw that the trail he was leaving coincided with the marks of your running shoes in the dust along the path, it gave me a turn, since I supposed you weren't exactly having a game of hide-and-seek with a critter like that."

"I can't tell you how grateful I am to you," Bob murmured, somewhat abashed.

"There's no reason to thank me. The only thing I ask is that you be more careful next time. You can see now that there are no one-way street signs in the jungle, and you never know when you may run into trouble."

"Don't worry. I'll keep it well in mind from now on."

"And remember: this isn't your fantastic fake 'Jungle Cruise' with its cardboard wild beasts and its Coke machines. This is the real damned jungle."

All the rest of the way back to camp, neither of them said another word. It was only when they arrived at the ranch and Lawrence got out of the car that Bob noticed that the hunter always had a loaded rifle within reach, on the other side of the steering wheel.

The Vultures Take Wing

JUDGE McGREDY had gotten up early that day to do some on-the-spot investigation on Mackinnon Road. Although he carefully reconnoitered the place where the accident had occurred and the area around it, all he found was the charred skeleton of the car and a few nuts and bolts scattered amid the bushes by baboons. It was as though the sun that was already beginning to beat down like a hammer on the anvil of the Tsavo had reduced all other traces of the accident to dust—that red dust that was rising in swirls of hot air toward the copper-colored sun.

Meanwhile, the copies of the bills of lading that had been stolen from Bruno Toffani the night before had arrived that morning, via the well-greased machinery of the Special Branch, to the hands of one of Munyoka's aides who sent the documents along in the envelope of correspondence that he dispatched to his chief daily on the first morning plane. And thus, through one of those paradoxes that the Universal Humorist invents for his amusement, as the Judge dug about in the dust, trying to unearth some clue that might incriminate Muriuki, the concrete evidence that a plot was afoot was winging its way through the air thousands of feet above his head, in a plane headed for Mombasa.

When the Judge arrived at the Nyali Beach a few hours later, feeling crestfallen at his lack of success in turning up any real evidence and covered with dust from driving up and down the bone-dry trails of the Tsavo, the Minister received him with uncontainable excitement, hopping about the room like a dwarf who's just found a talisman.

"Here's the proof I needed!" he exclaimed, waving the rumpled papers in the Judge's face, as though he were shoving an article of clothing belonging to the murderer beneath the nose of a bloodhound. "This is proof that the arms shipment that Muriuki went to Europe to arrange has actually been sent, definite proof that there's a conspiracy afoot. Have a look," he said, handing McGredy the documents. "You'll see with your own eyes."

The Judge examined the bills of lading, holding them a fair distance away because of the pungent smell they were giving off, a blend of Toffani's odor and the scent of cheap perfume.

"Interesting, interesting . . ." he muttered, in a voice husky from all the dust he'd swallowed on his trip to the Tsavo.

"Wouldn't you like some tea?" the Minister said hospitably, handing him a cup still sitting on the table after his late breakfast.

"Thanks, thanks very much. . . . This is most interesting," he repeated, after clearing his throat. "But I doubt that these documents can be used as proof. The name of the consignee of the shipment is missing, and even the name of the boat is practically illegible: Nos–fa–ler? Nur–fa–ther? Admittedly, the nature of the merchandise is quite clear: arms and explosives, sent CIF—Mombasa."

"Doesn't that strike you as sufficient proof?"

"To be frank with you, I don't believe these documents could be presented as evidence against Muriuki in a court trial," McGredy concluded, handing the documents back to Munyoka.

The latter remained silent for a few moments, holding the papers in his hand, with the expression of a child who's just been given an electric toy as a gift and all of a sudden discovers that the batteries for it are missing. The onionskin copies were badly rumpled, to be sure, due to the many different hands through which they had passed, and the writing on them so blurred as to be practically illegible. Two things, however, could be made out quite plainly: the name of a well-known European arms factory in the upper right-hand corner and the list of merchandise, which included a considerable quantity of automatic rifles and machine guns, along with the ammunition for them.

"Allow me to say that I disagree completely with you," the Minister finally answered, trying his best to conceal his irritation. "These documents in my opinion undoubtedly constitute sufficient proof, sufficient enough to put J. M. behind bars. It's of little moment that the name of the consignee is missing on them. After all, we couldn't expect Muriuki to be stupid enough to sign his name at the bottom of a list of contraband of this sort. But the date of these documents and other details coincide exactly with the period when Muriuki was in Europe."

"However, the date, even an approximate one, of the arrival of the shipment in Mombasa isn't shown. So how are we going to manage to seize this shipment?"

"There won't be any major difficulty if we keep a sharp eye out. What's more, I have a rather good idea of when J. M. plans to make his move: during the conference that UNICORN will be holding in Nairobi, attended by delegates from all over the world. What better sounding box could he hope to have for his hidden ambitions?"

"I don't want to appear to be a wet blanket, but before making any official use of these papers," the Judge said, pointing to the bills of lading that were fluttering in the breeze like doves about to take wing, "I would want proof that they were authentic and make certain exactly where and how they had turned up."

"These documents were stolen just yesterday, in a Nairobi nightclub, and one of our usual informers who works there passed them on to our Special Branch, whereupon they were immediately turned over to me: As you will note, my men couldn't have been more efficient."

"Has the person who 'lost' the documents been interrogated?"

"It hasn't been possible to locate this individual yet, although he is known to have visited the brothel in question, and hired the services of a woman. She was the one who took care of relieving him of certain of his belongings. The problem is that the man in question was not one of the usual customers. It was someone who doesn't live in Nairobi. He may even be a foreigner."

"But I trust that the prostitute could at least identify him. Has she provided you with a description of him yet?"

"Strange as it may seem, the whore has also disappeared without a trace."

"Can she have been deliberately rubbed out? Muriuki's men wouldn't think twice about bumping off a girl in a case like this."

"That's possible, but it may also be that she's simply gone back to her village. As you know, a number of such women come to the capital to make a little easy money, and as soon as they've put enough aside to buy a few new pots and pans and a couple of chickens, they go back home to work in their garden, their *shamba*, and regain their status as respectable matrons, with a little *toto* hanging from each breast."

"Possibly she also relieved the individual in question of a sum of money that was more important to her than those documents. But even so, all this arouses my suspicions," the Judge said, stubbornly shaking his leonine head. "Experience has made me mistrust the type of evidence that falls into your hands as though by sheer chance, at the very moment you need it. . . . Bear in mind that Muriuki may be leaving a trail of false clues for us to cover up his real intentions."

This time the Minister was unable to conceal his impatience.

"Come, come, my dear McGredy, let's not go out of our way to invent difficulties. What motive would Muriuki have for putting us square on the track of this shipment? In fact, we already suspected that he had contacted arms dealers."

"For that very reason. This may be a way of drawing our attention to a particular place, while the contraband enters the country at some other point."

After thinking for a moment, Munyoka's sharp eyes lighted up as another idea occurred to him: "It so happens that there's another fact that would fit in perfectly with all the rest: the American's accident. Let's not forget that his death came about as he was heading down to the coast, perhaps for the precise purpose of investigating the arrival of that arms shipment. After all, the Yankees may not be as badly informed as we think. It's more than likely that their agents and contacts in Europe have gotten wind of this contraband shipment before we did."

"That may well be, of course," McGredy admitted, nodding in agreement as he sipped his tea, and thinking that English civilization had even managed to teach some of these Africans how to use their heads.

"That would also explain why the Americans sent their new agent to the Tsavo area—not only to investigate the death of their colleague, but also to watch for the arms shipment," Munyoka went on, his eyes gleaming more and more brightly.

"If all this is true, I wouldn't give two shillings for the life of that fake ecologist. The Tsavo isn't a very safe place, especially if Muriuki's men are dogging his every footstep. It won't be long before the lure catches the falcon's eye."

"That's precisely what we must prevent. This is no time for another incident involving Americans. So do keep an even closer eye on the lure, as you call him. Moreover, if we watch his every move, he may lead us to the eagle's nest, that is to say, the place where the arms have been cached."

"Don't worry, I'll keep a sharp eye out. I intended to go to Malindi this very day, and if it's necessary, I'll go to Galana to talk to the American," the Judge replied. "Youngsters like that don't know what the word discretion means."

"And I for my part will make it a point to inform Ambassador Poire of the discovery of these documents. It will be interesting to see what his reaction is. Incidentally, I forgot to ask you: Did you find anything on Mackinnon Road that might be useful?"

"Not one thing. Between the real vultures and the human scavengers prowling about in the area, they've carried off practically every nut and bolt of the car. And in the villages round about, they're all so involved in smuggling charcoal and poaching that they can smell a policeman a hundred miles off. For the moment, I don't think we can turn up very much information as to the circumstances of the accident."

"In any event, Poire's going to prick up his ears when he hears about those documents."

And picking up the telephone, Munyoka put in a call to Nairobi.

126

The Hospital

LAWRENCE BROWN went down to the coast to pick up the safari party, and Bob took advantage of the trip to visit Lewis Patterson, who had been sent to the hospital in Malindi, suffering from a severe attack of malaria. Brown dropped Bob off in front of the hospital, on the outskirts of the city.

"If you like, we can meet for lunch on Watamu Beach, at a hotel called The Seafarers. Any taxi will take you there, but watch out that they don't gyp you."

The building looked like one of those field hospitals in old movies about the war in the Pacific, a wooden hut with a veranda covered with bougainvillea. Farther in the distance was the blue sea and the harbor of Malindi, surrounded by little whitewashed adobe houses, like a Nativity scene. On the other side of the harbor the Galana dumped into its estuary the load of reddish mud that it had carried off from riverbanks in the Tsavo, forming a sharp contrast to the indigo of the sea, like two dabs of color on the same palette.

After having him wait for a few minutes on the veranda, an African nun, whose dark skin looked even darker against her snow-white coif, led him through the labyrinth of the hospital to Patterson's room. They went down narrow, impeccably waxed red-tiled corridors smelling of chloroform and chrysanthemums and across a rectangular inner patio with ugly black birds hovering overhead that struck Bob as sinister creatures. Finally, in a dark room, he found the man who was to act as adviser for his study at Galana, his forehead beaded with sweat and his eyes fever-bright.

"So you're Professor Fender," the sick man said to him in a feeble voice, extending a burning hot hand through a slit in the mosquito netting. "My usual luck. The day before you arrive, I come down with this confounded attack of malaria, damn it all. Just as I have a

chance to share my experience at Galana with a scientist and exchange impressions with a civilized human being, what do I do but
take sick."

The good man went on railing against his bad luck for some time,
in such a feeble voice that Bob didn't dare interrupt him, for fear that
they might be his last words.

"And what infuriates me most," Patterson concluded in that barely
audible voice, "is that that beast of a Lawrence Brown is going to end
up getting his way, as usual, and will be the one who'll show you the
secrets of the ranch, and the new Oryx Project that I've fought so
hard for."

"Lawrence Brown asked me to pass on to you his very best wishes
for your speedy recovery. And don't worry about me, because I'm in
no hurry. I'll just wait patiently till you're better."

"I was thinking just this morning," the sick man said, raising himself up slightly in bed so as to be able to speak more easily, "that there
are those who have it in them to survive in Africa and others who are
licked by this continent. Unfortunately I'm one of the latter. The
others are people who were either born here or came to live here at a
very early age, and have absorbed the wild telluric forces of these
environs. When I called Lawrence Brown a beast a moment ago, it
wasn't meant in the least to imply contempt, but rather, admiration.
Brown shares the vitality and the fierceness of the animals that he's
been contending with ever since he was a little boy, and naturally the
animals know it. The buffaloes and the elephants that he runs into
every day without ever getting so much as a scratch know it, the
snakes that crawl by within inches of him without biting him know it,
and even the mosquitoes know it. . . . Can you explain to me why
Lawrence has never had malaria, whereas I, who take tons of quinine
every day, come down with it?"

"I couldn't tell you, but it does seem odd," Bob said, somewhat
surprised by the turn that the conversation was taking. He had been
hoping that Patterson would give him some pointers as to how he
should go about gathering data for his study.

"The reason is that the mosquitoes don't dare bite him. Have you
seen his tough, scaly skin like a crocodile's, a reptile's skin? What
insect would dare penetrate that armor? I certainly wouldn't try it if I
were a mosquito. On the other hand, look at these arms of mine"—
and he thrust one of his skeleton-like, dead-white limbs outside the
sheet. "They're the arms of a civilized person, a scholar, a scientist:

128

They're not a sign of any brute, elemental force, which is what prevails in this primitive land."

"It's odd that you should say that, since you've no doubt been here quite a while, because even though I for my part have just arrived, I already have the same impression that a special force emanates from this land, something profound and mysterious that is somehow disquieting to those of us who set foot in Africa for the first time. Even the air and the vegetation have a curious odor, of humus, of vegetable decay, in a word, of death. . . ." He paused, looking at the sick man, wondering if he hadn't said more than he should have in trying to explain, and hastened to add: "The circumstances in which I arrived were quite unfortunate, naturally: The first thing I learned, even before I'd left the airport, was that Murphy had had an accident. As you know, apart from being the person with whom I'd made all the arrangements for my trip, John Murphy was my only contact in Nairobi."

"I know. Murphy was a good friend of mine too, of course, and you have no idea how much I regret his untimely death." Patterson paused, and sat up in bed again. The conversation seemed to be having a tonic effect on him; his voice was clearer and firmer. "Don't forget, though, that Murphy's case is different from that of others of us who are devoured by Africa; he had the qualities necessary to survive. In his own way, he was a wild, strong man."

"I'm well aware of that. When we were in college together, I went on hunting trips with him a number of times. I'm not a great hunter myself, as you can imagine, but I noticed that John, on the other hand, felt quite at home in the midst of nature."

"John was really tough and hard, and he could have survived here . . . if he had wanted to. But his problem was different; in one way or another, he was out to destroy himself. If it didn't sound so sinister, I'd say that John had already chosen exactly the sort of death that he in fact met with. To be burned to a cinder in the middle of the remote, barren Tsavo desert—doesn't that strike you as a fitting death for an ecologist?"

"I'm afraid I can't follow your line of reasoning," Bob said, wriggling in his chair; he was beginning to feel uncomfortable in the stifling atmosphere of that tiny cubbyhole of a room.

"Let's be frank with each other. You've surely heard some of those strange theories about John's death that are making the rounds. Well,

I warn you that they're all false rumors. I won't go so far as to say that John didn't perhaps devote his spare time to nosing about a bit here and there; I think all diplomats enjoy playing at being spies now and then, isn't that true?"

"I suppose so; but I'm not a diplomat."

"In any event, in Murphy's case it's clear that that was what he was up to. But at the same time I'm convinced that he wasn't killed for that reason. What's certain fact is that John Murphy lived too intensely; he was always ready to set out on some new adventure—a hunting expedition, a love affair, a political intrigue, it didn't matter —but always something that would take him to the limit of his possibilities, to the brink of the abyss. This colonial, or postcolonial society if you prefer, is a closed one: There are any number of human vultures—worse than those of the Tsavo—who are always ready to sink their beaks into other people's mishaps and poke around; that's why people have gone around inventing a thousand cock-and-bull stories about Murphy's death."

"The Embassy Counselor told me not to pay attention to those rumors, in Nairobi."

"The truth of the matter, however, is that Murphy died because that was his fate, one that he himself had chosen. If he hadn't crashed into a tree in the Tsavo, some jealous husband would have blown the top of his head off, or he would have been trampled to death by one of those buffaloes that, as he himself admitted, he used to wound in the belly so as to experience the kicks of chasing a raging wild beast through the heart of the jungle."

"Really!" Bob said, a bit taken aback. "I didn't know that John indulged in that sort of thing."

"He had many sides to him, of course. Nonetheless, what he was seeking was to make himself one with the earth again, and in the end he contrived to do exactly that. He is one now with the red earth of the Tsavo. His spirit will rise in the dense dust devils that darken the sun when the south wind blows."

The two of them fell silent, as though the sea breeze had suddenly brought with it something of the spirit that that delirious old man had just conjured up. Bob looked out the window. The blue waters of the ocean had darkened as a cloud passed overhead and the streak of muddy water that the Galana was emptying into the bay had now taken on a more intense, and more dramatic, tone.

At that moment the nurse came into the room to announce that visiting hours were over, and the wings of her coif fluttered in an odd sort of way in the sudden draft. Bob was reminded of the dark birds hovering above the hospital patio: the same ones he had seen in the airport in Nairobi, just after learning that Murphy was dead.

The Counselor

AMBASSADOR W. D. POIRE was pacing up and down his office in great long strides, unable to keep the imposing silhouette of the Conference Center from following him across the picture window. That building, which had grown larger and larger till it completely obstructed Ambassador Poire's view of the great plains, had turned into the symbol of his frustrated African dream. The frequent meetings of UNICORN attracted swarms of ecologists who, with their scientific vibrations, destroyed the harmony of that little colonial city, surrounded by golf courses and natural parks.

At that moment, there were a couple of almost inaudible taps on the door, and Maguire, the Embassy Counselor, poked his head into the room, with his usual expression of a wary reptile ready at any moment to disappear with a rapid flick of its tail into its hole.

"Did you call me, Ambassador?"

"No, I don't believe I did, but come in anyway."

The Counselor stepped into the room then, in one of his double-breasted Brooks Brothers plaid suits, looking as impeccably neat and well-groomed as though he had just stepped out of the lobby of a Wall Street bank. He was holding a newspaper in his hand, which he proceeded to unfold and spread out on the Ambassador's desk.

"I don't know if you've noticed this news item," he said, pointing. "I find it interesting."

In a box on the third page was a photograph of J. Muriuki, leaving The Red Bull amid an applauding crowd: "Our photographers surprise the leader of the opposition dining in a luxurious restaurant in Nairobi," the caption read. As if by chance, there was

131

another photograph on the same page showing the President visiting a school on the coast, surrounded by various members of his Cabinet, and the faces, half-delighted and half-terrified, of the schoolchildren.

"Though it may not appear to be very important," the Counselor went on, "knowing the political customs of these people, invading the government's territory can be considered to be a grave provocation. As you know, The Red Bull is the favorite hangout of a number of Ministers."

"Do you really believe it's that important that Muriuki came to have dinner in one place rather than in another? Maybe he couldn't get a table at another restaurant," the Ambassador said jokingly.

"The proof that it's really a serious matter is that it was reported by this newspaper, which, as you know, acts as a sentry, alerting the government the moment it sees an enemy in sight, so that the guard dog knows who to attack. I don't know if you remember how it carried news of the strike at the University, and later on the workers' meetings in Thika . . . a few days before the police went into action."

"That may well be, but it strikes me that in this case you're exaggerating. You seem to me to be a bit too obsessed by Muriuki's activities. To be frank with you, I, too, think he's up to no good, but it's better not to anticipate events. What point is there in being an alarmist?"

At that very moment, the phone rang, and the Ambassador reached over to pick up the receiver.

"A call from Mombasa from Munyoka? Yes of course, put him through."

Maguire stood there in silence as the Ambassador spoke on the phone, trying to guess from certain questions and words that he kept repeating, what Munyoka was telling him. He guessed enough to turn pale, and his nervousness was evident from a number of little tics, which in turn had the effect of disconcerting the Ambassador.

"Please stop fidgeting. Can't you see you're distracting me?"

When he hung up the phone, the Ambassador repeated Munyoka's information regarding the discovery of the bills of lading and Muriuki's possible participation in the plot. The Counselor listened to all these new developments, vigorously wiping the lenses of his glasses and starting to make other nervous movements that he immediately cut short after a sternly reproving glance from the Ambassador.

"All this information seems interesting, very interesting," said Maguire, after putting his glasses back on; the sunlight reflecting off

the windowpanes of the Center was making him blink his eyes painfully. "You'll note that it rather clearly justifies my grave concern as
to what Muriuki may be up to." He paused so as to give the Ambassador a chance to duly acknowledge the point. "Nonetheless, there is
one thing concerning this arms shipment that I find incredible: They
suppose that the contraband is going to arrive at Mombasa and then
be transported across the Tsavo to Nairobi, I gather."

"Yes, that's what Munyoka said. What's so unlikely about that?"

The Counselor rose from his chair and walked over to a large map
of Kenya on the other side of the room.

"If I had to transport shipment of this sort to Nairobi, the very last
route I'd choose would be via the Port of Mombasa, the place most
closely watched by the authorities, and the tortuous back roads
through the Tsavo, where there's a great possibility of having a run-in
either with the police or with the bands of poachers that infest that
area."

"But that's precisely the point. It's the route that has traditionally
been used by ivory and charcoal smugglers to get contraband *out* of
the country, whereas this time it will be used to smuggle contraband
in. Doesn't that seem logical to you?"

"No, because we're long past the early days of the Uganda Railway, when that was the only means of shipping goods to the interior.
There are other means nowadays—small private planes that can land
in any open spot, trucks traveling at night with their headlights
off...."

"I was aware that you knew this country well after having been
here for a number of years, but I had no idea you were so well
acquainted with the secrets of smuggling," Poire said jokingly.

"What I'm really acquainted with is the contacts that Muriuki has
with Tanzania and Uganda. In view of the sympathies of the Socialist
countries toward Muriuki, there'd be nothing easier than to arrange
for a shipment from Libya to the Kampala Airport; it would then
enter Kenya via Lake Victoria, following the route of the coffee
trucks, which is shorter and safer," the Counselor said, pointing out
the itinerary on the map.

"That sounds rather interesting. Why don't you pass it on to
Muriuki?" The Ambassador's smile faded as he remembered something else. "Incidentally, I forgot to tell you something Munyoka
mentioned that worries me. He led me to understand that the authorities think—as we feared they would—that the ecologist who left for

the Galana a few days ago is in fact a spy that we've sent to investigate Murphy's death. He even told me that the man ought to watch his step, because Muriuki's men are already on his trail."

"Well, what can we do?" the Counselor answered. "Let them think whatever they want to."

"That doesn't seem to me to be the proper attitude for us to take. In the final analysis, we sent Fender right into the thick of things."

"We didn't send him anywhere," Maguire replied, almost vehemently. "He had to go to the Galana, because that's where he's going to do his study on grass."

"But don't you think we ought at least to warn him of the risk he's running? We could recall him, on one pretext or another. . . ."

"That would only attract more attention to him. It seems to me that it's better to leave things as they are. When you come right down to it, what he does is none of our business."

"As the American Ambassador, it's my duty to keep an eye on the safety of my nationals in this country, and I am not about to allow an unfortunate misunderstanding, for which I feel that I myself am partly responsible, to endanger the life of a poor scientist who surely doesn't have the least idea that at this very moment he's landed square in the middle of a dangerous political plot."

"With all respect, Ambassador, it strikes me that you're the one who's exaggerating in this instance. As things stand, we don't have any indication whatsoever that Fender's life may be in danger. That's just a pipe dream of Munyoka's."

"All right, all right, we won't do anything for the time being. But at the least sign that Fender's safety may be threatened, I'll call him back immediately and inform him of the trouble he's unwittingly gotten himself into."

The Cemetery by the Sea

THE BEACH AT WATAMU formed a half moon, protected on the open side by a small atoll; the line of the coral reef stretched across it like a bowstring, leaving inside it a pool of transparent shallow water with mooring buoys for leisure craft and fishing boats. The Seafarers Hotel, where Bob had arranged to meet Lawrence Brown, was simply a large hut with a straw roof built on bamboo pilings driven into the sand of the beach, with a number of "bungalows," also with straw roofs, scattered among the palms. When Bob asked for Brown at the main hut, they told him that he'd find him down where the boats were moored.

And indeed, some hundred yards out from shore, where the water was only a few feet deep, he recognized the profile of the hunter, bending over the engine of a boat, whose bowels he was poking around in with the aid of a few tools and resounding imprecations, uttered at regular intervals. He was so absorbed in what he was doing that he didn't even realize that Bob had rolled up his pants legs and walked out into the water to where he was; he continued to wield his wrench and heap insults on the nuts that had refused to come loose. Only when he straightened up to ease the strain on his back did he see Bob, who was silently watching him work.

"Oh, it's you," he said, pushing back the lock of hair dangling down over his forehead, which was streaked with black where he had wiped away the sweat with his greasy hands. "Here I am, struggling with this contraption—I curse the day I ever bought this piece of junk! I don't take it out more than a few times a year, and I spend far more time getting it ready than I do on the water. The last time I was here, I managed to bend the propeller on coral as I headed out around the reef."

Despite his protests it was plain to see that he was enjoying himself

135

like a child taking a toy apart, and didn't mind in the least being smeared with grease and standing in water up to his knees. Bob, who would not have suspected the hunter of having a love of the sea, immediately understood, on seeing the gleam in Brown's bright blue eyes reflecting the transparent water, what a thirst for vast open seas, for deep salt water a man might feel if he lived almost continually in the wastelands of the Tsavo, where the reddish horizon blends indistinctly with the color of the dry bush and the ocher soil.

"It doesn't look too badly damaged," Bob said, taking a look at the dented propeller. "I don't think it's necessary to remove the entire shaft. Just removing a few nuts and bolts, you can dismount the propeller and straighten the bent blade; and it will run all right. I can give you a hand if you like."

The hunter stood there for a few moments staring at him with such a skeptical look on his face that it was almost comical: The word "You?" was plainly written in the transparent mirror of his eyes.

"May I say that, unlikely as it may seem, I know something about boats? I had a piece of junk like this one when I was studying at Yale, to take out on the lakes."

"I believe you, I believe you," Brown said, somewhat abashed that Bob had read his mind. "But I don't think I need your help, and besides, I have very few tools."

He turned back and buried his head in the engine, anxiously sniffing the effluvia of fish and crusted salt in the bottom of the hull. Bob remained standing there in the middle of the water, with his shoes in his hand, feeling silly; the sun beating down on the bay was so strong that the odor of evaporating salt and iodine was dizzying. At that moment, someone hailed them from the shore: There was a phone call for Lawrence Brown, from Nairobi.

The hunter went hopping off over the water like a frog, skirting the sea urchins feeding on the rocky bottom. Bob took advantage of Brown's absence to look at the bent propeller and feel the coupling of the drive shaft below the water; there were some nuts, near the shaft, that could be loosened in order to remove the propeller blades, so there was no need to poke around in the engine. He didn't want to spoil Lawrence Brown's fun, however. The latter returned in a few minutes, with a look of joy on his grease-stained face.

"It looks like I'm going to have time to repair the damage; the clients aren't coming today. I've just talked to Tony Allen, the professional hunter who's taking them out on safari, and he told me they'd

136

missed the plane for Malindi. I imagine they went out on the town last night in Nairobi, and naturally, they didn't get up in time to catch the plane this morning." His face lit up with a roguish smile. "I know Tony very well, he's a good kid, and a good professional hunter, but he can't resist painting the town red."

"Are we going back to Galana then?"

Brown shook his head and looked up at the sun directly overhead, beating down on the beach.

"I was thinking—it may not be worth the trouble. The clients will be arriving tomorrow, in a private plane, at a landing strip that's halfway between Malindi and the ranch. We could spend a nice quiet day here and leave early tomorrow morning. What do you say to that?"

"That's fine with me."

"Okay then. I know the manager of the hotel and he'll put us up in one of the bungalows free of charge."

"Great. In that case, I'd like to get my bathing trunks out of the car. Could I have the key?"

"It's open. Mungai, the boy, is there."

"All right. See you later." Bob walked off a few steps, and then came back. "Sorry to bother you, but I wanted to ask you: Is it all right to leave my money and my camera in the Toyota?"

"They'll be perfectly safe there. This is not Nairobi, where they'll steal something from you before your back is turned. These Africans on the coast may be a little thick between the ears sometimes, but usually they're honest. In any case, with my people, you needn't worry."

Bob went to get his bathing trunks and put them on in the car. Again he felt that marvelous sensation of running across white sand and plunging into the clear warm water. As he swam out toward the coral reef, the water became deep enough to dive amid the rocks; he could see perfectly under water, but his eyes smarted from the salt. He went back to the beach and lay down under a palm tree, being careful as before not to let the sun's powerful rays fall directly on his skin. He half-closed his eyes to shut out the reflection of the sunlight on the sand, and he immediately remembered the scene in the cemetery that he had visited after he had left the hospital.

Before going to Watamu, he had asked the taxi driver to take him to the cemetery where John Murphy was buried. He thought the grave would be hard to locate, but he had no difficulty finding it. The cemetery was a small plot of land partially overgrown with grass and weeds, but there was one side on which the grass had recently been cut, and Murphy's brand-new gravestone glistened in the sun. At the other end of the cemetery was a stone wall, covered with bougainvillea, and behind it he could see the sea. Bob sought out the shade of a bush, for the sun was reflecting off the white walls, concentrating the heat, and he remained there for a time, not knowing what to do, looking back and forth from the gravestones and the flowers to the gentle slope leading down to the water's edge. What he really would have liked at that moment was to already be at the beach.

It was hard for him to realize that the body of his friend—or what the scavengers had left of it—was buried beneath that very green grass, protected by that gleaming white stone somehow mindful of a baptismal font. He had been impressed by what Patterson had told him about Murphy's having long deliberately sought death. That was not how he himself remembered John from his student days: He had never known anyone more vital, more sure of himself, more devil-may-care. He must have changed a great deal. In any event, he reflected, if it were true that John had been seeking to return to the earth, he had ended up in a beautiful, quiet place, full of the scent of the forest and of flowers and swept by a sea breeze.

And again he felt a knot in his stomach, that distress precisely because he did not feel distressed, or not sufficiently so. What was the point of this sentimental journey in search of a person whose traces in his life, although profound ones, had long lain buried in the past? Had it not been for this study on grass, he might well have lost all track of John Murphy. Their paths would never again have crossed, and he would have had no way of knowing whether John was dead or alive. In any case, he didn't feel like prolonging this visit to the cemetery; what he wanted was to be swimming in the clear water, washing away the dust and the sweat of the journey from Galana.

He was about to get up from the spot where he was crouching beneath the shadow of a bush for shelter from the sun when he heard the creak of gravel along the little road leading up to the cemetery. He looked toward the road and saw the nose of a blue Mercedes appear at the top of the little hill and park in the shade of the same tree underneath which the taxi driver had taken refuge. A tall woman with chestnut hair blowing in the breeze got out of the car and opened the ironwork gate with a steady hand; she was wearing jeans that showed her slender silhouette to advantage and a loose blouse, of the same color as the bougainvillea. She strode resolutely along the little path running through the cemetery and went over to place a small bunch of mixed wildflowers on a grave near John's. From his hiding place, Bob watched as the woman muttered a few words that the breeze carried off as her eyes stared vacantly into the distance; her profile was regular, perhaps slightly angular—high cheekbones and an aquiline but well-proportioned nose—and the sun was bringing out coppery highlights and gold glints in her shoulder-length chestnut hair.

She was unquestionably an attractive woman, although what most impressed Bob was the way she walked as she headed back toward her car: He had not noticed when he saw her coming toward him, but seen from the back, the rhythm of her stride seemed extremely mechanical, like that of a sleepwalker, and her head seemed to bend neither downward nor sideways, as though she were still absorbed in her prayers or lost in her memories.

Bob rose from the spot where he had been crouching, and followed along after her powerful hips and copper-colored hair, which continued to give off strange glints in the sunlight. It was only as he walked past John's grave that he realized that the woman had in fact left the flowers on his friend's grave and not one nearby, as he had thought. So that woman had known Murphy. Bob quickened his pace to catch up with her, but then he hesitated for a moment: He was going to speak to that stranger, but what would he say to her? "Did you know John Murphy?" The answer would obviously be yes. "I knew him too," he would answer, and that would end the conversation. His moment of indecision allowed the woman enough time to cover the distance separating her from her car, which took off at a fair speed.

Bob stood there enveloped in a cloud of dust, feeling rather frustrated and curious to know who the devil that young woman might be. He had half a mind to shake the taxi driver, who had fallen fast asleep, and give him the classic order: "Follow that car!"—but he was sick of the entire aura of adventure and mystery that had surrounded him ever since he had set foot in Nairobi Airport; he was eager to escape that bizarre atmosphere, so contrary to his whole lifestyle, to his temperament. As a scientist with an orderly, methodical turn of mind, he had a natural aversion to the unexpected and the extravagant. Even so, once he had managed to rouse the taxi driver and they started off, he could not keep his eyes from following the blue Mercedes through all the traffic and around each curve in the road. It got farther and farther ahead of them and soon disappeared down a side road, before they too turned off the main highway and headed for Watamu.

The Ozone Layer

WITH HIS EYES HALF-CLOSED—he could still feel the salt on his eyelids—he lay watching the movements of an army of whitish crabs emerging from their hiding places, taking up positions when the line of foam withdrew toward the sea and retreating to the dunes each time a wave thundered in and broke on the shore. Bob knew that a large part of the harmful ultraviolet radiation that reaches the earth's surface falls on equatorial regions, between the latitudes of thirty degrees north and thirty degrees south, due to the fact that the ozone layer is thinner there. The effects of harmful radiations on animals other than man had not yet been studied; it had been assumed that animal species are protected by hair, feathers, scales or shells. But as a matter of fact, unlike humans, the majority of animal species do not expose themselves to full sunlight: Marine species hide during the day in rock cliffs or in deep water, and wild terrestrial animals are either nocturnal or stay beneath the shade of trees during the day.

The cry of the seagulls overhead mingled with the screaming of a band of monkeys that was shaking the branches of the palm trees. In all the years that he had devoted to the study of biology, Bob had never felt as close to nature as he did now.

"If you don't want a bad case of sunburn, I advise you not to lie sleeping in the sun," a hoarse, unknown voice, that seemed to be coming from the heavens, said to him at that moment.

Already half-asleep, Bob raised his head to see who was addressing him in such a peremptory tone of voice; but the stranger's head was directly superimposed on the dazzling glare of the sun, thus creating a

140

peculiar halo effect round about his abundant head of hair. Bob realized however that it was a man of very short stature, since when he sat up a little farther, leaning his back against the trunk of the palm tree, the individual's massive head was very nearly level with his own. He was accompanied by a small, ugly-looking dog—it seemed to be blind in one eye. It began to sniff impertinently at Bob's extremities, and not content with that, piddled on the palm tree against which he was leaning, so that he was obliged to shift slightly to one side in order not to get splashed.

"Come here, Bush, don't bother the gentleman," the stranger said then.

"Don't worry, the dog's not bothering me," Bob commented, in a tone of voice that implied: "But you are."

The stranger's head then moved into the shade, and Bob was able to get a good lock at the man's features, as hard as though they were carved of wood, framed by a reddish mane that made him resemble a lion. That head was unquestionably all out of proportion to the rest of the man's body, which was lean and stringy, and his shorts revealed a pair of very bowed little legs, the result of long service in a cavalry regiment, or maybe some deformity dating back to his childhood. But the most surprising thing about the man was undoubtedly his piercing eyes, which were now examining him closely from head to foot. Bob noted the intensity of those black pupils, and had the curious sensation that they were drilling through his body and even leaving a mark—scorched bark, perhaps—in the tree trunk that he was leaning against. The stranger's gaze was so powerful that when he had finished scrutinizing him, Bob rose to his feet and began to tuck his shirt into his bathing trunks, as though instead of lying on a beach, he had just found himself lying on a table in a hospital lab being thoroughly X-rayed.

"It was not my intention to disturb you," the stranger went on, "but I wanted to warn you, inasmuch as you strike me as a newcomer to these latitudes, of the dangers of the sun this close to the equator; its rays are more intense than they appear to be, and many tourists end up in the hospital at Malindi suffering from serious cases of sunburn."

Bob, who was already burned up, so to speak, because everyone had been giving him advice and suggestions ever since his arrival in Kenya, or perhaps because he was annoyed by the stranger's bold scrutiny, answered him with a curtness that was not usual with him:

141

"First of all, I am not a tourist, but a scientist, and I know very well what a powerful effect the rays of the sun at the equator have: The reason they are capable of producing serious burns is not because they are more intense, but because the ozone layer is thinner in equatorial latitudes, thereby allowing harmful radiations to reach the earth without having been filtered through this protective layer. And secondly, I should like to know why you concluded, even before exchanging one word with me, that I am a foreigner. I had the impression that the majority of us human beings are about the same, especially when we're lying in bathing trunks in the shade of a palm tree."

"That is precisely the reason I took you to be a foreigner. Nobody who has lived in Africa very long would dream of lying asleep on a deserted beach: If you have anything of value with you, you could easily be robbed," he said, pointing to the travel bag lying alongside Bob.

"Well, it's precisely because this is a nearly deserted spot that it seemed to me that there was very little likelihood of my being robbed."

"It's more likely than you think. Take a look at those Africans sitting over there. It looks as though they're busy mending their fishing nets, but in reality they're spying on us and taking in every word we're saying . . . providing they understand English."

Bob had noticed these fishermen as he passed by; they had been walking along the water's edge dragging their wicker nets behind them. Their heads were shaved bare and every bone in their emaciated torsos stuck out; their arms and legs were covered with a crust of sea-salt, and their cracked skins—the result, doubtless, of toiling for many hours at a stretch in the water—looked more like the rough, scaly skin of reptiles than that of human beings. They had come and sat down some hundred yards away from where he was, silently mending their fishing gear, their dark bodies very nearly indistinguishable from the stunted trunks of the palm trees.

"You surely don't think that those poor wretches would be likely to rob me while I'm sleeping?"

"Those of us who have lived in Africa long enough know that on principle Africans are not to be trusted."

"Doesn't it strike you that that way of thinking is a little outmoded? Are whites any more trustworthy?"

"Well, here on the coast there are also undesirable Europeans, especially certain Italians or Portuguese—though, incidentally, I am not at all sure that the latter belong a hundred percent to the white race. But the majority of us have a certain social standing, a position, and none of us would stoop to coming down to the beach to rob you of your wallet. An African, on the other hand, would, and in point of fact they very frequently do so."

"So, according to what you said, all blacks are potential thieves?"

"They may perhaps not all be professional ones; but in any case it's best not to offer them the opportunity."

"How strange, just a little while ago a person who knows this area well happened to remark to me that the blacks here on the coast tend to be more honest than those in Nairobi, for example."

"It is in the cities, naturally, that Africans take on the worst vices of civilization; unfortunately, they do not assimilate the virtues of our culture as readily."

At that moment Bob saw that the man's ugly-looking dog, an unusually curious canine, was nosing about inside his travel bag, where, among other things, were the documents for his study.

"Don't stick your snout into my things," Bob said, pushing the dog's back away from his bag with his hand. "They're in enough of a jumble already."

The dog started to give a fierce growl, but then docilely walked off.

"That's odd," his master said, lightly scratching his unruly lion's mane. "I'm surprised at his behavior."

"Don't worry, he's not bothering me, but I do have documents in my bag that could easily get all mixed up."

"It's not that. What strikes me as odd is the fact that he didn't bite you," the man said in a puzzled tone of voice. "He doesn't like strangers, and never allows anybody to lay a hand on him. I can almost guarantee that he would have bitten anybody else who did what you did. I can see that you have a way with animals."

"Luckily!" Bob muttered, saying to himself: "In other words, on top of everything else, I ought to congratulate myself that that hound of yours didn't attack me. Thanks a lot!"

The dog did seem irritated: It began to growl, the hair on the back of its neck bristled and it even bared its teeth, but its short ears were pointing toward the beach the while.

"Don't worry. He's not doing that on account of you. It's because he's caught the scent of those African fishermen and is watching their every move. But you may rest assured. No African is going to come within twenty paces of you with Bush here."

The poor fishermen meanwhile hadn't budged an inch during this entire conversation, and went on mending their gear in silence, as though they had been sitting beneath those palm trees for several generations.

"I don't know why you mistrust the natives," Bob said, "but I assure you that after living in New York for several years, I often feel safer here than I did there."

"Yes, but the difference is that in a big city like New York, if something bad happens to you, there are always doctors and hospitals —places where they can put you back together again. But in Africa the moment you get very far away from one of the few civilized towns, you're totally helpless. Think for a minute: If somebody has an accident in the middle of the Tsavo, for example, who's going to sew him up if there's no telephone within a thousand miles? The first ones to get there are the vultures."

"It's curious that you've mentioned the Tsavo, since that's precisely where I'm going to be doing my work. I've come here to make a study of the grasses in semi-arid regions, and I'm planning to concentrate on the Galana Ranch and its environs."

"Well, regardless of the nature of your study," the Judge said with a knowing wink of his eye, "I recommend that you watch your step. As you know, the Tsavo is crawling with smugglers and undesirables involved in the illegal traffic in ivory and charcoal. You have every chance of having a run-in with a bunch of rough characters!"

"I know. We almost had an encounter with poachers, but since my study deals only with grasslands and vegetation, I don't imagine my activities are going to bother people of that sort very much."

"When you said that you were a scientist, I took it that you'd come here for the UNICORN Conference that's beginning next week in Nairobi."

"No, everybody keeps asking me if that's why I'm here, but my work isn't directly connected with the activities of the Center, though I will say that I intend to utilize the documentation available from the Center with regard to the subjects I'm dealing with. But the most important part of my study is the data that I'll be gathering in the field myself."

"In any event, I advise you to be careful. In order to save your skin in these parts, it takes something more than seeking out the shade of palm trees!"

"I'm grateful for your advice, and you may rest assured that I'll keep it in mind."

Unexpectedly, without so much as a wave of his hand to bid Bob good-bye, the man called to his dog and walked off across the sand in great long strides, despite his short legs, throwing stones into the water and glancing out of the corner of his eye at the African fishermen who were still mending their gear beneath the palm trees. It was only then that Bob noticed that Lawrence Brown was walking up the beach toward him, and he wondered if the stranger's abrupt departure had been due to the hunter's arrival.

"Well, isn't it time we went and had ourselves a beer and something to eat?" Brown asked as he came up to him.

He was holding the propeller in the air with his arm outstretched, with the pride of an athlete bearing the Olympic torch. It was plain to see from the parts he was holding in his other hand that in the end Brown had decided to follow Bob's suggestions, but Bob very carefully refrained from making any sort of comment.

"What did Judge McGredy want of you?" Brown asked as they headed for the hut at the Seafarers.

"Judge? What judge?"

"The fellow you were talking to—McGredy. I saw the two of you having a long conversation together."

"As a matter of fact, it didn't occur to me to ask him what his name was, and I had no idea he was a judge," Bob answered.

"And a very famous one at that. They used to call him Bwana Maximum during the Emergency; McGredy had a reputation for applying the security laws with the utmost rigor, and even a certain perverse pleasure, people say. That man signed, in his own hand, a number of death sentences."

"I'm amazed to hear that. He struck me just as an eccentric old man, though a bit too garrulous perhaps and something of a racist. So that's it—I understand now why he's so mistrustful of blacks."

"He's quite a sinister figure, who can smell the carrion from miles away, like vultures or hyenas. Are you sure you're not in any trouble with the law?" Brown asked, standing stock-still for a moment and looking at him intently.

"Why should I be? I've just arrived in this country, after all, and I couldn't possibly have had time to get into any trouble."

"Well, I assure you that if that man has been talking with you, it's because he wanted to pry some information out of you. Knowing what sort of person he is, I'm certain he wouldn't waste a single minute of his time idly chatting, not even with his wife."

"I haven't the vaguest idea why he might have been interested in me, unless he mistook me for somebody else. . . ."

"That's possible," Lawrence Brown said, shaking his head. "But try to keep away from McGredy—he's a bird of ill omen!"

The Meeting

THE ATMOSPHERE of the Seafarers Hotel was casual and informal, as was the bamboo hut that constituted its main building. Hanging on the walls were mounted sailfish, sharks' jaws, and a number of yellowed photographs of outsized catches. The bar at one end of the hut was crowded with old-time colonials who had come from Nairobi or from other places along the coast to spend a weekend at Watamu, gorging themselves with food and drink with the excuse of a fishing excursion. The manager of the establishment, a red-headed Scotsman with a big pot belly, was handing out generous rounds of beer, taking a big swig from his own mug each time he served one of his customers.

The dining facilities were also rudimentary: a few tables with cracked marble tops and some wicker chairs placed out on the veranda overlooking the beach. But the buffet that was set out—assorted seafood, salads, and tropical fruit—was fresh and copious. Bob helped himself to an avocado stuffed with delicious crab salad, and a plate of oysters, small and delicate though perhaps a trifle tasteless, noticeably improved, however, by a drop of Tabasco sauce and a squeeze of lemon. The cold beer went down well after the time he'd spent lying on the hot sand, and a cool breeze suddenly ruffled the straw fringes of the hut, bringing with it a pronounced odor of seaweed and foam from the reef.

When he had partially satisfied his appetite, Bob asked about something that he had been mulling over in his mind: "If that McGredy

146

served as a judge during the Mau Mau rebellion and sentenced its guerrillas to death, how come the government kept him on as a magistrate after independence was declared? Weren't the ringleaders of the rebel movement the ones who later became the leaders of the nation?"

Before answering, Lawrence Brown wiped his hands and his mouth with his paper napkin, and his forehead as well, still streaked with grease from the boat engine.

"In the first place," he said, after letting out a genteel belch, "the ones who won the country's independence aren't exactly the same ones who fought the guerrilla campaign in the forest; the British placed the current president in power precisely because they regarded him as a moderate, as in fact he's turned out to be, though in his day many people accused him of masterminding the Mau Mau. The truth of the matter is that those who took up arms are not the ones in power at the moment; they have assumed, rather, more extremist positions —J. Muriuki, for instance."

He paused again to wet his whistle with a swig of beer, and then went on:

"As for the reason they kept McGredy on in his post after he'd sentenced a fair number of rebel leaders to be hanged, that too can be explained, if one keeps in mind the African mentality. Although in certain respects these people may strike you as simple and primitive, their logic might be different from ours, yet very practical in the final analysis. Knowing the diversity of interests in a new country such as this, they may have wanted to guarantee the independence and impartiality of the judicial process by having someone who is above tribal rivalries and petty traditional rancors because he hates them all! The tougher and more unbending that man is, the more guarantees he offers them."

After lunch, Brown went off to the workshop of the hotel to fix the propeller he had dismounted, and Bob went back to the spot where he had had the conversation with McGredy and lay there contemplating the tide that was beginning to come in and the seagulls hovering just above the foam of the reef, occasionally flying straight up from the water with a small fish gleaming in their beak.

Between the big lunch he had just eaten and the gentle breeze stirring the fronds of the palm tree above his head, he felt a pleasant lethargy begin to steal over him once again. He had drunk too much beer on a nearly empty stomach. Much too much beer. The judge's

147

warning was still ringing in his ears, in that voice screaming above his head like the cry of a bird of ill omen: "I don't advise you to lie sleeping in the sun . . . sun . . . sun!"

He staggered to his feet, and the creak of the sand beneath the soles of his feet resounded in his head; if he continued to walk along the row of palm trees, he would get his feet burned, and if he went down to the edge of the water where the sand was cool, the sun would sink its fingers in his hair and rake his back through the thin cloth of his shirt. His knowledge of ultraviolet rays, the ozone layer, the whole scientific rigamarole was of very little use to him. Incoherent phrases, admonitions and prophecies that the chorus of colonial fauna had been offering him one by one reverberated in his feverish head like the piercing cries of seagulls. Maguire: "Above all don't get strange ideas in your head. Murphy died on a deserted road, the hyenas tore his body to pieces and the monkeys scattered his clothes all about, but there was nothing unusual about the accident." Patterson: "Don't worry, if John hadn't crashed into a tree, a jealous husband would have blown the top of his head off, or a buffalo would have disemboweled him." Lawrence Brown: "This isn't the 'Jungle Cruise' at Disney World, it's the real damned jungle." And how!

The ribbon of beach joined the line of palms in the distance, like two straight parallel lines converging at infinity, and at that very point the already oblique light of the late afternoon sun was breaking up above the mist of the crashing waves, forming the stripes of a rainbow. He headed toward it like a man possessed, reluctant to admit to himself that the mirage kept moving ever farther toward the horizon line as he walked on.

Although he sought out the firmest part of the beach, where the sand was still damp, his feet sank deep into a warm mud, and the surge of the waves washed away his footprints. Heavy dark clouds were gathering on the horizon beyond the palm trees, portending a storm.

As he rounded a little curve of the beach that narrowed as it passed beneath a rocky promontory covered with vegetation, Bob saw an apparition making its way toward him. For the space of a few instants, he thought that it too was a mirage, like the faint rainbow of sea mist that kept receding as he walked toward it; but then he realized that it was real. It was the young woman he had seen in the cemetery; she was walking toward him with the same steady, mechanical rhythm of her shapely hips, enveloped now in a multicolored

148

kanga; and despite the fact that the strip of sand was narrow in that spot, her eyes again had such an absent gaze that she did not even blink as she passed by him. And again her hair had a reddish glint, accentuated this time by the setting sun.

Bob spun round on his bare heels like a top, so fast that his ankles nearly creaked, and headed after her. He wasn't going to let her escape this time. Even so, he followed for a long way the line of her footprints being erased by the tide. In a place where the beach again widened, the woman left the water's edge and began walking in the direction of a large white bungalow surrounded by a bright green lawn, clearly visible between the palm trees. He caught up with her just as she was starting up the little gravel path leading up a slope from the beach to the house.

"I beg your pardon, but it seems to me I've seen you before. Did you by any chance know John Murphy?"

There was something sad and evasive about her eyes as she glanced momentarily at his face, and then her gaze immediately skipped like a flat stone over the crest of the waves and the sea-foam from the reef, finally losing itself in the dark storm clouds looming on the horizon.

"Yes, I knew John Murphy," she finally said, in a somewhat gutteral voice, swallowing hard. "Was he a friend of yours?"

"Yes, we went to college together."

They remained standing there facing each other for some time, not knowing what to say. Fortunately, at that very moment it began to rain. A few very fat warm drops, like bird droppings, fell first, forming little balls of sand as they touched the ground. Then the heavens let out a prolonged belch and spewed out a heavy warm rain on the beach. Such a dense downpour that it formed a white curtain, hiding the grove of palm trees, the house, the sea from sight.

The two of them ran up the gravel path—an uncomfortable sensation in bare feet—to the house. By the time they reached it both of them were soaked to the skin, Bob especially. His hair, his shirt, and his bathing trunks were dripping wet, as though he had just dived into the sea.

"You look like a wet hen!" the woman said, breaking into hearty, contagious laughter. "Come inside and dry off."

"But I'm going to get everything all wet," Bob said, trying to shake the water off himself, like a hunting dog.

"It doesn't matter. It's a tile floor and they'll mop it up."

They went through a spacious entry hall, decorated with African art, and crossed a large living room that was nearly dark, from the shadowy corners of which there emerged the heads of buffaloes, the jaws of lions. They ended up in a library, on the shelves of which there were more bottles of liquor than books. Sprawled out on a sofa, a glass of whisky in his hand, was a man of about fifty, reading a novel with the aid of half-glasses resting on the tip of a patrician nose slightly red from the sun or from alcohol. Or both.

Alex Townsend-Reeves had a noble profile, a broad forehead, regular features that might even be described as handsome were it not for an aura of flabbiness, of premature senility surrounding his person. His large blue eyes, gazing at the visitor from above the half-glasses, were somewhat watery and dull as well, like those of someone who has drowned a great many sorrows in drink.

"My husband. Alex, I'd like to introduce you to a gentleman I've just met. By the way, what's your name?" the woman asked Bob.

"Fender, Robert Fender."

"I'd like you to meet Mr. Fender."

As Guni made the introduction, she remained some distance away, standing just inside the room, as though the better to appreciate her husband's reaction to this visitor. She had the look of mingled shyness and pride of a young retriever that has just deposited an unusual piece of game at its master's feet, not yet knowing whether it is about to be petted or scolded for its exploit.

"Delighted, I'm sure, Mr. Fender," Townsend-Reeves said, barely rising to a sitting position and extending a slender hand with slightly puffy fingers. "Do pour yourself a drink and come sit down. Whiskey hits the spot in stormy weather like this."

"Thanks very much, but it's still too early in the day for me. Moreover, I just got up from the lunch table, practically speaking."

"Why are you holed up inside here instead of going out on the veranda to read?" Guni asked her husband, with an insolent note in her voice all of a sudden. "You're going to go blind reading in the dark like this."

"I came inside here to escape the downpour. You know very well that bad humidity like that ruins my books. I'll go back out when it clears up. That heavy rainstorm yesterday lasted only a few minutes."

The downpour in fact soon subsided, and as abruptly as it had started, it stopped lashing the windowpanes. Alex and Bob went out onto the veranda then, as Guni went off to change clothes.

150

The Tag End of a Race

THE CLOUDS HAD BURST like ripe figs, leaving the earth impregnated with a sweetish smell of nectar and resin. There were now only a few wisps of haze still floating in the blue sky that was slowly taking on the deep red tinge of twilight. The rain had washed the air, and the various odors of seaweed, vegetation, and pollen had now become particularly sharp and distinct, as though filtered through that soft, transparent light. The breeze nonetheless brought with it a more powerful odor, of wet earth, of fermenting leaves, of rotted flowers: the smell of Africa.

Bob and Alex sat in hammocks on the veranda overlooking the sea. The latter had brought along his drink, which seemed like an extension of his right hand, and every so often he raised the glass to his lips, with great solemnity and devotion, as though he were draining a chalice in celebration of some secret ritual.

"I can tell by your accent that you are an American, Mr. Fender. What brings you here to the coast, if I may ask?"

"Certainly; there's nothing secret about it. I'm conducting a study on grass for the Food and Agriculture Organization. . . ."

"What sort of grass?" Alex asked with a smile.

"I should say, rather, that it's a study of grasslands in semiarid regions. I've come to the Galana Ranch to collect the field data I need. I came down to the coast today just to see what it was like, and to visit Patterson, who's in the hospital in Malindi. He's the person who'll be orienting me when I begin gathering data for my report."

"A report on grass? What an interesting subject! When I was in charge of cattle raising on my uncle's ranch—that was some years ago—we always went at the whole pasturage business blindly, because there were no reliable studies on how to make the best use of grasslands, or anything like that. Moreover, that was rich land, in the Rift Valley."

"That's precisely why I chose the Galana region. But I suppose that the problems of overgrazing, and of the interrelationship between the needs of wild animals and domesticated cattle for grazing land, are problems common to all of Africa."

"That's a fascinating subject. When I first began to come down to the coast one couldn't get here by way of the Tsavo, since at that time it was an almost impenetrable jungle of *nyka*. But today the animals have destroyed the forest, turning it into open range. I don't believe you could have chosen a better place for your study."

"To tell the truth, the person who organized everything and put me in contact with the people at Galana was John Murphy, the officer in charge of environmental matters at the Embassy. Unfortunately, he was killed a few days ago in an automobile accident."

Bob paused, waiting for Townsend-Reeves to offer the usual remarks about Murphy on hearing this. But he remained silent, merely burying his nose in his glass, slowly sucking up the vivifying liquid like a thirsty pachyderm. When he raised his head from the glass, Bob noted that his hand was trembling even more than it had been a moment before, but he attributed this to the effects of the alcohol. The rays of the setting sun turned the tops of the palm trees to gold, and the rose-colored stretch of horizon before them gradually took on the soft mauve tint of twilight.

"I presume that Bwana Game is still lord and master of the Galana, is that right?" Alex asked, although the question did not appear to be particularly relevant to the subject at hand.

"Bwana Game?" Bob asked.

"I'm referring to Lawrence Brown. Is he still refusing to bury the hatchet in his war with the poachers?"

"As a matter of fact, he's still quite concerned because they're killing his animals. He says that if he and his men didn't keep a sharp eye out, the poachers would clean out the entire Tsavo region."

"I've known that old grouch for some time. In his day, he was the best professional hunter in all Kenya, but now he's joined the ranks of the conservationists. He only allows a party of hunters to enter his territory from time to time, merely in order to offset some of the running costs of the ranch. And even so, he goes around scaring the game away from his own clients so that they can't get one shot at anything that's worthwhile! Don't you think he's going a bit far?"

"Perhaps so, but the subject of animals is only of peripheral interest to me as far as my study is concerned—large mammals in particular, since they're browsers rather than grazers."

"Yes, but don't forget that by clearing away the trees and trampling down the bush they enable grass to grow, since otherwise it would be choked out by excessive vegetation."

"I can see that you know a great deal about these things. Have you had training as a scientist?"

"No, not really. But I've lived in these parts for a good many years, and a person gradually picks up certain things here and there. If you'll allow me to offer you a piece of advice, I recommend that you try to study grass, animals, and even men as a single, interrelated whole. In the final analysis, who determines the ecosystem? Animals, and man—the latter in particular. Fire, for instance, is an important factor in controlling grasslands and preventing all other types of vegetation from choking out the grass. But who is it that sets fire to the grasslands? Africans, honey-hunters or poachers, in order to concentrate the game in certain places or to open up passable trails through the bush."

"I agree, but this is not an important fact for my study. I don't share Lawrence Brown's obsessions about hunting or poachers."

"Don't forget that even in my own lifetime, we colonized this area with the British flag in one hand and a hunting rifle in the other. In the days when I first came to Africa, participating in that sport was practically obligatory; if you weren't a hunter, you were regarded as an odd sort. But I don't share either the obession of certain longtime colonials concerning poachers; they speak of the natives as though they were vermin. I for my part regard them as merely another element of the environment. Do they kill animals? Of course they do, but they don't do any more damage than a stubborn drought or other natural accidents. As I told you before, life in Africa evolves on different planes, but they are all textures, on different levels, of the same warp and woof."

"You may be right."

They sat there for some time discussing ecology, grass, animals. From time to time Alex submerged his lips in his glass, with the same eagerness and delectation with which a hummingbird sips the nectar of a gorgeous tropical flower, and went on expounding his theories, which became more and more confused and complicated; meanwhile the dusk and the dampness little by little crept over the terrace. Bob smiled to himself, reflecting that it was rather ironic that he had had his first interesting conversation about the subjects of his study under such odd circumstances—thanks to his following an unknown woman to her house—with this British toper who looked at the world with a

153

certain perspicacity, through the double enlargement of the lenses of his glasses and the bottom of his glass of whiskey.

Before darkness had completely fallen, they saw the silhouette of a man coming toward them along the water's edge, following the footprints left in the sand by Bob and Guni. Alex recognized him as soon as he spied him:

"Speaking of the devil, isn't that Bwana Game himself—that is to say, Lawrence Brown in person?"

Bob wasn't sure whether he should be annoyed or amused by the fact that the hunter had followed his trail, as though he were a mere antelope, but decided to call out to him. "Mr. Brown, we're up here, on the veranda."

The Electric Ray

WHEN HE CAUGHT SIGHT of Bob on the veranda, Brown walked up the gravel path, grumbling and muttering incomprehensible phrases.

"Whatever became of you, Mr. Fender?" he asked on reaching the veranda, in the tone of voice of someone admonishing a child. "I've been looking for you for an hour, and was beginning to think that something might have happened to you."

It was only then that Brown noticed Alex, who had remained seated in his hammock with his head in shadow; the hunter appeared to be somewhat ill at ease in the presence of the Englishman, who bade him welcome with a vague wave of his trembling hand.

"I'll get you a whiskey. I need to freshen my own drink."

Bob sensed hostile vibrations between the two old-time colonials. From their distant, impersonal manner, he had the feeling that they had known each other for years, but that it had been some time since they had been on friendly terms. The hunter nonetheless accepted the glass of whiskey he was offered, and when a servant dressed in white appeared on the veranda, announcing that dinner

154

was served, he accepted without further ado Townsend-Reeves's invitation to join them.

The dinner took place amid alternate moments of animated conversation and heavy silences. The lady of the house did not appear until the second course; the three of them were obliged to rise to their feet as she entered the dining room. She had on a *kanga* much like the one she had been wearing that afternoon, though this one was in shades of black and white that harmonized with a dark silk blouse loosely buttoned down the front. Her hair gave off even brighter copper glints in the light of the kerosene lamp, and even the stuffed animal heads mounted on the walls seemed to be leaning forward to look down the low-cut neckline of the blouse. The woman murmured a few polite phrases, and then retreated into a hermetic silence.

"Before you arrived," Townsend-Reeves said, trying to revive the conversation, "I was trying to convince Professor Fender that in order to understand the reality of Africa, he would have to set aside many preconceptions and try to study all the available data as an interrelated whole."

"I told him the same thing the day he arrived," Brown chimed in, nodding his head. "To study this country—either its grasslands or its wastelands—requires large doses of realism, and things that can be learned in books and at universities aren't much help at all."

"You see?" Alex said, turning to Bob. "Forget everything you've learned thus far, and throw all your documentation into the muddy waters of the Galana River. All that is going to be of very little use to you: Africa is different!"

"I think I've come to realize that already," Bob murmured, casting a curious glance at the woman, who was still sitting there taking no part in the conversation.

By then the two Britishers had drunk impressive quantities of alcohol, creating a certain air of complicity and understanding between them that, as Bob assumed, did not exist when the two of them were in their normal state. After a while the subject of Judge McGredy came up again in the conversation. Apparently the Judge aroused great interest among old-time colonials.

"I have no idea what's brought him here," Brown commented, "but he was prowling about the beach this morning. I know he has a house in Malindi, but this is the first time I've seen him around these parts."

"When Bwana Maximum pokes about at his leisure, he's not always on an official assignment. Despite his inquisitor's eyes and that stern mask he assumes, he likes a good time. Only recently he was seen in the Florida Club in Mombasa, surrounded by Somali whores. It's almost as though he liked Africans only at exceptional moments: in bed or on the gallows!"

Lawrence Brown greeted that bad joke with his gutteral laugh that sounded more like a big dog growling, and added, "Fender was just asking me, as a matter of fact, how the African government could have kept a character such as McGredy on in his position after the role he played as a judge during the Emergency; I explained to him that despite their resentment, Africans trust a white judge more."

"Of course, and it also suits those in power that the bad guy, the one who metes out punishment, should continue to be a white; in that way they manage to have a European continue to be the target of people's hatred, while at the same time law and order are maintained. You'll notice that nearly all African leaders have a renegade white who's close to them, a man with whom they plot their worst atrocities, and at the same time a man whom they can denounce publicly before their fellow citizens the minute they need a scapegoat. Look at Amin Dada's or Bokassa's white advisers, for instance."

"Up to a point, that seems quite logical," Bob replied.

"As it so happens, African logic is sometimes more realistic than our European logic. And more different still from American ways of thinking . . . Incidentally, how did Washington ever get the idea of sending a black ambassador here? I can assure you that Poire's appointment has not been very popular in African circles."

"I don't work for the State Department, but I see nothing wrong in sending a black representative to Africa. Moreover, I think he is a good ambassador; he was very kind to me, anyway."

"Yes, but don't forget that in these developing countries, the hierarchy of values of the colonial era are still deeply engraved in their memories. They need to have you send them your best people, so as to confirm their status as nations. And I guarantee you that here, the fairer, the more Waspy your ambassador looks, the better."

"Hear, hear, I think he is right, he's damn right," asserted Lawrence Brown, with his muffled laugh, "otherwise African people's reaction is to think: Who do they take us for, anyway?"

Bob was beginning to tire of this conversation. The two men were trying to be clever, but by this time they were far too thick-tongued for that. The woman, who had left the room as the men took their traditional after-dinner glass of port together, appeared again and

156

announced that she was going out to get a little fresh air. Bob took advantage of the opportunity and offered to come with her, leaving the other two to drain the bottle of port in the stifling atmosphere of the dining room that reeked of pipe tobacco and kerosene fumes from the lantern.

They went walking along the beach, in the bright light of a full moon, obscured only by an occasional passing cloud traveling in the same direction as they were. They padded along in silence, listening to their own footfalls on the wet sand; every so often, a cool, gusty breeze rippled the surface of the water and shook the tops of the palm trees. Remembering his conversation with the Judge, Bob couldn't help glancing out of the corner of his eye at the movements in the underbrush bordering the beach. Suddenly they heard a noise caused by something other than the wind, and a moment later a monster with limbs covered with wrinkled skin came bursting out of the bushes, its huge carapace gleaming in the moonlight. The woman, walking barefoot at the water's edge, was terrified and instinctively drew closer to her male companion.

"It's only a tortoise . . . an enormous tortoise," Bob said, feeling his heart beat faster.

The amphibian was waddling across the sand, a few feet away from them, its heavy shell swaying from side to side; it slowly covered the distance separating it from the water and plunged in with a loud splash, momentarily disturbing the calm surface of the bay. Only then did Bob realize that Guni had huddled up so close to him that he could feel her nipples, grown hard and erect from the cold, against his shirt, and her thigh peeking out of the half-open *kanga*, touching the calf of his leg. Almost instinctively, his lips brushed the woman's forehead, whereupon she clung to him even more tightly, deliberately pressing her warm belly against his. Bob could scarcely breathe, and he could feel the blood at his temples pounding. He realized, in terror, that it would be possible for him to possess this woman at that very instant, throwing her down onto the cold sand, or dragging her to the warm water's edge, or pushing her hot body into the underbrush where the tortoise had just laid its eggs.

But voices echoed in the night—they seemed very far away but they were very close at hand. "Mr. Fender, where are you?" "Guni, we're over here." The breeze brought with it the hunter's stentorian voice and the slurred call of the drunken husband; they were searching for them.

With mingled despair and relief, Bob slipped out of the woman's feverish embrace just as his hand was sliding up the smooth soft skin of her leg, opening the *kanga* even wider. He shook his head, as though to free his mind of confusion and desire, and took a step backward into the warm water. At that moment, the soles of his feet touched something that glided away along the sandy bottom, and he suddenly felt an intense pain like the lash of a whip, an electrical discharge that made him leap into the air. He stumbled out of the water and sat down on the sand clutching his injured foot. He saw that the sole of it had the same burn mark it would have had if he had stepped on a bare high tension cable. He wondered what in the world could have caused such a sharp pain. Despite all his knowledge of biology, he failed to remember at that moment that tropical seas are haunted by stonefishes and electric rays. The woman had remained standing there stock-still, overcome with surprise too, with her strong legs still spread apart and her skirt half open.

The voices sounded even closer now . . .

Nocturne, with Flute

VAGUE FAREWELLS on the veranda began to die away in the night fog. Lawrence Brown and Bob Fender still had to get back to the hotel at the other end of the beach. Brown was tottering from the port, and Bob was limping from the pain in his foot. Halfway back, they stopped to piss. Brown waded out into the water up to his knees, pointing his stream of urine up at the moon, and Bob remained at the water's edge to avoid any more mishaps.

Between the walk and the breeze that was making the palms applaud, the effects of the alcohol were wearing off, and as they covered the last stretch, they began to comment on the events of that evening.

"That Alex fellow struck me as a rather decent sort, and he seems to know a fair amount about the African countryside and its ecology," Bob said.

"Bah! Don't believe even half of what he tells you. He's a fraud, likable enough perhaps, but a fraud nonetheless. Everything he has to say about the forest and its animals he's no doubt read in those books in his library, because I assure you he's never gone more than twenty yards off the Nairobi–Mombasa highway."

"Well then, how did he acquire that magnificent collection of trophies? He couldn't have come by them shooting from his car. . . ."

"Alex has never known how to shoot, from a car or from anywhere else. Trophies like that can be had for very little on the black market, and they say he's on excellent terms with the traffickers."

"That's curious. I would have sworn he was the real thing, and a real gentleman too, of course."

"It's all a false front. A goodly number of Europeans won't even say hello to him because during the Emergency he abandoned his house, leaving his firearms behind, and they fell into the hands of the guerrillas. I accepted his invitation to dinner tonight only because it seemed awkward for me to part company with you once we'd gotten here, but in all the time I've been coming down here to the coast I've never set foot in his house before."

Bob remained silent for a moment. Although what Brown had said might well be true, Townsend-Reeves's having bought trophies to decorate his living room, or even his having abandoned his house out of fear of getting his head cut off didn't strike him as really heinous crimes. It was anybody's right to be afraid, wasn't it?

Meanwhile, they had arrived back at the hotel, and Brown searched around in the clump of palms for the number of the bungalow that they'd been assigned. After working the key in the lock, the wooden door opened with a creak of rusty hinges. The hut was not exactly spacious, and it smelled musty, but it had two bedrooms and a small toilet. Brown did not deign to sleep in his dingy cubbyhole of a bedroom and took his bed out onto the veranda, saying that it was cooler out there. He sat for a long time on the wooden steps of the bungalow smoking his pipe and trying to fix a rusty fishing reel that he'd found in one corner of the hut. There is nothing more stubborn than a slightly drunk man endeavoring to prove his manual dexterity to himself, even under the most adverse circumstances—in this case in dim light and with a pocket knife as the only tool—and at a time when his fingers do not respond properly to signals from his brain.

Bob, however, went into his bedroom and lowered the mosquito netting, leaving a crack of the door open to let in air. From his bed, he could see the massive, reassuring silhouette of the hunter fixing the reel in the dim light on the veranda, not even noticing that he was being surrounded by swarms of vicious mosquitoes, as Patterson would have put it.

Between the heat, the humidity, and the palm trees outlined in the frame of his window and casting strange shadows on the wall, he again found it hard to drop off to sleep. There suddenly came back to his mind that disagreeable sensation that he had felt, just before dawn, in the Hotel Norfolk on the day that he had left for the coast. He was able to recall that, just before he had heard the rustling sounds of the birds, he had been startled by the click of the sliding door leading to the garden, which he had imprudently left open the night before; he could even play back the muffled sound of bare feet running over the lawn of the main courtyard of the hotel. He had not even had time to give the incident a second thought, in the hustle and bustle of catching the plane, arriving in Mombasa, and getting out to the Galana Ranch. But now, he thought he was hearing again the muffled sound of some steps on the sand, and the crackle of a window somebody was trying to open, from the outside.

Brown must have already fallen asleep, because the light on the veranda was no longer on, and Bob noted that an irresistible drowsiness was stealing over him too, although the room was quite stuffy; he turned his head the other way, and there then came to him a puff of breeze saturated with a strong sweetish smell. That odor! He made a desperate effort to open his eyes, to sit up, but he was unable to. With one sweep of his hand, he managed to brush the mosquito netting away from his face. He was too tired and the bones at his temples were pressing in on his brain like a metal clamp. He frantically dilated his nostrils, fighting for air, but the air he managed to breathe in was poisoned with an overpowering, nauseating perfume. He felt that his head was about to burst, but it was utterly impossible for him to sit up. By making a valiant effort, he managed to, open his eyelids slightly, and then he saw the shadow of a man in the window frame, in sharp outline against the bright moonlight. It might have been the trunk of a palm tree, or an odd fold in the mosquito netting, but it wasn't; it was a man.

Trying his best to focus his eyes as his vision began to cloud over—all the objects in the room seemed to be distorted and turning round and round, growing fainter and fainter in a thin cloud of smoke—he concentrated on what that shadow was doing. The man had somehow managed to pierce a hole in the window screen, and using a hollow bamboo stalk, he was blowing a vapor with a penetrating, sweetish odor into the room. This was what was making the furniture dance about and the walls gyrate, and was about to cause Bob's skull to explode. There was nothing he could do, he was unable to move, and possibly he was going to die of asphyxiation; so he devoted himself to contemplating with morbid delight the spirals formed by the smoke as it left the blowpipe, the way it was gradually filling the entire room, and the movement of the mosquito netting, drifting like an immense fishnet, blurring the perspective, enveloping all the objects within that poisoned fishbowl.

Suddenly the door of his room was flung wide open, and the bulky outline of the hunter, stark naked, appeared on the threshold, carrying his sheet bunched up in one arm. He crossed the room in one leap and drove his fist, with all the force of a drop hammer, into the silhouette in the window. The glass shattered and the splinters flew in all directions, and the body of the intruder could be heard thudding to the ground below amid the fallen leaves, like a sandbag. The hunter then left the room, coughing and holding his nose. Making a super-human effort, poor Bob, as limp as a rag with vertigo and nausea, staggered out after him.

When he reached the door, his knees gave way and he collapsed on the bed out on the veranda, dragging it along as he fell and hitting his head on the wooden crossbar. He lay there unconscious, bleeding copiously, till Brown came back from chasing after the shadow, which had vanished in the night, and tied a strip of sheet around Bob's head to stanch the wound.

PART FOUR

Shadows at Dawn

NIGHT OWL THAT HE WAS, Bruno Toffani had left Nairobi after dark, driving along the trails of the Tsavo Park with his headlights turned off, taking advantage of the bright moonlight. All day long, he had combed the city in search of the fat prostitute who, the previous night, had relieved him of his clothes, his wallet, and the copies of the bills of lading, leaving no stone unturned. But she had disappeared without a trace. Though he did not reject other possibilities that made the thick hair on his forearms stand on end, he was finally inclined to suspect, as the shrewd Munyoka had also surmised, that the woman he'd caroused with had assumed a second identity. Dressed in different clothes, with an ample peasant's turban wound around her head and enveloped in a loose-fitting tunic that hid her outsized breasts and bulging hips, she might have sat right in front of him at some market stall, and even bargained with him over the price of a wicker basket and he would never have recognized her.

By nightfall, after having tramped through all the bars, rooming houses, and brothels where they might have known the thief, he admitted defeat and abandoned his search. And after having stopped by his hotel to pick up his belongings—how glad he was, given the circumstances, that he had signed the register with an assumed name! —he started back down to the coast. The African boys who worked for him curled themselves up in blankets, in the back of the van, and fell asleep as soon as he hit the main road.

In those moments of emptiness just before first light—when night has ended and the new day has not yet dawned—Bruno felt a tremendous anxiety suddenly grip him by the throat. As he approached the Galana, great black storm clouds completely hid the moon, which was now a mere fleeting, thin, pale disk, and for a time he was obliged to turn on the headlights. The shadows of antelopes flitted among the bushes like ghosts, and every so often the headlights revealed the phosphorescent pupils of buffaloes, half-hidden in the underbrush, their horns gleaming in the darkness. On a level stretch of ground at the end of Mackinnon Road, a long line of elephants slowly filed by along the roadside, still enveloped in mantles of fog, like members of an eerie brotherhood.

As he drove on toward his house, his dark forebodings took on more and more concrete form—like the silhouettes of the animals that were beginning to stand out more and more clearly against the dawning light—and his sudden anxiety became more and more sharply focused. He had good reason to feel anxious, since Muriuki's men, who regarded themselves as the heirs of the Mau Mau guerrilla fighters, practiced the same barbaric rituals as those hard-core rebels bound together by a blood oath, mutilating their enemies' cattle and setting fire to their crops and dwellings. Though Toffani had not experienced the upheavals of the Emergency at first hand—its worst effects had been felt in the highlands, in Kikuyu territory—tales of the atrocities committed in isolated villages and on remote farms by the freedom fighters (often, it was said, under the influence of halluncinatory drugs) had reached the coast.

Toffani was so impatient to get home that when he reached Garsen, instead of skirting the village and crossing to the other side of the river by way of the tree-trunk bridge a mile or so farther upstream, he drove the Land Rover straight across the river at the spot where it widened, just in front of the gentle slope in which his house was located. The ford was a deep one and it was difficult to calculate how

166

high the water was running, so that there was always the risk of sinking into an unexpectedly deep pool; but the current at that hour was flowing gently along, and the reflections of stars were still gleaming on the surface of the gray water amid the rushes on the shore. A few herons flew up from the canebrake, their white wings blending with the wisps of fog hovering above the current.

His heart suddenly leaped for joy as he saw that his shack was just as he had left it and everything outside quiet and peaceful. The whole place looked perfectly normal. Even the light on the veranda, which was always left burning when he was away, was welcoming him home, its beam falling on the empty hammock where he was in the habit of taking his afternoon naps. But a few seconds before the Land Rover braked to a complete stop, he saw something jump onto the running board, and at almost the same moment, the dark eye of a gun was thrust through the window; he felt the cold touch of the barrel on the nape of his neck.

"Stop the car and don't do anything dumb or I'll blow your head off." The voice sounded calm but icy; the click of the firing pin of a revolver, pressed to his ear, constituted a most convincing argument.

Bruno was sitting with a loaded shotgun underneath him, but he knew that before he could touch the seat cover, that man would have dispatched him to the next world to meet Mussolini. Two or three more silhouettes immediately leaped out of the shadow, aiming their weapons at the "boys" who were riding in the back of the van. In the semidarkness Bruno recognized the man in the Panama hat he'd run into in the Hotel Hilton, who now walked over to him with a sinister smile on his lips.

"And now you and I are going to have a little talk there inside your place, and don't try any funny business because my men have already gone in there."

On hearing those words, Bruno felt an ice-cold chill run up his spine, and his blood froze as he went up the steps and saw the dead body of old Pogo, the Neopolitan mastiff, lying on the veranda with his belly ripped open; his neck had been nearly sliced through with a machete, his belly was slit straight down the middle, and his genitals had been lopped off: It seemed to Bruno that his own guts were spilling out as he thought of the scene that might greet him when he opened the door of his house. Fortunately, when he turned the light on, he saw Rosa and his daughters sitting at the dining room table, guarded by two henchmen standing alongside them. Rosa and the two girls sat there with their arms around each other, not saying one word. The girls merely rolled their expressive eyes in their little round faces, realizing that this was not the time for effusiveness or warm greetings.

"If you're going to do anything to me, you can take me outside. I don't want it to happen in front of them," Bruno murmured.

"You're not the one who's running this show," one of the guards said to him, lightly smacking him in the belly with the flat of his rifle butt. "But don't worry. We'll send the womenfolk to bed so we can have a nice quiet chat together."

They thereupon led Rosa and the girls off to the bedroom, and he could hear their sobs, muffled by the drapes curtaining off the sanctuary with his Fascist relics. The men made him sit down at the table with his hands extended on the wooden board, and the young rascal in the Panama hat sat down across from him and lit a cigarettte before beginning to talk. During all that time, Bruno tried his best to think fast, to make up some story or excuse that would sound convincing, but there was one question that kept hammering away in his head, making it nearly impossible for him to think at all: How had they gotten wind so quickly of what had happened?

"We don't have much time. It's getting light and we have to get back to Nairobi—and we don't know the shortcuts through the Tsavo as well as you do," Muriuki's henchman said, leaning forward and pushing his hat back. "Why did you do it?"

"Why did I do what?"

"Come on, don't play dumb. We know that the documents we gave you have fallen into the hands of the police, and so do you."

Bruno thought quickly, knowing that no matter what he answered he was risking his neck; his instinct told him that the only thing that could save him was to own up to the truth.

"If you know so many things, you should also know that I didn't lose them on purpose. And what's more, only part of the documents have gone astray. The originals of the bills and the shipping documents, with all the information, are still in my possession, hidden in a safe place. . . . I needn't mention that if you do anything to me you'll never find out where they are." And at that point he purposely took off his hat and set it down on the table in front of his interrogator, his thought being that if they searched him that would be the last place they'd think of looking.

Bruno then recounted the whole unfortunate incident and told of

168

his search for the woman who'd robbed him. As he went on speaking, he gradually recovered his self-confidence and a tiny little ray of hope began to dawn in the back of his mind: Something told him that, despite everything, he just might get out of this whole mess alive. As Bruno was telling his story, the man in the straw hat had risen from his chair and was pacing up and down the room in great strides on his long, lithe antelope's legs, halting every so often in front of the window to take a look outside. A round sun was slowly rising on the other side of the river, tinging the fog hovering above the shoreline with its rosy glow.

"All right, all right," the man said, suddenly turning around and cutting Bruno's story short. "You needn't go into any more details. I think what you're telling me is true, but you're still responsible for what happened, since a person has to be really stupid to go off painting the town red and getting dead drunk with such sensitive documents in his pocket. You were careless and you deserve to pay for it," he said, giving the butt of his revolver a threatening pat. "But all fools are lucky, and that's what you are—a fool. You deserve to have us slit your belly open and throw your dead body along the roadside somewhere to feed scavengers. That's how we had to get rid of that fat whore who robbed you"—he smiled as he saw Toffani give a shiver of fear.

"But for this time, we're not going to do that. Bear in mind, however, that this is your last chance. Don't get the idea that just because we let you off easily this once, you can go on doing dumb things. The next time . . ." and he finished his sentence by drawing his index finger across his throat.

Toffani felt so relieved, he almost began to cry. All the effort that he had put into holding himself together when he thought that they were going to kill or torture him suddenly collapsed. Once he realized that he'd cheated death yet again, his whole belly began to heave with nervous convulsions; but he soon regained control of himself and put his hat on again, as a symbol that he'd become a human being once more.

"From now on, don't expect us to trust you completely," the henchman went on. "And in view of this unfortunate incident, we've changed the instructions for the delivery of the merchandise. We're not going to tell you where it is that you're to go to pick it up until the very last moment. One of our men will go with you to the place, to make sure that everything goes smoothly."

Toffani rose to his feet and went outside with the man. With a wave of his hand, the latter ordered his men to set Bruno's servants free, and they came out from behind the bushes rubbing their wrists, badly swollen from having been bound for so long. Before climbing into the car that was waiting with the motor running, the henchman turned around and said to Bruno:

"Incidentally, I advise you not to continue to stash important documents in your hat. It's not a safety deposit box. And what's more they stick out from underneath the lining," he added with a wink.

Bruno was dumbfounded. How had he guessed? They caught on to everything, they could even hear the grass grow. If at any time Bruno had entertained the idea of going to his father-in-law to tell him the story of the contraband arms shipment and place himself in the hands of the authorities, the way in which these people had learned in practically no time that the bills of lading had been stolen from him was sufficient reason for him to decide not to do so. It was useless to try to play a double game, since whatever their source of information might be, Muriuki's men knew fully as much as the authorities did. He began to wonder whether Patel hadn't been right, after all, to think that the time had come to change mounts.

And as he watched the car disappear in a cloud of dust, Bruno thanked his lucky stars that he was still alive, in one piece, and able to contemplate the dawn of that new day. Then he went back inside his house to calm his daughters down and polish his Fascist relics once again.

The Dung Beetles

THE SAME RED SUN that Toffani was contemplating on one side of the Tana was lighting up the dust that Brown's Toyota was leaving behind it along the Tsavo trail that led to the landing strip. Bob had fallen asleep despite the jouncing and jolting that was making his bandaged head bounce against the window glass, and on the front seat beside him Bush the bull-terrier was also asleep, with his muzzle docilely resting on the calf of Bob's leg, though his permanently open blind eye gave him an air of continual vigilance and ferociousness. In fact, when Lawrence Brown had braked to a stop in front of the Park gate to show the car papers, Bush had given a fearsome growl as the African guard stuck his hand through the window to return the documents. But what the devil was Judge McGredy's dog doing in Lawrence Brown's Toyota as it headed for the Galana Ranch?

Lawrence Brown had come back empty-handed from his chase after the shadow that had attempted to knock Bob out with the narcotic vapor. When Brown saw the ecologist unconscious with a head wound on the veranda, and realized that the bleeding couldn't be stanched simply by pressing down on it with a handkerchief, he had put him in the Toyota and taken him to the hospital in Malindi, where he had been given emergency treatment. When Bob came to and saw, by the light of the little bedside lamp, the white coif of the same nurse who had shown him the way to Patterson's room when he had come to visit him, he thought he was dreaming: He certainly hadn't intended to come back to that dreadful hospital so soon! After letting him rest for a couple of hours on a cot there in the emergency room, the doctor on duty had discharged him and informed Brown that he could safely drive him back to the Galana Ranch if he took it slow and easy.

But just as they were going down the steps of the clinic, Judge McGredy appeared on the scene as if by magic, and asked to speak with the injured man for a few moments. Thinking that what the Judge was after was a statement from Fender for the judicial inquiry, Lawrence discreetly withdrew, though before leaving the two of them alone together he whispered in Bob's ear: "Remember what I told you? He's like a vulture—he can smell the carrion from miles away."

The interrogation took place in a stuffy hospital room that smelled of chloroform and used bandages. After ordering Bob to tell him everything he remembered about the incident, the Judge sat there staring at him intently, with a reproving expression in his penetrating eyes.

"Don't say I didn't warn you. I hope you've at least changed your mind about Africans."

"But if the only thing we saw was a shadow, how can we be sure that it was an African?"

"Bah, that narcotic smoke technique has been used for years and years by the natives on the coast. It knocks the victim out, so that they can then proceed to rob the victim at their leisure: It hardly matters if he's gone to the trouble of hiding his money under the mattress or tucking it away under his pillow, and even if they man-handle him or yank his rings off his fingers, he won't be aware of a thing."

"In any event, they would have found very little in my room: my camera and some research papers."

"I prefer to think that whoever did the deed was just a thief and not someone paid by someone to search through your papers or try to find out more about you."

"What could they discover of any interest?"

"Come off it, Professor Fender, don't play dumb," the Judge said, with that knowing look that so irritated Bob.

At that moment, they heard the horn of Brown's car begin to blare. He was becoming impatient, fearing that he might not arrive at the airstrip in time to meet Tony Allen and his clients. So Bob and Mc-Gredy broke off their talk. Just as Bob was about to climb into the Toyota, however, the Judge called him back.

"Look, this may strike you as an odd request, but I have to go to Nairobi for several days, and I don't want to leave my dog here alone. Would you mind keeping Bush for a couple of days for me? I could come by Galana myself to pick him up on my way home, and I don't really think he'd be much trouble to you out there in the wide open spaces at the ranch. He'll just follow you wherever you go. I've noticed that he's taken a liking to you, something that doesn't happen very often, and quite frankly, you'd be doing me a great favor."

Bob was so surprised by this request, made in an almost pleading tone of voice, that half out of boredom with the whole business and half out of weakness, he said yes. The dog, who had been sitting in the Judge's van watching them, leapt through the window at a gesture from his master, and sat down at Fender's side.

"Bush, you're to stay with this gentleman and not pester him." And to Bob: "You'll see how nicely he behaves: He's almost human. What's more, he's a first-rate watchdog; that I guarantee you!"

Bush settled down on the front seat of the Toyota, between Brown and Bob, as though that were his usual place. The hunter grumbled a little when he saw the dog leap into the car, but then he calmed down.

172

"If you're able to look after him, I don't mind taking him with us. All I ask is that you see to it that he doesn't go after any of my boys. Dogs like that are trained to hate Africans, and naturally, seeing that it's Judge McGredy who's his master, he hates them worst than most."

Shortly thereafter Bob was fast asleep, exhausted by the dramatic events of the previous sleepless night, and he didn't wake up until the car was well inside the Tsavo. He was awakened by the dust that was blowing in through the window and clogging his throat, making him cough; it took him a few moments to realize where he was, where they were going, and what the Judge's dog was doing sitting there beside him, watching every twist and turn of the trail with his one good eye, and resting his cold nose on Bob's forearm. Bob fingered his bandage to see if his head wound was still bleeding, and realized then that his head still ached, though he wasn't sure whether it was because of the concussion he'd received when he fell against the bed or the narcotic fumes he'd breathed. He then remembered the scene on the beach, half erotic and half farcical, that had ended when he had stepped on the electric ray; he could still feel the burning itch on the sole of his foot.

"The odd thing," he said, after clearing his throat to rid it of the dust he'd swallowed, "is that I knew that the night was going to end badly. I felt it in my bones when I left to take that stroll along the beach with Guni, and as I was walking in the shallow water along the shore, some strange creature stung me or gave me an electric shock in my foot. It could have been an electric ray."

As his only answer, Lawrence Brown gave two or three of his low muffled laughs that sounded like a big dog woofing, causing Bush to prick up his ears.

"What is it? Why are you laughing?" Bob asked.

"Nothing, nothing. I was just thinking that the night could have ended more badly still if I hadn't gone out to look for you and Townsend-Reeves's wife. I had the distinct impression that she was putting the make on you all during dinner!"

"What nonsense! It must have been your imagination!" Bob replied, blushing to his earlobes. He hoped that Brown wouldn't notice, what with the double camouflage of the Mercurochrome and the red dust.

"Imagination or not, take my word for it. That female is asking for trouble. I saw from the footprints on the beach that she had led you to her house, and that strikes me as an even riskier business than following a lioness into her den. If I were you, I'd keep my distance if you don't want to get yourself into hot water. As a friend of mine says: 'If it weren't for the fact that women have a cunt, they'd have long since been put on the vermin list.' And this female especially strikes me as one who's on the prowl: Don't have anything to do with her!"

Bob was at a loss for an answer. But Brown went on in the same vein. At that moment they were driving by a pile of dung that elephants had left as they crossed the road, and a cloud of insects and scarabs had descended upon it. The hunter braked to a stop for a few moments: "Listen, the relationship between a man and a woman is comparable to that of those pairs of scarabs, who live on elephant dung," he said, pointing to one of the beetles that was rolling, with visible effort, a ball of dung several times its own size.

And then, starting the Toyota up again: "If you're a scientist you doubtless know something about all this. Look at how the male rolls the ball of dung along, like an imbecile, for more than thirty or forty yards sometimes, all the while running the risk that a bird of prey will spot him, and at the same time fighting off all the other males that try to get the ball away from him. And what's the point of it all? It's because the stupid idiot has decided to seek out a lady friend, and he knows that his success at finding a female depends on his contriving to accumulate the very largest ball of shit so as to offer it to her as a wedding present. When he's managed to attract the female by doing this, she latches onto the ball, and the male rolls it along, with her on top of it, to a spot where he then laboriously digs a hole so that the female can devour the ball of shit in peace, three feet or more underground. The male, however, has been exposed to a whole series of risks and encountered all sorts of difficulties. Doesn't all that remind you of the behavior of a great many human males and females?"

"As an interpretation of the animal world through your macho ideas, it strikes me as an ingenious analogy," Bob replied. "But as a scientist, I'll answer that the behavior that you're describing is characteristic only of certain species of scarabs. It's the female of the *Kheper platynotus* that rides, during the mating ritual, on top of the nuptial ball that the male has prepared. But not all species of ball-making scarabs behave in precisely that fashion."

"You know that the details aren't important. What I'm trying to do is point out to you that those miserable insects are like men: They accumulate treasures for the females, who inevitably end up devouring us."

174

"I think in this case you're confusing dung beetles with praying mantises, the female of which does indeed eat the male after the wedding."

They had arrived in the meantime at a clearing in the bush which apparently served as the landing strip. It was simply a stretch of ground without trees, but overrun with thistles and rank weeds, and with enormous holes and towering anthills here and there. It seemed impossible to land a kite, much less a plane, on that overgrown patch of ground, but it was in fact the landing field. Soon after they arrived, they saw another car coming toward them. It was the safari car with Tony Allen's crew that had left the day before from Nairobi and was coming to meet the hunter and his clients at the rendezvous point. The African drivers and trackers in the two vehicles, who appeared to know each other from previous hunting expeditions, greeted each other effusively, giving each other great cuffs on the head and smacking each other's palms; then they went off and squatted down on their heels, in the shadow of a bush, telling each other stories punctuated by loud whoops of laughter, while Lawrence Brown and Bob remained in the Toyota, suffering from the intense heat, with their eyes fixed on the sky.

They did not have long to wait. A little black dot soon appeared on the horizon; it could have been a vulture soaring on the updrafts of hot air, but it very quickly took on the configuration of a small plane. Tony Allen's men immediately started the safari car up and raced across the landing strip at top speed, both to clear away as many thistles and bushes as possible and to catch the pilot's eye by raising a cloud of dust. The pilot soon spotted the signal, and changing course, described a broad circle above their heads, searching for the best landing approach.

"Who are the clients who are arriving with your friend?" Bob asked Lawrence. "Have you already met them?"

"No, of course not. But since this bunch is Italian, however, I intend to keep a close watch on them, because usually Italians pay very little attention to the hunting regulations."

Before the plane had even set down in that weed patch, from the moment he caught a glimpse of their indistinct faces as they waved from behind the windowpanes, Bob sensed that they were the same Italians he had seen at the airport in Nairobi a couple of days before, with that arsenal of weapons of various calibers, and accompanied by that corpulent "white hunter" with straw-colored hair. Despite the endless prairies and vast savannas, life in Africa was carried on in circles—as flocks of vultures come flying through the sky from every direction and end up wheeling round and round above the same prey.

What nobody was expecting, on the other hand, was the highly original welcome that Tony Allen's boys and trackers extended his clients. As soon as the plane had set down—raising a whirlwind of dust and dried-up thistles—and the engines stopped, the blacks formed a double line leading from the landing stairway. And when San Miniato's tanned face peeked out the door, they broke into a deep-throated, melodious, primitive chant. At least that was what Bob thought for the first few seconds, until he caught a few badly pronounced Italian words and realized that the gutteral voices were singing a song that had been popular the year before in Rome:

> Here comes Gianni, the Latin lover
> flying like a gracious dove
> his arms are delicate and tender
> but his heart is burning hot

After a few moments of stupefaction, the clients burst into cheers and applause.

"Where the devil did they learn that?" Bob asked Lawrence Brown.

"I have no idea. They must have heard it from other clients on some previous safari, or in a cabaret on the coast. These Africans would be capable of learning to play the violin if it would earn them a good tip from the clients."

"What do you think of the woman? She strikes me as quite a good-looking number," Bob said to the hunter, nudging him in the ribs with his elbow.

"Too good-looking," Brown answered, shaking his head. "Too good-looking."

The Cable

AMBASSADOR POIRE received news of what had happened to Bob Fender at a luncheon given by the Italian Ambassador. Despite his typically Italian name, Francesco Pastramino, the Ambassador, had so thoroughly absorbed the British manners and mores that had permeated the former protectorate that he dressed in typical English fashion, wore the mustache of a colonel of the Raj, took tea at three in the afternoon, and stuttered so badly that a person felt like giving him a good hard slap on his chubby pink cheeks to see if it would make him spit the words out whole.

After receiving a message from the servant, Ambassador Pastramino leaned over to Ambassador Poire, who was seated on his right, and said in his ear, in a tone of voice that was meant to be discreet, but that everyone at the table heard clearly: "There's a phone call for you from Mombasa. I think it's the Minister of State himself."

It was indeed Munyoka on the other end of the line. He immediately informed Ambassador Poire of what had happened the night before at the Seafarers Hotel: "It may be just a coincidence, an attempted robbery of no importance, but I thought that you ought to be informed, in view of Mr. Fender's special status."

"As far as I am aware, Mr. Fender has no special status," Poire answered. "But the fact that he's an American citizen is quite enough for me to be deeply concerned about his security."

When he returned to the Embassy, Poire immediately called Maguire into his office and reprimanded him as severely as though the Counselor himself had been the person responsible for what had occurred: "Didn't I tell you that I was concerned about Fender's being allowed to wander about loose in the midst of this whole mess? Didn't I advise you that it would be more prudent to call him back to Nairobi on one pretext or another?"

The Counselor blinked his eyes nervously behind the thick lenses of his glasses, without answering; he had never seen the Ambassador in such a rage.

"All right, let it pass. I know that nobody ever pays any attention to me. You career diplomats think that we political appointees are a bunch of ignoramuses. . . . I agree that in certain instances we may be all wrong, but this is one situation at least that I sized up correctly from the very beginning: The Galana Ranch was the last place to send Fender when an investigation into Murphy's death was under way in the same area, and as if that weren't enough, a possible contraband arms shipment as well."

"If you'll allow me to repeat what I said to you the last time we discussed this," Maguire finally answered, stammering slightly, "the fact is that we haven't sent Fender to the Galana, or anywhere else. . . . He's gone there on his own to carry out his study on grass. Please pardon my stressing this essential point, but if I don't do so we'll end up talking like the people who believe that Robert Fender is really a secret agent."

"Such subtleties are of little importance at this point, if there are people eager to lay a trap for him. Furthermore, in talking with the other Ambassadors who were at the luncheon today, I noted that the tense situation that has arisen between Muriuki and the Government is a matter of genuine concern. I therefore want you to do two things. First, send a cable to Rome to the effect that, in view of the present circumstances, they would be well advised not to send the agent; that would merely contribute to increasing the tension. If you don't mind, I'll dictate the text to you so as to save time:

TOP SECRET.
DURING RECEPTION ITALIAN EMBASSY HAVE HAD OCCASION TO DISCUSS POLITICAL SITUATION HERE WITH VARIOUS WESTERN AMBASSADORS— NETHERLANDS, SWEDEN, FRANCE, GREECE—AS WELL AS U.K. HIGH COMMISSIONER. ALL AGREE SITUATION DELICATE: DUE BOTH TO INCREASING INDIFFERENCE PRESIDENT, ISOLATED FOR SEVERAL MONTHS IN MOMBASA, AND TO INCREASING ACTIVISM J. MURIUKI, WHO, FROM ALL INDICATIONS, WILL ATTEMPT TO PROVOKE DISORDERS COINCIDING WITH UNICORN CONFERENCE.

"With regard to this latter point," Poire added, "please refer to my previous cable, and then we'll end as follows:

FOR ABOVE REASONS, I DO NOT, REPEAT NOT, JUDGE IT ADVISABLE TO PROCEED WITH PLANS TO SEND "AFRICAN BIRD" TO INVESTIGATE ACCIDENT

178

"I think that's clear enough as it stands. Please make a fair copy of
it and send it as soon as possible."

The Counselor, who had carefully noted everything down on a
sheet of paper, nodded, and the Ambassador then went on: "The
second thing that I would like you to do is to contact Professor
Fender, however you can, and tell him to return to Nairobi immediately."

"To return? On what pretext? And where can we contact him?"

"The reason—it's no longer just a pretext—that you're to give him
is that he's being offered a seat in our delegation at UNICORN. Since
Murphy's no longer on hand and since the fake ecologist is not going
to appear on the scene, we could use a real scientist. As for the way to
get in touch with him, I leave that up to you."

"I don't think there's a telephone or even a radio at the Galana
Ranch," Maguire said in desperation. "How am I going to get in
touch with Fender then?"

"You can cope with the details on your own, and if not, I presume
that you have a safari hat and a pair of shorts, don't you?"

"Yes, of course. . . . But you're not suggesting, I hope, that I go
looking for him myself," Maguire said, turning pale.

"I don't see why not. It would do you good to get out in the open
air for a while. How long has it been since you've spent any time on
the coast? When the conference begins next week, I want to see Professor Fender in the delegation. That's an order."

It took Maguire some time to get hold of himself, once he was back
in his office with the door closed; this time he had to take two long
swigs from the bottle of vodka that he kept in the drawer of his desk.
Then he sat down at the typewriter himself to copy out the cable,
using one of the embassy's cable forms, with copies for various files
attached. But when he'd finished, he tore out the blue copy, the one
used by the encoding officer to send the cable, and carefully burned it
in the glass ashtray.

Later on, sitting on the veranda of Walter Seago's house in Langata as the afternoon sun played over the hills, he told the naturalist
about his discussion with the Ambassador and was amazed when
Seago commented, in his soft voice:

"You see, when you don't pay too much attention to it, a problem

179

can settle itself almost by itself; everything is now under control, with no interference from our side."

"What? Everything is now more complicated; what are we going to do with Fender, once he's working for the Conference? This will only confirm the suspicions of the people who think he is, in fact, an agent."

"Well let's not make too much fuss about it; after all, there is nothing wrong in sending an ecologist to an environmental conference. That is exactly where he belongs."

"Not after having told everybody that the only purpose of his trip to Kenya was his study on the grasslands of the coast."

"Look, Maguire, don't worry so much about what other people think. A possible mistake over Fender's identity is none of our business. On the other hand, what is really important is that the Ambassador has eventually realized that sending an agent to investigate the accident, at this stage, would only increase the tensions. When we advised Washington to stop African Bird, without telling Poire, we were only anticipating his final decision. As a career diplomat, you should be proud of yourself!"

"I hope he will never know about the cables I've been sending without his consent, or those whose copies I've filed, which were never coded and forwarded to the State Department."

"Come on, Maguire, don't tell me an old hand like you cannot find some explanation about misplacing some documents!"

"In the meanwhile, I have to buy a safari suit, take a four-wheel-drive car, and look for Fender in the middle of the jungle. I don't think it's funny!"

"Hopefully," said Walter Seago, "with a mischievous smile, knowing very well Maguire's apprehensions, the grass rain won't come in advance this year; otherwise, at the coast, you might be surrounded by veritable swarms of mosquitoes and have a good chance of catching malaria!"

A Gentleman's Agreement

THE PARTY AT THE GALANA ranch spent their first evening dining on the veranda with the trophies, and then gathered around the campfire that had been built on the open stretch of ground overlooking the river. Although not many animals came down to drink, and the dark storm clouds driven by the wind frequently hid the moon, Bob noticed that the Italian clients were as thrilled as he had been the night he had first arrived. Finding a receptive audience, Lawrence Brown came out with the best stories in his repertoire, tales of hair-raising hunting adventures and chasing after legendary poachers; he even sent one of the boys to fetch a wrinkled leather pouch from which he extracted a handful of arrowheads that, as he explained, had belonged to a famous Waliangulu hunter who had decimated the elephant population of the entire district.

"Nowadays, however," Brown went on, "lots of the poachers have modern weapons, even automatic rifles, that they come by heaven only knows how. But up until just a few years ago they did all their hunting with primitive bows and poisoned arrows, that incidentally are quite effective. If an arrowhead hits a vital spot, it can kill a huge bull elephant in two hours."

"Can an arrowhead like that really kill an elephant?" Paolo asked, his eyes as big as saucers.

"Don't forget that they're smeared with an extremely powerful poison," Brown answered. He took one of the arrowheads in his hand, and with the aid of a knife slit open the corn husk wrapped around it to protect it, and then pointed to a blackish, gelatinous substance smeared on the metal. "This is the poison," he said, "which is extracted from the bark and the leaves of a species of *akkokantera* tree by boiling them for several hours in a pot into which they throw a number of live snakes and salamanders as well so as to enhance the magic powers of the ointment. To test whether the poison is strong enough, they traditionally wet a splinter in the liquid and stick it into whatever small animal they can capture at that point."

"And it dies?" It was Julia who asked the question this time, in a horrified tone of voice.

"Naturally—in a matter of seconds. When the poison is fresh, the effects are nearly instantaneous. The poachers seek out those particular *akkokantera* trees that for some reason have a greater concentration of the poison, keeping a sharp eye out for the telltale sign, a number of dead birds nearby, from eating the berries."

In that atmosphere of a witches' sabbath, created by the flickering light of the campfire and the shadows of the trees, which took on giant proportions in the moonlight, the clients were dumbfounded, and the arrowheads were passed from hand to hand with mingled repulsion and fascination. Soon, however, exhaustion overcame them, and they went off to their tents one by one, after bidding the others good night.

Back in his own tent, Bob stayed up for a time reading and going over the plans for his study. After a while, however, he heard the sound of footfalls and voices outside his tent; it was Lawrence Brown and Tony Allen, having a rather heated discussion. Their silhouettes stood out on the wall of the tent in the moonlight, and their voices came through the canvas so loudly and clearly that it was well-nigh impossible for Bob not to hear every word of what they were saying:

"I thought we had come to an understanding, before we made the arrangements for this safari, that you weren't going to shoot any rhinos," Brown was saying. "It was a gentleman's agreement!"

"That was my understanding too," Tony answered. "But you know how it is with safari clients. Almost the first thing that San Miniato asked after getting off the plane in Nairobi was how he could secure a permit to bag a rhino."

"And how exactly did he secure it, may I ask? You know very well that the authorities hand them out with an eyedropper."

"Don't ask me how, but he managed to get one. He phoned the Italian Ambassador, who put him in touch with I don't know who in the Ministry of Tourism, and that official in turn called somebody in the Game Department. . . . When I saw him standing there with the permit in his hand, I couldn't believe my eyes."

"Just think for a minute about what this means to me; this whole system I've managed to organize so as to fight the poachers and preserve the couple of dozen rhinos that are still alive on the Galana Ranch—only to be obliged now to put up with my own clients shooting them down!"

"Rhinos are on the list of animals that can be hunted at Galana, according to the brochure that the Nairobi office sends out."

"I'm not the one who puts that brochure together. The people in the Nairobi office are responsible, and all they care about is money."

"Well, anyway, don't worry. I'm not going to be the one who deliberately sets out to track down a rhino, but on the other hand, if we're unlucky enough to run into one, I'm not going to put my hand over the barrel of my client's rifle to keep him from shooting. And as you know, rhinos are pretty stupid animals!"

"And don't you worry either. I'm going to go out ahead of you every morning, to make sure you don't run into one by accident."

"Okay, I'll look the other way. As you can see, I'm quite willing to go along with the agreement between us."

Bob remembered then what Townsend-Reeves had told him about the manager of the Galana Ranch, that he scared game away from his own clients. So that old toper had been right after all!

"I can't understand why this San Miniato fellow is so hot to bag himself a rhino. I imagine it's because he's trying to impress his young lady friend. I don't blame him: she's a first-rate trophy!"

"I hope you'll keep your hands off her. I don't want two rutting male lions in my territory."

"Don't worry, I was only joking. You have to admit that I've changed a lot when it comes to skirt chasing; I respect the unwritten white hunter's rule now, I swear. 'You are not to try to sleep with the woman of the man whose whiskey you're drinking.' "

"Exactly. That too is a gentleman's agreement."

When Bob woke up, it was already daylight; for once, he had slept like a log, and felt rested. The strong, mingled odors of damp earth and vegetation filtering through the slits of the tent seemed familiar now. He was suddenly aware of something moist touching the sole of his foot. It was Bush's nose: He was lying fast asleep at the foot of the bed. Bob remembered his injury then; he fingered the bandage. It felt dry to the touch, and he realized that his head no longer ached; the queasy feeling and the dizziness that had lingered on all the previous day were also gone now.

He could hear people stirring in the nearby tents, and the boys going in and out, bringing tea and basins of hot water. Bush now awakened too, and began to growl on hearing the Africans padding about. To avoid any unfortunate incidents, Bob had left word the night before that they were not to bring him tea in his tent in the morning. He washed his face in the hot water that the boys had left outside and then walked over to the lodge where the Italian clients were already eating breakfast on the veranda, along with their professional hunter.

A mere glance at Paolo's face sufficed for him to see that the boy must not have slept a wink all that night, what with the noises of the wild animals and the shadows playing on the canvas of his tent—exactly what had happened to him on his first night at the Galana camp. Massimo San Miniato, on the other hand, had a glowing, relaxed look on his face. Bob had to admit that Julia was an extraordinarily attractive woman, even at that early hour in the morning, with her face freshly washed. He found it hard to keep from staring at the movements of her long, shapely limbs, the gleam deep within her dark eyes, the ample, firm curve—was she wearing a brassiere?—of her breasts. The hunter too was staring at this woman in utter fascination. Unlike San Miniato, who had appeared dressed to the teeth and equipped with various cartridge belts and leather pouches, Tony Allen was wearing only a T-shirt, shorts, and tennis shoes. No bullet pouches, no hunting knife, nothing of the sort, merely a small pair of binoculars suspended from his neck: He looked more like a bird-watcher all set for a walk through the woods of Long Island than a famous "white hunter."

"Hey, aren't you coming with us?" Tony asked Bob as they got up from the breakfast table.

"No, thanks anyway, but I've a great deal of work ahead of me that I've hardly even begun to tackle yet."

"I realize that you're a scientist, and quite possibly you aren't very much in favor of hunting, but all we're going to do today is take a turn around the ranch and do some target shooting to try out our firearms. At most, all we'll do is shoot an antelope for bait."

"Thanks very much for the invitation, and I may very well accept it some other day, but I must work this morning."

And in fact he settled down to work at one of the tables on the veranda and began to go over the documents he'd brought with him. After a while, he was distracted by the sound of shots echoing loudly along the river, though they were coming from far off downstream. Bush, who had settled down underneath the table in search of a cool spot in the shade, darted out barking and ran to the edge of the rise,

184

standing there for a moment with his ears pricked up in the direction from which the shots had come. "The war is on," Bob muttered, and concentrated once again on his documents.

The first casualty of this outing, however, was Paolo San Miniato, who came back to camp in midmorning with a black eye. He had a small cut over one eyebrow, where the telescopic sight of his rifle had hit him as the gun recoiled when he fired it.

"I got hurt in the dumbest way," Paolo said. "Papa insisted that I take a shot with one of the largest caliber rifles, I don't know why, and I must not have handled it right because when I fired it, it hit me in the eye—they have a terrible recoil!"

That same afternoon, the hunters were so insistent that he leave off working and come with them that there was nothing for Bob to do but agree to join them. The fact was that until Patterson returned to the ranch, he wasn't going to get very far with his program for gathering data on grass. So he slung his camera around his neck and climbed into the Toyota, taking a seat on the middle bench between Paolo and one of the gun-bearers; Tony Allen, Julia, and San Miniato were sitting in front, and in the back, poking their heads out of the sunroof to spot game, were two other trackers.

The sun was beginning to go down, but the heat was still stifling, and it was only when the trail ran along under a patch of trees that a breath of air came in through the windows of the safari van. Shortly after leaving camp, the trackers riding in the back banged on the roof of the Toyota, as a signal to Tony that they had spotted something, and in fact, at a certain distance off the trail, peacefully grazing in the shade of some acacias, was a herd of impala. At first, all Bob spotted was a group of females, but by looking closely in the direction in which the Africans were pointing, he was able to make out, half-hidden in the vegetation, a superb male, with the characteristic horns of its species curving in the form of a lyre, standing guard a little way away from his harem. "*Ndume, ndume,*" the Africans murmured above the heads of those sitting on the benches.

After observing the male through his binoculars, Tony Allen decided that the trophy was worth going after and that they would try to bag it. He backed the Toyota up till it was hidden in some bushes, and then they all climbed out and got ready to creep up on the antelope without being detected. After a few moments' hesitation, Massimo San Miniato decided to pass up the chance for a shot at the impala in favor of his son Paolo. Paolo tried his best to decline this offer, saying

185

he was sure he'd miss, but his father insisted: "If you miss, there'll be another chance later, but I want you to be the one to bag the first trophy."

Bob, who was following the safari group with his camera as they described a circle, concealing themselves in the bush so as to approach the herd upwind, noted that Paolo was a bundle of nerves, and was sure that the youngster would, indeed, miss the shot. In fact, when they got to within about a hundred yards of the animal, Tony Allen decided to halt, since there was an open stretch of ground ahead of them, without bushes, and the impala was beginning to move his head and sniff the wind, sensing the danger. Tony pointed to a horizontal branch of a dry tree trunk that Paolo could rest the rifle on to steady his aim.

The animal was a perfect target, facing them with his head raised haughtily, the oblique rays of the sun making him stand out clearly against the foliage in the background and highlighting his superb horns. But when Paolo squeezed the trigger after taking a few seconds' aim, the bullet passed several feet above the male's head, shattering the branch of a tree, in the shade of which the females were grazing. "Try again," Tony Allen whispered. The impala was still frozen in exactly the same position, disoriented by the echo of the rifle report and not knowing which way to run. Another shot rang out, this time raising a cloud of dust at the animal's feet. He detected which way the danger lay, and rearing up on his hind legs, whirled round with incredible agility and raced off. The females followed him instantly, bounding through the bush in prodigious leaps.

Then San Miniato, who was immediately behind his son, swore in rage, and grabbing the rifle out of Paolo's hands, aimed it at the impala, shot one last bullet at it, and also missed. Tony Allen spoke up then: "Don't shoot again because you might hit one of the females; besides, the whole herd's a fair way off now, and hidden by the vegetation." Bush had stood watching the shooting without a whimper, but when he saw the prey escaping, he started to chase after it, barking as though possessed, though he stopped short when Bob called him and turned back, joyfully wagging his tail. It was plain to see that he loved to hunt.

"Don't worry," Bob whispered to Paolo, as the young man sat down alongside him in the van, with his head hanging down. "You'll have another chance." It appeared, however, that the one who felt most humiliated by that minor fiasco was Massimo San Miniato.

A Flight of Sand Grouse

THE FOLLOWING DAY they got up very early to go off to shoot sand grouse coming down to drink at the river's edge. Bob had overheard Tony and Lawrence Brown, who had fallen into the habit of holding their strategy-planning sessions in the immediate vicinity of his tent, agree that it would be a good idea for the clients to work up to big game by shooting at birds first. "It's absurd," Brown had remarked, "for these people, who are used to shooting pheasant that beaters have flushed out of the underbrush for them, with gamekeepers in livery on hand to pick up the dead birds with a flourish of a hunting horn, to head off all of a sudden into the middle of the African bush, in the blinding sunlight and the suffocating heat, on the trail of a dangerous big game animal. We have to take them out to shoot small game first, till they become accustomed to the light and the insect bites and swallowing dust in the Toyota."

Before dawn, they were all in the van, still half-asleep, jouncing over the potholes and the rough stones of the trail running parallel to the river that cut through the forest. Bob had joined the hunting party again, taking his notebook with him on the day's excursion so as to record data on the flora and species of grass which might prove useful to him for his study. The intimate atmosphere inside the Toyota, as they sat squeezed together on the benches, was not at all unpleasant. A humid breeze, mingled with the odor of mud and vegetation, came drifting in through the window, and along with Julia's perfume, he also recognized the smell of saddle soap given off by the leather equipment, the oil used to lubricate the rifles, and the scent of goat's milk and damp wool coming from the back of the vehicle, where the African trackers were squatting, wrapped up in their red tunics.

It was still dark when they arrived at the drinking pools. Tony handed round the shotguns and the ammunition, and proceeded to

187

position the clients in a broad semicircle at the edge of a broad sandy stretch along the river's edge. At dawn the sand grouse would be flying down to drink in the pools that dotted it, though they were already half-dry after the last freshet. Along with Paolo, Bob was assigned a shooting spot covering one of the ends of this sandy stretch, and both of them sat down alongside a bush, waiting for day to break and the birds to appear. They had left Bush shut up inside the van so that he wouldn't raise an uproar with his barking on hearing them shoot.

The sky looked like a leaden bowl pulled tightly down over the blurred line of the horizon; but soon the garish light of dawn began to break, staining the mist with bloody reds and filling the sky with spurts of acid-yellow splendor. The canebrake, the shores of the river that lay only a hundred yards or so from the drinking pools, and on the banks of the stream, the patches of bushes and vegetation that followed the meanders of the current began to take on more definite outlines. At almost the same time, even before the sun had risen, they heard an odd whistling sound, and the first flocks of sand grouse, still flying very high—like little black dots against the sackcloth-gray sky, began to circle above their heads. The sound of their beating wings grew louder and louder, and the gutteral call of the birds resounded along the barren stretch of sand.

"Don't shoot till they fly down to drink," Tony Allen shouted from the spot where he had stationed himself. In fact, with the first glowing light of the rising sun, the flocks of sand grouse began to dive down to the drinking pools, landing some distance away from the hunters. But in a few moments they took wing again, flying only a few feet above the ground now, on a trajectory that would take them just above the spots where the hunters were waiting with their guns. "Now!" Tony exclaimed. "And aim well ahead, they're flying like demons!" Several shots rang out, but only two birds were hit, remaining suspended in the air for a few seconds like limp rags, and then falling to the ground in a flurry of feathers, plunging downward like a whirling pinwheel.

Paolo, his mind elsewhere at that moment, tried in vain to aim his shotgun as a flock of the birds passed directly over his head. "Shoot, Paolo, shoot—they're right above you!" San Miniato shouted to his son from his station. Bob couldn't help but remember John Murphy's "Shoot, you idiot!" on their hunting trips on Long Island.

Other flocks of birds flew down to drink, and still others took wing again, until the sky—now filled with light—swarmed with black dots wheeling at dizzying speed. A hail of shots came from the spots where the others were stationed, and the breeze carried downstream the smell of gunpowder and the feathers that hovered above the cane-brake before falling into the water. Tony Allen shot at the birds when they were still high in the air, and it seemed like a magic trick when one of the sand grouse, which appeared to be completely out of range, disintegrated in the air. It seemed easier to shoot them down as they took wing after drinking and headed within short range of their shotguns, almost grazing the bushes with their wings; but in fact they kept leaving their shots behind, misjudging the birds' speed.

Paolo took a number of shots at them, with little success, where-upon he handed his gun to Bob: "If you'd like to try, go ahead, I've had enough of this." Bob had a strange sensation as the gun slid underneath his forearm and he felt the warm barrels and the smooth wooden stock: The last time he had had a shotgun in his hands had been when he'd gone hunting with John Murphy in the woods on Shelter Island.

He didn't have much time to think about that, however, because at that very moment a flock of sand grouse that had just finished drinking on the river's edge took wing again and, describing a broad curve, headed in his direction. His heart beat faster on seeing the birds' silhouettes looming larger and larger, and the reddish sunrise glow illuminating the delicate filigree of their feathers. The flock shifted its line of flight slightly, passing with their wings unfurled between the branches of a nearby acacia, like quartz crystals filtering through a sieve. When the first one poked its beak out the other side of the tree, Bob raised the shotgun to his cheek, and aiming at least half a yard ahead gently squeezed the trigger. The bird disintegrated in the air, as though it had just crashed into an invisible glass wall.

The other birds began to fly even faster, but Bob had time enough to give the one that had fallen farthest behind the second barrel, and once again a bird exploded into a mere ball of feathers.

"Fantastic shot!" Tony Allen exclaimed from his stand. "Congratu-lations, Paolo!"

"It wasn't me, it was Bob," the youngster hastened to say, with great pride.

"Fine shooting, whoever it was."

Bob had been a little surprised himself by this spectacular double shot, and was looking at the smoke pouring out of the barrel of the gun, as though he found it hard to believe that he was the one who had fired it with such consummate skill. But the smell of gunpowder and the sound of gunfire had excited him. He asked Paolo for two more cartridges, and tried his luck once more. He continued to shoot again and again, till the hot barrels of the shotgun burned his hands, as flights of sand grouse continued to pass overhead. By the time the last one flew off, tracing concentric circles very high in the sky, Bob had bagged more than a dozen birds, with long, accurate shots.

All the others in the hunting party rushed over to congratulate him.

"Hey, you didn't tell us you were a black-belt champ with a shotgun," Tony Allen commented, with an edge of annoyance in his voice. "I haven't seen shooting like that for a long time!"

"Neither have I," Bob answered, a bit abashed. "I haven't had a shotgun in my hand since my university days, when I used to go hunting on Long Island."

As the trackers were gathering up the downed birds and Paolo and Julia were walking back to the van, Allen suggested that San Miniato and Bob took their shotguns and had a look around the riverbank with him. "There are usually yellownecks and guinea fowl in the bush down there, if they haven't been scared off by the shooting."

Cutting through the canebrake along a narrow path, well-trodden by many hoofs, they came out at a place where the riverbed narrowed; on the other shore the river had formed a beach of fine sand and the straw huts of an African village peeked about above the forest. At that very moment, a young woman dressed in a bright-colored *kanga* came walking down from the village to the river with a wicker basket on her head, accompanied by two naked boys who went chasing down the path. When she reached the water's edge, the woman set the basket down, took off her clothes, and plunged into the river, as the youngsters, one on either side of her, beat the surface of the water with willow rods.

"They think that that will chase away the crocodiles," Tony explained in a whisper so as not to frighten the woman, who had begun bathing herself directly in front of them.

The sun's rays filtered obliquely through the branches of the trees, backlighting the river and reflecting off the water, making the African woman's lustrous skin, her long thighs, her high buttocks, her incredibly firm, erect breasts gleam. The woman could scarcely have imagined that male eyes were intently contemplating her ablutions from the other side of the stream; the scene seemed to have leapt from the sensual palette of a Gauguin, and when Bob looked at San Miniato out of the corner of his eye, he noted that the Count was very excited.

"What would happen if I crossed the river and had a go at her?" the Italian whispered in the white hunter's ear.

"I don't know if she'd be eager to fuck with you or would take off at a run," Tony Allen answered, slightly taken aback. "These native women react in the same unpredictable way that gazelles do." And on seeing that San Miniato was beginning to unfasten his boots, he added: "If I were you, however, I'd think twice before going out into the river: Huge crocodiles have been sighted around here, and I assure you they don't pay any attention to stop signs!"

But San Miniato already had his boots off, and taking no heed of the hunter's warning, he removed his shirt and ventured out into the water, expanding his chest like a chimpanzee in heat. The woman soaking herself in the warm water was so relaxed she didn't see the Italian in rut until he was practically on top of her. On spying him, she let out a guttural shout, dashed out of the water, and ran across the sand. In no time she had snatched up her belongings and disappeared in the bush, like a wildcat, followed by her cubs.

San Miniato remained standing there in the middle of the stream in water that came up over his knees, still waving a ten-shilling bill he'd taken out of his pocket. Not knowing what else to do, he crossed over to the other side of the river, sniffing like a stray dog all around the spot where his prey had vanished.

Irritated by his fluvial erotic fiasco, San Miniato was quiet for a while. They went on along the path, which became narrower and narrower as the cane thicket grew denser and denser until finally it formed a barrier between them and the river.

Suddenly from beneath a bush there came a tremendous din of branches breaking, and a huge rhino came rushing out of the thicket, barely twenty paces away from them. "Don't move," the hunter murmured, standing there paralyzed like the others. But the rhino had been frightened by something and came dashing in their direction, shaking its enormous carcass and letting out terrifying snorts. San Miniato was about to shoulder his gun and aim, but he remembered just in time that it was loaded with pellets that wouldn't even have scratched the hide of the immense creature. Fortunately, as it came to within ten paces of where they were, the rhino dug its four hoofs into the dirt and with one last snort went back into the thicket, leaving

191

behind it a cloud of dust and the deafening sound of bushes being trampled on.

The charge and the retreat of the rhino probably hadn't lasted more than thirty seconds, but it had seemed like an eternity to Bob. When the cloud of dust had settled, he noted that his heart was pounding madly, and his feet felt as though they were nailed to the ground: If he had had to run, he might well have been unable to move them. The rhino had been so close that he had left the thicket impregnated with an overpowering odor of urine and dung, like the smell of a circus from the ringside seats.

Once the danger was past, San Miniato's first reaction was to go chasing after the rhino.

"We'll have to follow close behind it if we don't want to lose it. It's a magnificent specimen!"

"Take it easy," the white hunter said, holding him back by one arm with a firm grip. "If we follow it now, all we'll do is frighten it more. The first thing to do is send one of the boys back to the car for the rifles. I trust you're not planning to get the rhino with birdshot!"

"And what will happen if it takes it into its head to cross the river? We'll lose the trail!"

"If the rhino crosses, we'll cross too. Where we are now, the Ranch's hunting concession extends to the other side of the river."

An Extraordinary Coincidence

AFTER FLOWING THROUGH the cane thicket, the Galana opens up and gives birth to two little twin streams, separated by islets of bush. Following the track of the rhino, the group came out on a stretch of open range, dotted with acacias. On reaching the top of a gentle rise that then sloped down toward the river bank, they could see that the hoofprints disappeared in the water.

"The rhino did cross the river," the hunter conceded, wiping the sweat from his face with the back of his arm. "But this is a bad place to cross for us, because the bottom is nothing but mud here. We'd better go get the car."

Two hours later, they were still on the trail of the rhino. To find a spot where the safari van could ford the river, they had had to make a long detour, and it took them quite a while to pick up the trail again, since on the other side of the river the look of the landscape and the ground surface changed completely. On the bank of the river on the Ranch side, the grass gave off a little moisture, and the rhino's hoofs left sharp prints in the damp clay soil; on the other side, however, the ground was very dry and hard, with red sand that crunched under the soles of their boots like broken glass, and the tracks were harder to follow. Along the border of the Tsavo Park, the *nyka* forest stretched bare branches threateningly toward the sky, which was already enveloped in a shroud of dust and fog; through a slit in the haze, the bloody ball of the sun appeared like an open heart.

All at once, the hunter stopped short, spat on the ground, and cursed in white-hot fury. He had just discovered the trace of a bare foot following the trail of the rhino—a poacher. The trackers milled about the footprint, plainly excited, muttering phrases in Swahili. Tony Allen made no further comment, but Bob noticed that he had exchanged the light rifle he had in his hand for the heavy double-barreled one that the bearer was carrying.

What Tony Allen could scarcely have suspected was that Salim the Somali had been spying on his every move ever since the hunting party had arrived early that morning at the sand grouse drinking pools. The poacher had been following the big rhino along the Galana and had crossed the river after it the night before as it went to wallow in the mudholes on the Galana Ranch side. He had been close enough to be able to shoot a poisoned arrow between its ribs, but just at that moment the moon had come out over the open range with not so much as a bush that might serve him as cover, and Salim had decided to wait till dawn when he would be able to lie in wait for it in the bush.

On hearing the roar of Tony Allen's Toyota, Salim hid in the canebrake and remained there, keeping a close eye on the hunting party and taking in everything, including their halt on the riverbank to watch the African woman bathing. Salim thought that all their shooting at the sand grouse would have frightened the rhino off and it would be a long way away by then, but as he was slipping stealthily through the cane thicket the animal suddenly took off, practically out from under the poacher's feet, heading straight for the other hunters. Salim took advantage of all the confusion and the wait for the trackers to return from the safari van with the rifles to get a head start on the party and cross the river again, following the trail of the big bull rhino.

Sensing that it was being pursued, the animal had gone deep into the *nyka* forest, with Tony Allen and his clients following after it. From outside, the forest did not seem very dense, but on trying to make their way through the bushes, the thorny branches clung to their clothing like monkey paws: A thin cloud of dust hung in the air, making breathing difficult and the rhino's trail hard to see. The heat was becoming more and more stifling in that clay bowl, and the bushes swayed back and forth before their eyes as though moved by mysterious forces.

The only one whose spirits did not flag was Allen, who had become completely absorbed in tracking the rhino. Even his expression was no longer the same: He was on the alert now for the slightest change in the traces left by the animal, eyeing every broken branch, sniffing the shifting wind, touching the rhino's dung to determine whether the trail was still fresh. In the beginning, he had hung back a little, no doubt remembering his conversation with Lawrence Brown the night before, but he soon forgot the gentleman's agreement not to shoot at a rhino; and once he was hot on the animal's spoor, he would have followed it to the very gates of Hell.

At just about noon, they emerged from the *nyka* forest, coming out at a dry riverbed, along the edge of which there was a bit of greenery.

"We'll stop here for a while to rest," Tony said, leaning his rifle against the trunk of a thornbush. "If you like, you can have some tea and something to eat if you're hungry. But I warn you not to take in too much liquid: The more you drink, the more you sweat."

"As far as I'm concerned, the rest of you can go on without me," Julia said, collapsing on the ground. "I'm not budging."

The woman was worn out, and had gone on only so as not to betray what they might call a feminine lack of stamina. Paolo too was extremely pale, and even San Miniato had stopped puffing out his chest and was sweating from every pore; even so, he found strength enough to protest: "If we don't want the rhino to get too far ahead of us we shouldn't stop for very long."

"At this hour of the day, the animal will have undoubtedly sought

194

out a good bush to take shelter under for an afternoon nap," Tony said. "If we leave him in peace, we'll be able to move in on him more easily."

"Providing the poacher doesn't find him before we do," the Italian answered, snorting like a seal.

The sudden appearance of Bruno Toffani in that desolate, parched setting had something magical and totally unexpected about it—as though a genie had abruptly popped up out of a bottle in a puff of smoke in the middle of the desert. On the far side of the plain, a cloud of dust raised by a vehicle materialized; for a few moments it blended with the dust devils being borne skyward on the reddish horizon by the updrafts of hot air. After crossing the open expanse of sun-scorched grass the van turned into the dry riverbed and headed its way at a good clip, stopping a few yards away from the acacia in whose shade Tony Allen and his clients had taken shelter from the noonday sun.

When the wake of dust raised by the Land Rover had settled, they saw a short, thickset man, with an outsized ranger hat perched on his head and shod in half-boots, climb out of it. The man was also wearing a sleeveless hunting vest with nothing underneath, so that luxuriant tufts of very dark curly hair were peeking out through the neck opening and the armholes, and a cartridge belt loaded with large-caliber bullets that shifted up and down as he walked, revealing the flabby folds of his belly and a hairy navel as deep as the cavern of the Cyclops.

Toffani stopped short two steps away from them, arms akimbo. Tapping the ground with the heels of his seven-league boots, he barked: "Halt in the name of the law! This is a game sanctuary! I'm an honorary warden, and I must see your hunting permits and your identity papers."

For a few moments, nobody moved. On seeing that fearsome apparition striding toward them, Bush had taken refuge under Bob's knees and lay there growling in terror. Behind Toffani, two young African rangers leaped out of the back of the van, their emaciated arms and legs making them look like scarecrows dressed in starched uniforms many sizes too big for them, and holding their rifles as though they were brooms. They seemed less like representatives of law and order than like pirates straight out of the pages of Robert Louis Stevenson, all set to dig up some treasure buried in those red sand dunes.

The professional hunter was the first to react.

"My name is Tony Allen and these are my clients," he said as he went on imperturbably taking tea mugs and hard-boiled eggs out of the food hamper. "We've come here on a hunting trip from the Galana concession which, as you no doubt know, extends on this side of the river as far as the border of the Park. . . ."

"Tony Allen," Toffani repeated, interrupting him. "That's good enough for me! Your reputation as a hunter is well known, and if these people are your clients, I'm quite certain you possess the necessary permits," he added, as though bowing to the obvious. The sly fox had dropped his overbearing manner in favor of a conciliatory, almost humble tone of voice.

"I and my boys," he said, pointing to the young rangers who were moving their heads from one side to the other on their long necks like ostrich pullets, "have been following the trail of a dangerous poacher who's been operating along the banks of the Galana lately, and according to our calculations, he may be somewhere right around here today."

As he spoke, he knelt down, sketching a rudimentary map on the ground with a little tree branch, indicating the various directions involved with the long, filthy fingernail of his little finger.

"As a matter of fact, when we crossed the Galana we did see the footprints of a poacher, following the trail of the same rhino we're following," the hunter replied. "But I couldn't say whether he's the poacher you're looking for. Unfortunately, there is no lack of undesirable elements in these parts," he added, looking straight at Toffani.

The latter pretended not to have heard him, and went on scratching in the dust, as though trying to get his bearings.

"Seeing the direction the poacher was heading in, it wouldn't surprise me if it was the same one. If you run across him, I advise you to watch your step. We think it might be Salim the Somali himself!"

"But you people came from the south, from the very area the poacher's heading toward," the hunter observed, pointing to the map on the sand. "So you're more likely to have seen him than we are. When you crossed that stretch of barren range, you were bound to have run across his trail."

Toffani scratched his head for a few seconds before answering.

"As a matter of fact, we've come a long roundabout way, trying to intercept him, but for the time being the wretch has managed to slip out of our grasp. However, now that you mention it, we did see a

196

huge bull rhino some miles upstream. We scared him off and he headed toward the Tsavo. I don't imagine the poacher will dare follow him inside the Park!"

"Well, if the rhino's gone inside the Park, we've lost him!" the hunter exclaimed. "I'm glad you told me, though. It'll spare us the trouble of following his trail for the rest of the day for nothing."

At that moment San Miniato, who had followed the conversation between Toffani and Tony Allen without saying a word, exclaimed, "Don't tell me that these imbeciles have scared off the very rhino we were tracking! Couldn't it be another one?"

"I regret to say that there aren't that many rhinos left on this side of the Galana. I think we'll have to wait for the next chance that comes along."

At that, San Miniato let out a string of insults and curses in Sicilian dialect, never dreaming that Toffani might be able to understand them. But the freebooter, far from being enraged, listened to that flood of abuse with a blissful expression, as though he were standing in a refreshing downpour beginning to fall on the parched range.

"For the merciful love of God, either this pitiless sun beating down has just softened my brains, or else I'm hearing the blessed tongue of the very place where I was born!" he exclaimed, and then, addressing San Miniato: "Aren't you Italians—or to be more precise—Sicilians?"

Once the Count had recited all his names and surnames in reply, Bruno knelt before him, covering his hands with kisses and tears, as though he had just run into the King of Italy himself in the middle of the jungle. The aristocratic Sicilian, who wasn't at all certain of the reason that lay behind this explosion of affection, struggled in vain to free himself from that repellent embrace.

Toffani explained, once he had recovered his composure, these people, through a coincidence little short of miraculous, were not only compatriots of his, but in fact the little village of Cortinaldo, where his family hailed from, was located within the large landed estate held by the Marquis de Castromonte, who was undoubtedly related to the San Miniatos. And he, Toffani himself, as a child had accompanied his grandfather at Easter to take a basketful of eggs and capons to the manor house of the Marquis, who had been so kind and asked Toffani his name and presented him with a package of caramels.

In view of the disreputable Italian's gift for tall stories and his talent for coming up with different origins and family antecedents suited to his purposes, there might be those inclined to doubt the veracity of this tale. But it must be granted that on this particular occasion, Toffani played his part so convincingly that anyone would have swallowed his story. In any event, the sleeve and the bottom edge of the Count's safari jacket were completely covered with slaver and tears, as damp testimony to the miraculous nature of this encounter in the middle of that wasteland.

For his part, once the Count had recovered from the shock of this naturally disconcerting moment and furtively wiped his hands on his silk handkerchief, he was visibly pleased to have come across a serf of his in the heart of Africa.

"The Marquis de Castromonte," he explained, his chest expanding once again despite the murderous midday heat, "was my grandfather's brother, that is to say my great-uncle. And as a matter of fact it was in the hunting preserve at Cortinaldo that I bagged my very first game, with a 12-millimeter shotgun that my grandfather had given me as a present."

Toffani was clever enough to take immediate advantage of the general atmosphere of warm cordiality to invite them, one and all, to have a glass of Chianti and a bite to eat at his house, remarking that it would be a shame to be content with a few sips of tepid tea and a dreary hard-boiled egg when, just a few miles from there, his wife was waiting for him with a delicious stew that it would be an honor to share with such illustrious guests. Anything, he said, rather than to have his grandfather's curse fall upon his head; that forebear would turn over in his grave if he knew that a descendant of the Marquis had passed by that remote corner of the world without Bruno's having offered him so much as a cool glass of wine.

The Italians soon let themselves be talked into accepting the invitation, dragging the hunter along with them; in any event he had realized that the day's hunting was ruined. They followed after Toffani as he took off at top speed in his ramshackle van. Bruno was delighted to have been able to get that pack of idiots off the trail of the valuable rhino, and to have prevented a confrontation between the poacher Salim and Tony Allen, which might well have had serious consequences. Once more, a clever stratagem of his had worked.

Ali Baba's Cave

THROUGH A LABYRINTH of narrow trails and dusty cattle paths, they arrived at the Tana, crossing to the other side of the river over the tree-trunk bridge. On the far side of the sloping stretch of ground in front of it, Toffani's shack shimmered through a halo of humidity, and the tin roof gleamed in the sun, as though the dwelling were made of frosted gingerbread. Heedless of the heat, two little mulatto girls were playing in the shade of the big acacia whose horizontal branches stretched all along the veranda of the dwelling.

Inside, something about the dark, mysterious atmosphere reminded Bob of the shadowy lair of Patel. The roll-up blinds were closed, but every so often a few puffs of breeze came drifting in through the slats, along with smells that hinted of the sea; and in fact, they were not all that far from the coast. From the very first moment, Toffani outdid himself to make his compatriots feel at home, and went to dig out his very best bottle of Chianti from the depths of his cellar. A tall African woman with regular features, her head swathed in a blue turban and dressed in a long tunic of the same color, padded silently about, bringing glasses and plates and setting the table.

"That's Rose, my wife," Toffani confided with a sheepish smile as she went off again toward the kitchen. With a shrug of his shoulders, he added, "She's not bad, is she? She's the best I was able to find in these godforsaken parts."

By some miracle, the wine was cold, and slid down their parched throats easily; moreover, it soon loosened their tongues, especially Toffani's. Without having to be asked twice, he began to tell the story of his life and incredible fortunes, making no effort to hide his brushes with the law or his Fascist past.

"I lived the most glorious hours of my life during the Ethiopian campaign, when I was wounded in combat in the service of Il Duce," he proclaimed, and proudly lowered his dirt-encrusted pants to show them the scar of a bullet wound in his buttock; he could scarcely have received it while advancing toward the enemy, unless he had been doing so backwards. "But the English made me pay dearly for my political convictions, keeping me shut up in the prison camp longer than the others and forcing me to put up with all sorts of insults and abuse."

Weaving together the real and the imaginary, he went on to tell them of the many vicissitudes of his life in Africa—from the time he got a traveling circus together that ended up being wiped out by a terrible storm that blew the tent down and let his trained animals loose to wander all over the countryside and be devoured by wild beasts, down to his last attempt to set himself up in an honest business, a fish hatchery that also ended in disaster, this time on account of a severe drought that left his fish asphyxiated in the mud. "Don't get the idea that before coming out here to stagnate in these wastelands, yours truly didn't fight to carve out a decent niche in life for himself," the man said with a sigh. "But in Africa, the elements are uncontrollable, and sometimes because of too much water and at other times because of too little a person ends up stuck in these dry gulches."

The Italians were fascinated by Toffani's story. He had suddenly appeared before them like a ghost from the past, a living fossil from a world that none of them had known, except for San Miniato, who may have had a secret nostalgia for the glories of Fascism. Allen, on the other hand, could scarcely bear Toffani's bragging about his life as a petty gangster and was repelled by his stories of his heroic Fascist exploits—not out of any political convictions but out of solidarity with his friends, the British colonials of the old days who had fought in the African campaign during the Second World War.

As Toffani went on talking Tony Allen became more and more certain that the man was undoubtedly not an honorary game warden at all, and very probably a smuggler; the gleam of the tips of ivory tusks, peeking out from underneath a burlap cloth in the farthest corner of that den of thieves, had not escaped his alert eye. Toffani soon noticed the Britisher's cold reserve, and emboldened by floods of Chianti, he made a special effort from that moment on to dwell on details of his life's story that would annoy him most.

"The day we arrived in Nairobi after getting out of prison in Mombasa, a friend of mine and I managed to hide a couple of shotguns and some ammunition in our baggage. We rented a car and took off over back trails after nightfall, and knocked off a few zebras and giraffes by blinding them with the headlights."

"What sportsmanship!" the hunter muttered, trying to be sarcastic. But subtle slurs such as that scarcely made a dent in the Sicilian's thick skin.

"We didn't do so badly, considering the circumstances. The only trouble was that we soon began to hear sirens wailing and flares started to burst over our heads, and in less time than it takes to tell, we had all the police in Nairobi on our tails. Do you know where we'd been hunting?"—laughing till tears came to his eyes, Bruno had to interrupt his story—"Right in the National Park of Nairobi, a hundred yards from the guards' booth!"

"Where else?" Tony murmured, his face beet-red with indignation.

"Imagine, after spending three years locked up, the very day they let me out of jail, I land straight back in the slammer," the bandit went on, still laughing fit to kill.

"Force of habit . . ." the Englishman said dryly. He would gladly have left that very minute, except that just then Rose came into the dining room with a bowl of steaming hot stew.

Before they got to dessert, they had emptied the second bottle of Chianti. Toffani got up from the table, and with a melodramatic gesture, suddenly parted the red curtains that separated them from the alcove, revealing his precious Fascist trophies. It was a very effective theatrical gesture, one he'd perhaps learned in the days when he was a circus ringmaster—like the moment when the magician unexpectedly pulls out of his handkerchief a golden cage full of fluttering doves.

The guests couldn't believe their eyes, and got up from the table without a word and walked over to the fabulous gallery of relics that Toffani proudly proceeded to show them: the perfectly lubricated Mauser hanging on its support of nails, a swastika delicately carved on the butt with the point of a knife; two hand grenades, so shiny and new looking that it seemed as though they might explode at any moment, carefully placed on a lace runner on top of the mahogany chest of drawers; the German soldier's helmet, with its little bullet hole at the level of the forehead. The sepia photographs of the Ethiopian campaign hanging on the wall looked quite alive in the reddish light of late afternoon; and the portrait of Il Duce, somewhat faded and haloed with a damp stain around the head, acquired the beatific expression of a martyr.

While Tony Allen and Bob remained seated the Italians had entered that sanctuary on tiptoe, and gazed intently at each one of the pieces, not daring to touch anything and scarcely daring to breathe. Julia very nearly crossed herself as she entered, and the Count, unable to restrain himself, found great tears beginning to run down his cheeks in a sudden access of emotion, mingled perhaps with the effects of the Chianti. Seeing a propitious atmosphere, Toffani performed his last magic trick, giving a tug on a silk cloth covering the statue of Hitler, revealing him standing like a classic demigod on his marble pedestal, with the nape of his neck shaved completely bare and his bristling little toothbrush mustache. Bruno stood at attention before the image of the Führer and, with his arm outstretched, began to sing the Italian Fascist hymn, in a soft, deep voice, as his compatriots, almost unconsciously, began to repeat the stanzas that came bursting forth from some secret corner of their memory:

> *Salve oh popolo d'eroi*
> *salve oh patria immortale*
> *son rimasti i figli tuoi*
> *con la fede e l'ideale*
>
> *Giovinezza, Giovinezza*
> *primavera di bellezza*
> *nella vita, nell' ebbrezza*
> *il tuo canto squillerà.*

The voices soon increased in volume, and Rose and the girls came running from the kitchen, their little round eyes rolling with curiosity as the Italians went on singing at the top of their lungs, in tones grown slightly hoarse from the wine and the dust of the trails, until the walls of the shack vibrated, and the rifle and the helmet of the German soldier began to jingle on their supports, keeping time once more to the Fascist anthem.

As their patriotic ardor cooled down a little and they began to drink their coffee, the hunter insisted that they should leave, since they all had a long ride back to the Galana Ranch ahead of them. He eventually managed, with the greatest of difficulty, to drag them away from there.

Before taking off, he had to let Bush, who had been shut up in the safari van for fear he might bite the little girls, out for a few moments. The dog sniffed about and urinated on all the bushes in the scraggly garden, and finally began to dig about at the foot of the big acacia, in a spot where the ground had been turned over.

Toffani, who had come outside the house to say good-bye to them, said sorrowfully, "That mutt is really smart. That's the very spot where I buried Pogo, my faithful Neopolitan mastiff, who died in a regrettable accident."

A Rogue Buffalo

ON THE ROAD BACK to the Galana Ranch, the river threaded its way for a time between steep cliffs, and the trail ran along some distance away from the stream, winding up and down hills with various crops growing on little banked terraces of red earth; on the hilltops overlooking the valley were villages of straw huts. As they drove through one of these settlements, leaving a cloud of dust and terrified chickens in their wake, a boy came out and began chasing after the car, desperately waving his arms to signal them to stop.

"What can he want, I wonder?" Tony said, stopping the car at the foot of the slope so that the boy could catch up with them. He came running down as fast as his legs could carry him, and although still out of breath as he reached them, he began to recount something in Swahili, with his face still covered by a mask of dust. Tony translated for his clients: "He says there's an old buffalo that's been wandering about here terrorizing the villagers, eating up their crops and attacking the women going down to do their washing in the river. This very afternoon, he says, when his father went to fetch water down by the riverside, the buffalo charged out from under a bush, sent his father scrambling up a tree and the dog that was trying to defend him flying through the air."

"And what does he want us to do?" San Miniato asked.

"He wants us to go after it and kill it; according to what the boy says, the beast is in a thicket down near the river."

"Why not do what he wants us to? I still haven't gotten myself a buffalo, and it could be a good trophy."

"We won't know whether it has good horns or not till we drive it out of the thicket, and it may well have taken refuge in the densest part of it. These rogue buffaloes that maraud round about villages are usually cunning and vicious, and I doubt that being all stirred up by a dog will have improved its temper. I warn you that it won't be easy to down. You'll have to take blind shots at it as it runs off into the bush—providing, that is, that it doesn't decide to charge us."

But San Miniato was all excited and just a bit fuzzyheaded—still feeling the effects of the Chianti—and insisted that they ought to try at all costs to hunt the buffalo down, if only to free the villagers from the marauding beast. The mounting rivalry and tension between Tony and San Miniato had reached the point where if one of them expressed an opinion the other immediately took precisely the opposite point of view. As for Tony, though he had not been exactly a devout admirer of the Count's earlier on, San Miniato's chumminess with that scoundrel of a Toffani and the Fascist emotional orgy had put an end to whatever respect he might have felt for his client.

"First of all, let's check and see whether that story about the buffalo is true," Tony said, reluctantly parking the safari van along the side of the road. "Sometimes these Africans have very lively imaginations, or maybe they just want us to kill an animal so they'll be left with the meat. Or it may have been yesterday that they saw the buffalo, and the creature is miles away by now!"

The light was beginning to fade, but the heat was still stifling; dark storm clouds, ripped apart by the razor strokes of the setting sun, hovered above the steep cliffs along the river. Tony had sent the trackers to talk with some women working on terraces halfway up the slope; the shadows the trackers were casting across the hillside and the road were growing longer and longer. Seeing them approach, the women began to wave their arms and waggle their heads like rag dolls. Everything was distorted by the hazy light, and everything seemed as though it were filmed in slow motion, as though time had coagulated in the suffocating heat.

The trackers finally came back to the van, confirming the boy's story. The leading actor in the drama, a toothless, half-witted old man, came back with them, explaining to the hunters in pantomime —with the water can still in his hand—how the animal had rushed out at him from under a bush near the stream and tossed the dog in the air, how he himself had barely escaped with his life. From a curve in the road, he pointed to the thicket where the animal was hidden.

"If we want to go after the buffalo, I think it really is in there," the hunter finally conceded. "But I'll warn you again that it's not going to be easy to down the beast. If the buffalo charges us, try a brain shot, just below the forehead; don't bother to get a shoulder shot, because even with a bullet in the chest, it can still trample us to bits."

"Come on, don't tell me an experienced professional hunter like you can be afraid of a poor old buffalo," San Miniato said jokingly, winking at Julia.

Tony sat there staring at him, his eyes blazing. "If we wound that buffalo and it takes off into the bush, you're coming with me. And I assure you it'll be an experience you won't forget," he shot back, and they could tell he wasn't joking.

Then he got out of the van, gave the necessary orders to the trackers and a few villagers who had offered to help drive the beast out of the thicket, and handed out rifles and ammunition to the hunters. He himself took his double-barreled rifle down from its metal support and loaded it with large-caliber bullets. The rifle slammed shut with a sharp clack, and it seemed as though the powerful barrels had suddenly absorbed all the sounds of birds and insects in the bush and the incessant chatter of the beaters. They followed the professional hunter in silence as he went down to the thicket by the riverside, and the only sound to be heard was their muffled footsteps on the sand of the path and the pounding of their own blood in their temples.

Tony arranged the hunters in a semicircle around one side of the dense thicket where the buffalo was presumed to be, and sent the beaters round to the far side so that by throwing sticks and stones into the brush they would drive the creature in the direction where the others were stationed. Tony posted himself and San Miniato in the spot closest to the forest where the beast would be most likely to take refuge; Bob and Paolo, the latter armed with a rifle, he put on the far edge of the thicket, closest to the village and the crops; and in the middle he positioned his bearer.

The scene, Bob thought, could be divided into two perfectly distince parts, like two juxtaposed photographs, one in color and the other in black and white: On one side, the picturesque, bright-hued panorama of the village, with the women working in the red earth of the terraces and the youngsters running along the path carrying baskets full of ears of corn on their heads; on the other side of the hill, already in deep shadow, the hunters, pale and tense, posted around the thicket, aiming their rifles toward the dense vegetation in complete silence, as the trackers advance from the opposite side of the thicket, gripped by the fear that the buffalo may charge in their direction at any moment. The echo of the beaters' voices, and the sound of the oil drums that they pounded with sticks seemed to be coming from somewhere else, from the bottom of the valley, as if it were the distorted sound track of a movie being shown outdoors.

Finally, thought Bob, reality breaks through the black and white screen and becomes one with the world of light and colors, and sounds and movements are synchronized. The buffalo took off in the direction opposite from where the hunters had been waiting for him, charging out among the beaters, who scattered in panic, flinging their sticks and their drums in the air. As though it sensed the trap being laid for it, the cunning creature crossed, like a puff of breath, the clearing separating the thicket from the dense woods covering the bottom of the hill and stretching down to the river's edge.

San Miniato shouldered his rifle and aimed in vain, for the buffalo dashed out so fast that the only thing the Count caught a glimpse of was a flash of copper-colored hide amid the bushes; he didn't even manage to focus in the telescopic sight, since in just a few fractions of a second the creature had disappeared once again.

"Damn!" he exclaimed in fury. "I wasn't even able to see it through the lens!"

"I told you not to use the telescopic sight when you're shooting in the bush," Tony reminded him. "The animal moves too fast and you have to shoot blind. A lens like that is just the thing, when you'll be shooting semidomesticated deer in an Austrian game preserve."

The Count felt as though he'd been taken down a notch and was at a loss for words. The hunter seized on the chance to rub it in.

"What, you don't care to follow the buffalo through that impenetrable tangle? Night will soon have fallen, but we still have ten minutes of light left."

To his surprise, the Count replied immediately: "Obviously, we must follow it while we can. . . . If you're not afraid, I'm not either."

The tension between the two men was greater than ever; their nerves were on edge in the face of the dangerous situation, and were it not for their egos as hunters, they would leave the buffalo in peace and fight it out then and there with their bare fists. The situation became even more dangerous, with the light fading fast, and in the dense vegetation where the animal was lurking, it was impossible for them to see farther than a foot or so in front of them. But once the challenge was laid down, neither was willing to back down.

Before entering the dense woods, Tony sent Julia and Paolo back to the car along with the trackers, leaving just himself and San Miniato and Bob, whom he asked along, with Bush, since the dog could be of help in following the buffalo's trail through that tangle. The three men and the dog entered the dark forest in which, in the last rays of the setting sun, each patch of foliage looked like the shape of a wild beast about to attack. In a whisper, the hunter gave his client some final instructions.

"Keep your rifle at the ready and follow directly behind me. And remember: Aim straight between the eyes! Try not to step on a single branch that might crackle; the buffalo knows now that we're coming after him, and he's the one that might be setting up an ambush for us. And another thing, try not to blow my head off, and for the love of God, take that telescopic sight off your rifle. If the buffalo charges, I guarantee you that you'll see him much closer up than you'd care to!"

This time, San Miniato obeyed without a word, removing the sight and stowing it in a pocket of his safari jacket. The tracks of the animal were clearly visible in the sandy soil, but the trail was nonetheless hard to follow, since the brush grew denser and denser with each step they took; in certain places the hunters were obliged to crawl on their bellies beneath the bushes. After the din of breaking branches created by the buffalo as it fled, a pregnant silence had fallen over the gloomy forest; from a little stream nearby a smell of moss and decayed tree trunks drifted their way.

Following in the rear, concentrating all his attention on holding Bush back as he tugged on his leash like a creature possessed, Bob was completely unaware of how dangerous the situation was, but Tony and San Miniato were quite plainly all on edge. Tony kept constantly wiping the sweat off his forehead, and with a mechanical gesture broke his rifle open at every third step to check that the bullets were in their proper place in the chamber and the hammers cocked. With his silk handkerchief San Miniato too wiped the sweat away and nervously fingered both the bullets in his cartridge belt and the telescopic sight sticking out of his jacket pocket, hampering his movements. The Italian kept turning his head and looking behind him as though fearing that the buffalo would attack him from behind, and when his eyes met Bob's placid gaze, a forced smile appeared on his face, which turned into a panicked grimace at the slightest crackle of branches or the sudden flight of a bird.

All of a sudden, Bush gave such a hard tug on the leash that Bob lost his grip on it. The dog took off into the bush in a flash, heading off at a right angle to the trail that they were following. Immediately thereafter, they heard a phenomenal bellow, and a great din of breaking branches and bushes being trampled underfoot as the buffalo came charging out of its hiding place. The hunters took aim in vain; the cloud of dust was too thick and blent with the oblique light of the setting sun and the movement of the branches: The entire forest seemed to come crashing down, but fortunately the buffalo, on being pursued by the dog, had not charged in their direction, but instead headed for the little stream flowing down to the river. And for a few minutes that seemed like centuries, the echo of its hoofs galloping over the stony stream bed, accompanied by the dog's barking, filled the air, amplified by the hollow basin formed by the river.

"The buffalo had turned around and retraced its steps, so that it was behind us," Tony said, looking at the bush beneath which it had lain lurking. "And undoubtedly it was about to attack when Bush caught its scent. It seems to me that that dog saved our lives, because if the buffalo had attacked us from behind from higher up on that hill, we would have been hard put to stop its charge," he said, shaking his head in a gesture fraught with meaning. "It strikes me that we've played hide-and-seek with that beast long enough for one day."

A while later, Bush reappeared, wagging his tail. He was covered with dirt from head to tail, and hairs of the buffalo's hide were still clinging to his muzzle, but he appeared not to have a single scratch on him. They slowly made their way back out of the dense woods. Tony looked a bit crestfallen since he hadn't been able to down the buffalo and since he realized that, when all was said and done, it was the dog that had gotten them out of a rough situation. San Miniato, on the other hand, was all puffed up with pride, since he'd followed the trail of the dangerous creature through that impossible tangle of vegetation, thereby giving proof of the same courage and coolness in the face of danger as the professional hunter; of the two of them, it was he who had won the moral victory.

"It would have been sheer madness to follow the buffalo any longer, since we had only five more minutes of light," Tony commented, as though to justify himself, as they emerged from the jungle.

"What's more, one dog alone isn't enough to corner that creature in dense vegetation such as that; if there had been two or three dogs, it would have been a different story."

To his misfortune, at precisely that moment the old man was coming down again to the riverside with his can to get water, followed by his limping dog.

"There's another dog for you. Shall we go back after the buffalo?" San Miniato remarked sarcastically.

"As a matter of fact, even two dogs wouldn't have been enough," the hunter said rather hastily. "We'd have needed three or four."

He had barely gotten the words out of his mouth when two other dogs appeared, trotting joyfully down the path. This time, Tony Allen did not venture a single word. After stowing the rifles away in the van and leaning on the horn to scatter the curious bystanders from the village who had congregated around it, he took off at top speed.

The one who had profited most from this entire adventure was Paolo. While his father was risking his life in the dense forest, he had gone for a stroll round the village, and on spying a little patch of marijuana growing half-hidden behind a wall of cane stalks, had made a deal with the owner of it and scored, for practically nothing, a fat packet of dried grass which he proudly showed Bob, putting a finger to his lips to signal to him not to say a word about it.

A Peaceable Man

THAT NIGHT, the thunderheads that had built up during the stifling hot day let loose a cloudburst on the basin of the Galana. In camp, Bob listened, half-asleep, to the raindrops drumming on the taut canvas of his tent, and smelled the now familiar odor of damp earth and plants, though this time it was cleaner, more aromatic. At dawn, he emerged from his tent to have tea with Lawrence Brown, who was getting ready to make his usual daily rounds of the ranch; Bob asked to go with him, and as they drove along they talked over the previous day's incidents, since the night before the hunting party had come back so tired after the long day that they had not met as usual to talk around the campfire.

The first rays of the sun found them already a long way away from the ranch, heading in the direction of the Park along the trail that ran parallel to the river. The Galana was swift and turbulent after the torrential rains of the night before. The water had a whitish cast to it, like coffee diluted with lots of milk, instead of its usual color and consistency of thick dark chocolate, the lighter shade harmonizing with the soft haze, the ocher tones of the Tsavo on the other shore, and the recently rain-washed pistachio-colored vegetation along the riverside, in that early morning equatorial pastry shop, with an odor mindful of fresh flour and yeast.

A brisk warm breeze was blowing off the plains of the Park, bringing other quite different odors, half-burned dung and remains of charcoal fires. And as the car went through the eucalyptus groves, the breeze tore away from the trunks long strips of bark that had been loosened by the dampness, which came away with a sound of wafers crackling and hit the hood of the Toyota or were run over by the wheels with a muffled sound.

"I didn't want to say anything yesterday in front of his clients, but Tony behaved very strangely. Who would ever dream of dealing with an individual like Toffani, the most notorious crook on the whole coast? Didn't they tumble to the fact that the only thing he had in mind was to get them off the trail of that poacher that he's surely working hand in glove with?"

"As a matter of fact, it was the Italians who accepted the invitation, and Tony couldn't refuse to come along."

"What nerve to pass yourself off as an honorary game warden, with two fake rangers! You may be sure that if I'd been there he wouldn't have tried that stunt. Toffani knows very well that if he dares set foot on the Galana Ranch, I'll clear him off the place immediately with a shotgun and a good load of rock salt."

"We didn't know he was a smuggler. You must admit that apart from his filthy clothes and his lies and tall tales, he's rather fascinating. And he looks familiar to me somehow. I'm one of those people who are quite likely to forget a name, but never a face."

"I may have mentioned his name to you myself when we were discussing the hunting situation and the poachers; thanks to people like Toffani, they're decimating all the animals, even in the national parks. The first thing I asked Tony to do was not to go after a rhino; there are so few of them left that I want to keep all of them alive, but you can see how little attention he pays to what I tell him!"

"All I can say for certain is that it was the rhino who came after us, and not vice versa. We weren't tracking it. When we were through shooting sand grouse, we were having a look around down at the river's edge, carrying our guns with us, and the beast suddenly came charging out at us from underneath a bush. I think that in the beginning Tony wasn't very enthusiastic about following its trail, but then later he warmed up to the idea."

"He warmed up, did he? That's where the whole problem lies—he's hot. I think it's that woman who has him all worked up."

"What woman? Julia?"

"Of course: Who else? I don't like putting such attractive females up at the ranch; all women like that do is create problems. Have you noticed the look in Tony's eye every time she walks through the camp with just a bath towel wrapped around her after she's showered?"

"Well, I don't think any of us mind seeing such a gorgeous woman a bit lightly dressed," Bob remarked with a smile. "I for my part think she adds a feminine touch and a bit of class to the camp. I'm not surprised that San Miniato's so proud to have a woman like that with him."

"Tony and his client are like two rutting male lions prowling around that female, and I fear the whole thing's going to end badly. Do you think it's normal for a hunter as experienced as Tony to go into dense forest as night is falling, chasing after a mad rogue buffalo? That's downright crazy!"

"To tell you the truth, I didn't realize at the time how dangerous it might be."

"All right, when you're hunting an animal, you have to give it a fighting chance. But under such conditions, the hunter is at a serious disadvantage."

"This may seem absurd to you, but the place where they organized the ambush struck me as so beautiful and so picturesque that it didn't even occur to me that we might be gambling our lives."

"Rogue buffaloes that maraud round about the villages are usually old bulls that have been driven out of the herd by younger and stronger males, and ordinarily they're resentful and bad tempered. The very fact that they've become accustomed to the presence of

211

human beings makes them more cunning and aggressive. I assure you that Tony Allen knew all this very well, but wanted to look like a real he-man in the eyes of that woman!"

"All of us were no doubt somewhat to blame. It seemed only natural to us that a group of well-armed hunters should try to free those villagers from that marauder. And I remember that till the very last moment, Tony was the one who was most reluctant to get out of the car."

"He shouldn't have allowed himself to be persuaded. On safari, the professional hunter is like the captain of the ship, and it's his duty not to endanger his clients' lives. Tony especially should have known better, after the run-in he had with—as it so happens, a buffalo." The hunter paused for a moment before going on. "I know he doesn't like the story to get around, but now that I've mentioned it, I'll tell you that Tony had an accident, not so very long ago, as he was following a wounded buffalo in the bush. He was with an Argentine client, a diplomat whom you may have met; he's well known in social circles in Nairobi."

"I spent only a few hours in Nairobi, and I didn't meet him."

"Never mind. To go on with the story, the Argentine wounded a buffalo, and on following it into a thicket, it charged them at such close range that Tony couldn't even get a shot at it and the buffalo sent him flying through the air. Tony was badly bruised, and I think the client was also knocked about rather badly. That's why I said that Tony ought to be the last person in the world to go rashly chasing after buffaloes."

Brown paused, because the trail sometimes passed through deep puddles or runoffs from the heavy rain, and he had to shift into four-wheel drive to get the Toyota out of the mud. When they got past these low spots, he went on.

"Look, Fender, hunting in Africa is like any other sport that involves a certain risk. Everything is fine as long as a person keeps a cool head and doesn't take unnecessary risks. But it can become something really dangerous if the professional throws caution to the wind and allows himself to be carried away by passion or pride."

The hunter braked once again, this time to examine some tracks, sharply imprinted in the mud, crossing the road.

"A pair of lions passed by here early this morning, heading for the water holes. They'll have a hard time catching even an antelope, because after a storm like the one yesterday, all the prey scatters. They drink at puddles here and there and don't turn up at the usual water holes. For human predators on the other hand, rain is a blessing; as you can see, the tracks remain clearly visible in the mud, and following a trail is a piece of cake.

He stood there a moment studying the lion tracks, before going on, with a hearty laugh: "A propos of what we were just talking about, I'm reminded of an experience I had some years ago while hunting in the Mara area—close to the Tanzania border. My client, who was an Austrian prince or something like that, wanted to bag a fine lion. And in fact there was a splendid male in those parts, with a nearly black mane and a magnificent head, but the animal was now very old and too cunning for the hunters. We'd despaired of laying traps for him, because the beast was very clever and didn't ever touch the bait, knowing that going after it would get him into trouble. The safari was almost over, and I had my doubts that we'd ever be able to get our hands on that magnificent trophy, when all of a sudden the right opportunity presented itself: the animal began rutting. We soon started seeing his tracks in the company of two young lionesses, and I immediately thought: The male's in rut, and maybe we can get him!

"And in fact one day we baited a trap again, with a zebra, and the lion went for it, accompanied by his two girl-friends, wonderful young lionesses with lustrous pelts and sharp white teeth. The poor old chap needed to provide food for his harem! I was watching him through my field glasses from the blind, and I noted that at the last moment, the lion hesitated before entering the clearing where we'd placed the bait; he must have caught our scent, or perhaps it was just the instinct of an old animal that senses danger. But the lionesses were already going for the meat and were calling him with voluptuous growls. He finally decided to come out of the bush, but he kept looking around out of the corner of his eye, and I think that I knew precisely what was going through that feline's mind at that moment: 'I'd never dream of being here if it weren't for these whores!' Just a few seconds later my client downed him with a shot through the heart."

In the meantime, they had almost reached the paved bridge that crossed the Galana, on the border of the Park; after a curve in the road, the terrain descended abruptly to the river. Lawrence stopped the car to look at the lovely panorama of the wooded river-edge, which had miraculously turned green again after a single night's rain; the storm had caused a freshet, with many pools of water and little water courses that ordinarily were dry trails and gullies down which the animals came to the river to drink.

On the other side of the Galana, however, the wastelands of the

Tsavo had soaked up the water, and the vast plains lay before them, bright red, like the huge oil canvas of a saint, drawn and quartered, with vultures hovering overhead like archangels, scanning the blue horizon. A halo of steamy mist was beginning to rise from the flooded woodland along the riverbank, a shroud about to envelop the holy corpse.

"That road runs from the entrance at Voi to the Sala gate," said Brown, pointing to the road of beaten earth crossing the Tsavo plains, "where we went into the Park the other day. And if you take a good look, that side road was the one used by the poachers we tried to stop; that denser patch of jungle, to the right, is where that swamp where we saw the elephant carcass is; with all this floodwater, it looks like part of the river. It's hard to see because of the reflection of the light on the water," he said, squinting. "Will you let me have the binoculars for a minute?"

Bob handed them to him, and after a few seconds he saw the expression on the hunter's face suddenly change.

"By the horns of the devil, don't tell me they've come back, the bastards!" he exclaimed, shoving the binoculars into Bob's hand and starting the car. "That white van is here again, in almost the very same place. What nerve!"

Bob, too, was able to make out the outlines of a vehicle on one of the trails, and although it was difficult to tell for certain because of the light reflecting off the water, as they came closer he could see that it bore a certain resemblance to the poachers' off-white van. And come to think of it, it also looked a good deal like Toffani's van; as a matter of fact, all safari vans looked more or less alike.

Lawrence Brown went racing down the slippery slope, convinced that it was the same van that had given them the slip before, the day Bob arrived at the Galana Ranch. Nonetheless, Brown had to brake when he arrived at the bridge, since floodwaters almost two feet deep covered the asphalt surface, and make his way very cautiously across. On arriving on the other side, he noted that there were recent tire marks—clear imprints in the mud—leading up to the same bridge from the other side; but then the vehicle had turned round and taken off down one of the side roads of the Park.

"I think we have them trapped this time!" Brown said jubilantly. "That's a blind road, and there's no way to get off it—especially with all this flooding."

The road entering the forest had, in fact, turned into a quagmire where even Lawrence Brown's Toyota, despite all his driving skill,

214

pitched and rolled like a ship about to capsize. But he continued to grip the wheel like a man possessed, even though at times the van lurched dangerously close to the embankment leading down to the river; in that spot, the waters looked deep and turbulent.

They finally reached the crest of a little hill, and the white van was down below. The road crossed a gulley a foot and a half under water, and the vehicle had bogged down there, stuck up to its fenders in the mud.

"We've trapped them, we've trapped them!" Brown kept shouting. "I'm going to get out and go after them. Don't move from that seat, and if there's shooting, duck down."

In one second he had taken down the rifle from its support alongside the steering wheel, and stepped out onto the ground, or rather, into the mud. The van looked empty but he approached it gradually, taking cover behind bushes, with his rifle aimed in that direction. They heard a sort of splashing noise, however, coming from the rear of the vehicle.

"Halt, whoever you are!" Brown shouted. "Come out with your hands up or I'll shoot. I'll only wait till the count of three!"

A man, his face and clothes completely covered with mud, emerged from behind the vehicle with an armload of mud-caked branches, that he was trying to put underneath the rear wheels. The hunter again ordered him, in Swahili, to put his hands up, and on obtaining no response, said in English:

"Up with your hands, and no tricks! If you don't step away from that van before I count three, I'll shoot."

"Don't shoot! Don't shoot! I'm a peaceable man!"

"Just a minute," Bob said, climbing out of the Toyota. "I think I know this man."

Although the man was smeared with mud up to his eyes, that silhouette looked familiar to Bob. On seeing him approach, the man waved one of his raised hands.

"Ah, it's you, Fender. I'm happy to see you."

Bob still didn't know who the individual was, and didn't recognize him till he took a handkerchief out of his pocket to wipe the mud off his metal-framed glasses.

"Maguire, for heaven's sake! Whatever are you doing here?"

"As a matter of fact, I came looking for you, but I couldn't find my way to the Galana Ranch on account of these flooded roads. I have a message for you from Ambassador Poire."

PART FIVE

The Story of the Chicken

Two DAYS LATER, Bob woke up in his room in the Hotel Hilton, in Nairobi, missing the smell of damp earth and rotting vegetation. At that very same hour, back at Galana, the hunters would be getting ready to leave the camp, and the boys would be going from tent to tent—Bob thought he could still hear their feet quietly padding about on the sandy path—bringing hot tea; in vain he tried to hear the echo, far in the distance, of the herds of antelope running from the water holes. He even missed Bush's damp muzzle affectionately resting on the sole of his foot.

But he was many miles away from the Galana, shut up in a hermetically sealed, air-conditioned room on the twentieth floor of a hotel. The first soft light of day was not filtering through the canvas, but through curtains with a garish pattern of big orange diamonds. He got out of bed and drew back the drapes; the city was still veiled in fog and from behind the Ngong Hills, looming threateningly in the distance, the first rays of the sun were breaking through, striking the monolithic, oppressive tower of the UNICORN. From there the view of the streets of Nairobi and the plains in the background had the flatness and impersonality of a giant postcard.

Bob drew the curtains closed again and got back into bed, covering his head with the pillow; he felt trapped. He regretted having come to the city, having accepted Maguire's offer. However, in view of the way in which it had been put to him, it would have been difficult to refuse.

Ambassador Poire's proposal had come his way with the same shocking suddenness as the heavy rainstorm which had flooded the lowlands of the Galana the evening before, depositing Ralph Maguire. Once they had hauled the Counselor's car out of the gully and brought him to the camp, where he was able to wash the mud off himself and have breakfast, Maguire explained to Bob the mission that had brought him over such rough trails, hardly the usual routes that diplomats were accustomed to follow in order to get down to the coast. The Ambassador was offering Bob a seat on the delegation as an expert on the environment, since it had been impossible to send, from Washington, Rome, or any other place, anyone who could substitute for Murphy as the Embassy Counselor in charge of such matters.

"People here imagine that Nairobi is in the center of the world because it has three decent hotels and four golf courses; but in fact it's hard to persuade anyone who lives in a civilized place to come—it's a long way from anywhere," Maguire explained.

The offer was tempting: While Bob had taken part in other ecological conferences from behind the scene—preparing the reports and documents that were needed for the Secretariat—he had never participated in an important meeting seated behind the placard bearing the name of his country. What Bob did not know was that the decision had in fact already been made for him: The Ambassador had had a telephone conversation with one of the big wheels of the Food and Agriculture Organization in Rome, arranging for the agency to "lend" him Fender for the duration of the Conference. But Maguire, as an experienced diplomat, didn't mention this detail; he merely stressed how valuable it would be for the delegation to be able to count on the collaboration of a person with Bob's knowledge.

Bob went off for a walk along the river's edge, sitting for a time in the shade of a baobab; the sky was hidden by the usual layer of fog, but the air was cooler after the storm, and Bob allowed his thoughts to drift peacefully along, keeping pace with the grayish waters of the Galana as they bore along the trunks of trees and bushes uprooted from the riverbank by the floodwaters. After a while, he realized that there was no need to think things over any further, and climbing up the path to the veranda where Ralph was still sitting in his bare feet as his boots dried in the sun, Bob accepted the offer. They decided to leave very early the following day, allowing the trails a little more time to dry out so that they wouldn't repeat the Counselor's epic adventure and end up stuck in the mud in the middle of the Tsavo.

That night, however, as he was packing his few belongings and sorting out the documents that he would leave at the camp in a trunk until his return, he had a sudden hunch that he shouldn't interrupt his stay at the Galana Ranch; this wild region had gotten into his blood, and the experience of the safari—even Lawrence Brown's constant grumbling and the undeclared war between Tony Allen and San Miniato—had fascinated him. Sometimes one could come to feel more attached to a place or to certain persons in a few days than in an entire lifetime.

The tent flap at the entrance opened and San Miniato's son stepped inside. Bush began to growl from under the bed, but quieted immediately on seeing that it was Paolo. The boy was holding the bag of grass he had bought.

"Is it all right with you if I come in here to have myself a joint?" he asked conspiratorially. "I'm afraid my father will come into my tent and notice the smell of dope."

"You can do as you please, as far as I'm concerned," Bob answered. "But leave the flap open a little, otherwise we'll suffocate."

Paolo nodded and, sitting cross-legged on the floor, began to roll a joint, whistling softly; the light from the lamp fell directly on his face, and Bob realized that it was not the first joint he'd smoked that day; he had the pallor and the dreamy expression of someone who is already a little high.

"Good stuff, really good stuff," the boy said thickly. "In Rome I would have had to pay more for this one joint than I paid here for the whole bag. Wouldn't you like to sample a little?"

"No thanks. I don't go in for that sort of thing very much, especially when I have work to do," Bob said, going on with the task of sorting the documents and stowing them away in the metal trunk.

They heard the call of a night bird, and from the water holes came the echo of loud snorts and the sound of animals galloping off, muffled by the damp sand of the riverbank. Then everything was still again. After a long pause, Paolo broke the silence once more:

"I don't like your going away, you know. I think we've come to be good friends, and I'm going to miss you. To tell you the truth, I don't have very much in common with the hunters, Tony Allen and Lawrence Brown, and as for my father and Julia, they're busy doing their own thing. . . ."

"I'm sorry to be leaving the Galana too," Bob said, sitting down on the edge of his cot. "But I don't mind telling you that I'm really wasting my time here. I came to Africa to complete my research, not to chase buffaloes in the forest. Anyway, don't worry; we'll see each other again before you all take off from here. I don't intend to stay in Nairobi for more than a few days."

Paolo sat looking at him with a beatific expression on his face. The pupils of his eyes were very dilated.

"Above all, watch your step. *I* don't think you're a spy, but if you are one, be on your guard."

"What's that you're saying—me a spy? Wherever did you get that idea?"

"This afternoon I overheard Lawrence Brown and Tony Allen talking in their tent, saying something about you and the arrival of that American diplomat. They were saying that odd things kept happening whenever you were around. What seemed oddest to them was the fact that an Embassy big shot like Maguire should come all the way out to the Galana looking for you. . . ."

"There's nothing odd about that," Bob interrupted him. "They need an expert for the Conference, and they haven't been able to come up with anybody but me."

"Tony was also surprised that you were such a good shot after saying that you had no experience with guns. He suspects that you have a double identity."

"I was amazed myself at what a good shot I turned out to be with the sand grouse. But something strange happened to me: I used to go out hunting a long time ago with my friend John Murphy, the man who was killed in an accident on Mackinnon Road near the Tsavo. . . ."

"Yes, I've heard about Murphy. They say that he was an agent too."

"People's imaginations are working overtime. Anyway, when I had the shotgun in my hands the other day, I suddenly remembered everything that Murphy had taught me, things I could never manage to do when I was out hunting with him, perhaps because he intimidated me. But yesterday with the sand grouse it was as though *he* had the shotgun in his hands."

"I see what you mean," Paolo said staring vacantly at the darkness outside.

"Well anyway, I think you ought to go to bed now and let me finish packing my things, because we're leaving very early tomorrow morning. And don't give another thought to all that nonsense. People really enjoy running off at the mouth."

"Okay, I'm willing to believe whatever you say. And above all, please don't tell my father that I've been in here smoking dope. He'd kill me!"

Although he did not want to take Paolo's fantasies too seriously, Bob remembered how he had had to explain over and over again that despite being an ecologist he had not come to attend the UNICORN Conference, nor was he going to take John Murphy's place on the American mission. And now he'd be taking part in the conference after all, and moreover—even though Maguire had not said it in so many words—he'd also be acting as John's replacement.

Bob had a horror of ambiguous situations; they were liable to cause more talk, require more explanations. He was going to get out of bed and talk with the Counselor again. He knew Maguire was awake; Bob could see his shadow on the canvas of his tent. The diplomat was fighting a fierce battle against imaginary hordes of mosquitoes with the aid of a huge aerosol can of insecticide he was wielding as though it were a machine gun. But at that very moment Maguire turned his lamp off, and Bob did not want to bother that squeamish character, probably causing Maguire to suffer an attack of insomnia.

Besides, why attribute so much importance to what other people might think? To whom did he owe an explanation of this change of plans? To Patel, the dealer in contraband trophies? To poor Alex Townsend-Reeves, consumed by his abuse of alcohol and the sexual appetites of his beautiful wife? To the sinister Judge McGredy, who suspected everything and everybody? To hell with them all.

It occurred to him, just before he fell asleep, that it was strange for Maguire, who was supposedly familiar with ecological problems, to use insecticide with such a heavy hand: Had he forgotten that the excessive use of pesticides and aerosol sprays was one of the causes of

223

the gradual destruction of the ozone layer in the upper atmosphere?

Judge McGredy was one of the first persons Bob visited after his return to Nairobi. He wanted to give his dog back to him. Though Bob had eventually become used to the presence of that ugly, cranky hound, there was no denying that he was a real nuisance in the city; Bob couldn't leave him in the hotel, for fear the dog might bite an African boy who happened to wander into his room, and he certainly couldn't take the creature out with him. In the five minutes that Bob had spent at a garden party in Ambassador Poire's residence, the dog barked at the black guests and even growled at the Ambassador when he approached Bob with arms extended.

Judge McGredy lived in a modest little house, on the heights of Nairobi, with a view of the sun-scorched plains of Jamhuri Park, the Parliament building, and toward the north the dark hills that formed the spurs of Mount Kenya, whose snow-covered summit could apparently be seen on unusually clear days. The veranda was behind the house, overlooking a slope covered with eucalyptus and sycamores; at the foot of the slope lay the greens of the municipal golf links, whose fairways, waiting for the rainy season, were only showered with ashes and red-hot cinders all along the railway line that ran straight through the middle of the course. The local train, which went only as far as the Kajiado district and the Konza station, passed through the grove of trees every now and then, bringing with it dense clouds of smoke which, when filtered through the eucalyptus branches, gave off a medicinal, aromatic odor. The afternoon light that lingered amid the branches gave the mountain range in the background a strange animation, like a giant caterpillar crawling along the edge of twilight.

McGredy received him with a mug of Pimm's Cup in his hand, smoking a cheap cigar that kept going out. The Judge was energetically fiddling with a primitive tow-wick lighter, trying to keep the coarse tobacco lit.

"Welcome back to Nairobi!" the Judge greeted him. His nose was slightly red. "I knew that your study on grass wouldn't keep you on the coast very long. I hope my dog hasn't given you too much trouble. But before you tell me how things went, do sit down and pour yourself a good big mug of Pimm's: it makes up for all the errors of British colonization; the cucumber and the mint are from our very own garden."

224

There were two other people on the veranda whom McGredy introduced as his wife and son—an elderly woman, who reminded Bob of a suffragette, and a skinny adolescent with acne scars on his face, dressed in an impeccable professional hunter's outfit. The old suffragette devoted her entire attention to serving the drinks and emptying the ashtrays, as though she were a servant. The boy's uniform was so stiffly starched, his leather chest belts so highly polished that, with the bracelet of elephant hairs around his frail wrist and a lion's fang dangling on his hairless chest, he looked like a child at a costume party. The Judge growled twice; his family left. He wanted to chat with Bob alone. Bob gave him a brief account of his days at Galana—with special emphasis on the adventure with the buffalo when the dog saved them from what might well have been a serious mishap—until Maguire arrived to take him to the Conference. The Judge kept looking at Bob with those eyes of his, as piercing as drills, but with a smile hovering at the corners of his mouth.

"So you finally decided to take part in the Conference, did you? That's fine, that's fine. And you say that this mutt very nearly saved your life," he remarked, patting Bush's back and adding (in the tone of voice in which one might say, 'I can't keep my dog from chasing the neighbor's cat.'): "He loves to chase after buffaloes and other wild animals—he's a born hunter! But I see that you, too, don't spend all your time measuring the length of the blades of grass on the range; your predecessor, Murphy, also greatly enjoyed following a dangerous wild animal through the thickets. . . ."

Bob, who was prepared for a remark of this kind, shot back: "Hold it a minute. Let's clear the air. The other day when we met on the beach, I didn't know who *you* were and I don't believe you knew who *I* was either, and I'm afraid you're barking up the wrong tree. Look, it's true that I knew Murphy some time ago, and that he was the one responsible for my visit to Kenya, before his tragic accident. But I assure you that any sort of relation or connection between John and me ends right there. I don't know if Murphy merely served as an adviser on ecological matters or—as certain people suggest—whether he also had other duties at the Embassy. And I really don't care. I assure you that I have absolutely nothing to do with such things; I came here to do my research. Period. And if for some peculiar reason it's crossed your mind that you ought to tail me or keep me under surveillance, I can tell you that you're wasting your time. I'm neither a spy nor a secret agent."

The Judge continued to stare at him, his eyes as beady as grape-shot, and he was no longer smiling; before he answered he took a long swig of his drink.

"Let's presume that I believe you. There are countless circumstances that tell me I ought *not* to believe you, but I could forget them. What's certain is that in this situation what matters most isn't what you or I believe, but what the others think of you; and I can tell you that there are people who think that you're something more than you appear to be."

"But that's absurd. Why should it matter to me what other people think?"

"Look, Fender, let's not be naive. What other people think has a very great influence on our lives, to the extent that we end up being what others think of us."

"I don't accept that, at all. What happens to individual freedom in that case?"

"Don't forget that we live within society, and that what others think or do has a decisive influence on our lives. When all is said and done, it's the chicken that's right."

"What chicken? What are you talking about?"

"Don't you know the story of the chicken?" Bob shook his head and the Judge went on: "There's this man, see, who's a patient in a psychiatric clinic, suffering from a persecution mania. He thinks he's a grain of corn, so he's afraid that any duck or hen that comes along may gobble him up. After months of intensive treatment, it appears that the man has recovered, and the head of the clinic calls him in to his office to release him. The patient thanks him for the excellent care he has received, and especially for having cured him of his stupid mania and given him back his real identity. But to the vast surprise of the head of the clinic, ten minutes after he's left, the same patient bursts into his office and takes refuge, in utter terror, underneath the doctor's desk, muttering incoherently. When the doctor asks him why he's in such a panic, the patient, who can barely get the words out, answers: 'Something terrible happened to me just as I was leaving here. I was walking down the street, minding my own business, and suddenly I met a chicken—a chicken, can you imagine!'

" 'But look,' the doctor says to him, 'didn't you tell me before you left that you were completely cured and that you no longer think that you are a grain of corn?' 'Of course,' the patient answers, '*I* know I'm not a grain of corn, but what about the *chicken*?' "

The Judge laughed at his own joke, coughing from the smoke of his reeking cigar; seeing that Bob didn't find his story very funny, he turned serious again.

"That's the problem, my dear Fender. You know very well that you're not a grain of corn, that is to say an agent, and perhaps with a little effort I could bring myself to believe it too. But the question is: Does the chicken know it?"

The Presidential Motorcade

THAT MORNING, Bob had been going over the conference documents in the little office assigned him in the embassy when the Ambassador came in without knocking: He was obviously quite excited.

"If you want to witness an interesting spectacle, stop whatever you're doing and come with me. They've just informed me that the date of the solemn ceremony marking the opening of Parliament has been moved up and it's to take place today." He hesitated. Bob was still wearing his safari outfit. "I don't think they'll allow you onto the diplomatic balcony dressed like that, but once we're inside we'll get you a seat in the public gallery."

There was great excitement around the Parliament building. A motley crowd had collected, carrying placards bearing the President's name and political slogans in Swahili on which words such as *uhuru* (independence) and *harambee* (unity) appeared again and again. The Ambassador's car, with the American flag waving on the fender, made its way through the multitude—roughly shoved out of the way by the city police, dressed in impeccable navy blue uniforms—and entered the courtyard of the House of Parliament. Bob had not noticed until then that the entire building, and the clock tower in particular, was actually a crude copy of its British counterpart; the clock was a duplicate of Big Ben with a cloisonné face and hands pointed like lances.

As they headed for the Parliament building, Bob remembered see-

227

ing the presidential motorcade pass on the road when he and Maguire were coming back from the Galana. They had left camp very early in the morning, taking off down the Tsavo trails at daybreak; round about noon, as the sun beat straight down on the bone-dry plain, they came out onto the main Nairobi-Mombasa highway. The ribbon of asphalt paving reflected the metallic sunlight, flattening out in the little gullies and slithering between towering rocks, like a snake skin. The Counselor had glanced back at the road behind them in the rearview mirror, and Bob saw him pale; a line of motorcycles was bearing down on them at top speed, with headlights blinking furiously. In the middle of that wilderness the sudden appearance of the presidential party seemed like a mirage sprung from the heat, and the motorcycle escorts, with their dark leather uniforms and gleaming helmets, looked like fantastic warriors from outer space. But the escort cars, loaded with bodyguards poking their hands out the windows and imperiously motioning them to move over into the ditch, were quite real; Maguire jammed on the brakes, the car skidded onto the sand along the roadside, and they nearly went off the road.

And then the majestic presidential Rolls Royce, enveloped in a halo of sunlight and dust, passed by with the shield of Kenya on the hood. Through the heavily tinted windows they could see only the dim shapes of the illustrious occupants. Maguire sat for a few seconds with his head resting on the steering wheel, still trembling; after taking off again he stopped at the nearest gas station to make a phone call.

A few minutes after the Ambassador had taken his place on the platform with the other diplomats and Bob had found a seat in the public gallery the ceremony began. After a shrill trumpet blast followed by a sepulchral silence, the chamberlains began to file in, followed by a long procession of high-placed government officials, political leaders, and magistrates who, one by one, took their assigned places on the platform. It was only when he turned around to sit down that Bob saw Judge McGredy, whose magistrate's wig made him look more leonine than ever; but the most picturesque contrast was provided by the black magistrates, who wore snow-white wigs reaching down to their shoulders.

The scene was like a negative of the familiar image of the opening of the British Parliament: it had the curious air of a ceremony from an age long past. The kings-of-arms marched through the chamber with maces on their shoulders, with a bearing meant to be martial,

228

though the effect was somewhat spoiled by the looseness of their arms and legs. When the spiritual leaders took their seats they received a warm ovation; the witch doctor in particular, who mounted the platform magnificently arrayed in a monkey-skin mantle and a headdress of ostrich feathers and hippopotamus teeth, carrying a ritual fly whisk with an ivory handle and the tail-hairs of a giraffe.

There was a deep silence, and at last the President entered the chamber, poured into a snug double-breasted pinstriped suit with a full-blown carnation in his lapel. All those seated in the chamber rose to their feet, greeting him with thunderous applause and cheers, which Mzee acknowledged by waving back at them with his solid gold fly whisk. The murmurs on the platform had scarcely died down and the speaker had just cleared his throat to deliver his words of welcome to the President when J. Muriuki materialized at the main entrance and headed for the platform with a supple, defiant stride, like a young bull just let loose in the bullring.

There was a tense silence, then the entire chamber broke out into a frightful uproar: Some whistled and applauded, others booed or drummed their heels against the legs of the benches, and, above all the hubbub, the words *"Ndume, Ndume"* could be heard, repeated in a frenzy by the audience, like a breaking wave ebbing and then surging forward once again with renewed force.

Bob remembered vividly the hunting at the Galana, when the trackers beat on the roof of the safari car to announce that they had spotted an animal worth hunting, muttering those same words, *"Ndume, Ndume,"* meaning that the creature was a male. Muriuki was a magnificent specimen; he suddenly stood absolutely still, his gaze insolently sweeping the entire chamber before he sat down. Bob thought of the impala that Paolo had taken a shot at as the splendid animal stretched his neck, sniffing the wind, haughty against the afternoon light sifting through the forest.

At the Galana, that morning, the hunters had gone out to kill an antelope for bait. They were crossing a broad expanse of grazing land, where puddles from the recent flood were still standing, when the trackers had begun to beat on the roof of the Toyota to signal that they had spotted something. A hundred yards or so away downstream, where the underbrush grew denser, a group of female waterbucks with their young was grazing amid some bushes; the male was a little farther away, lying under an acacia, but it rose to its feet at the sound of the motor.

229

Tony looked at it for a few brief moments through the binoculars. "It's not an exceptional trophy, but it's perfectly shootable," he said to San Miniato. San Miniato climbed out of the car and slid a bullet into the chamber of his rifle; and when he focused the telescopic sight on the shoulder of the animal, he was certain that this time he wasn't going to miss. The rifle report resounded in the thicket, and almost simultaneously, the dull thud of the bullet as it penetrated the animal's hide reached his ears, like the muffled "thunk" when a bullet sinks into a sandbag. The antelope tensed at the impact and took off at a very swift gallop, but within a few yards its legs gave way and it suddenly collapsed, sinking its curved horns in the sand and raising a cloud of dust with its feet.

They all got out of the car and walked over to the antelope. The animal lay motionless, its eyes set in a rigid stare. The trackers went to work on its back with their sharp knives, carving up the hind quarters after having peeled away part of the hide to be able to cut up the flesh more easily. Before leaving the body of the animal behind, one of the trackers sank his knife into its belly and made a deep gash which left the entrails visible.

"Why did they do that?" Paolo asked, averting his eyes in horror.

"That will make the hyenas smell carrion and come running to devour the carcass. If you pass by this way tomorrow, there won't be anything left of the animal except bones—if that."

The opening session of Parliament went on at a slow, ritual pace, and the light of midday, pouring through the stained glass windows on either side, cast colored patterns on the gleaming parquet floor and bounced off the bald heads of the ministers. The time had now come for Muriuki as leader of the opposition, to take the floor. He strode smilingly to the dais, empty handed, with neither a prepared text nor notes for his speech, and after offering the customary formal salutation to those about to hear his words, including the President (whose face seemed to be carved out of a massive block of wood) he began to speak in a deep, vibrant voice:

"On other occasions I have often made mention of the problem of land in our country, the land for which we fought against the colonialist forces, the land that our valiant guerrilla fighters drenched with their blood, the land that is now being monopolized and usurped by a group of ambition-ridden merchants and politicians.

230

"I wish to speak to you today of the wildlife situation, of the animals, whose existence is threatened by the same circuits of avarice and corruption that cause hundreds of acres of land to fall into just a few hands when many wananchis are forced to live without possessing a single acre. The word that we use in Swahili for game—nyama—has a double meaning, referring as it does both to meat as food and to the wild animals that range freely in the parks and countryside of Kenya. The question that I wish to pose today is this: What is happening to these animals, why are there fewer and fewer of them? Why are these innocent creatures being slaughtered indiscriminately, when they constitute an important resource of our country, when the profits realized from them by selling their hides, their tusks, their heads as trophies do not end up in the hands of poor wananchis but in the hands of unscrupulous merchants who sell such trophies to tourists at an exorbitant price and very often export them illegally, depriving the country of the hard currency vital for other projects.

"And by that I do not mean the poor villager who kills a gazelle to feed his family, but professional killers who have made a business of illegal hunting and realize substantial profits from it. What ought to be brought home to these unscrupulous individuals is the fact that, by sacrificing, as they are, hundreds upon hundreds of animals in order to line their own pockets, they are endangering one of the greatest potential sources of wealth of the nation: They are killing the goose that lays golden eggs, destroying the heritage that our forefathers have left us.

"It is a phenomenon very much like that of the bad farmer, of whom I have spoken on other occasions, who hastens to pick the fruits of a tree before they are ripe, thereby killing the tree. In this parable that I put before you, the tree is the nation and the fruit the product of the recently won uhuru!"

This resounding phrase, with emphasis on the Swahili word for independence, called forth a murmur of approval that swept through the rows of seats in the public gallery and a number of parliamentary benches as well. J. M. paused for a moment to take a sip of water and prove to himself, with a glance that swept the entire chamber, that he had totally electrified his audience.

"I remember that when I was a little boy living in a tiny village in the Rift Valley, near the forest of Kibaki, I used to see the armored cars of whites on safari passing by, followed by trucks loaded with the

231

equipment necessary to set up camp and the arms and ammunition to shoot down wild animals. Many years have gone by since then, we have won our independence, and yet I am certain that another youngster, there in my very own village, is watching other white hunters like the ones I saw pass by. And I ask once again: Why has nothing changed? Why do the same white hunters that we saw in our youth, that our fathers and grandfathers saw, continue to roam about at will over our plains and through our forests, with their arrogant air and their powerful firearms, as though they still were bent upon forcing the symbol of colonialism upon us? Like the landless farmers probably think that the white settlers are still on the fertile highlands, the wananchis looking at a safari party crossing the plains must think that the game still belongs to the muzungus.

"All this, my friends, could be and should be a problem that has a solution, a simple solution: a hunting ban. By declaring a total, absolute ban on all hunting, the problem of illegal hunting and the contraband traffic in trophies and the activities of white hunters who continue to lend a false colonial atmosphere to our country would be resolved."

A thunderous ovation followed; and again there was that sweeping glance of Muriuki's, like a bull in complete control of the ring, and then he went on:

"I regret to say, however, at this point that those who rule our country today are doing nothing to control illegal hunting, or the contraband traffic in trophies, or the forays of white hunters. The reasons behind this inactivity are very simple: ambition and profit. Unfortunately, too many powerful interests are involved in the whole business of hunting, and the government is unwilling to rock the boat, since there are high-placed officials who earn fat profits from the illegal traffic and they are afraid that the truth could come to light."

This aroused a loud murmur of disapproval from the Government benches, and someone shouted, in a voice boiling with rage: "Enough of your slanderous insults, you've held the floor too long, go back to your seat!"

Bob's eyes were fixed on the President's face. He was seated directly below where Bob was sitting in the gallery, and despite the distance separating them, Bob could clearly see the President's jaw set in a grimace of intense anger, and he thought he saw a convulsive

232

movement of his hand, tightening its grip on the giraffe tail of his fly whisk.

"*Although somewhat irritated voices are being raised and perhaps some esteemed members of the Government would prefer to see me return to my seat,*" (A wave of repressed laughter ran through the chamber.) "*I must confess that I'm in no hurry to regain my seat, since the bench is very hard and my backside can still feel the effects of the forty-four strokes of the cane that the English gave to me when I was in detention.*" (The murmur of laughter became a loud ovation.)

"*Before I conclude my remarks, I want to mention the great Conference Center that has been erected in the center of the city, towering over our heads like a new tower of Babel built by human pride. We all admire the clean lines of this edifice and doubtless it provides excellent shade for the vagrants taking their afternoon siesta in Jamhuri Park*" (another wave of laughter) "*but has anyone asked: What purpose does it serve, other than providing a place for a handful of delegates of various nationalities to discuss esoteric subjects of no importance to anyone, as meanwhile the* wananchis *die of hunger and disease and the countryside is parched by drought. My question is: Will this Conference bring us rain, or bring a more equitable distribution of wealth among Kenyans? My question is: Why do foreign delegates need so many floors and so many windows when on a clear day the view of Kilimanjaro can be seen by any humble Masai shepherd lying on the crest of the Ngong Hills? I'll tell you what purpose that great tower serves: It acts as a sounding board for the present Government, a music box that's out of tune.*

"*I call upon the Government, I challenge it, to oblige the Kenya delegation to propose at this Conference that just one effective step be taken, one step capable of bringing genuine international prestige to the host country: Let them offer to forbid all hunting. Let them pass a hunting ban. Isn't that organization called the International Center for the Conservation of Nature and Other Resources? Well then, let them pass a measure to save animals, which are one of our most valuable natural resources.*

"*As I have already said on other occasions, our watchword must be: Freedom for everyone or for no one. And when I say that I am merely repeating the words of a valiant freedom fighter who also fought for the independence of his country, Abraham Lincoln, when he said, 'Government of the people, by the people, for the people.' I*

233

wish to declare from this platform a ban on great landed estates, on nepotism, on corruption. I want our people to be able to roam freely through the country, like the herds of antelope that cross the plains between Kenya and Tanzania when the season changes. I want the game to be for everyone, or for no one."

The vibrant voice had gradually risen until the speech became a passionate harangue, and at the end Muriuki received a delirious ovation; not a soul dared now to boo or stamp his feet. The very people who had merely murmured when he had made his appearance were now shouting, *"Ndume, Ndume"* at the top of their lungs; and the public gallery seemed about to cave in with the thunderous vibration of the applause and the cheers for the leader of the opposition.

On the diplomatic platform, the Ambassador of Italy, who was sitting next to W. D. Poire, his chubby red cheeks growing even more flushed in his excitement, leaned over and whispered in Poire's ear:

"The Old Man will have to react forcefully or I suspect the new Ambassadors will be presenting their credentials to a new President. J. M. is playing a dangerous game, but if nothing untoward happens to him, it may be that there will be important changes in this country sooner than we thought."

The American Ambassador answered, also sotto voce, "Whether or not we like his ideas and his demagogic logorrhea we have to take our hats off to him! With just one kick of the ball, he's demolished a fair amount of the prestige the Government was likely to garner by hosting this Conference, and by appropriating the idea of a hunting ban for his own purposes, he's effectively prevented the government from taking such a popular measure precisely at the time when all the foreign ecologists are in Nairobi."

The Blazer

THAT SAME AFTERNOON, Bob—still without his luggage—went in search of clothes he could wear for the opening of the Conference the following day. In Nairobi a safari suit was worn even on formal occasions, but it didn't seem proper for a member of the American delegation to appear at the Conference Center dressed as an explorer.

In a shop near the New Stanley Hotel, he was waited on by an East Indian clerk possessed of the gift of persuasion, and a special talent for making the wrinkles in the fabric disappear, magically, smoothing it with deft little touches of his hand across the shoulders.

"This jacket is an absolutely perfect fit," he said to Bob, brushing an imaginary speck of dust off the lapels. "Made to order for you! It's a classic cut, the height of elegance. Just look in the mirror."

"It's not bad," Bob said. He liked the unobtrusive conservative tailoring, but the blazer had a shield over the upper left-hand pocket; a bullseye with two crossed rifles in the center, and the initials L. G. C. embroidered in gold thread.

"Don't you have a jacket like this without the emblem?"

"I'm sorry, but it's the only one we have left in your size. But allow me to say that that's the shield of the Limuru Gun Club, one of the oldest and most prestigious sporting associations in the country. This blazer was a special order for a client of ours who is a member of that club and had to leave the country unexpectedly."

A young woman, with very white skin and dark hair, dressed in European clothes, had come into the shop. She sat down near the counter, waiting for the clerk. Turning slowly in the blazer, Bob saw her big blue eyes reflected in the mirror. He thought she looked approving; he decided to buy the jacket.

"I'll take it. And give me a tie as well, one something like the one that young lady has in her hand."

235

The tie was a pretext to talk with her. She had a pleasant voice and an odd smile, half-shy and half-mischievous. Her accent was more British than American, with the trace of an intonation that was either French or Italian. They left the shop together, chatting casually about the exorbitant prices of European things in Nairobi. The afternoon sun shone down on the crowded streets. A strong breeze carried powerful odors from the nearby market, mingled with the smell of dust and human bodies. To his surprise, Bob found himself asking the young woman to have a drink at his hotel with him. She turned him down politely, blushing, but something about her attitude hinted that she would have liked to accept. Bob's eyes followed the slim, delicate figure and the dark wavy hair till he lost sight of her in the crowd.

Later, as he stood on the terrace overlooking the swimming pool of his hotel, Bob thought of the young woman whom he had just met—he'd forgotten to ask her what her name was—and the other women he'd met in Kenya, Guni and Julia. For different reasons, both of them intimidated him. He realized that the sweetness and the touch of naiveté that he'd sensed in the unknown woman seemed more attractive to him than the striking, almost aggressive beauty of the other two. He hoped he'd meet her again—that might not be difficult; in that city everyone seemed to end up in the same places.

He'd agreed to have dinner that night with Lucio Luz, an Argentine diplomat and a friend of John Murphy's whom he'd met briefly at an embassy reception. He wore his new jacket and tie. At the Red Bull Lucio was waiting for him, leaning on the bar with that indolent and blasé air of his, belied by his large dark eyes, whose expression was so kindly and ingenuous. When one meets an Argentine one always hopes that his personality will correspond at least to some degree to the stereotype of the Spanish gentleman, half idealist and half decadent. In Lucio Luz's case, however, the reality surpassed one's most optimistic expectations. With his impeccable blue suit, his hair going silver at the temples, his slender pianist's hands, and his eyes fringed with long drooping eyelashes, he could well have been an instructor teaching ladies to tango in the best belle epoque tradition.

Bob ordered a Pimm's Cup.

"Well, I see you've adopted the local drink and joined the Limuru Gun Club," he said, pointing to the emblem of Bob's jacket. "You certainly don't waste any time!"

"Not really," Bob said, embarrassed. "This shield was already on the jacket when I bought it. I was left with just the clothes on my back when the airline lost all my luggage."

"My word, what a shame! I still have all my suits made in London; the English, despite all their faults, have the only decent tailors left in the world."

Despite the Argentine's air of self-importance and a few racist remarks that he no doubt thought were the "in" things to say in that colonial atmosphere, Bob immediately sensed that he was basically a kind and decent man. He was perhaps the first person who had spoken to him of John Murphy with genuine affection, without that mixture of admiration and envy that he had found in Ralph Maguire, who during the return trip from Galana had spoken almost obsessively of his dead colleague. Bob was curious to know the Argentine's opinion about the American diplomat.

"I think Maguire is an interesting character; he insisted so much that I shouldn't believe all the gossip about Murphy's death, that he made me think there was something odd about the accident.

"In fact, there are many stories going around; the last one I heard was that John was heading to the coast to meet his lover, Townsend-Reeves's wife, and it was the jealous husband who did him in. In fact, nobody knows what happened on Mackinnon Road; we'll probably never know what really happened."

"But, is it true that he was sentimentally involved with Townsend-Reeves's wife?"

"Yes, I suppose their *liaison* was no secret to anybody, including the husband, but in this colonial society, this sort of thing is not taken very seriously. Knowing Alex, I can't see him waiting behind a bush, in the middle of the Tsavo, to ambush John Murphy. I admit he could have felt uncomfortable, at some stage, about the whole story, but his reaction would probably have been to have an extra drink."

At this point, Bob tried to change the topic of discussion, switching to some environmental issue. But the Argentine interrupted him almost violently. "Look, Fender, we are going to have more than enough time to listen to any number of high-flown ecological speeches in the next few days. I would be more interested in knowing how your trip to Galana was; I heard that, in spite of the poachers' ravages, they have managed to keep quite a few animals around."

"Well, the only thing I know is that, for different circumstances, I went out to Galana for my study on grasslands, but ended up with a group of hunters, chasing buffalo through the forest."

237

"Ah, so you were hunting buffalo, were you? That's my favorite game. Perhaps it's my Spanish blood—hunting buffalo is the African version of bullfighting."

Bob felt obliged to tell him the story of his adventure with the rogue buffalo, which Luz found so fascinating his dinner grew cold on his plate; he drank glasses of wine, and his eyes began to gleam as brightly as the glass pupils of the mounted buffalo looking down on the dining room.

"Very interesting, very interesting," Lucio said, his voice cracking with excitement. "I find it incredible that that imbecile Tony Allen committed exactly the same clumsy mistake a second time; when he was with me a similar incident occurred in very nearly the same circumstances, though it had more serious consequences."

Bob remembered then that Lawrence Brown had mentioned something about another accident Tony had had, also involving a buffalo, when he'd been out with an Argentine client. And Bob realized that Lucio Luz had been so fascinated by his story because he was reliving his own adventure. He told Bob the story.

"We'd left camp, somewhere around the Tana River—Block Eighteen, as I remember—early in the morning, and I had shot at a buffalo that I wounded but didn't manage to down. We followed the wounded animal all one morning through pretty impenetrable bush, till its trail led us to a dry riverbed—a lugga, as they call them around here—where the hoofprints could be seen clearly in the soft sand. The heat was unbearable, that suffocating heat that sticks to a person's skin, and the buzzing of the horseflies was getting on our nerves. Tony had long since lost all interest in following the trail, and he was dragging his feet over the sand, after having handed his rifle to the bearer. As we approached a clump of brush where the beast might be hiding, I told Tony that if he didn't mind, he should grab his rifle, just in case the buffalo was lurking in there and charged us. 'Why don't you shoot it? You've got a rifle too, haven't you?' he answered, the stupid fool. 'You're the professional, aren't you?' I shot back. 'Since I've heard so many times that you have so much experience as a professional, now's a good time to prove it,' Tony replied. He always was jealous of my reputation as a hunter."

Luz paused to take another long swallow; his throat was bone-dry from excitement. It was obvious that he had told this same story at least a hundred times and that each time he relived it just as intensely.

238

*"The words were no sooner out of my mouth when the buffalo,
which had been hiding on the very edge of the thicket all the time,
charged—just as the bearer parted the first branches with his hand to
see if the beast was there. All the poor man could do was throw
himself on the ground as the buffalo went by him like a locomotive;
Tony's desperate reach for his rifle attracted the beast's attention, and
with just one butt of its head it sent him flying ten paces through the
air. When the cloud of dust raised by the buffalo's sudden attack had
settled, I saw that Tony had fallen amid the bushes, without his rifle,
and that the animal was heading toward him again. With no time to
take careful aim, I shot off the two bullets in my rifle, one right after
the other. I could see the animal through the branches, with its head
down ready to gore Tony, so I tried to hit it in the shoulder. Though I
didn't succeed in downing it, I at least made it swerve as it charged.
Do you know what Tony said to me afterwards, the bastard! That if
I'd been a real professional, I'd have waited till the animal charged
me before shooting the second bullet—despite the fact that I'd just
saved his life!"*

"That hardly seems appropriate, given the circumstances," Bob said.
"But wait, that isn't the end of the story. Once the shots hit him, the
buffalo did turn on me, and since my rifle was now empty, the only
thing I could do was run."
"With the buffalo on your tail?"

*"Precisely. As I was running I could hear the monster snorting
behind me. Those are things you think happen only in a nightmare,
until they really do happen to you. As I was running through the
bushes, thinking of putting as much distance as possible between the
beast and me, I suddenly stumbled into a hole and fell flat on my face
in front of the animal. Some bastard of a poacher had camped there
the night before and had made a hole to bury the embers from his fire,
which of course were still red-hot. I didn't realize that till later; for the
moment I had a two-thousand-pound beast on top of me, leaning its
muzzle on my chest and trying to rip my balls off as I tried to get it off
me by pounding desperately on its boss with my hands. Fortunately, it
didn't manage to gore me, no doubt because my body had sunk into
the sand, and after a few minutes it went off, since it had been badly
wounded."*

"So the buffalo didn't do anything to you after all?"
"He didn't do any harm to me directly, but I was so unnerved when

I fell I didn't realize that some of the coals from the fire, still red-hot, had gotten into one of my boots along with the sand. When I finally tumbled to the fact that they were live coals, I had bad burns on that foot that made me walk with a limp for months and months. The scars still ache when the rainy season comes."

"That's a shame," Bob said, not knowing whether he was supposed to laugh or to express sympathy.

"If you talk to Tony, he'll surely tell you a completely different version so as to safeguard his reputation. But the truth of the matter is that on that occasion at least, it was the client who had to save the professional."

"Now I understand why, when we began to follow that buffalo through the dense forest, Tony was deathly pale, and sweating bullets."

"But he's the one who's responsible if he gets his clients in unnecessarily dangerous situations. An incident like that would never have happened to me with a reliable professional—one like Lawrence Brown, say, when he was working as a hunter."

"Ah, so you know Lawrence Brown too?"

"I certainly do. I was one of the last ones to go hunting with him at the ranch, in the days when he still took his own clients out, before he became completely possessed by that conservationist mania of his and turned into the self-appointed sheriff of the Galana. They say that every time an animal gets killed on the ranch now, it's as though his very own body felt the impact of the bullet."

"It's true that he's obsessed by the fact that they're killing his animals, but after spending some time at Galana, I understand how he feels: The poachers are literally wiping out all the game in that whole district. He has other manias that I don't understand nearly as well—his hatred of women, for instance. I've never once heard Brown mention 'females' except to denigrate them."

Lucio Luz looked at him with eyes slightly out of focus.

"If I were in his shoes, I wouldn't trust women very much either, after what Vanessa, his former wife, did to him."

"I didn't know that Brown had been married. I thought he was a confirmed bachelor!"

Again he had the impression that in Kenya life proceeded in circles that gradually became smaller and smaller the more people one met and the more intimately one came to know that city, which was where the clues to the labyrinth lay.

"I presume that you'd like to see a bit of nightlife here in the city. There's a place that's usually quite lively, the New Stanley grill. Some friends who are there tonight suggested we come join them after we'd finished dinner. Unless you'd rather go to the Casino?"

"No, I'm not much for gambling. But I'll gladly go with you to have a drink at the New Stanley."

In the New Stanley nightclub a motley, decadent crowd of dispossessed colonial landowners were whooping it up, men dressed in white and women with long dresses hauled out of some old trunk. The orchestra platform was decorated with gilt palm trees and the only missing touch of fake splendor was a moth-eaten lion lurking in the plastic underbrush. In posthumous homage to their lost dominion, the best tables in the place were reserved for the old-timers, whose stridently uproarious bursts of laughter were punctuated by repeated orders in Swahili to the black waiters to bring them yet another round of drinks. The tourists and the hotel guests found themselves relegated to the sidelines, and each time they timidly tried to venture out onto the dance floor, they were brusquely elbowed aside by the corpulent ex-colonials who needed all the available space to kick up their heels in some ancient foxtrot with their partners, often their friends' wives.

Lucio Luz headed for one of these privileged tables, followed by Bob. The svelte figure and the reddish hair of Guni Townsend-Reeves was conspicuous even in the semidarkness; she was dancing with a man who wasn't Alex. When another dance began, she returned to her table and saw Bob immediately. She deserted her partner and came over to say hello, kissing Bob affectionately on the mouth and sitting down next to him.

"How great that you were able to come! Lucio told me he might bring you. Isn't it a marvelous surprise to meet again?"

"Yes, it's really something," Bob answered, absorbing a little energy from the Pimm's Cup that the waiter had brought him. "I thought you were still down on the coast!"

"Oh, no, Alex couldn't survive for very long without going to the Casino to fritter away the little that's left of his fortune, and as if that weren't enough, the horse races start next Saturday . . . and I wanted to see you again," the woman said, lowering her voice and pushing her long hair back: A wisp of it brushed Bob's cheek and he recoiled.

A black singer with a deep, rich voice had just appeared onstage, and Guni dragged him out onto the dance floor, to the rhythm of a sad and supersensual song. Without a word, she drew him to her and began to dance. Every inch of her body was pressed against his; her head leaned on his shoulder, covering part of his face with her heavy reddish hair. Her heavy perfume almost suffocated him.

Bob felt someone tap him on one shoulder, and turning around found himself face to face with Alex Townsend-Reeves, who was out on the dance floor too, locked in the arms of another woman. The Britisher beamed a broad smile in his direction and winked, as though encouraging Bob to go on dancing cheek to cheek with his wife. Guni didn't notice; she was clinging to him so tightly that he could feel her nipples through the thin dress, and her thighs brushed provocatively against his knees.

When they sat down again, Alex came over to greet him once more and remained at the table for a time chatting with him. Bob's cheeks were still burning and his hands sweating after all that heat that Guni had poured on. He didn't understand how Alex could behave as though it was all perfectly natural.

"This is quite a lively place," Bob finally said after taking a long swallow of Pimm's. "And that black singer is one of the best I've ever heard. Her song has such a mixture of sensuality and sadness; one can see she really feels it."

"The poor girl is from Uganda," Alex said, with an odd smile, "and in view of the present situation in her country, she can never be sure she'll live very long."

"Are things that bad in Uganda?"

"They're worse than bad. We complain of the violence here and the lack of security, but this is a paradise compared to Kampala. Human life there has no value. It doesn't have very much here either, but nonetheless it's still worth just a little bit more," he added with the same vague smile.

Would this man with such exquisite manners and such a phlegmatic temperament have been capable of ordering the death of his wife's lover, as someone had hinted to the Argentine? Beneath the hysterical gaiety of that nightclub, in the languid, plaintive song of the woman from Uganda, Bob sensed a deep current of sadness and fear, as if all that lightheartedness was a desperate attempt to blot out the threat of death.

The State of the Environment

THE PLENARY MEETING ROOM of UNICORN was circular; at one side stood the raised dais, beneath the illuminated world globe bearing the emblem of the United Nations. The various delegations were seated together along the row of the circular amphitheater whose diameter gradually decreased, leaving at the very bottom an empty space, also circular, like a bullring; a ring where absolutely nothing was happening.

The Conference sessions dragged on endlessly. A delegate from the Ukraine was reading in Russian his speech on the state of the environment, which was being simultaneously translated into various languages by the interpreters, who were yawning desperately in their glass booths, like fish gasping for oxygen. A ray of sunlight was entering almost vertically through the main skylight, leaving areas of semi-darkness in which a number of delegates were napping, having disconnected their microphones and earphones so as not to have their snores stereophonically amplified. Others, pretending to listen, were idly sketching geometrical designs and naked women in their notebooks, and the most ambitious doodlers were trying their hand at architectural drawings of the conference hall, the perspective of which turned out to be difficult to reproduce due to the absence of right angles. A Japanese delegate suddenly let out such a huge yawn that he attracted the attention of his neighbors, whereupon his jaws shut with a snap; he looked as satisfied as a chameleon that has just swallowed a butterfly.

Leaning back in one of the seats assigned to the American delegation, Bob was listening to the speech on the environment with a faraway look, having given in to that pleasant sensation of lethargy, of light-headedness, of immersion in deep waters that he had felt more than once since his arrival in Kenya. Quite possibly this was not a conference on ecology—and the exotic delegates who stirred in their seats were creatures who moved their limbs as though they were antennae and tentacles; no, it was really a subaquatic assembly of rare crustaceans, the epicenter of the universal aquarium, the supreme temple of an underwater world.

From the very first day of the Conference, Bob had realized his presence there was unnecessary. The other members of the delegation —which had turned out to be a fairly large one—had cornered the most interesting committees and working groups for themselves, leaving Bob stuck in the session, listening to boring speeches. In the afternoons, he was assigned a working group on firewood, which did not even meet in the main conference hall, but in a UNICORN building located on the far side of the city. An Embassy car had been put at his disposal; by one of those coincidences that Bob had by now become quite accustomed to, it turned out to be a Toyota with a canvas roof that John Murphy had used on some of his combined ecological and hunting expeditions. The oilcloth on the floor still smelled of the dried blood of game, like the safari cars at the Galana Ranch, and every so often an empty shell turned up in the folds of the seats.

Despite all that, Bob was not sorry he had come to Nairobi: quite the contrary. He had seen the woman from the clothing shop a second time. Her name was Melissa Turner. On the opening day of the UNICORN Conference, Bob was finishing his solitary lunch on the terrace of the Hilton when she came up to his table, and with that same half-timid, half-mocking smile, asked him if his invitation of the day before still held good. He asked her to sit down, and this time hastened to ask her what her name was and where he could reach her. As she talked, the thought occurred to Bob that the night of noisy dancing at the New Stanley had left few traces—except for a vague feeling of depression and perhaps a few smudges of Guni's makeup on the collar of his jacket, but his brief encounter with the unknown young lady, and the memory of her delicate figure melting into the crowd, amid the mingled sunlight and clouds of dust filling the streets, had persisted.

Melissa had come to Nairobi a couple of years before with her husband, Philip Turner, who worked for a firm that exported commodities and was overseer of a coffee plantation in the Eldama district, which he visited frequently. Bob liked the natural way in which Melissa referred to her husband—with genuine affection, while at the same time, with very feminine subtlety, leading Bob to understand that the fact that she was married did not prevent her from being interested in, and even attracted to, a person of the opposite sex.

Bob in turn told Melissa his reason for having come to Kenya, and how he had had to interrupt his stay on the coast because he'd been called back to Nairobi, only to discover that his presence on the delegation was far from indispensable.

"As a matter of fact," Bob said, grateful for his first opportunity to tell someone about his confusion, "I still haven't found out why they made me come back. The other delegates, who are on the diplomatic list of the Embassy, pulled rank on me and grabbed all the seats on the committees dealing with the most important issues, no doubt to add it to their service record. And meanwhile I've been exiled to a secondary working group that meets in a place miles away called Rosslyn, which must be practically in the middle of the jungle since they've lent me a safari car to get there. . . ."

Melissa laughed, a sensual, contagious, throaty laugh.

"I don't see what's so funny," Bob said.

"That weird area called Rosslyn, that you describe as though it were the end of the world, is the district where we live. The road that leads to the UNICORN buildings passes right in front of my house."

"Well! I hope I'll be able to drop in for a visit."

Melissa seized upon that happy coincidence to invite him to lunch the very next day. Her husband would pick him up at the Center at noon to take him to their house, after which he could go on to his meeting.

They lingered at the table for quite some time, drinking coffee and talking. When she left him, an aura of simplicity and freshness still lingered in the air around him.

Bob thought with pleasure of the gentle, graceful movements of her hands, the very pure lines of her nose and lips, her deep blue eyes framed in very dark eyebrows, the exquisite, slightly rounded forehead, which gave her a certain remote, mysterious expression. And her slender, boyish body was provocative; she wore skirts of a very simple cut and blouses like a schoolgirl's, emphasizing the androgynous charm of her figure.

As he sipped his coffee, Bob wondered again what there was about that slim, not particularly beautiful woman—who could have passed him a hundred times on the street without his looking at her twice—

245

that made him find her more attractive than the superb Guni, who offered herself to him so openly. Perhaps it was quite simply that Melissa was more his sort, more attainable, when you came right down to it. And his meeting her had all the charm of the unexpected; the relationship between them was not tainted by the morbid curiosity that led people to take an interest in him because he had been John Murphy's friend.

At the UNICORN session the following day, Bob waited impatiently for the chairman to adjourn the meeting, but he had to wait resignedly until various speakers had aired their points of view concerning the state of the environment. The debate lasted longer than the allotted time; when it was over Bob ran down the corridors and took the steps of the main stairway of the Center two by two.

Philip Turner was waiting, just in front of the main gate of the building, in a brand-new green Range-Rover, in the back of which was an intriguing mixture of sacks of coffee, riding equipment, and polo mallets; the horsy smell of the leather mingled with the smell of coffee beans, and on the back seat there was a white polo helmet and a black attaché case. He wore an impeccable suit tailored in English cloth. His skin was deeply tanned; and the wind ruffled his curly blond hair.

"Nairobi is still one of the most perfect places in the world; you can work, live a leisurely life, and engage in sports, and cheaply," Philip told him, after they had introduced themselves. "Someone like me, who can pilot a private plane, can easily be hunting buffalo in the morning in the thickets of Mount Kenya and in the afternoon go spear fishing in the waters of the Indian Ocean."

There was a spontaneity about Philip that was immediately attractive. He was one of those men who, when they enter a room, make women's heads turn and instantly arouse other men's distrust; after a few minutes' conversation with him, the women were utterly taken by him, and he had disarmed the suspicions of the other males. Despite the almost too-perfect oval of his face, his classic profile, and the fair hair lying in ringlets at the nape of his neck, he was thoroughly masculine; his limbs were long and muscular, and his prominent jaw gave him a virile look and an air of authority. But his eyes would gleam angrily with rather childish impatience, Bob noticed, when a truck suddenly cut across his path or a clumsy African driver got in his way. And, making some ironic or insolent commentary, his delicate

246

lips would contract in an unexpectedly cruel grin. He was striking and a bit overpowering, and as he drove, Philip delivered a series of short lectures on the political and economic situation in Africa, the coffee trade, the problems of agriculture, the increase in the crime rate and corruption in business circles—all of it a bit muddled and quite personal, but delivered with such conviction and vigor that it persuaded Bob before he could stop to consider whether the man's ideas had a firm basis in fact.

As they left Nairobi, they first followed the road that led to the American Embassy, then left the main street of the Muthaiga district and turned off to the left.

"Remember this turn-off, after the petrol station," Philip said, "because it's the same one you'll be taking to get to the UNICORN buildings; this road gets you to Limuru, and it's also the road that goes to Nakuru and Uganda."

Soon he turned off once more, into a gravel road that cut through fields of coffee trees. The area was already almost wilderness, with steep ravines along the sides of the road and dense clumps of bushes and thickets of oak on the crests of the hills. Along one side of the road were the fields of coffee trees, with rows of eucalyptus marking the boundaries.

"This is the Rosslyn area. Some people think that if you don't live in Muthaiga, or in the Langata and Karen area, it's like not living in Nairobi, but we've found a very pleasant house here, and since I take this same road to Nakuru quite often, it saves me from having to go through the city every time I make a trip there."

"Melissa told me that you have a coffee plantation."

"Well, I'm more the manager of it, though I also own a share in it It's near the little village of Eldama Ravine, a delightful place."

"What did you say the name of the place was?"

"Eldama Ravine."

"A pretty name."

The Painted Bird

GOING UP AN ASPHALT ROAD, bordered by a well-kept meadowland, they reached the house, which stood atop a steep knoll. With its slate roof, its veranda framed by delicate columns, and its large windows, the small mansion would not have been out of place in the middle of the cotton plantations of Virginia. Melissa came out on the porch at the back to meet them, and as she leaned over to kiss Bob, he noticed her soft fragrance, like that of a fruit kept in hay to stay fresh. She was wearing her hair in a ponytail, and a simple cotton print dress; the opening of it down her small bosom had two or three buttons undone.

They sat on the veranda, and Melissa brought them a delicious Pimm's with all sorts of fruits and tiny little flowers. Philip announced that he would be leaving for Nakuru right after lunch.

"There's a polo match this afternoon at Gilgil, which is halfway there; if I hurry a bit, I can get there in time to play in the second half. Melissa will show you how to get to the Center."

The dining room had a picture window that looked out over the vast sloping meadow and, farther in the distance, the rolling fields of the coffee plantations, green against the heavily wooded hills. In the northern part of the city, the landscape changed completely: The residential areas of Langata and Karen bordered on the parched pasturelands to the south, savanna and red-colored tablelands; while on the other side, in the direction of Limuru, the terrain mounted sharply toward the fertile, wooded highlands.

"On a clear day you can see Mount Kenya behind those hills," Philip said pompously.

"Don't pay any attention to him," Melissa interrupted. "That's the very first thing people tell you when you come to Nairobi. The ones in Langata say that on a clear day they can see Kilimanjaro, and those of us on this side of the city say that we can see Mount Kenya from here. I assure you that I've lived in this house for more than a year and a half, and I've never seen its snow-covered twin peaks. But I really don't mind, because the view is pretty enough as it is."

Bob had the feeling that this couple had captured perfectly the postcolonial style, enjoying what they found pleasant or interesting, but with enough detachment not to succumb to the obsessions of the old-time colonials.

"Is it true that there's a strong rivalry between people in Langata and those in Muthaiga?" Bob asked. "Apart from the business of the mountains, I mean?"

"It's quite true," Melissa answered. "These people have all sorts of manias. I can tell you that it's not easy for newcomers to make a place for themselves in this society. For people to have any respect for you at all, you have to have arrived in Africa in the days when they started building the Uganda Railway; otherwise they treat you like an outsider. Once, at a tea for lady members at the club, I told everybody that my family had arrived in Africa in 1912; it struck me as a nice-sounding date, and I think all those silly biddies were terribly impressed!"

"And how about the local people—the Africans, I mean?"

"Some of them can be perfectly delightful, but socially, you never know if you can count on them. You invite them to dinner one night and two days later they call you to apologize for not having turned up," Melissa said.

"That's true," Philip agreed. "My contacts with them are largely business ones, of course, and I find a number of them to be bright and efficient, even though corruption and unreliability are also rampant in the business world. But it's very difficult to be personal friends with them. A funny thing happened to us not so long ago: We'd invited a rather important man from the Ministry of Commerce to dinner, because I needed to talk over certain matters having to do with the coffee trade with him. Anyway, when we'd gotten tired of waiting for him to show up and were about to sit down at the dinner table, he called to say that he wasn't coming because he wasn't feeling hungry that night."

"That's quite a logical excuse, though it's a rather unusual one," Bob observed.

"And as for white society," Melissa said, "it clings to its old, male-dominated structure. This is true even among the younger people who come here to work; through his business and also by playing polo, Philip has been able to meet quite a few nice people and they've become friends. But it's been harder for me; there aren't many women my age here, and the first thing the men you meet try to do is seduce you. Maybe they think it's a social obligation, that they're perpetuating the old colonial tradition!"

Despite Philip's strong personality and his dominating presence, the one who conducted the conversation was his wife. When Philip delivered one of his seemingly brilliant but not very solid theories, Melissa deftly deflated his lofty arguments with a brief remark, like a sharp pinprick puncturing a balloon. A curious atmosphere of complicity had been created between Melissa and Bob; on several occasions, as she smothered her husband's verbal fireworks with her devastating logic, her foot lightly nudged Bob's shoe. Philip got up from the table before coffee was served, shook hands with Bob as he bade him good-bye, and as his lips lightly brushed his wife's forehead, he said to her:

"You can't complain; I'm leaving you in good company. What's more, Mr. Fender is a serious ecologist, not like those decadent colonials who try to seduce you the minute they lay eyes on you."

As Turner's car disappeared around the bend in the road, Bob thought that he had never wanted so much to be alone with a woman and here they were; though he did find it rather odd that the husband was the one to leave his own house in defeat. Bob felt extremely pleased with himself and emptied in one swallow the glass of brandy offered him by an African servant dressed in an elegant yellow uniform.

"I don't know what time your meeting starts," Melissa said, taking his arm, "but you're not leaving here till you've learned the secrets of this house; there are parts of it that are very dilapidated but on the whole I find it has a great deal of charm. And you'll see that the view from the upstairs bedrooms is even better."

Was it Bob's imagination, or had Melissa's hand touched his in a very special way as they were going up the stairs that led to the second floor? There was a large living room upstairs; on one side were the bedrooms and on the other a French door opening out onto a little terrace partially covered by a huge creeping vine, a luxuriantly flowering bougainvillea; there were wicker chairs and little low tables, and on one side a large pane of glass, like that of a conservatory, which protected the plants on the terrace from the wind and the rain;

250

the atmosphere in that sheltered area, saturated with humidity and the fragrance of flowers, was intoxicating. Suddenly, the smell of decomposing earth, of decaying compost that had previously so obsessed him, took on a new meaning for Bob; it was strong and sensual, like an aphrodisiac perfume. He felt terribly excited, and it seemed that he could also feel, through the cloth of his shirt, the heat of Melissa's hand resting on his arm.

"And now I'm going to show you my favorite corner. But you mustn't tell anybody that you've been in it; it's a secret room that I keep all for myself, and for very special friends." Melissa's voice was husky, and her cheeks were flushed.

At the other end of the terrace was another, separate room, like a tiny garret. Melissa led him to it, holding his hand. The touch of her fingers was very soft and warm. As she opened the door, he was surprised at how cool and dark the room was, unlike the terrace, where the ceramic tiles reflected the sun's heat. This garret had two small windows, the curtains of which were partly drawn: They were made of burlap and some light filtered through them. Little by little his eyes became accustomed to the semidarkness, and he could make out an odd jumble of furniture: a pair of leather-upholstered sofas, and a floor covered with the skins of various animals, felines, zebras, and many kinds of antelopes, including cinnamon-colored impalas, copper-colored bongos, and grayish kudus with markings that looked like white chalk stripes. There were also several cheetah and leopard skins, and even that of a black panther.

At the far end of the room where there was a bed covered with silk cushions and a zebra skin, Bob saw the glass panels of a huge aquarium; its diffused light filled the corners of the room with the stirrings of algae and the shadows of fish and eels. But he did not have time to look much longer, for Melissa gently slid her fingers down the hollow of his back and pressed her slim body to his, offering him her wet, open red mouth; Bob took her head between his hands—what thick, silky hair she had!—and kissed her eagerly. She pressed her body closer to him; beneath the thin dress, gaping open, Bob felt her soft skin. As they moved toward the bed, he began to undo the buttons, which seemed to melt in his hands. The dress slid easily from her thin shoulders, and to Bob's surprise, two little breasts with two pert little red nipples appeared—not a woman's completely developed breasts, but rather an exciting promise, what a libidinous doctor examining an adolescent girl might discover. He kissed them and drank in the milky, still childish aroma of those breasts; the dress fell away altogether, revealing a little pubes outlined in dark fleece, offered to him with a gentle movement of bony hips. Without taking time to remove his clothes, Bob slid his member between her thighs, which clasped it tightly for a moment, as though she were possessed of fingers inside her that could grasp; then she began to move back and forth in little spasms, as her hair and arms lay spread out on the zebra skin covering the bed.

The intense pleasure dizzied Bob: The movement of the woman's hair swayed in the same rhythm as the algae in the aquarium, and the softness and the warmth of her skin seemed to become one with that of the animal pelt beneath her. Something made Bob remember the sensation he had felt in the bungalow on the beach at Watamu, when the thief tried to drug him with that intense perfume. But at this moment, the feeling in the pit of his stomach was one of pleasure and desire. He could not remember ever having had a sensation of such intensity. Heat radiated from the woman's belly and spread through his whole body. When he himself reached the moment of orgasm, he withdrew a little, and his fingers stroked the woman's hair, her tiny breasts whose nipples had turned hard and as dark as blackberries, and searched through the fleece of her pubes, seeking the soft moistness. She drew him roughly to her, and with violent contortions, indicated that she was ready, and again the lips of her vagina contracted like a powerful pincers.

He was aware that he was about to come, when he heard a strange sound, half-clouded now by his intense pleasure; it was an insistent little sound, not very far away, like knuckles tapping on a pane of glass. His blood ran cold in his veins: It sounded as though someone were knocking on the French door of the garret! He had barely the strength to move, but turning his head just slightly, he realized what it was: At the nearby window, partially covered by the burlap curtain, a little bird was pecking violently at the glass, perhaps fighting the reflection of its own image. The woman had raised herself up a little: She, too, had heard. Their smiling mouths sought each other, and they were carried away by an orgasm that seemed endless.

Beneath him, the woman's body melted, and she moaned; her blue eyes were fixed, staring into space. Her head resting against the crystal base of the aquarium, moved violently, and the vibrations created a chaos of flickering tails, shifting sand, and quivering coral inside the aquarium. An eel glided along the inside of the glass, finally hiding itself at the bottom of a deep cleft.

The Karura Forest

FOR THE NEXT FEW DAYS, when the morning session at the UNI-
CORN was over, Bob would climb into his safari car and head for
Melissa's house, with the car windows open and the burning sun
pouring in through the windshield. As he entered the coffee plantation area, the smell of the red earth and the clumps of eucalyptus
overwhelmed his senses: It brought back to him the smells and sensations of the act of love. The landscape, the changes of light and the
fragrances, were colored by his sensual excitement, continually
renewed and continually satisfied. The sun, the flawlessly pure air,
and the luxuriant greenness were an aphrodisiac, and Bob suddenly
understood the follies and the excesses of the old colonials, the real
meaning of the hackneyed expression "Happy Valley."

Melissa and he would have lunch on the veranda, saying little and
behaving most circumspectly as the servants hovered about the table.
The great sloping meadow spread long and deep against the coffee
plantations and wooded hills. Perhaps they secretly hoped that the
power of love would suddenly cause the twin peaks of Mount Kenya
to appear above the haze on the horizon. As soon as the servants
retired to their quarters, they went up to the little room opening onto
the terrace, and without exchanging a single word, they made love,
more intensely each time. Melissa had the honesty not to hide her
eagerness for pleasure; her fragile little body surrendered fully and
completely to him.

At times, as he went back down the stairs, leaving Melissa still
naked on the zebra skin, Bob wondered if all this was not sheer
madness, if he was not irreparably compromising Melissa's reputation. But the house was far enough from the city for there to be little
chance of unexpected visitors, and the entrance to the grounds was
continually guarded by various *askaris* who protected them from any
unpleasant surprises while they were making love. Bob asked Melissa
the reason for these strict security measures. She answered vaguely; it

was because the house was so isolated, and to safeguard the sacks of coffee that were sometimes stored in a large shed at the far end of the garden.

He very seldom arrived on time for his afternoon meetings, though the UNICORN buildings were only a couple of miles away from the Turners' house, and once he took his seat, he rarely took part in the discussions; his thoughts were elsewhere. The chairman of the working group, a rather insolent Finnish ecologist, complained one afternoon of the lack of interest shown by the American delegation in the work of that committee. Bob answered that though the problem of firewood might seem an important question to UNICORN, when one traveled the country and saw entire forests and whole areas of savanna burnt to cinders by honey hunters and carcasses of elephants and rhinos scattered about everywhere, one realized that there were many other areas which required more urgent action. The Finn didn't lock horns with him again.

Meanwhile the political tension, which had increased steadily since the day Muriuki had delivered his impassioned speech in Parliament, was reaching the breaking point. As Muriuki had anticipated, the hypocrisy and the contradictions of the environmental conference became the target of the attacks against the government. The fact that the short rains were late this year, in the Nairobi area, was a perfect pretext for stirring up the people, who already looked with apprehension upon that mysterious building where groups of foreign magicians congregated day after day and were unable to find an effective exorcism for misery and drought. A local witch doctor came to the main gate of the Center every day, tracing magic circles and chanting magic spells, shaking his ceremonial baton and his monkey-skin cape, to counteract the curse of the foreign healers. The demonstrators carrying placards against UNICORN inspired by Muriuki's speech; the curious students, and the throng of idlers and vagrants, crowded outside the fences of the Center in such numbers that the police had to drive them off with billy clubs so that the delegates could push their way inside.

One morning, shortly after Bob left his hotel, a bomb went off in the government tourist office, very near the Hilton, where the majority of the foreign delegates were staying. No one was injured but another explosion occurred only a few days later, this time in a terminal for buses serving the Limuru district and the north of the country; since these *matutus* were jam-packed, it was a miracle that no more than twenty persons were killed. No one knew for certain the reasons for this brutal attack; while the government laid the blame for this act of terrorism on the opposition, J. M.'s followers spread the rumor that it was really an attempt on the part of the government to liquidate the leader of the opposition, since on the very day of the bombing he had rented one of the buses from that terminal in order to attend a political meeting that was to be held in Nanyuki, though at the last moment he had changed his plans. The explosion opposite the Hilton could also have been a move directed against Muriuki, since the hotel café was known to be the usual meeting place of the ring-leaders of the opposition.

Although Bob was still enveloped in that cloud of sensuality that floated above the coffee plantations of Limuru, the sound of these explosions had been close enough to shock him out of his lethargy. All this happened at the time of Philip's return to Nairobi; it was no longer possible for him and Melissa to use the house in Rosslyn for their lovemaking. Because of the widespread political unrest, the police had stepped up their control at various roadblocks along routes leading into the city, so that it would not have been prudent to meet in some little hotel on the outskirts. One day when Melissa came to meet him on the terrace of the Norfolk and they went for a walk in the grounds of the University, they found themselves suddenly trapped between a group of students with placards demonstrating against UNICORN and the police brigade trying to break up the demonstration. They took refuge in the car, but stones and tear-gas bombs filled the air around them; they barely escaped being taken off to a local police station. It was safer, they decided, not to see each other for a few days.

Meanwhile, the members of the government seemed to have vanished, or were afraid to appear in broad daylight. The Ministers scarcely showed their faces in their favorite haunts, like the Red Bull, which had become one of J. M.'s habitual hangouts. With the streets and the environs of the Center also invaded by Muriuki's supporters, the Ministers made only timid appearances, hurrying to their ministries or to official functions, and immediately hurrying back to hole up in safety. Even the President, who had always acted promptly and decisively when faced with a serious problem, was now hesitant as to what course of action to take. He too had entrenched himself—in the presidential palace, the former residence of the English Governor—and spent endless hours watching native dances and attending inane formal ceremonies, avoiding a cabinet meeting which might force a decision.

The truth of the matter was that the President was reluctant to admit that his former friend and ally in the days of the Emergency was in the process of snatching the reins of power from his hands. Nonetheless, he was beginning to perceive the situation more clearly than he had been able to on the coast—where he saw everything through a hazy blur of humidity, and a life of pleasures which included certain senile excesses which the licentious Munyoka encouraged him to enjoy. After the bomb explosions in Nairobi, he called together a Council of Ministers: It degenerated into a list of accusations against Muriuki, accompanied by a demand for a lightning blow against him from the President. The President, failing to calm his cabinet members, and finding himself at a loss as to what to say to them, at last fell into a rage and left the room in a fury, knocking over chairs and pitchers of water. The astute Munyoka, however, took advantage of the state of dejection that followed upon this stormy session to show the President copies of the bills of lading for the arms shipment, and managed to persuade him that this proof pointed directly at Muriuki, despite the fact that Muriuki's name did not appear on any of the documents. The Old Man inspected the documents carefully through his half glasses and thrust them in his pocket without a word.

Although no official decision had been made, that stormy cabinet meeting had crystallized the hatred of a number of members of the government who were eager to remove J. M. from the political arena. The evening after the cabinet meeting one of the ministers, a friend of Muriuki's, who wished to remain on friendly terms with the opposition, approached Ndume as he was leaving his office in the Parliament building. Dusk was falling. The Minister muttered only a few words in Muriuki's ear:

"Try not to go out alone at night."

"Come on!" J. M. had answered with a nervous laugh. "Don't worry—those hyenas wouldn't dare touch so much as a hair of my head. I'll bomb them, reduce them to ashes."

Later, since everything eventually came to light in the narrow confines of that aquarium, his words were to be interpreted as J. M.'s admission of guilt in the bombings.

After a few days it appeared as if the political storm had subsided, and the streets returned to normal, as though the brisk breeze from the Ngong Hills had blown away the smoke of the explosions and the burning hot equatorial sun had rapidly dried up the blood on the pavement. It had been only a week since Bob had visited the Turners' house for the first time, and only ten days since the Conference had begun, but it seemed to him that he had been in Nairobi for months. Melissa soon found a new place that was safe and convenient for them to meet: the Karura Forest.

The Karura Forest was actually a raised plateau covered with dense vegetation that stretched from the Muthaiga Club district to the coffee plantations of Rosslyn. Bob had only to make a short detour off the road he usually took to the UNICORN buildings, turning off along a dirt trail that started behind the golf course and led to a little local school, a wooden shack standing in the middle of a clearing in the woods. A little farther on, there was a half-abandoned cricket field, where students from a Hindu school sometimes came to practice.

He would park his car in the shade of a clump of eucalyptus behind the schoolyard. When Melissa failed to appear promptly, the curious little face of a schoolgirl would sometimes peek at him over the wooden fence, or the stern face of the white schoolmistress appeared for a few seconds at one of the classroom windows. Just as Bob had decided that Melissa wasn't coming, a cloud of red dust would appear at the other end of the little road, and a few minutes later, his heart would pound as he saw, through the windshield of her car, that characteristic smile of hers, half-timid and half-mocking, and perhaps a little guilty?

Bob would follow her in his car along one or another of the trails through the forest that crossed little clearings carpeted with thick grass and small streams flowing gently through the thickets: Melissa knew these winding trails so well that Bob wondered if this was her first adulterous adventure in Kenya. When they found a proper place they made love in the car, or walked a few paces into the forest and lay down, with almost all their clothes on, or leaned against the smooth trunk of a dead tree. They were surprised only twice, once by a group of schoolgirls in blue uniforms looking for insects in the grass who took to their heels in terror when they saw them; and a second time by some old woodcutters carrying bundles of dry branches on their heads, who stood brazenly staring at them, baring their toothless gums in a foolish smile and throwing stones at them before disappearing in the dense undergrowth.

One afternoon when Melissa came back from shopping in the city,

Bob took an antelope skin from her car and spread it out on the grass. They were so engrossed in each other they didn't notice a female bush-buck come out of the underbrush into the little clearing and slowly approach them—out of curiosity, or perhaps attracted by the odor of the freshly tanned antelope skin. When Melissa saw the gazelle, she whispered to Bob to turn around very slowly, and for a moment they were able to see the marvelous image of the animal illuminated by the light filtering through the foliage, until its eyes gleamed in sudden panic, and with one incredibly agile leap, it disappeared into the bush.

Two-Year Wanderers

THE ECHOES of recent political events were somewhat muffled by the time they reached the residential district of Langata, perhaps because of the distance, or because of the dense layer of fog that covered the lower slopes of the Ngong Hills. The old farmers or retired "white hunters" who lived there paid less attention to political developments than to the sound of the wind in the acacias, which might be a sign of a change in the weather; as the drought grew more severe, the antelopes broke through their fences and ate up their flowers and vegetables, and lions could be heard at night, prowling about behind the wire fence of the Park. Many ex-colonials, isolated on their little farms during the Emergency, had gone through some bad moments, and were not about to be frightened because two or three bombs went off in Nairobi, tainting the blue sky with faint shreds of smoke—like the thin clouds of smoke from the fires lighted by the Masai shepherds, as they settled down for the night on the hills.

Alex Townsend-Reeves, however, who had not lived through the worst moments of the Emergency, since he had fled to London very early on, saw the gravity of the situation much more clearly than the others. Though his mind floated almost continually in an alcoholic

258

haze, he remained sufficiently lucid to sense that those symptoms of unrest might lead, at any moment, to a full-scale rebellion. The day the bombs went off in the bus station, Alex was in the Muthaiga Club when he heard the news. He was leaning on the bar counter in the gentlemen's lounge downing a mug of Pimm's: "This," he said, raising his drink, "is the end of Happy Valley and the beginning of a second state of Emergency that could have more serious consequences than the first one." Alex's drunken remark about a Second Emergency became common currency in the city.

The possibility that Muriuki might take power was viewed with horror, not only by the white establishment but also by the new African bourgeoisie, which preferred to cling to the ruling principles of the old colonial system rather than fall into the clutches of a group of Africans with a radical ideology and a thirst for revenge. To Alex, it all seemed a joke in bad taste; after having escaped unharmed—although with a certain loss of prestige—from the first one, destiny was putting him to yet another test: He now was older, and he was not prepared to pack up bag and baggage and start life over somewhere else; his future was indissolubly linked to that of this country—and where could he go? He had many debts and very few assets.

These worries had coincided with one of the worst crises of his marital career. His wife was terribly nervous and aggressive these days, and appeared to enjoy complicating his life on the slightest pretext. Although his British sense of respect for privacy restrained him from asking her why she was so tense and touchy, the reason was not that difficult to guess; though Guni had done everything humanly possible—and perhaps even a bit more—to try to attract the new ecologist, that Fender fellow, he hadn't paid the least attention to her. Alex knew that Guni had phoned Fender again and again, without having her calls returned; and by sheer coincidence—since the downtown section of Nairobi was so small—he had seen his wife prowling about the Hilton like a hungry lioness. The worst of it was that he was the one who was paying for this unrequited passion: early in the morning Guni would slip down under the sheets, contrive to stimulate his virility by means both licit and illicit, and consummate her little act of self-rape. Alex had sometimes heard it said that when certain men made love, they sometimes used the woman only as a means of masturbating, but this woman had always used him like a puppet, leaving him dry and as deflated as a punctured rubber dummy.

That early-morning sexual pantomime was often grotesque: More than once, Guni feigned spasms and moaned with pleasure, as though she had reached orgasm; when Alex lay back and relaxed with a vague smile of satisfaction, her expression would suddenly change and she would laugh uproariously or accuse him and insult him, but always taunting him because he didn't know how to make love and was half-impotent. The energy Guni brought to these acts of cruelty left poor Alex shattered and wondering what he could have done to arouse such hatred. Could she possibly think that he was the one who had killed her former lover, John Murphy, or hired someone to kill him?

Her fury preyed on Alex so obsessively that he unconsciously began to feel outrage at Bob Fender, and to feel as frustrated as Guni at Bob's lack of interest in her. Who did that imbecile think he was? He wasn't bothered so much that Bob hadn't shown any desire to occupy John's place in Guni's heart, contrary to everyone's predictions, as by the fact that that dolt was permitting himself the luxury of snubbing a woman from the very top drawer of society, married to a Townsend-Reeves no less, a relative, albeit a distant one, of the English royal family. An insignificant ecologist, a third-rate scientist, and even more humiliating, an American to boot!

When Alex finally learned the real reason for Fender's attitude—Bob's relationship with Melissa Turner (in Nairobi such things sooner or later became common gossip)—he was even more outraged. What did that woman, who looked like a cheap little china doll, have that his wife didn't? Alex had met her husband, that arrogant coffee merchant, at a polo match and the man had aroused his instant antipathy and scorn. And, he, Alex, could have an opportunity to tell the pitifully misled Fender what he thought about that sinister little couple.

One night Lucio Luz, who had appointed himself Bob's guide to nightlife in Nairobi, dragged Bob to the Casino, though Bob could hardly tell the difference between a roulette table and a blackjack table. The International Casino of Nairobi was located near the main street, Uhuru, right in back of the Mansarde Hotel, the usual stopping-off place of the one and only Bruno Toffani. Bob was surprised at the smoke-filled atmosphere and the tension in the air around the gaming tables. The flashily dressed and cosmopolitan clientele might be found in any of the great European casinos. But he was more surprised, the moment he entered, to see the Counselor of the American Embassy, Ralph Maguire, sitting hunched over at a roulette table and so absorbed in the game—eagerly counting his chips, and scrawling bets and combinations on a little piece of paper that shook in his hands—that he didn't even recognize Bob when he passed.

"I wouldn't have recognized him either, with this dissolute aspect; he looks very different from the unbending diplomat who comes every day to the Embassy, impeccably dressed, almost too correct and prudish."

"Well, you see, as we say in Spanish, 'wearing the habit doesn't make you a monk.' I knew that Maguire often played on the sly in big poker games organized by the Indian traders, but for some time now, he's been gambling openly. It may sound odd, but since Murphy's death, I think Maguire has been showing the other side of his personality."

"What's the reason for this change of image?"

"Because of his strong personality, John completely overshadowed Maguire, both socially and professionally. As you well know, the Ambassador is not in very good terms with his deputy. Since the beginning, they felt a mutual scorn and mistrust for each other. Even if John was below Maguire in diplomatic ranking, Poire always trusted John and discussed all sorts of important business with him. Maguire then felt relegated and took revenge by hiding interesting information from his boss and organizing complicated secret operations Poire never deigned to participate in."

"How do you know all this, not through Maguire himself, I suppose?"

"In Nairobi you end up knowing everything; for some time, I was involved with an Austrian nurse, from "The Flying Doctors," who lived in the Langata area, just opposite the house of an interesting British character, called Seago, who apparently has masterminded the British intelligence operations since the time of the Second World War. Almost every afternoon, I could see Seago and Maguire chatting conspiratorially over tea, in the veranda overlooking the Athi plains."

At that moment Alex Townsend-Reeves, who had been playing at another table, came to say hello, and suggested that they have a drink in the bar. But Lucio was tempted to try his luck at blackjack—there were several quite attractive female croupiers in the Casino—and Alex and Bob went on to the bar without him.

"I say," Alex commented, drawing his stool closer to Bob's, "since the last time we saw each other at the New Stanley, it seems as though you don't want to have anything more to do with us. My wife has phoned you several times at the hotel to invite you to dinner, but you never returned her calls."

Bob mumbled a vague excuse about his crowded schedule at the Conference and how tired he was at the end of the day.

"Come on, don't hand me that," Alex answered with a knowing smile. "I've learned that you find the time to visit certain friends of yours in Muthaiga, almost every afternoon."

"If you're referring to the Turners," Bob said, flushing, "I might remind you that they don't live in Muthaiga but in Rosslyn, and that their house happens to be very close to the UNICORN buildings where the taskforce meetings on firewood I attend every day are held."

"Firewood, firewood," Alex repeated. He seemed drunker than usual. "As though all of us hadn't been thirty years old once upon a time too. From the very first days of the colony, the siesta hour has always been the favorite one for assignations, for the simple reason that that's when the servants retire to their quarters to rest. Don't try to teach an old fox like me how to steal hens!"

Bob was shocked: He did not feel like discussing the details of his love life with someone he barely knew, someone whose wife had been trying to seduce him since the first day they met. But Alex took advantage of Bob's silence to go on:

"Look, Fender, you may tell me it's none of my business, but if I were you, I'd be more careful about the people I chose for friends. Why hang around with those vulgar people in Muthaiga? They're a pack of parvenu traders and newcomers, what we call two-year wanderers around here. Remember that Kenya is still 'a sunny place for shady people.' There are still lots of drifters who've come here from heaven knows where, or for heaven knows what reasons, and who soon disappear just as mysteriously, maybe leaving a sting and a couple of months' unpaid rent behind them. Mrs. Turner may be an attractive woman, in her own way, but allow me to tell you, in all confidence, that her husband doesn't have any too good a reputation in the business world; they say that some of the coffee he deals in comes from the contraband traffic with Uganda."

"I'm afraid," Bob interrupted him curtly, "that you're breaking one of the rules of etiquette you British are so fond of by making personal remarks about people you scarcely know. And furthermore, when I need references concerning my friends, I'll ask for them myself."

Alex let out a loud but artificial laugh, and gave Bob a slap on the back.

"Come on, don't be angry. There's no need to get your back up. Let's drop the subject of the Turners, if it upsets you so. Practically all of us who are of the right sort, with a certain social standing and interests not unlike your own, the kind of people you'd enjoy spending time with, live in Langata and Karen. We're close to nature, close to the Park; every night we can hear lions coughing, and the people who live in that section have always been close to wildlife, to the land; they're former farmers, old white hunters, writers perhaps, or naturalists, the people John Murphy spent his time with, people who are your sort."

Alex reached for his glass, and had a long swig; he went on, in a different tone. "And now, if you've gotten over being angry, I'm going to tell you something, very confidentially. Guni, my wife, is going through a bad time right now; she's very nervous and depressed. It's no secret to anybody that she had a very close relationship with John Murphy," he added, staring at the floor, "and his death affected her terribly. I think that when she first saw you, knowing that you and John had been at the university together and that the two of you had similar backgrounds and similar tastes, she thought, almost unconsciously, that she could somehow bring the friendship that had been so tragically interrupted by his accident back to life with you. . . ."

Alex was so overcome with emotion he was unable to go on. Big tears welled up in his eyes, which were bloodshot from liquor; a tear overflowed and rolled down to the tip of his nose. Bob didn't know what to say; there was something pathetic about the man's plea for help, despite the reek of alcohol on his breath and the scabrous tone of the conversation.

"But what is it you think that I can do?"

"I don't know, I really don't know," Alex answered, wiping his nose with the back of his hand. "But if you'd offer Guni a little friendship and share some of your time with her, I'm certain she'd feel comforted. Take her to lunch one day, or for a drive through the park; you'll see that she's an exceptional woman. And I assure you that I wouldn't have any objection. I've seen too much and lived too long to start being a possessive, jealous husband at this late date."

263

They were obliged to interrupt their conversation; Lucio Luz was heading toward the bar after having lost several hundred shillings. Alex stood them all another round of drinks and took advantage of the convivial moment to invite them to dinner at his house the following evening. Bob didn't have the heart to decline the invitation.

"What were you and Townsend-Reeves plotting together tonight?" Lucio asked as he was driving Bob back to his hotel. "I saw that the two of you were having a real heart-to-heart talk."

"Well, believe it or not," Bob sighed, "he was reproaching me for not paying enough attention to his wife. Since John Murphy and I were friends, and since she had an intense relationship with John, it seemed only natural to him that I should take John's place...."

"And how does that strike you? You agreed, of course?"

"You're wrong there. Guni is an attractive woman, but I don't care for the idea of substituting for my dead friend, especially in an affair of the heart. What's more, ever since I've arrived in Nairobi, I've had the feeling that I'm living a borrowed life. The work they've found for me to do, the friends I've met and all the experiences I've had—it seems to me that I'm living my whole life here inside somebody else's skin."

"I wouldn't make such a big deal out of it. As I mentioned before, John was a man with a strong personality: Being his friend, and arriving here just a few days after his death, it's reasonable for people to assume you would inherit some of his relationships, good and bad. People might even think you've taken over *all* of John's concerns, including his penchant for nosing around and playing at being a secret agent."

"I wish to God he'd kept to ecology," Bob said.

"I found some of his eccentricities hard to understand, his friendship, for instance, with that insolent nigger who likes people to call him Ndume. But if you have followed in John's footsteps, with some good stretches and some rough ones, why don't you go ahead and take advantage of the good ones? If you feel like having a go with that smashing German woman, and if that lily-livered Englishman doesn't object, what's stopping you? If anybody told me that he wouldn't have to repeat it twice."

264

The Second Emergency

DURING HIS NUMEROUS MARRIAGES Alex Townsend-Reeves had managed to maintain a certain style of sober elegance in the residence he had inherited from his uncle, Lord Delaware, at the outskirts of Nairobi. Had he bowed to the tastes of his various wives—each of whom had been of a different nationality—and acquired new things and new furniture with each female incumbent—the house would have become a kind of international bazaar. The residence was located on magnificent property, on the border between the Langata district and the Karen area, with a large garden, a greenhouse, a guest house, several large, perfectly kept stables, and a soft dirt practice track for the horses. The house itself was becoming shabby, but had retained the look of an old colonial mansion; inside there were no mounted trophies, no African folk art; nothing but signed paintings— a few empty places could be seen on the walls, witness to times when he had been hard-pressed by creditors—and Victorian mahogany and rosewood furniture, in the tradition of the best British country residences.

Lucio Luz had come to pick Bob up at his hotel, and although they got lost for a while in the labyrinth of little roads and dirt trails, they eventually found their way up to the house, thanks to the row of acetylene lanterns the servants had lighted all along the gravel drive that led to the house. That night Alex had invited—in Bob's honor perhaps—the most select and picturesque of the Nairobi fauna: As the pièce de résistance there was the famous Peter Malone, the white ex-minister of one of the first cabinets after independence; despite his cardboard-looking skin, his great shiny bald pate and the Franciscan-friar's fringe of hair across the back of his neck (which made him look a little like a ventriloquist's dummy), Malone had enormous vitality and energy; he was still involved in any number of schemes and engaged in several sports, of which his favorite was courting women much younger than he. He had, according to what people said, a special sense of smell—like vultures—that enabled him to detect the first symptoms of a marriage that was falling apart, and began to hover about its victims, diving down to feast on the remains as soon as the definite break took place. With his hyena smile and his long nose, like a bird of prey, he would console the disillusioned woman, offering her understanding and company.

Nobody knew for certain how far he got, but he never lacked for the choicest female company, and was given to embracing and affectionately fondling his lady friends, like the sly priest who takes advantage of the embrace of condolence to feel the widow's breasts. That night he was accompanied by a beautiful, young, svelte Norwegian girl, with very black hair and intense blue eyes; the girl had smoked several very strong joints before arriving, and hardly opened her mouth during dinner.

Also present were Jean-Humbert and Vivienne d'Alembert, a French prince and princess of dubious lineage, who had arrived in Africa quite some time before, escaping from the bankruptcy of values of *la vieille France*, and perhaps from some personal, less historical bankruptcy as well. The Prince was a tiny but well-proportioned man, like a miniature, and held his glass of sherry in just two fingers, the better to display the rings with ducal seals on the other fingers; when something did not please him, he thrust his lips forward in a tight little pout. The Princess had a masculine manner and was slightly bow-legged from having ridden horseback a great deal, but her features were regular, and her deep-set black eyes stared at Bob as brazenly as though she were measuring him to see if he would fit in her bed.

"Have you noticed how the Princess is staring at you?" Lucio whispered in Bob's ear. "Women are always running after you. What's your secret?"

"Is she *really* a princess?" Bob whispered back, quite impressed.

"In the colonies, everyone passes himself off as whatever he cares to; these European aristocrats add a new title to their names every time they cross a frontier, and just think how many countries those two must have gone through to get here," Lucio answered.

And finally, there were also a genuine Austrian count and countess, Mathias and Rosvita Rosbingratz. He was a giant of a man who had to duck his head to pass through doorways; she was thin and fragile, like a Sevres porcelain. From a very early age Count Rosbingratz had declared a holy war on all species of animals, particularly those that were scarcest and most endangered, and had traveled halfway round the world to hunt and take fabulous trophies; as he admitted, with pride, the inclusion of several species on the list of protected or extinct animals was due to his marksmanship. One would have thought that he would be a wonderful raconteur, brimming over with tales of exciting encounters with wild beasts and descriptions of exotic places, but in reality the Count seemed to have been left speechless by his own hunting exploits and deafened by rifle detonations. During the entire evening he opened his mouth just once, to say, "Even today, on a two-month safari, it's easier to down a hundred-pounder than a buffalo whose horns are in the book." This may have been perfectly true, but it had nothing whatsoever to do with what was being discussed at that particular moment.

Another guest, who arrived after they had sat down at the table, was a woman, middle-aged but well preserved, named Leda Lesbos, the widow of a Greek businessman with a colossal fortune. She wore a long dress with a great many ruffles and a starched stand-up collar; it gave her a certain resemblance to Snow White's wicked stepmother.

Dinner was served in a huge dining room, lighted only by candles in a sumptuous candelabra. Large picture windows opened onto a vast terrace and an immense impeccable lawn; the garden was ingeniously lighted so that the century-old trees, draped with moss and lichens, stood out, ghostlike in the night mist. Breaking the rules of precedence, Guni had seated Bob on one side of her and the Austrian count on the other, thus arousing the jealousy of the French prince, who felt his rank had been slighted; the Prince sat through dinner pouting and making conspiratorial gestures in the direction of Lucio Luz, who, as Chargé d'Affaires, also deserved a more important place at table, although he for his part couldn't have cared less. The lady of the house—who looked especially beautiful that night, in a white dress that set off her deep tan to perfection—fluttered around Bob, like a moth around a lamp, trying to attract his attention and laughing at everything he said.

Dinner went smoothly until the conversation turned, inevitably, to the latest political events and the future of the country. Alex had been sitting lethargically at one end of the table, concerned only with seeing that the waiters kept everyone's wine glass, including his own, filled at all times. Hearing the first comments on the political situa-

267

tion, he gave a violent start as though some secret inner spring had been released, and vehemently joined in the discussion. Someone mentioned the idea of a Second Emergency, using the phrase Alex was proud to have coined.

"If we wish to compare the present situation with that prior to independence," Alex said, tapping his glass with his knife to attract everyone's attention, "the first thing that we must remember is that back then the British Government, faced with the need to control the insurrection, could count on a perfectly disciplined army, with officers and men trained and battle-hardened by the campaigns of the Second World War. Thanks to that army, we were able to win without difficulty. But then the British Government arbitrarily decided to hand the colony over to the leaders of the rebellion. Because, let us make no mistake about it," he went on, his bloodshot eyes gleaming and his voice hoarse with excitement, "what today goes by the name of the war of liberation was really a walkover for us. We jailed their leaders and petty chieftains, we drove them out of the cities, we exterminated them in the forest, we cleaned them out of the fields"—to underline his words, he made a sweeping gesture, knocking over a glass of wine and spilling it on the dress of the widow, Mrs. Lesbos, who was seated on his right. Guni darted a poisonous look in his direction. Alex went on doggedly:

"They make me laugh when they talk about the gallant Mau Mau freedom fighters. Where were they? Most of them dead, or in prison, and the few remaining ones wandering through the woods dressed in rags and eating roots and berries like the giant forest hogs. Because, even though the English authorities wanted to exaggerate the danger that the guerrilla fighters represented and the savagery of their acts, and to demonstrate that this campaign was a struggle of the civilized world against barbarism, other than maiming a few cows and burning the harvests, the truth of the matter is that the rebels killed very few Europeans; perhaps some thirty all told, whereas on the rebels' side around ten thousand died and ninety thousand were imprisoned. Those are the figures, and they speak for themselves."

Although no one dared to interrupt this heated outburst, there were winks and smiles exchanged across the table, since all of them knew that at the very first signs of the outbreak of a rebellion he had cleared out of the country. They did not know that during his voluntary exile, Alex regularly received the *East African Standard* at his club in London and read it faithfully every afternoon, to keep himself

268

informed as to what was happening in the former protectorate. The only one who responded was Peter Malone, a man who had played a very active role in the political events of that turbulent era.

"I agree absolutely with Alex that, militarily, it was a clearcut British victory; moreover, it couldn't have been otherwise, since the forces confronting each other in the conflict consisted on the one hand of a modern army, well-armed and supplied, and on the other of a group of guerrilla fighters armed only with shotguns and homemade pistols, which more often than not exploded in the faces of the men using them; and despite the fact that they were better acquainted with the trails through the bush and had the support of the civilian population, especially in the Kikuyu areas, there was very little they could do when they came face to face with the experienced platoons of the King's Rifles.

"Nonetheless"—Peter Malone paused to drink a sip of wine, barely parting his lips—"nonetheless, while the numbers of victims of the conflict that you've cited are quite accurate, you've forgotten to mention the fact that, along with the relatively few casualties among white army personnel and civilians, the number of *African* troops loyal to the British Government who were killed was more than two thousand. All of which is proof, yet again, that these 'wars of independence' turn out to be civil wars between the natives themselves rather than an armed conflict between the colonial power and the liberation movements."

An attempt on the part of Jean-Humbert d'Alembert to draw a comparison between the Emergency era in Kenya and the French Revolution was rudely interrupted by Alex Townsend-Reeves, eager to take the floor again. The air was laden with the smell of food and the smoke from the men's cigars; the candelabra were dripping great hot drops of wax onto the gleaming varnished tabletop without anyone making the slightest effort to do anything about it. The women, in accordance with traditional British custom, retired to the drawing room while the men stayed on at the table to enjoy their port; although, in view of the decadence into which traditional customs had fallen, the ladies were more likely to be sniffing a line of coca than powdering their noses.

"Everything you've been saying strikes me as most interesting," said Alex, "but what I still can't understand is why, after having won such a decisive victory over them, the British Government decided that the time had come to hand the country over to the rebels. If we hadn't been so magnanimous then, perhaps we would not now be on the brink of seeing a character like Muriuki seize power. He has managed to combine the corruption of the present Government with a Marxist-radical ideology: A winning combination if ever there was one! I assure you that if that bird comes to power, all of us sitting around this table—now that the ladies have left I feel free to say it—are going to be hunted down like rats. We're in for difficult times, and I'm not surprised that the expression 'Second Emergency' has become so popular."

Malone interrupted this tirade. "May I say that I'm not at all certain that when J. M. comes to power—if in fact he does—this presupposes a total rupture with everything that has gone before, and that they're going to throw all us whites into the sea. When the President was established in power, the old colonials thought then, too, that it was the end of the world, yet as you can see we're still here. The Africans know that they need us, and don't forget that Muriuki, apart from being an ambitious and intelligent man, is first and foremost a Kikuyu, and in his tribe what predominates in the end is their practical side, their sense of business, above and beyond any other political or ideological consideration. I might remind you that the President, himself, was accused of being the spiritual leader of the Mau Mau and he was imprisoned and exiled. And yet, once in power, he's given evidence of being a more moderate and pro-Western man than many of us ever dreamed he would be."

This brought forth an avalanche of argument, since the subject of the President's possible participation in the Mau Mau rebellion, with its sordid oaths and acts of cruelty, was a favorite topic of discussion among the Europeans. Opinion fell into three categories.

One group believed that the President, finding himself unable to reach power by any other means, had created the Mau Mau sect and directed its activities, even after he was imprisoned.

A second group believed that despite having played the principal political role in the fight for independence, he had never been involved in the secret activities of the Mau Mau, and in fact would have disavowed them.

The intermediate, or eclectic, position was that the President, who for obvious reasons had not directed the activities of the Mau Mau— he had been put in prison the very night that the State of Emergency was declared—had nonetheless acted as their spiritual leader, and knew all about their rituals and activities.

Unfortunately, just as these interesting theories were beginning to take shape at various corners of the table amid the general din (everybody was talking at once) Guni burst into the dining room; they had talked long enough about politics and the ladies requested their company. The men all rose from the table, except Alex. He had collapsed in his chair, the victim of his oratorical excesses, and was muttering incoherently about the Mau Mau and the Second Emergency, while great drops of hot wax from the candelabra fell in his outstretched hands, apparently not bothering him in the least.

As usually happens in such situations, efforts to get the party going again in the living room were fruitless, though Guni had lowered all the lights and put on soft music to create a more intimate atmosphere. The guests soon left one by one, Lucio first, then Peter Malone, who carried his limp young girlfriend out in his arms—she had been lying half-stoned on a sofa after one last joint. The French prince was still pouting because they had "seated him badly" and had not let him get a word in edgewise at the table, something that, by this time, he must have become quite accustomed to, since almost everything he said was utter nonsense. His wife had struck up a lively conversation with Bob, doing her best to hypnotize him with her great, dark eyes; the Prince gestured to her to rise to her feet and leave with him; he looked like an hysterical schoolmistress.

The Rosbingratzes stayed longest, not because they wanted to but because they hadn't tumbled to the fact that the party was over; when the Count at last managed to lift his gigantic frame, he stepped out onto the terrace for a moment, murmuring: "It's a good moonlit night, just right for waiting in ambush for a leopard, though to tell the truth I wouldn't like to have to track one of those wounded felines through the forest, what with this terrible fog." Outside the summit of the hills was perfectly clear, with all the folds in the terrain and even the trails and the arroyos standing out sharply in the moonlight, while down below, as though cut sharply in half by a pair of scissors, a dense fog covered the entire plain.

Bob realized that he was now alone with Guni; the living room was half in shadow; the reflection of the flames from the fireplace crept over the thick rug. If it was dangerous to track a raging feline through the dense forest, it was no less perilous to remain in this intimate atmosphere with a woman whose pride was hurt and who was suffering from a chronic lack of sexual satisfaction, while her husband was sleeping himself sober in the next room. Bob would have chosen a prudent retreat, but since Lucio had slipped out without a word, he had been left with no means of transportation; it was clear that Guni would be obliged to drive him back to his hotel in her car, a stratagem that she had perhaps carefully planned. When she came back downstairs with the keys of the car, her face had the happy expression of an adolescent whose parents have just given her permission to go out at night for the first time.

They went back into the dining room. Alex was still there, toppled over onto the table, snoring; Guni very carefully snuffed out the wicks of the candles, floating now in pools of melted wax and, taking her husband by the arms, pushed him gently back into his chair and planted a kiss on his forehead. The ritual reminded Bob of a wake.

They climbed into an old Bentley and Guni took off at top speed with all the windows open; a brisk breeze cleared their heads of the fumes of wine and smoke. Though it was not easy for Bob to tell which way they were going—despite the moonlight, so bright that it made the headlamps of the car almost unnecessary, the roads were still unfamiliar to him—he thought that Guni was taking a roundabout way back to Nairobi.

The sand trail crossed through the middle of a grazing ground of tall, dry grass, where the headlights made strange traceries; it was a great open space free of fog that he and Lucio had not crossed on their way to the house; and the profile of the hills, so close that it seemed he could reach out and touch them, was to their right now, not behind them. Before he could ask where they were going, Guni had turned off along a little dirt road and braked to a stop amid a clump of bushes. The moonlit brightness of the night was filtered through branches. Bob, who had been preoccupied with inventing a thousand plans to keep Guni from dragging him to a discotheque or going up to his room in the hotel for a drink, suddenly found himself unable to resist that rape in the middle of the countryside. Everything was suddenly so familiar—the smell of dry, scorched grass, the fragrance of the eucalyptus, the branches of the bushes nearly creeping through the windows of the car—and yet so different; through a fog of alcohol, he remembered his first meeting with Guni in the cemetery, his walk along the beach, the electric ray; this merged with Melissa's very pale face as she was about to climax, the clearing in the forest of Karura, and the antelope approaching them as the sun warmed his bare back.

The German woman's strong, agile fingers had untied his tie and

272

unbuttoned his shirt, and her tongue began to brush his nipples and navel as it traveled downward; it was a hard, slightly rasping tongue, but skillful, provoking a wave of sheer, brute pleasure. The woman's skin was sleek, and Bob slipped one finger across the soft, delicate hair at the back of her neck, then traced the line of her throat down to her breasts, which swelled in his hands, warm and hard. But Guni had managed to unbuckle his belt and her tongue searched avidly about once again; Bob's back stiffened and his whole body tensed, as though trying to pierce that medusan tongue with his penis.

He was about to let himself go when he looked up and saw that the windshield of the car was alive with horrible deformed faces, lips pressed against the glass in monstrous grimaces. Were they too the phantoms of his brain projected onto the glass or creatures of flesh and blood? Was this the same nightmare of the great aquarium, teeming with evil tadpoles and humanoid sea bream with slit lips, that had come to haunt him in the forest of Langata? No. They were real. A hideous black hand thrust itself through the car window and came to rest on Guni's white shoulder. She gave a start and instantly turned on the headlights. The vapor blurred the windshield, and monstrously enlarged shadows projected onto the foliage. The terrifying faces belonged to a group of vagabonds in rags and tatters that surrounded the car; their eyes—smiling and cruel—reflected the light.

Bob sat petrified, unable to react, as though his whole body had stiffened in a panicked erection. But Guni remained admirably cool and collected; seeing her lebensraum threatened by the beggars crowded around the car, she reacted as quickly as though mounting a blitzkrieg: She threw the car in gear as she bit down hard on the hand of the creature who had reached through the window and was trying to seize the steering wheel. She took off at top speed, sending a pair of bandits who had climbed up onto the hood flying through the air; the branches of the bushes, whipped violently backward as the car passed by, knocked out the rest of their pursuers, and just before the car skidded back onto the sand trail, there was a sinister crunching noise, which might have been broken branches or broken bones.

Beneath the clear, cold moon, a white Bentley, its passengers completely naked, majestically crossed the crackling grazing ground, heading for the hills.

PART SIX

The Grass Rains

WHEN ALEX WOKE UP the next morning—despite his hangover—he had an unusual feeling of well-being; Guni was sleeping like a log at his side, and the serenity of her face led him to suppose that his wife might have finally found what she was looking for. He inhaled with the greatest pleasure the air coming in through the window: clean, pure air, just a little cooler than the day before, with a smell of damp dust and scorched grass that presaged the arrival of the rainy season, the grass rains of early October.

In his sleep he thought he heard the sound of a car on the gravel drive. The bathroom window overlooked the rear of the garden and the esplanade where cars were parked. Getting out of bed, he went to have a look out, walking on tiptoe not to wake Guni. All he could see was their labrador Tinka's two puppies playing on the lawn, and near the porch, the faithful Kamanthe, polishing the fenders of the Bentley; but leaning a little farther out the window, he saw the hood of a black Mercedes parked on the esplanade. He was apprehensive: Who could be visiting him at this early hour?

He walked slowly down the stairs that led to the entry hall, but as he went past the bar he was unable to resist the temptation to pour himself a straight vodka over ice, a drink that always went down well in the morning. As he stepped into the living room he almost dropped the glass on the floor; stretched out on a sofa, calmly reading the paper, was none other than Joseph Muriuki. Muriuki raised his eyes from the paper, and without even rising to his feet, extended an arm in his famous gesture of greeting.

"I apologize for having burst in on you like this, but as you know, I live not very far from here, and it occurred to me that the quickest way to talk over certain subjects of mutual interest to us was to come over to see you."

"Of course, I quite understand," Alex stammered. "My door is always open to all my neighbors in this district . . . particularly such a distinguished person as yourself."

"Please know that I told the servants not to disturb you if you weren't up and about yet, but I'm not certain that they heard, since at the very sight of me they took to their heels as though they'd run into the Devil himself."

The living room did appear to have been suddenly abandoned in the midst of being tidied: There were still dirty glasses and ashtrays from the evening before stacked on a table, a dustcloth tossed on the floor, and a feather duster left lying on one of the shelves. The sight made Alex smile; he regained his composure.

"I trust you'll excuse my servants. I'm sure you're aware of the tension that is gripping the country at present, and your own increasingly important role in political developments at this moment is too well known not to arouse a sacred respect for you among these humble people."

"Ah, yes, of course," Ndume replied, smiling in turn. "I'm the one who's provoking—what's the expression?—ah, yes, a Second Emergency; that's your favorite phrase, right? It's certainly an appealing idea, not only to your Europeans, but also to that gang of African thieves who see their interests threatened the moment that anyone dares to speak out for a little justice and social progress. So the country is faced with a Second Emergency, is it?"

Alex had flushed to the tips of his ears: How could this scoundrel be so well informed? Could he have spies among the servants—which

278

happened frequently during the first Emergency? Or could some hypocrite like Peter Malone—who had always played a double game at the political gaming table—have gone to him with the story?

"However, my dear friend," Muriuki went on, "the thought may not have occurred to you that these moments of tension and upheaval might have a positive side, if one takes them as a sign of the struggle of a people aspiring to genuine independence, opening its wings in search of freedom. You, I am told, are a nature lover; undoubtedly you know the meaning of the word *emergence* in the biological sense: the passage from the embryonic state to that of the mature adult—as in the case, for instance, of dragonflies?"

"Hmmm: Emergence-emergency. That's an interesting concept that hadn't occurred to me. The two words do complement each other, inasmuch as every change of state, every metamorphosis, implies a certain painful rending and tearing."

"But," said Muriuki, "it will all turn out to have been worth it if the nation finally succeeds in escaping from its cocoon and takes wing. It seems to me that not only Kenya, but also many other African countries whose ideals of justice have been frustrated stand in need of a second emergence. Otherwise, I fear that like the larva that cannot break through the cocoon, they will be fated to grow stiff and cramped in the hard shell that confines them, and will eventually die."

As he listened to Muriuki, Alex tried to guess the reason for his visit. At a moment when the political situation was close to the boiling point, when each minute and each movement of a single pawn counted in order to win the political game, Muriuki would not have wasted half a morning coming to his house to deliver a homily on the similarities between the words *emergence* and *emergency*. The African also was perfectly aware that each minute that went by made Alex more nervous, but he was enjoying the game, and employing a typical Kikuyu stratagem: Before getting to the real subject he wished to discuss, he brought up a secondary problem to confuse his adversary even further.

"Although I came here to speak to you of another very important matter, I should like to take advantage of my visit to put you on your guard against certain inquiries being carried out by Judge McGredy concerning the death of John Murphy, the American diplomat who, as you know, was killed on Mackinnon Road as he was going down to Malindi."

"To Malindi?" Alex answered, as though he'd been bitten by a poisonous snake. "Why have the authorities been so certain that he was going to Malindi? Mackinnon Road, as you know, is a shortcut with many side roads leading off to the coast and to the interior; that's why it's so frequently used by hunters, charcoal smugglers, poachers. . . . As far as I know, John never told anybody where he was headed. Knowing Murphy, it's more than likely that he didn't know himself; every so often he gave in to his adventurous and romantic inclinations and went wandering about in the most remote places—not forgetting, of course, to gather information here and there that might prove to be useful to his Embassy. And don't ask me if the information was ecological or political—might it not have been both?"

"Quite possibly. Murphy was a many-faceted man," Muriuki answered with a smile.

"I know that people have been speculating wildly about Murphy's accident, but I'm of the opinion that they're doing so just to add some excitement to their lives; I am convinced that it was simply what it appears to be: an accident. I might, however, accept the *possibility* that he had a run-in with some of the criminal types who use those shortcuts at night and who immediately fled from the scene after they'd collided with Murphy's car; though there's nothing to prove it, I think that that's what probably happened, if one assumes there had been foul play."

"It's curious that we've arrived at very similar conclusions," Muriuki commented. "But at this point you and I are the principal suspects with regard to this *accident*. Or to be more precise, I'm the prime suspect and you're number two. That's why I've come to warn you. At the moment, Bwana Maximum, at the instigation of Munyoka, is leaving no stone unturned, trying to prove that I'm the one behind the whole incident; that would be a very convenient excuse to ruin my name and discredit me politically. But sooner or later Mc-Gredy is going to get tired of not finding any evidence against me—and I can assure you in advance that he's never going to find any—and since you're second on the list of suspects, you'd best start preparing your defense. So don't say I haven't given you fair warning!"

Muriuki said this with such conviction that it sounded like an accusation.

"How can you be so sure that they're going to go after *me*?" Alex's voice trembled with indignation. "You yourself have said that you're the prime suspect, and you know very well that when the authorities want to find evidence against someone, they find it, especially in this country."

"Not in my case. I assure you that it would be extremely easy for me to prove that neither I nor any of my men would ever have made an attempt on Murphy's life. . . .That would have been killing the goose that laid the golden eggs," he added meaningfully.

"I don't follow you. What is it you're trying to tell me?"

"Look, Alex, I think that you and I are going to reach an understanding about certain things, so I don't mind telling you something that up to now has been a carefully guarded secret: Murphy was on our side." Seeing the look of utter astonishment on Alex's face, he added, "He was one of us. Perhaps at the very beginning, when he made friends with us, he was acting under instructions from his Government to gather information about the opposition, but I assure you that in the end he became our adviser and confidant, because he was convinced that our cause was just. So what reason would we have had for killing him?"

Alex was speechless, not so much because of this surprising revelation—if it was in fact true—but because he couldn't imagine what J. M. wanted of him: Why was he making *him* a party to such momentous secrets?

"Would you mind if we took a walk around the garden?" asked Muriuki. "We ought to take advantage of the few days of good weather ahead of us, for those clouds rolling in from the east are a sure sign that the seasons are changing. And it's about time the grass rains began. It's said that they bring good luck."

Muriuki expressed interest in seeking the stables and the training track; this did not surprise Alex, knowing how fond Muriuki was of horse racing. But they had taken only a few steps along the path to the stables when J. M. explained to Alex, in the most straightforward and specific terms, exactly what he wanted of him. J. M. knew that Alex kept in the bay at Watamu a boat with a fairly deep draft—an old fishing dhow that he had renovated—which Muriuki needed to transport a delicate shipment, to be unloaded from another larger boat on the open sea and brought to a deserted beach somewhere along the coast. Before Alex could tell him whether he was willing to carry out such a mission, Muriuki quickly explained the details of the operation to him: The boat from which he was to unload the shipment would anchor a few miles offshore from the Kilifi inlet, where there were many small bays and coves, at one of which Bruno Toffani would be waiting; Toffani was in charge of picking up the merchandise and transporting it overland to a safe hiding place. Alex was too shocked to answer, but he realized that by telling him this, Muriuki had compromised him: Muriuki had offered him this dirty work knowing that he would be forced to accept the proposal. And, in case he had any doubts, Muriuki explained why he was counting on Alex to keep his mouth shut.

"Although it may strike you as odd, you and I are in fact in the same boat. For different reasons, we're both on the Government's black list: It's obvious why they want to silence me, and they want to get you out of the way because it bothers them that you continue to maintain a most enjoyable life style, despite your apparent bankruptcy; this strikes them as being the privilege of a culture and a class that they don't enjoy. Basically, it's a question of sheer pettiness. Moreover, they have their eye on the few things you have left; the hotel in Naivaisha, which the Minister of Commerce would like to take over, and the beach house at Watamu, which has caught the eye of Munyoka himself, who's been looking for a private, discreet place on the coast for wild parties."

"How on earth do you know all this?" Alex asked.

"I know, and that's all that matters. Moreover, helping me out with this shipment, which as you may have guessed, is an arms shipment, is not only a patriotic act, but a humanitarian one as well; this Government is old and ossified, and remains in power only through sheer inertia. It's like a wounded animal awaiting the coup de grace to end its suffering. I already have the support of the people and sooner or later I could seize power. But I want above all to avoid a major upheaval; I want to bring down the Government without giving it the time to react, so that the changeover will be less traumatic. Otherwise, a move like that could turn into another civil war."

"However bad things may be in this country, you're asking me to participate in something very serious," Alex said, trying to maintain a shred of dignity. "What would happen to me if I refuse to lend you my boat?"

"You don't have very many alternatives left. You must realize that there are many lives at stake, and my men are well aware of that. No, really, I don't recommend that you turn down my proposal. On the other hand, if you accept it, and we come to power, as we foresee that we will, your situation will be considerably improved. Just think, for example, of what would happen if they were able to put me out of circulation by other means; they'd keep hounding you, using Murphy's accident as an excuse. And you must admit that there are reasons that would point to you as the prime suspect: the relationship between Murphy and your wife, and your connections with dealers in contraband on the coast, such as Toffani. But you may rest assured that if I'm in power, I'll see to it that that particular matter is buried. . . ."

So it was Toffani who had put the whole idea in his head! The damned bastard: He should never have dealt with him! So this was how Toffani repaid all the favors he'd done him. Alex had even loaned Toffani his boat on several occasions to take ivory out of the country.

"The important thing now," Muriuki went on, "is that the operation go smoothly. You'll have to leave for Mombasa today; the cargo might be arriving at any moment." Seeing that Alex still hesitated, Muriuki put before him one last argument, the proof of his psychological acumen: "I suggest that you stop turning the idea over and over in your mind. And don't let it even enter your head that you can get out of it by flying the coop; you've spent your whole life escaping, and the results haven't been all that good. When you took off right in the middle of the Emergency, you earned yourself the enmity of those who later took over the country as officials in the Government, and even your own friends, the old-time colonials, looked down on you for having proved yourself a coward. There are times when one has to take a stand; and you may consider yourself fortunate that I'm offering you the chance to be associated with a new Government, with a country in a state of emergence; for once in your life, you'll be ahead of events instead of being caught up in them."

Alex nodded his head, a gesture of acceptance and defeat. They had now reached the training track where the jockey was warming up a horse. It was a yearling; almost without a sound it galloped slowly over the soft dirt, stretching its slender legs in a wide stride.

"A magnificent piece of horseflesh," Muriuki commented. "Before six months are out, he'll already have made a name for himself."

But Alex was in no mood to watch anything, not even his colt's performance. His eyes, fixed on some distant point of the horizon, filled with tears as his gaze swept over the layer of swollen clouds, as black and ready as ripe figs to burst open, unleashing a downpour at any moment. Through the dark storm clouds the pale sunlight was

283

enveloping the Ngong Hills in a grayish mantle. Was this the good luck that the change of seasons was bringing him? Alex thought to himself. He'd have been better off if the drought had continued!

He hadn't been mistaken when he had suspected that it had been Toffani's idea to get him into this whole mess. In the Mansarde Hotel just a few days before—perhaps the very night that Alex had been talking with Bob in the Casino—there had been a secret meeting between Bruno Toffani and Muriuki's lieutenants to settle the details of the unloading of the shipment. They needed a boat, and had rejected the idea of renting or chartering one from an African owner, who might have ratted to the police at once. It was then that it had occurred to Bruno that Alex was up to his neck in debt and sufficiently compromised by his dealings with smugglers to be forced to agree to any proposal made to him; he had no choice. *Yellow-Tail*, Townsend-Reeves's boat, was the right size, had the necessary range, and enough maneuverability to enter small bays. It looked like an ordinary dhow on the outside—though Alex had had the interior lavishly and luxuriously decorated—and it would not attract attention. Alex had used the boat to go up and down the coast with his friends, anchoring wherever the fancy struck them and drinking themselves blind on the beach.

In the course of that conversation in the Mansarde Hotel, Toffani had also gotten the green light to take action against the Galana team, to make sure that the intractable and ill-tempered manager of the ranch wouldn't come sticking his nose in their business while they were transporting the illegal shipment. If they didn't want to put the entire plan in jeopardy, it would be necessary to neutralize that bunch, who continually patrolled the area through which the arms must be transported—even if they had to kill Lawrence Brown or kidnap some of his clients.

Crocodile Skin

AT THE GALANA tensions were building; Tony Allen and San Miniato continued to have bitter disagreements at the drop of a hat, like two schoolboys with a crush on the same girl; Julia felt flattered by that rivalry and did nothing to stop it. Young Paolo spent most of the day trying to hide from his father to be able to smoke the almost inexhaustible stash of marijuana that he had bought in the village. Lawrence Brown went on obsessively spiriting away the most interesting trophies—rhinos and elephants—like a sleight-of-hand artist making his trained doves and rabbits vanish. But he had not been able to prevent the hunters from downing a few of the animals included in their permit: a pair of good impalas, a lesser kudu that was almost record size, and even an old buffalo, with a huge, rough boss, that San Miniato had downed with a single shot from an ambush alongside a water hole.

Brown had realized that if he let Tony Allen and his client go out hunting together, taking that woman with them, there would inevitably be trouble, and to prevent this he had begun to take the hunters out in two different groups. This afternoon, Brown had taken Massimo San Miniato with him to a spot in the river where they had seen huge crocodiles; he was more familiar than Tony with the twists and bends of the Galana and the sandy banks where the reptiles stretched out to bask in the sun. The big bull crocodiles could grow to ten or twelve feet; it was necessary to hit them square in the brain, otherwise the bullet might ricochet off their hard scaled carapace; even if one of them were wounded, it could reach the water with two vigorous lashes of its tail and sink to the bottom of the river to die, whereupon it would sometimes be devoured by its own fellows.

The other group, consisting of Tony, Julia, and Paolo, had gone out to place bait for the leopard; they were using the hindquarters of an antelope, which they would set out in different places since leopards were also becoming scarce because of the traffic in their skins; they would thus increase the probability that a feline would go for one or the other of the pieces of bait. The Count was not very happy when Tony and Julia left in the same car, but he was reassured that Paolo would be with them; he presumed that the white hunter wouldn't try to dally with his rival's mistress in front of the man's own son. What the Count couldn't have guessed was that Paolo was the worst chaperone in the world, since what he wanted most was to be left by himself, to dip into his sack of grass and have himself a few joints, giving Tony and Julia splendid opportunities to whisper sweet nothings into each other's ears. And Tony was marvelously ingenious at thinking of ways to get rid of his helpers, the bearer and the trackers, sending them on ahead to look for animal prints or setting them to work at some task while he and Julia went off under an acacia to have a cigarette and an intimate little chat.

That afternoon, Tony had chosen an ideal spot for the leopard bait. It was a little valley between two small plateaus along the river. A small arroyo—dry at the moment—descended from the ridgeline to the Galana, and they had found the tracks of a large leopard on its sandy bottom. The bed of the little stream ran directly beneath some trees with thick, rough trunks; the leopard could climb onto one of them as though it were a staircase, up to one of the horizontal branches on which they would set out the bait. The hunter's expert eye chose exactly the right tree, close to the arroyo, with an open space between it and a patch of bush where they would locate the blind.

On the pretext that he was going to look for the best angle to shoot from, Tony disappeared into the bushes, accompanied by Julia, as his bearer and the trackers took charge of placing the bait in the tree. It was a long and tricky job; one of the boys was obliged to climb, catlike, up to the same spot in the tree where the leopard would sit to eat the bait, so as to make sure that the branch was wide enough and sturdy enough to support the animal's weight, and at the same time choose another suitable branch from which to hang the thigh that they were using as bait. After that, he threw a rope down to the boys below, and with all of them hauling on the thick rope, they hoisted the piece of meat up to the right spot in the tree. Once the bait was securely tied to the firm branch, he had to lop off some of the smaller branches so that the animal would have easy access to the lure, while

286

at the same time he had to take care to keep it well concealed from above so that the vultures wouldn't see it.

As the boys concentrated on this procedure, Tony and Julia had gone into the little thicket; sunbeams filtered through the bushes and a breeze from the other side of the river made the heat in the bosky bush less suffocating. Without leaving their hiding place, Tony would grab his binoculars every so often to check that the job of placing the bait was proceeding as it should, according to his instructions: The knots in the rope tying it to the branch had to be hidden from sight and the meat had to peek out from amid the branches; though the feline would be guided above all by its sense of smell, it was also necessary that the food be enticingly visible.

It did not occur to the hunter, however, to focus the binoculars on the spot where he had left Paolo, who had stayed behind in the car, pretending to be tired. Tony had left the Toyota in the shade of an acacia down by the Galana, a fair distance away from the arroyo where they had seen the tracks of the leopard; he had not wanted to take the car very close to the valley where the blind would be set up, so as not to leave tire marks in the sand or the smell of gasoline in the thicket, since this might scare off a wise and wary old male, which was what this feline appeared to be, judging from the size of its tracks and the deep marks of its claws on the trees round about. Sitting down comfortably, Paolo opened all the windows of the safari car and took out the bag of grass he kept carefully hidden in the inside pocket of his bush jacket. From the very first drags he noticed that he was really feeling the effects of the marijuana; perhaps it was partly the heat and the heavy humidity coming up from the river. He began to lose himself in pleasurable contemplation of the flowing water and to follow in fascination the drifting tree trunks and other floating objects which his imagination began to turn into fanciful forms. It didn't take much of an effort to identify a bump on that tree trunk as the snout of a hippo or invent evil little beady eyes at one end of a length of rough bark, which might well be the skin of a crocodile.

But after the second joint he began to have wilder hallucinations. He envisioned himself involved in an exciting adventure in colonial Africa; the car was a fort where a group of brave legionnaires under his command, confronted by vastly superior numbers of fanatic dervishes, were prepared to séll their lives dearly. Soon the bushes around him began to sway, and with surprising clarity he saw through the rearview mirror the shadows of turbaned blacks crawling toward him across the grass, and surrounding the car. The one who appeared to be in charge of the operation was holding a razor-sharp knife in his teeth, the blade of which glinted when the sun's rays hit it. The hallucination was almost too real for him not to feel anxiety. He was about to turn round to look behind him when a gnarled, bony hand was clapped brutally over his mouth. The skin was very dark, covered with deep wrinkles and what looked like scales: crocodile skin. Several pairs of arms lifted him bodily out of the car, preventing him from making the slightest movement. This was a real bad trip, he thought; the bushes scratched his face and he had to close his eyelids very tightly to keep the thorny branches from getting into his eyes; he struggled desperately to free himself, but the arms holding him gripped his limbs like vises and an evil-smelling rag was pressed over his nose and his mouth. He could not breathe; from lack of oxygen and out of sheer terror, he lost consciousness.

When Tony could see through his binoculars that the trackers had finished their work, it occurred to him to have a look through the glasses at the place where he had left the car; he saw that the door of the Toyota was open and that Paolo wasn't inside: That idiot had again disobeyed his orders not to leave the car by himself! He couldn't see Paolo sitting in the shade of the acacia either, or anywhere else; impatiently he lowered the binoculars and emerged from his hiding place.

"Where are you going?" Julia asked seductively. She had thought that the white hunter was going to pursue this golden opportunity, but he didn't even bother to answer her question.

In a few swift strides Tony reached the car. When he saw the trampled grass and the trail of broken branches leading into the bush, he realized what had happened; before the poachers had fled, carrying Paolo off with them, they had punctured all four tires, and had taken two rifles from the gun rack, plus several boxes of ammunition.

"Shit, shit, shit!" Tony muttered. More than the danger the kid was undoubtedly in, the one thought that was resounding in his mind at that moment was: What was he going to tell Paolo's father? "They kidnapped your boy while my attention was elsewhere, flirting with your woman?" Great black thunderheads were gathering above the plateau along the river; the setting sun made deep red gashes of color on the trunks of the acacias.

Massimo San Miniato had gone out on foot with Lawrence Brown to look for crocodiles along the banks of the Galana. At a spot where

288

the river widened, they saw a dead cow, its belly swollen, floating down the muddy waters till it bumped into one of the banks and got caught in some bushes, with its legs in the air. The current in that particular spot was not strong enough to dislodge that carcass—which was mostly skin and bones—but it was causing the inert body to rock back and forth, so that it looked alive. The hunters, who were watching from the opposite bank, saw several long shapes emerge from the water; they could have been drifting tree trunks, but looking at them through the binoculars, two tiny holes with bubbles coming out of them could be seen at one end, and a hand's breadth beneath them, a pair of evil-looking little beady eyes: They were crocodiles.

For a few minutes the reptiles made no move to reveal their camouflage except for the tiny flicks of their tails in the water which enabled them to remain in the same place; soon at least fifteen of them of different colors and sizes had gathered around the cow: some were yellowish, others were yellow with greenish speckling; others were a darker color, wonderfully mimicking the muddy waters of the river. Suddenly one of the largest dove beneath the cow's body and the carcass shook violently, bitten from underneath. As though this were the signal for a rush for the spoils, all the other reptiles launched an attack on the cow's abdomen, tearing off great strips of hide in their strong jaws; the most skillful of them, once their jaws had clamped down on their target, gave a violent twist of their entire bodies, spinning in the water and furiously lashing their tails till a great chunk of carrion fell off, which they then devoured, returning to the attack again a few minutes later.

Brown did not want San Miniato to shoot at any of the crocodiles, since only a part of their bodies was visible and hitting a moving target from the opposite shore would have been very difficult, but he promised to come back to that very spot the following day to see if any of the great reptiles were still there, basking in the sun on the sandy riverbank after the banquet.

San Miniato was properly impressed, remembering how imprudent he had been to have crossed that same stream to try to seduce the good-looking native woman; his foolishness had been the cause of one of his first arguments with Tony Allen, and he was forced to admit that on that particular occasion the hunter had been right. After the scene he had just witnessed, he wouldn't have waded into the river up to his knees for all the money in the world.

Back at camp, San Miniato took a shower, and after changing into clean clothes, sat by the campfire with a drink in his hand, waiting for the other group of hunters to return to talk over the day's events. But darkness had fallen and the others had not returned. Lawrence Brown, sitting next to the fire, holding his glass of whiskey between his knees as was his habit, saw that the Count was becoming more and more nervous; his eyes were glued to his watch.

"It must have gotten dark while they were placing the bait, and they probably had to come back by way of the concrete bridge; the water level has risen these last few days and it's not possible to get across by way of most of the fords," Brown said, hoping to relieve the tension.

"Even so, I'm surprised that they're not back yet. We never came back to camp this late, not even that afternoon when we were chasing the rogue buffalo."

"That's true, but when you go out hunting, there can be a thousand unexpected delays getting back—anything from a mechanical breakdown or getting stuck in the mud to having wounded an animal and being obliged to follow it till you've killed it. Something as simple as a flat, which can be fixed in half a minute on a highway, may prove to be a tough job in the middle of the bush."

San Miniato was not reassured.

"If you don't mind, I'm going to ask that dinner be served. They'll get here in their own good time, and that'll be that," Brown said at last.

The Italian said barely a word all during dinner; he didn't eat but drank whiskey steadily. At the slightest sound on the road, or the sight of lights moving anywhere in the camp, he got out of his chair, thinking it might be Tony's car.

"You can set your mind at ease. Paolo and Julia are in good hands. Tony Allen is one of the most competent professional hunters going, and his boys are first-rate too. There's no reason for you to worry; they've no doubt had some minor mishap that's held them up."

"What annoys me most," San Miniato confessed finally, "is that this has happened on the very day that Julia went out hunting with Tony."

"I wouldn't let that worry me either. After all, she's not alone with Tony. Your son Paolo and Tony's boys are with them."

"You don't seem to understand," the Italian exploded. "My son is a naive kid, and that scoundrel Allen wouldn't have any trouble getting rid of the boys to be alone with Julia. . . .I have my reasons for not trusting him. He's never missed the slightest opportunity to make advances to her, sometimes before my very eyes."

"That's probably because she allows him to," Brown argued, with his usual directness. "No woman gets herself in a compromising situation unless she wants to. I assure you that when a woman isn't interested she knows very well how to make a man stay in line!"

Brown went on to explain his famous theories regarding the intrinsic evil of womankind, repeating the anecdote about the lion in rut, once again transposing that well-worn parable from the animal world to the human realm and concluding his tirade with his favorite proverb: "If women didn't have cunts they'd long ago have been included in the vermin list!"

The conversation was the one least likely to reassure San Miniato, who got up from the table and began to pace up and down the camp, stopping every so often to refill his glass with whiskey. Lawrence Brown remained on the veranda, repairing the firing pin of a rifle, till he began to get sleepy.

"There's no sense in both of us staying up waiting; if they were really in trouble, they'd fire a shot at regular intervals so we could locate them; otherwise it would be the height of foolishness to go out looking for them when it's pitch dark." With these words Brown calmly strode off to his tent, and ten minutes later was sound asleep.

Not poor San Miniato, who stayed up waiting and imagining the thousand ways in which that sly fox Tony Allen could have given Paolo and the boys the slip to be alone with Julia and try to seduce her. It never once crossed his mind that it might be his son who was in trouble, or that anything more serious than the predictable consequences of the mutual attraction between Julia and Tony Allen might have occurred.

At four in the morning, however, Lawrence Brown was awakened by strange sounds coming from the rear of the camp, as though a hard hollow object were being pounded with something metallic—an axe or a hammer. Or might it be a hyena that had gotten into the kitchen quarters and was dragging off a metal pot full of meat? Brown grabbed his rifle and his flashlight and hurried off to see what was causing all that noise. Not far from the tents there was a wooden shed there the trophies and the skins were stored until they could be mounted. The lights in the shed were on: It seemed to be the source of the furious blows. Opening the door, Brown found Count San Miniato in his pajamas, clutching an outsized machete, with which he was shattering to bits all the horns and other trophies stored there.

"What are you doing, you fool?" Lawrence Brown exclaimed, doing his best to keep out of range of that dangerous weapon.

The Count stared at him momentarily with the expression of a man plastered to the gills, and then continued his furious efforts to destroy everything in sight.

"Leave me alone, leave me alone!" he bellowed, lashing out with incredible rage at the trophies that were still intact.

"What in the world has gotten into you? Have you gone crazy?"

"I'm not crazy, not in the least!" he shouted, cleaving with one two-handed slash the skull of the buffalo that he had gone to so much trouble to down. "The only trophy that will be left here are my own horns!"

It took a moment for Brown to understand that phrase uttered by a thick-tongued, very drunk man; but he suddenly remembered that the Italians used the expression being given horns to describe a husband who's been cuckolded by his wife, and realized that for San Miniato those trophies had become a symbol of Julia's supposed infidelity with Tony Allen.

Several camp boys had come running, and Brown was at a loss as to how to end the whole episode; it was no easy task to discuss the matter rationally with a very drunk man armed with a machete a good five inches wide. They heard voices from the road, and a few moments later they saw Tony Allen and his boys in the light of the lanterns, walking into camp, looking dejected and utterly exhausted. Julia was leaning on Tony's shoulder; he was almost carrying her; she looked haggard and was limping. San Miniato ran to meet them, brandishing the machete like a maniac:

"What's this I see? What in the world has happened?"

Then, pointing at Allen with a look of intense hatred: "What have you done to this woman, you bastard, bringing her back to camp in such a state?"

Tony's mouth was so dry he barely got the words out: "Poachers damaged the tires of the car so badly we couldn't fix them, and we've had to walk all the way back from the other end of the Ranch."

"That's a lie, an outright lie!" San Miniato screamed, brandishing the machete. "I knew I couldn't trust you; this is all a trick to get what you're after. You ought to be really proud of yourself!"

It was then that Tony Allen understood what was on San Miniato's mind.

"Instead of being so concerned about the two of us, you ought to be asking what's happened to your son."

"My son? Ah, that's right." The Italian's eyes searched about for a few seconds in the darkness. "Where's Paolo? Where have you left my son, you bastard?"

"I don't know where he is. I'm very much afraid that the poachers have kidnapped him; we left him alone for a while in the car, and when I came back he was gone. If it had been an animal that got him, I would have seen traces of blood or some other sign, but all I found was some trampled grass. I think it was poachers that carried him off with them and punctured the tires so that we wouldn't be able to follow them; they also stole two rifles that we'd left in the car."

"And why didn't you go after them?" San Miniato roared, having recovered some of his ability to think clearly. "Did you need a couple of dogs to follow the trail this time too?"

"This is no time for stupid jokes," Tony answered, trying to control his temper, "when what we should be doing is thinking about how we can rescue Paolo; I'm very much afraid he's in grave danger. I willingly admit I'm partly to blame; I shouldn't have left him by himself."

San Miniato, who was gradually calming down, realized the seriousness of the situation. He flung the machete as far away as he could and took a few tottering steps and finally collapsed, sobbing, on the floorboards of the shed, amid the shattered horns.

Magnus Coleman

AT ABOUT FIVE O'CLOCK in the afternoon, on the same Friday that Alex had been visited by Muriuki, a small four-passenger light plane took off from Wilson Airport, near the Langata district and the National Park. It was piloted by Magnus Coleman, a farmer and cattleman, who had been a professional hunter in his day, and now had a small farm near Mount Kenya. Sitting at the pilot's right was Lucio Luz, and in the back seat Bob Fender, a bit uneasy because of the pitching and rolling of the small plane—he had never liked flying. The rear of the cabin was loaded with cases of rifles and ammunition, for when Lucio went hunting, if only for a weekend, he took a veritable arsenal with him. What the devil was Bob doing taking off on another hunting expedition? Even though he sometimes complained that he always ended up doing what other people wanted him to do, he couldn't really claim that he had been kidnapped at knife-point. Two days before, Lucio Luz had offered to take him to Coleman's farm, where he would be able to see the Mount Kenya area and a terrain quite different from Galana. Though Bob would have liked very much to go with him, he had been planning to spend the weekend with Melissa, who would be home by herself in Nairobi. But the situation had changed, unexpectedly.

Bob had hurried out to the Karura forest that noon to meet Melissa as they had arranged; as usual, he had parked the car in the shade of the tree next to the fence around the school and sat peacefully reading the morning paper, knowing that Melissa almost never arrived at the hour they had agreed on. But this time she was later than usual; the schoolgirls had already come out for recess and were taking turns climbing the wooden fence to giggle at him, and students from the Hindu school had arrived for a practice game of cricket on the nearby field, discussing each play in loud voices. He was just about to leave, thinking that she wasn't coming, when a cloud of dust appeared on the trail that Melissa always used. What would happen if some day, instead of its being Melissa, it was her husband who came, or a gang of hoodlums paid by Philip to beat him up? The incident with the vagrants in the Langata forest had made him realize that a romantic rendezvous in the midst of nature was not as safe as it might appear.

But it was Melissa who was at the wheel. After one look at her, he realized that something was wrong.

"I apologize for being so late, but I've just had a terrible argument with Philip. He asked me to go with him to Eldama Ravine and was so insistent I couldn't refuse. I've just come to tell you that we won't be able to see each other this weekend."

"You mean you have to leave this minute? Can't we at least take a little walk or talk together for a moment?"

"It was lucky I managed to get away at all: I told him I needed to get something at the market. He's home waiting for me right now, with all his things already in the car!"

"What a drag! I'd already arranged everything so that we'd be able to be together this whole weekend. I was even thinking of taking you on a little trip to Naivasha on Sunday; I've been told that there's a hotel on the shore of the lake."

"I don't know if that would have been a very good idea—that's the place Philip eats his meals on his way to or from the plantation at Eldama," she answered with an odd hard edge to her voice. "We'll have to put it off to another time. What's more," Melissa added with a very strange smile, "I have to admit that I never go with him on his travels, and he's always let me do as I please. And now that he's asked me for once to go with him—I simply couldn't refuse!"

"I understand, I understand. Don't worry on my account," Bob said, thoroughly annoyed.

Melissa got back into her car after kissing him, coldly, on the cheek.

"I have to leave this very minute, because if I'm gone any longer, he'll be angry. Call me Sunday if you like; we may be back fairly early. 'Bye now—see you soon."

She was very tense and nervous, and something told Bob that, apart from the fact that she was afraid her husband might be angry, something had suddenly come between him and Melissa, an obscure barrier that destroyed any possibility of tenderness and passion between them. As she drove off, and the car disappeared around a bend in the trail, he had the presentiment that he'd seen Melissa for the last time; he tried his best to blot out the memory of her drawn face, her forced smile.

He was crushed, but what could he do? On the way back to his hotel, he stopped at a gas station to call Lucio; he caught him just as he was going out of the house. "Zoom out to Wilson Airport; we'll wait for you there," Lucio told him. "But remember that we can't leave any later than five o'clock; those light planes aren't equipped for night flying."

They took off with just enough time to reach their destination—a little landing field near the ranch—while it was still daylight. As they left behind the circle of clouds surrounding Nairobi, the visibility improved, and in a little while they saw the skirts of Mount Kenya and the snow-covered peak in the background. Magnus Coleman even had time to make a few passes over the steep hills covered with dense bush that bordered his ranch, which he said were the hiding place of the buffalo that came down into the valley at night to eat his crops; and after a low-altitude pass over the clumps of trees, they spotted a herd of some twenty or thirty buffalo, peacefully grazing in a little meadow still lit by the setting sun; only the oldest bulls raised their heads and shook their tails on hearing the plane engine. "If you stay there till tomorrow, maybe I'll bring you a nice surprise," Coleman muttered. From there he headed straight for the landing field, which was simply a meadow with a fence around it to keep the cattle out; the little plane made a soft landing on the grass and rolled to the far end of the enclosure. While they waited for the ranch car to come for them, night fell.

The house was not very large, but it was warm and comfortable. The Narumoro—a little trout stream flowing down from the snowy peaks—ran through the middle of the garden; the light from the veranda illuminated part of the lawn, and at the far end of it they caught a glimpse of the clumps of trees bordering the little stream and could hear the water splashing over the rocks.

Once the sun had set, the temperature dropped abruptly. The night air was extremely damp: It was too cold to have a drink out on the veranda before dinner. During dinner, the conversation turned, as was inevitable, to the subject of hunting. After Magnus and Lucio had told their favorite stories—Bob was obliged to listen for the third time to Lucio's tale of how he'd been charged by the wounded buffalo —they asked Bob what hunting incident in his life he remembered best; Bob told them about the time he'd gone goose hunting on Shelter Island and how he had been so impressed by the beauty of the geese on the frozen inlet that he'd forgotten about shooting them. He thought the little episode was scarcely dramatic enough to interest those two veteran hunters, accustomed to going after buffaloes and elephants, but he was wrong: "That's one of the finest hunting stories I've ever heard," Coleman said; he seemed genuinely moved by it.

"I can just see the whole scene," said Lucio, "and that bastard of a Murphy—may he rest in peace—shouting from the blind: 'Shoot, shoot, you idiot!' Now there was a guy who was a born hunter and a magnificent shot; though I must say that I heard the other day that you yourself impressed the bunch at the Galana with your shooting the day you went out after sand grouse."

"I was lucky," Bob said, surprised at how quickly news spread, even from the Galana. "I'd gone out just to keep the other hunters company, but I found myself with a shotgun in my hands and remembered the times I'd gone out hunting with John."

"Well, when we go out hunting tomorrow," Magnus said solemnly, "you'll come with us, and the first buffalo will be yours, in honor of John Murphy, who was our friend, a great hunter, and a great person. To John!"

They rose to their feet and drained their glasses. Bob didn't bother to try to explain any further; it was obviously hopeless to insist that his own personality was quite different from the one assigned to him. That night, however, he didn't sleep well, lying awake wondering what the next day's hunt would be like; going out after a flock of harmless sand grouse with a shotgun wasn't quite the same thing as going into the bush after a buffalo.

He lay sleepless in the dark, remembering the look on Melissa's face earlier that day. Usually Melissa's face reflected an inner serenity and sweetness, but the woman he had seen a few hours before had looked hard and drawn, and her ironic smile had turned into a sarcastic grin. Outside, the piercing cry of a hyrax rose over the lamenting sound of the wind.

Magnus Coleman awakened the others long before dawn; before leaving they drank steaming hot tea in front of the fire. Outside a cold wind was blowing down from the mountain. It had rained a little during the night and there were little puddles in the road. It was bitter cold inside the car, but Bob remembered with pleasure the mornings at the Galana Ranch, when the whole safari party had piled into Tony Allen's car, and he wondered what they were doing at that moment. The beaten earth trail wound around up the hillside; it was beginning to get light now. Bob heard a little sneeze; until that moment he hadn't noticed Moses, the tracker, in the back of the car, cold and silent. He wore a dark overcoat with the collar pulled up around his ears and a cap with the visor pulled way down; all Bob could see was a pair of bright, inquisitive eyes. After turning off onto a muddy trail leading into a cultivated field, Magnus stopped the car. He stepped out, and in the light from the headlamps they saw him gesticulating as he leaned over to inspect the tender corn shoots just coming out of the earth. He climbed back into the car, cursing.

"The buffaloes were here last night, and they've trampled down the crop I just planted, the bastards! But with the drizzle that fell during the night, they've left a clear trail in the mud that'll be easy to follow. Those blasted beasts aren't going to get away this time, damn 'em!"

The trail climbed more steeply now as they started up the skirts of the mountain; it soon turned into a narrow forest path boxed in by the dense trees; the front bumper could just barely squeeze between the trunks on either side, and they could hear low branches crackling on the canvas roof. The sun was beginning to filter through the dense foliage and the morning mists. When they reached a clearing covered with grass and ferns, Magnus stopped the car.

"We'll have to go the rest of the way on foot," he said. "We're going to try to head off the herd before they go any higher."

As they took the rifles and buckled on the cartridge belts, Bob remembered the thicket on the banks of the Galana, when they had followed the trail of the rogue buffalo. But this time he was not just a spectator, but one of the hunters.

"I put four bullets in the magazine," Magnus said to him as he handed him a rifle. "They're solid—458s. I hope you'll only need one of them; you'll be the first to shoot if we run into a bull that's worth the trouble."

Bob had never used a heavy-caliber rifle before, but he had shouldered one a few times at Galana; he knew the mechanics of placing a bullet in the chamber and how to put the safety catch on.

"I'm ready when you are," Bob said. It seemed to him the voice that he heard wasn't his own but someone else's; from that moment on, it was as though all the sensations, the tastes, the smells he experienced had a sort of echo effect, as if they were coming to him through someone else's skin. He felt a curiosity in the face of danger that was quite foreign to him; he found himself chewing on a pine needle, savoring the flavor of resin, as he had seen Murphy do when he was out hunting.

They walked at a brisk pace across the thick grass; in front of them, on the hoarfrost gleaming in the early light of the sun, the tracks of the buffaloes were clearly visible; there were also heaps of dung, still steaming. The tracker unabashedly stuck his finger in the warm shit and then sucked it clean, as though it was the most natural thing in the world.

"If we don't get to the top of the hill before they do, they'll enter the dense bush up there and we'll have lost them," Coleman said, stepping up the pace.

They were almost running now, straight uphill, and despite the cold and the dampness, Bob began to sweat in his hunting jacket; he felt fine and the rifle didn't seem at all heavy in his hands. A few yards behind him, Lucio Luz was puffing and panting, and blaming it on whiskey and tobacco. He was also complaining about a sore in his ankle, from the hunting accident, which he had suddenly remembered.

On the top of the slope they found that the wind was blowing hard on the crest of the hill, dispersing the morning fog. Before them lay a vast meadow, with a patch of bright blue sky behind it; from amid the clouds the snow-covered peak of Mount Kenya emerged, so clear and sharp in the transparent dawn air.

Coleman tapped Bob on the shoulder. "There they are! Get ready to shoot!" A herd of buffalo was coming out of a little grove of trees on their left and calmly crossing the meadow, heading toward the denser forest. Squatting on the ground, Magnus took a close look through the binoculars.

"None of them has very good horns but the third one to the right, in the group that's farthest in front, is shootable. Wait till he turns sideways, and try a shoulder shot. You can use that bush for a support."

Bob positioned himself and prepared to shoot, resting the barrel of the rifle in the fork of the bush to steady his aim.

"Wait a minute; I think they've caught our scent now," Magnus said.

The wind on the crest of the hill, which had been fluttering the leaves of the bushes and blowing straight into the hunters' faces, had suddenly shifted and was now carrying their scent in the direction of the herd of buffalo. The biggest of them, leading the herd, made a complete turn, raised his muzzle, and sniffed the wind; his boss, wet and gleaming from grazing in the damp grass, shone in the sun like a bronze helmet.

"Don't shoot that one," Magnus whispered. "He's too old, and one of his horns is splintered; it's the third one back we want; wait till he turns around." As though he had heard the hunter, another buffalo, a younger one with wider and better-shaped horns, turned all the way around to look in the direction from which he sensed danger. "Ndume, Ndume," said the tracker. Although his heart was beating furiously and he was so excited he could scarcely focus his eyes, Bob was reminded of Muriuki, his neck tense and thrust defiantly forward, as he spoke before Parliament.

"All right, go to it, aim just below the boss, between the eyes, and you've got yourself a buffalo."

Bob tried to steady the gun in the fork of the bush; when he pressed the trigger, his eardrums nearly burst from the detonation, and he could feel the powerful kick of the rifle against his collarbone. The

299

animal hunched over, and for a few seconds his hind quarters tottered, as though he were about to fall, but he unexpectedly recovered, and turning swiftly around, galloped up the slope and disappeared in the bush. The rest of the herd had stampeded off too, but were taking a straighter line as they headed for the top of the hill. "Well," Bob said, ejecting the empty cartridge, "I missed him."

Coleman stared at him.

"Not completely, unfortunately; from the way he hunched over, I'd say you've wounded him in the chest. I told you to try a brain shot! We're going to have to track him down in the bush now."

"I'm sorry. He moved his head just before I shot."

This was a lie, but he'd heard Paolo come up with that excuse when he'd missed that beautiful impala.

"We'll stay here for a few minutes and have ourselves a cigarette, to give him time to let his wound get cold; he'll separate himself from the herd," Coleman said, sitting on the stump of a fallen tree. "I don't like it that the bastard's taken off among the ferns."

The wind had now blown the clouds away completely, and the sun was beating down on the mountain; the light on its snow-covered slope was blinding. Still sweating from the swift climb, Lucio Luz's hand shook as he lighted his cigarette, as though he had a fever.

"This is the part of hunting I like least," Luz muttered, averting his eyes. "To tell the truth, I don't like it one bit."

Coleman was silent. He stared fixedly at the spot where the wounded buffalo had disappeared; then he began to concentrate his attention on the whorls of smoke from his cigarette as the wind carried them off. Bob realized that Coleman was trying to determine exactly which way it was blowing; but it kept shifting, at times sending the smoke upward toward the hilltops in long streaks, and at others sucking it downward in wispy spirals that slowly drifted across the grass, until they broke up on contact with the hoarfrost.

"Well, let's get on with it," Coleman said, putting out his cigarette. "Moses will go first and Bob will follow behind to finish the buffalo off. You and I, Lucio, will go off to the right, in case the buffalo tries to reach the thick bush above; he's wounded, though, and I think he'll take off toward the valley instead."

At that moment Bob realized that they had only two rifles for the four of them—the one he was carrying and one belonging to Lucio Luz, who was muttering to himself, and limping ostensibly. Why didn't Coleman, who supposedly had the most experience in tight situations like this, have a gun? Bob realized that Magnus thought that he, Bob, might have taken it as an insult if his gun had been taken away from him because he'd missed his first shot. Magnus was giving him proof of his confidence in him as an expert shot. Once again, that confounded reputation he'd inherited from Murphy! Bob felt sorry for the poor tracker who, following the orders of his boss, had resolutely started off in front of him to follow the trail of the wounded buffalo. If he was trusting Bob's marksmanship to get him out of trouble, he'd had it!

The stretch of open ground they were crossing before reaching the thicket made Bob think of what a bullfighter must feel like as he makes the tour of the empty ring before the bull is let loose; he would willingly have wandered off to gather daisies and wildflowers to postpone the moment when he would be obliged to enter the dense bush, which looked terribly dark and forbidding, though the sun was now bright in the sky. But rather than lovely little wildflowers Moses found a splatter of blood on a little stone, and farther on, a great dark clot, hanging from the stem of a fern.

"He's been hit in the chest; there's no doubt of it," Coleman said. "But he can't go very far if he's coughing up this much blood."

The buffalo's trail cut obliquely across the middle of the slope, heading downward, just as Coleman had predicted. They reached the top of a ravine and came out on the edge of a valley, in the bottom of which was a ditch. The sides of it, though covered with brush, were very steep and even.

"These ditches were dug during the Emergency to keep people out of the forest and we've left them so as to keep the wild animals in the forest. But to tell the truth, they haven't fulfilled either purpose," Coleman said, lighting another cigarette.

Though badly wounded, the buffalo had managed to climb up the opposite side of the ditch; there was more blood and the deep imprint of his hoofs on the red earth.

"He's still got some wind left, the bastard, but he can't be very far away. We'll separate now to cover more territory."

Entering the bush again Bob heard the Argentine mutter in Spanish and the rancher swear in English, urging him to keep his mouth shut. Under that thick canopy of greenery barely penetrated by the sun, Bob was overtaken by a strange sense of serenity; he was no longer anxious. He remembered that once he had had to leap into an icy lake with all his clothes on to save a dog from drowning; though he had dreaded the chill shock of the water, once he'd jumped in, the lake didn't seem all that cold. In much the same way he had been more terrified just before entering that cage of dense foliage, where he knew that a wild beast, concealed in the darkest corner of it, lay waiting for him.

He had inserted another bullet in the chamber and his thumb was resting on the safety catch of the rifle, ready to release it at the slightest sound. All his senses were concentrated on detecting the smallest sign—a noise, a smell, a contact—that would warn him of danger; he had taken an immense leap backward in the evolutionary scheme: He was prehistoric man clutching his axe, or a primate evading the attack of a leopard. For perhaps the first time in his life he was faced with a real threat, with a concrete, powerful enemy—not merely the trivial annoyances of everyday existence—an enemy that could destroy him in a single charge, but one that he could best if he kept his head and his self-control. At last he understood John Murphy perfectly, and felt comfortable in his skin.

They had just come out onto a narrow firebreak that came to an end at the bottom of a little incline covered with dense brush; as he started up that little slope Bob heard a creaking sound up above, and he saw that the tracker had stopped dead, his body as tense as the string of a bow. Silence once again; but an artificial, frozen silence, with not a sound of insects or birds in the forest. Bob held his breath as Moses leaned over very slowly to peer under the bushes. As he bent over, from a nearby bush there came a muffled snort, like a death rattle, like a warning of mortal danger. Bob leaned one arm on the African's shoulder; his hand was shaking so badly that he was afraid the rifle might go off. It was almost comforting to see that the African's eyes were rolling in their sockets in mute terror; with a shaking forefinger he pointed to a darker patch underneath the bush. "*Ndume, Ndume,*" he whispered.

There was a sudden violent explosion; it seemed as though the entire hill were coming down on top of them in a great din of broken branches and crushed clods of earth; a dense bush, less than fifty yards away, spat out, like a volcano, the incandescent mass of the wounded buffalo; he went streaking down the hillside, enveloped in a huge cloud of dust, dislodging stones with his hoofs. It seemed as though no human force could be capable of containing that avalanche of gleaming horns and hoofs, crimson hide and bloody snout.

Bob stood petrified, hearing, as though from a great distance away,

Moses's hysterical voice shouting in Swahili: *"Piga, piga!"* Shoot, shoot! For a few moments that seemed to be forever, Bob saw that image of death tobogganing down his retina, growing larger and larger, bringing with it a curious sense of vertigo, compounded of horror and fascination.

To his right, he heard the report of Lucio's rifle as the Argentine hastened to his aid, then immediately afterward, a second shot. But though the shots had come from not very far away, the bush covering the hillside made an accurate hit impossible. Lucio had fired both bullets in his rifle in close succession, and Magnus stood watching helplessly as the enraged beast lowered its horns and charged; but Bob didn't raise his rifle to his shoulder. The rancher suddenly remembered the magic words that he'd heard the night before: "Shoot, Bob!" he shouted. "Shoot, you idiot!"

When the beast was only five paces away from him, Bob shouldered the rifle, closed his eyes, and pulled the trigger; the bullet hit the buffalo straight between the eyes, and after stumbling for a few seconds, he dropped dead in his tracks. His head rolled forward, and the tips of his horns plowed a deep furrow in the moss and the damp earth.

Bob turned to the others as though asking them what happened. The only one in sight was Coleman, who rushed to congratulate him; Lucio had disappeared, and it was several minutes before he appeared again, climbing up out of the bottom of the ditch, his face and his rifle completely covered with mud.

"Well, Lucio, it looks as though you'd rather battle the elements— fire, water, and even mud—than be gored by a buffalo . . . despite your Spanish blood and your love of bullfighting," Bob said. He was shivering slightly though the sun was beating down mercilessly on the valley.

Lucio tried to laugh, but his lips were caked with mud and his teeth were chattering. Coleman shook Bob's hand and said: "You were really terrific; even John couldn't have done better!"

It took them a while to find Moses, the tracker, who had scurried up into the highest fork of a tree. The flies were already beginning to buzz about the dead body of the buffalo.

The Hunting Ban

THAT SAME SATURDAY at daybreak, vehicles with their license plates covered with strips of burlap had arrived at the President's ranch near Kiambu; the occupants of the vehicles had set fire to the crops and brutally maimed the cattle, a tactic the former Mau Mau guerrilla fighters had used when they were trying to drive the European colonials from their lands. That ranch was one of the President's favorite places for relaxing; it was a symbol of what had led him to fight for independence: his passionate love of the land.

The moment he was told, the President had set out for the ranch, and had reached Kiambu while grayish-black clouds of smoke were still rising from the cornfields, which had been set afire and were burning on all four sides. Waving his aides aside, the President stepped out of his car and, sinking into the mud up to his ankles, leaned over to pick up a few of the seared ears of corn. The set of his lips and jaw betrayed an irrevocable decision.

That same morning, an emergency meeting of the Council of Ministers was held in the little house in Kiambu. Munyoka, who had taken it upon himself to call the meeting, had carefully refrained from getting word of it to those ministers who might have had more doubts and scruples than he with regard to the adoption of a hard line. The President himself did not even attend the entire meeting of the Council, leaving it up to the Minister of State to see that the necessary measures were taken in order to put a definite stop to the wave of terrorism and violence unleashed by Muriuki's followers. There was no discussion as to what should be done—only how and when; it was decided to move against Muriuki that very day, taking advantage of a perfect opportunity. After attending the horse races, as he did every Saturday, Muriuki was in the habit of dismissing his ever-present praetorian guard of henchmen and bodyguards and joining a few friends in the cafe of the Hilton Hotel. That was the right time and place to nab him; there would be crowds on the streets on Saturday night and the police action would not attract attention.

Munyoka himself, as the official responsible for state security, took charge, with a certain pleasure, of arranging the details. He left no loose ends. The area where Muriuki was to be taken would be cleared beforehand of the itinerant peddlers and beggars who were in the habit of hanging around the hotels, to avoid the presence of embarrassing witnesses, and the arrest would be made to look as official as possible, so that J. M. would not resist accompanying the agents escorting him—supposedly to a police station. He would be told that it was necessary for him to make a deposition with regard to a shipment of arms, if necessary showing him copies of the documents. As a last clever touch, it had occurred to Munyoka to inform Judge McGredy of the arrest and ask him to be present, though he would be told nothing about the real purpose behind it; the presence of Bwana Maximum would reassure Muriuki, since J. M., while by no means a fervent admirer of the Judge, nevertheless recognized that, after his own fashion, McGredy was honest and fair-minded.

It was also decided at the meeting that in order to avoid major upheavals, the necessary arrests of certain of Muriuki's followers would be made during the weekend, and the security forces would be given orders not to hesitate to use violence to break up any demonstration or disturbance that might be forthcoming in the days following his disappearance. The strategy had been thoroughly discussed previously without the President's knowledge—the only possible drawback was the fact that those dates coincided exactly with the period when UNICORN would be in session, and many foreign delegations would be in Nairobi. It would be much more difficult, if something went wrong, to silence international public opinion than to order that the necessary measures be taken to silence the opposition and nip a possible mass popular protest in the bud. Those in the Government, like Muriuki himself, were of the opinion that it was necessary at any cost to avoid a civil war. Unfortunately, the Government was dependent on its good relations with certain powerful Western democracies in order to secure extensions of loans and the creation of social programs vital for the country. As the Minister of Foreign Affairs observed rather bitterly: "That pig of a Muriuki has pushed us too far at the very moment when hundreds of ecologists from all over the world are watching us. If we declare open season on the opposition at this time, those idiot conservationists are going to scream their lungs out."

Though reason was on his side, Munyoka, sly as ever, was not about to allow an inconsequential detail such as a meeting of ecologists to interfere with this excellent chance to rid himself of his hated rival, and he had improvised a smoke screen which would conceal the political crime from the ecologists.

"You yourself, without realizing it, have already pointed to the solution," Munyoka said to the minister who had articulated the problem. "You mentioned an open season, didn't you? Well, the answer is a hunting ban. To make the ecologists happy and keep them from sticking their noses in our business, all we need to do is make a gesture that will ease their consciences and allow them to boast to the entire world of their beneficial influence on environmental policy. If, coinciding with the UNICORN Conference, we decree a total ban on hunting, it will be looked upon as a victory for the conservationists, and will, at the same time, leave us a free hand to do whatever else we please."

The other ministers—even those who had been the most reluctant when the question of a hunting ban had arisen on other occasions—applauded Munyoka's brilliant idea. Only Guichuli, the Minister of Defense, who had said very little during the meeting, seized upon the moment to reintroduce his old obsession with firearms control.

"If we're going to decree the ban, I feel it my duty to suggest that the use of all types of firearms be forbidden at the same time. Such a step would both reinforce the measures being taken to protect game, and contribute to the stability of the country. The quantity of hunting guns in this country—not counting the unregistered ones used by poachers—add up to a veritable arsenal. This can be very dangerous in a time of political tension like the present one!"

"Guichuli is right," Munyoka agreed. "A total hunting ban must be accompanied by the cancellation of all arms licenses, and we'll be killing two birds with one stone. Furthermore," he added with a cynical smile, "I do not believe that the members of the opposition will raise any objection to this measure, since they themselves proposed in Parliament that a hunting ban be declared."

After a superb lunch on the veranda of Magnus Coleman's house, highlighted by a magnificent 1964 Spanish wine, Bob and Lucio were ready for the flight to Nairobi. Flying over the outskirts of Kiambu,

Magnus saw the spiral of black smoke rising high in the sky; it was not the familiar whitish smoke that blanketed pasturelands when grass was being burned off.

"Strange. That fire must be very near the President's ranch," Magnus said, tilting the wings of the plane for a better view. "I hope I'm wrong, but I fly over this area all the time, and the field crop that's burning down there is right on Mzee's property. I wouldn't like to be in the shoes of the ranch manager when The Old Man discovers that he's been asleep on the job."

It had rained in Nairobi the night before, and once again great dark thunderheads were gathering over the plains and being driven toward Langata by the wind. As they flew over the Ngong Hills the tail of the light plane was badly buffeted by the turbulence, leaving Bob with his heart in his mouth. All around the airport of Embakasi on the other side of the National Park a dense curtain of water was beginning to fall. As the plane touched down and taxied toward the hangars, the first fat drops had begun to spatter against the windshield; they had to unload the equipment and the guns in a great hurry and make a run for it to the hangars.

They took their leave of Magnus in the airport offices. Lucio brought his car around to take Bob back to his hotel; the downpour caught up with them, and though Lucio turned the wipers on full-force, the rain almost covered the windshield.

"What's come over you? You've gotten very quiet all of a sudden," Lucio said to Bob. It was true: He'd said very little. Depression set in when he saw the tower of the Conference Center and the skyline of Nairobi dark against the stormy horizon.

"I don't know what's happened to me. Maybe my blood pressure's dropped. Abrupt changes of altitude have that effect on me sometimes," Bob said apologetically.

"Hey, come off it! We know each other well enough by now; you don't have to invent elaborate excuses. Something depressed you all of a sudden; you were as high as a kite till you got out of the plane— and you had every reason to feel elated. I've been here for almost five years now, and I've never had as perfect or as exciting an experience on a hunting trip as the one we had this weekend: You have every right to feel proud of yourself! And no doubt one of your female admirers is anxiously waiting for you to tell her all about it."

"It may just be that the woman who really interests me isn't waiting for me," Bob answered with a faint smile.

"Don't tell me that you've gone and fallen seriously in love when you could have every woman in Nairobi at your feet," Lucio said, letting go of the steering wheel for a moment to give him a slap on the back.

"I have quite a talent for complicating my life," Bob sighed. "The last thing I needed right now was a complicated love affair. But that's not the only thing on my mind. Ever since I set foot in this damned country, I've found myself at every turn doing exactly the opposite of what I set out to do. I came here to collect certain data and I ended up listening to the dreary clichés of the UNICORN delegates. I've always been a dedicated conservationist, and I found myself surrounded by hunters; this morning I killed a wretched wild animal that had every right to crush me to a pulp. *You* may think that everything that happened was just great, but *I* can see the headlines in the Nairobi papers: DELEGATE TO ECOLOGICAL CONFERENCE DIES ON MOUNT KENYA IN HUNTING ACCIDENT!"

"You only did what you had to do, and apart from your serious scientific concerns, which are entirely worthy of respect, it seems to me that you go through life with your eyes blinkered. You've been caught up in the world of hunting because that's the very breath of life in this country; it's still a symbol of what this society was like for so many years, and the old-time colonials cling desperately to that world."

"But it seems to me that they're wrong to do so; it's a world that's long past its prime and on the verge of extinction."

"I agree with you completely, but it's fascinating nonetheless to drain the last drops of this cup. Just think: At any moment now, the Government may ban all hunting; you've been lucky enough to have participated in what may well be one of the very last safaris in this country."

"I don't know if that's anything to be proud of. The very thing I reproach myself for is having allowed myself to be caught up in the fascination of this world; it's unreal, a fantasy. What I came here for was to discover an Africa that may have been much more simple and concrete, and more rewarding at least as far as my work was concerned. I'm not an adventurer or a conquistador; that's completely false. I think I told you as much the other day."

"Don't be naive. Do you think anyone completes the scenario he's laid out for himself? Do you think all of us are leading the life we really wanted?"

He paused, but Bob seemed completely absorbed in the monotonous sweep of the wiper blades back and forth across the windshield. The rain had slowed the traffic and a long line of cars and trucks waited to enter the city.

"Well, I'll tell you the answer," Lucio said. "In one way or another, we've all ended up doing what we like least. I'll give you an example: You noticed the terrible panic I was in this morning when we started following the trail of the wounded buffalo through the forest?" Bob stared at him, surprised at the complete sincerity in his voice. "Yes, I'm not ashamed to admit it: I was scared absolutely shitless. And I'm sure you're wondering: How is it possible that a famous hunter, who must have had any number of similar experiences, should feel like a coward in that situation? Well, I'm not a famous hunter, and I haven't had all that many experiences, and to be completely frank with you, the very idea of going into the forest, even to chase butterflies, makes me feel as though I'm wearing my balls for a bow tie, as the Spanish saying has it"—and he raised his thumb and his index finger to his throat.

"Well, I must say, I would never have thought so, knowing how you love to hunt."

"Love to hunt? Bullshit! If the truth were known, when my career in the diplomatic service took me to Nairobi—and let me say at this point that they might just as easily have sent me to Manila—I realized that the social elite of this country accepted you far more readily if you seemed to enjoy hunting. The women were much more interested in somebody like Murphy, who had the charisma of a man of action, an adventurer. John's example opened my eyes, and I did my very best to imitate him and hide my fear and apprehension at the very thought of going into the wilds and coming face to face with dangerous beasts. I'll even confess something else: I was scared stiff of sleeping in a tent! Every time I go to a safari camp, I have to take sleeping pills to get any shut-eye at all, and when I wake up I inspect my clothes and my shoes very carefully; I'm obsessed by the thought that some horrible creepy, crawly thing may have gotten inside them. Aaagh!"

Bob had hung on every word of Lucio's in complete sympathy. They had both had precisely the same reactions. The two friends exchanged glances, and were overcome with mad, irrepressible laughter; Lucio was obliged to stop for a moment on the side of the road for fear he'd lose control of the car.

309

When they had finally worked their way out of the traffic jam and reached Bob's hotel, they found the front sidewalk outside the main entrance and the lobby completely deserted; ordinarily, at any and every hour of the day, the hotel was surrounded by a mob of cripples and peddlers, begging for alms from the tourists or hawking necklaces of wooden beads and crude clay statuettes of wild animals.

"Well, well," Lucio commented, "it would appear that these first rains have driven them all off. I've never seen the streets as empty as this."

Bob was surprised when a policeman stopped him at the door of the hotel to ask him for identification; fortunately he always carried the card identifying him as a delegate to UNICORN.

The Oath

ON THAT VERY SPOT, barely half an hour before, Muriuki had been kidnapped. After an afternoon of occasional drizzles, which had not interfered with the races, J. M. had left the track amid the roar of the crowd; everyone wanted to greet him, to get close enough to him to touch him or to shake his hand, as they shouted "*Ndume, Ndume*" in chorus. Emboldened by these signs of popular fervor, J. M. dismissed his bodyguards at the exit of the racetrack, and arrived in front of the hotel at the wheel of his own Mercedes; he always drew up directly in front of the main entrance, whereupon one or another of the taxi drivers at the stand rushed over to have the honor of opening the door of the car and taking it round to the parking lot for him. It was unusual to see so few people around the hotel, but it occurred to him that it had probably rained harder in the center of the city than out at the racetrack, and people had no doubt taken shelter in the lobby; but the inside of the hotel was practically deserted too. This made him more apprehensive, and he was about to leave when two plainclothesmen approached him, showed their badges, and asked him to accompany them to the nearest police station.

"Why are you asking me to come with you?" J. M. asked, still calm. "Perhaps you've forgotten that I'm a member of Parliament, and therefore have immunity."

"We're not trying to arrest you," said one of the cops, having learned his little speech by heart. "We only want to get a statement from you regarding a contraband shipment in which some of your men may be involved. We've found certain bills of lading for an arms shipment, and you may possibly be able to give us some information about it."

Several of Muriuki's friends, waiting for him in the bar, approached: There were enough of them, all determined to see that no harm came to him, to have confronted the plainclothesmen if Muriuki had wanted them to. But there were so few police officers that J. M. felt confident; nearby there were other policemen in uniform, and he recognized, standing with them, the unmistakable person of Judge McGredy. This, too, reassured him.

"You needn't worry about me," he said to one of his aides, who was about to pull out his pistol. "If this were a trap, Bwana Maximum wouldn't have come with them; he wouldn't be a party to any underhanded business. I'm going to show those hyenas Ndume isn't afraid to enter their lair."

When another of his henchmen asked if he needed any help, J. M. whispered in his ear, "They won't dare touch a hair on my head. What's more," he said confidentially, giving him a little poke in the ribs with his elbow, "I think they've swallowed that whole business about the arms shipment hook, line, and sinker."

Leaving the hotel flanked by the plainclothesmen, he was surprised that the car they put him in was not a police van, but one of the unmarked cars used by the Special Branch. "Hey," he yelled to the taxi driver who was coming toward him to return his car, "I hope you're taking down the license number of this car." But it was too late; the agents had the barrels of their pistols in his ribs. Through the clouded windows of the car he saw several policemen surrounding the man who had parked his car for him. In a matter of minutes, they had put the taxi driver into a police van, and nobody was ever to see him again.

Although he could barely see the streets because of the steam on the windows and the rain, J. M. realized that they were not heading for a police station but were taking him beyond the city; at a crossroad, he saw a sign pointing toward Kiambu. Though he was uneasy, Muriuki preferred to think that the Old Man had wanted to have a conversation alone with him—perhaps an interesting political deal? —and that the President's pride had prevented him from summoning him to his ranch.

"If we're going out to see the President, there was no need for you to have lied to me; I would willingly have come to meet him anywhere he asked; you didn't have to make up some cock-and-bull story about contraband!"

No one answered, but one of the cops sitting in front of him held out a sheaf of folded papers: Muriuki recognized the copies of the bills of lading stolen from Toffani. As the car slowly climbed up the hills leading to the highlands, J. M.'s mind raced frantically—he was afraid. He remembered his adolescence and early manhood, the sufferings and privations that he had endured during the era of the Emergency; he remembered his recruitment when he was still a raw youngster into the first cabal of the movement, the KAU, to the time when he had taken the sacred oaths of the Mau Mau. His loyalty earned him a prison sentence and detention in concentration camps —Langata, Manyani, Aguthi; he remembered his visit to the President during the latter's exile in Maralal.

Of all those memories, the most vivid, which he relived now with a deep sense of foreboding, were the secret night meetings when he had taken the sacred oaths of fidelity to the cause. He saw again in this moment of fear the administrator of the first oath, the Oath of Unity —Ndemwa Ithatu—taken in the middle of a bare cornfield, near the Kabatini forest, with the full moon peering through the trees. The noninitiates filed back and forth several times beneath an arch made of cane stalks, then squatted down before the Master of the Oath, who held in his hand the entrails of a male goat with which he described seven circles above the heads of the novices. He rubbed the blood of the goat on the arms and wrists of the novices; small cuts had been made so that their blood would be mingled with that of the animal. Then the master of the oath had them bite into the entrails, which he had previously rubbed on the cuts in their arms and wrists, so that all those who took the oath would be united by the same blood.

The novices then repeated word for word the sacred oath:

> I speak the truth and vow before God
> And before this movement,
> The movement of Unity

The Unity which is put to the test
The Unity that is mocked with the name of 'Mau Mau',
That I shall go forward to fight for the land,
The lands of Kirinyaga that we cultivated,
The lands which were taken by the Europeans,
    And if I fail to do this
    May this oath kill me,
    May this seven kill me,
    May this meat kill me.

Later, he would take another more binding and more solemn oath, the Oath of Armed Struggle—*Batuni*. This time the initiate knelt, stark naked, before the thorax of a skinned young bull, and had thrust his penis in an opening in its flesh as he took, one by one, seven sticks that had been thrust into the ground and rubbed them slowly against the animal's ribcage, repeating the words:

I speak the truth and vow before our God
And by this *Batuni* oath of our movement
Which is called the movement of fighting
That if I am called on to kill for our soil
If I am called on to shed my blood for it
I shall obey and I shall never surrender
And if I fail to go
    May this oath kill me,
    May this he-goat kill me,
    May this seven kill me,
    May this meat kill me.
I speak the truth and vow before our God
And before our people of Africa
That I shall never betray our country
That I shall never betray anybody of this
    movement to the enemy
Whether the enemy be European or African
And if I do this
    May this oath kill me,
    May this he-goat kill me,
    May this seven kill me,
    May this meat kill me.

As Muriuki was recalling this awesome experience, the car arrived at the ranch, and his kidnappers led him toward the house. When he entered and they pushed him toward the cellar stairs, he felt that his dream was pursuing him, that it had become a frightful reality, like a nightmare that went on after one had awakened. The damp smell of that house reminded him of the abandoned hut where he had been given the Oath of Armed Struggle, but now there were other smells, of earth, of fresh blood, of marijuana smoke, not in his dream, but from the half-open door of the cellar.

In the cellar, the first thing Ndume saw, hanging from the ceiling, was a bull's thorax, slit completely open; the flames of an open fire made the shadow of the animal dance on the walls. Several men sat stark naked before a row of blood-smeared stakes driven into the floor of beaten earth.

The smoke was blinding him and the overpowering marijuana fumes were making him dizzy, but amid the Dantesque shadows dancing before him, he was able to discern a short, chubby man draped in a monkey skin and smeared with mud and blood staggering toward him. It was Munyoka. With all his strength, Munyoka struck him full in the face with the ceremonial baton he held. He shouted in a hoarse voice: "Kneel, you vermin; we are about to pass judgment on you as a traitor to the sacred vows of the Batuni; you have betrayed your country and your comrades in the struggle for liberation."

And like the roar of distant breaking waves, which gradually grows louder and then dies away, the moldy walls of the cellar resounded with the chorus of the novices:

> May this oath kill me,
> May this seven kill me,
> May this meat kill me.

Bob had gone up to his room after stopping in at the bar of the deserted hotel. What was the matter with the waiters tonight? They kept slipping behind the counter, like mollusks that feared exposing their bodies outside their shells. Despite his exhaustion, he found it impossible to sleep. He had turned off the little lamp on the bedside table, but the acid clarity of the neon street lamps came into the room through the half-open curtains. The silence was oppressive. The clock on the bedside table told him it was only midnight—on a Saturday night. There wasn't a soul on the streets. From the broad picture window the city looked as empty and aseptic as an architect's model. The rain was still pouring down, but there must be some reason, he thought, for that ominous calm.

He got up out of bed and watched the hundreds of dragonflies

314

hovering in the cone of light below the lampposts; he had no idea where they had come from, but it must have had something to do with the change of seasons. In a sudden emergence, the insects were celebrating the arrival of the grass rains. Bob saw human shapes moving, slipping away under the arcades like pairs of rats unaware that they are being observed by the scientist watching their cage. A few of the beggars and cripples Bob had missed seeing outside the hotel were coming out of their hiding places and furtively stealing along the sidewalk, leaning on their crutches till they reached the cone of light around the lampposts where the hovering dragonflies had congregated, like shining schools of sardines struggling in a transparent net. Whatever were those beggars doing? Eagerly they caught the insects with their hands and thrust them into plastic bags; once the miserable netting of their catch was done, they would go off to their hovels, reach their hands down into the sacks where the dragonflies still fluttered, and raise them to their mouths.

In the distance, on Uhuru, the main avenue, a dark-colored car is driving slowly along the deserted street. As it passes beneath the lampposts, the tires squash hundreds of dragonflies hovering above the wet asphalt, making a crackling noise—like countless little bubbles of chewing gum all bursting at the same time.

The car goes around the Langata traffic circle and heads up the highway bordering the National Park that leads into the Ngong Hills. Once past the residential section, it turns off to the left along a secondary road that crosses a vast grazing ground, where it slows down again; swarms of dragonflies dart up out of the grass, dimming the light from the headlamps and completely covering the windshield. Finally the car turns into a muddy trail that enters a little wood; beyond it the terrain descends abruptly, forming the side of a ravine in the bottom of which is a little arroyo swollen by the rains.

Men with flashlights get out and from the back of the car, lift out the broken wreck of a human being, covered with blood but still alive: what is left of Joseph Muriuki. He has cuts and bruises on his face, he is naked to the waist, and his hands are tied behind his back, but feeling the cool caress of the rain on his face he appears to revive and rises to his knees. His swollen legs feel the contact of the grass and the earth; he realizes where he is and what is happening. The dragonflies darting round and round in the light of the headlamps make him painfully dizzy.

He feels the need at this moment to recall something important, but

315

the dragonflies are distracting him, and other useless ideas crowd his mind. He remembers now: Someone once said that it is better to die on one's feet than to live on one's knees; but these bastards are going to force him to die on his knees. He will not permit such a thing; his brain makes a colossal effort to order his legs to tense and support his body for the last time; he is going to make it; his ankles and his knee joints flex and raise him up, and his powerful lungs eagerly breathe in the air and the rain. The miserable dragonflies swirl below, around the headlights. His neck stretches forward, tense and defiant, like a wounded bull.

Two shots ring out behind him: The bullets hit his body, but he does not fall. His legs totter: It is the dance of death of the bull about to collapse in the arena; but it is an eternal imbalance, teetering on imaginary points of gravity. The bull does not keel over. More shots ring out; the executioner has become nervous, the great body seems invulnerable. The gunner empties his revolver.

At last Muriuki collapses, his head falls on the grass and his teeth bite the earth in fury. They have executed him, but he is not dead yet; he can still see just a little, although his vision is very blurred. The trouble is the dragonflies, now that his body has fallen to the ground, hovering directly before his face. Who was it that mentioned a Second Emergence? Only insects are reborn out of the mud. A huge dark butterfly has alighted on his spirit.

The thugs drag his body across the grass to the edge of the slope, and a long knife gleams in the light of the headlamps; they are slitting his belly open so that the corpse will attract the scavengers that come down to drink from the arroyo. The killers give the body a shove that sends it rolling down to the bottom of the ravine.

The sound of the car engine has barely died away on the trail when the coughs and grunts of the hyenas echo in the ravine. They prowl round and round the corpse, and the boldest of them begin to sniff at its extremities. But human voices are heard from the little wood; dark shapes in rags appear at the top of the slope, and two or three stones fly downward, putting the scavengers to flight. The shadows approach the lifeless body spread-eagled on the bushes, and a match rasps in the darkness; the rain puts it out. Another match is lit, protected by several rough, scaly hands—crocodile skin—and for a few instants it illuminates the face of the victim. The second match has gone out now, but someone has recognized the dead man and there is a soft murmuring, a mixture of horror and reverence,

"Ndume, Ndume." They manage to drag the mutilated body to the top of the slope, out of the reach of the scavengers. Rending the silence of the curtain of rain, the echo of the hysterical laughter of frustrated hyenas resounds in the hollow of the ravine.

The False Scent

THE FIRST SIGN OF LIGHT dawned on the horizon above the open sea, but the leaden color of the water still blended with the deep amber of the sky, and from the sailboat heading toward the shore with the early-morning breeze, the Kilifi inlet appeared to be only a tongue of lighter-colored water licking the dark thighs of the rocks. In the hollow of the cliff, the seagulls were beginning to cry, plaintively, like sick children, in the semidarkness.

In one of the small coves of the inlet—still shrouded in fog—three men waited, hidden among the rocks and the bush covering the foot of the cliff, and the barrels of their rifles reflected the steely light of dawn. Lawrence Brown, Tony Allen, and Massimo San Miniato, had taken up different positions covering the stretch of beach separating the cliff and the sea; at the very edge of the water, the tire marks of a vehicle were visible in the sand, though the incoming tide began to wash them away. A muffled exclamation came from the dark as the tidewater rushed into a little channel and reached behind the rock where Tony Allen was hidden. On his hands and knees, he crawled to where Lawrence Brown crouched behind a pile of dry seaweed, calmly smoking his pipe, concealing its red glow between cupped hands.

"How long are we going to wait?" Tony whispered, crawling over the seaweed. "At the rate the tide's coming in we're going to have to swim out of here."

"If they're expecting a boat, I imagine they'll need a bit more light to enter the cove. And the higher the tide rises, the easier it's going to be to nab them. If we can't get out of here, Toffani surely won't be able to get his van out."

For two days in a row, barely stopping to eat or sleep, they had followed the trail of Paolo's kidnappers; their tracks had led upriver, leaving the edge of the stream for several miles at times in order to skirt a swamp or avoid a stretch of ground that was too open, and then continuing on, parallel to the stream bed once again. It seemed odd to Lawrence Brown that the poachers, so skillful at covering up their tracks and eluding their pursuers, should have left such an easy trail to follow, not even bothering to put out the embers of their campfires; rather than trying to give them the slip, the kidnappers were playing paper chase with them. They had even left an easily visible trail of roaches from the joints that Paolo had kept smoking—like the little pebbles that Tom Thumb kept dropping behind him—though the hunters refrained from pointing out this little detail to San Miniato.

"I don't know what they're up to," Lawrence Brown said on the evening of the second day. "But I think those guys are pulling our legs; they're leading us farther and farther away from the ranch. In this open terrain, where they can spy on our movements from any bit of higher ground, they can go on playing hide and seek with us as long as they want to."

"If they'd wanted to, they could have thrown us off their trail by crossing the river at some stony ford and then heading for Mackinnon Road, where a car could be waiting for them to take Paolo to a safer hiding place," Tony agreed.

"What can we do?" San Miniato asked anxiously. He had lost all his arrogance.

"The way the poachers are behaving reminds me of partridges that pretend to be wounded in order to lead hunters away from their nests," Brown said. "It seems as though they're using Paolo as a lure, to keep us away from some other place. I think we should go directly to Toffani's house. He's surely the one who's organized all this; he's the one who controls all the poachers' activities in this area, and they wouldn't have gone this far without his permission."

They reached the Tana that same night and hid the car in a clump of trees from which they could see the lights of Toffani's shack, on the other side of the river. They did not have to wait very long; through the binoculars they soon saw people entering and leaving the house, and the wind brought them the sound of a car taking off. In a few moments, Toffani appeared on the veranda of the house. He wore two bandoliers crossed over his chest and in his right hand was a double-barreled sawed-off shotgun; in the other hand he carried a large coil of thick rope and a lantern. His helpers were busy loading more lengths of stout rope and acetylene lanterns into the back of Toffani's light van; two heavy planks stuck out underneath the canvas top over the back.

"With equipment like that, I don't think they're exactly going crab fishing," Brown said.

"I think we did the right thing coming here," Tony answered, looking through the binoculars. "There's something fishy going on. And the one who's coming out now is Salim the Somali."

"There's no doubt that those guys know where they're hiding Paolo, and maybe if we follow them, they'll lead us straight there."

It wasn't easy for Tony to follow Toffani's van at a careful distance; Toffani knew every inch of the beaten-earth shortcuts and was driving at top speed without turning on his headlights. Luckily for Tony the moon had come out and the sand trail reflected its light; he could keep track of the car ahead by watching for the flick of the brake lights whenever Toffani took a turn too fast. After driving almost blind for two hours along those rough, twisting trails, they finally came out at the coast highway, beyond Malindi.

"You're going to have to follow closer behind them now, even at the risk that they'll sight us; if they reach the Kilifi ferry before we do, we'll have lost them," said Brown.

Just a few miles before they reached the Kilifi harbor, when they were already in sight of the lights of the ferry, Toffani turned off to the left, along a stony trail that wound down the side of the cliff to the beach. The hunters left their car hidden in the bushes at the top of the promontory and went down on foot, concealing themselves among the rocks, as the smugglers drove their car out to the end of the beach where the water formed a little natural cove.

"The only other access to the place they're headed is by sea," Brown said when he saw where they were going. "I've sometimes anchored my boat in that cove myself. They're undoubtedly waiting for a boat with contraband aboard, and if we watch every move we'll catch them red-handed."

Brown had not been wrong, for at first light a sailboat appeared in the distance, then, at the end of the beach lanterns blinked; their light barely penetrated the mist. Finally the breeze blew away the girdle of fog surrounding the cliff like a snake skin coiled around the rock; the sun broke through the cellophane of the horizon, separating the sky from the earth; a large dhow with a white sail appeared, cleaving the smooth waters of the bay. In the prow of the boat, almost as though he were riding astride the sea foam, stood a man dressed in ivory white, his blond hair ruffling in the wind.

"I'll be damned if it isn't that madman Townsend-Reeves!" Brown whispered.

It was indeed Alex Townsend-Reeves at the helm of the boat, with a couple of African seamen as crew. The dhow came in so close it almost touched the shore of the cove, and Toffani's men placed the big wooden planks on top of the collision mat on the side of the boat, improvising a ramp. They began to unload large, heavy-looking bales, wrapped in white plastic and protected by cord nets.

"Be careful, don't drop them in the water!" Toffani yelled. He was directing the operation from the beach, holding the double-barreled shotgun securely under his arm.

"We should move now, while they're busy unloading those bales," Brown said to Tony. "The only ones who have weapons with them are Toffani and Salim."

"I've already noticed. That bastard of a Salim is carrying the rifle he stole from my car! If I get my hands on him, he's going to wish he'd never been born. Let's go!"

Like a trained commando unit, the three hunters appeared from behind the rocks with their rifles aimed at the smugglers.

"Up with your hands and no tricks; if you move a muscle I'll blow your heads off!" Brown shouted. "And I'm warning you that my rifle's loaded with solid bullets that can drill through two or three of you at one shot."

No one moved. The breeze seemed to stop blowing and the seagulls seemed to suspend their flight; the only sound was the steady slap of the waves against the side of the boat.

"That's the way I like it, everybody nice and quiet, and I repeat: I don't want any funny business from you or I'll shoot to kill. I want you all to walk slowly toward the beach. You too, Alex; I'll kill you too if I have to. Easy does it; Salim and Toffani, you can drop your guns on the sand, and do it slowly"—and he repeated the order in Swahili.

Everything was going marvelously well, for Brown's powerful body

320

and his deep booming voice echoing off the rocks were as command-ing as his heavy weapon; all these poachers had heard of the manager of the Galana Ranch, and the mere thought that they might one day be within range of his rifle made them tremble.

"No tricks, Toffani. You know very well you can't bribe me with a couple of bottles of Chianti. If you had any idea how badly I've wanted to get my hands on you! Before we take a look at what's in those bales, you're going to tell us where you're holding San Miniato's son, because we know that Salim was involved."

San Miniato, who had behaved with exemplary discipline, could stand it no longer. Lunging at Toffani, he grabbed him by the neck and screamed at him in Italian:

"Bandit! Criminal! What have you done with my boy, you miser-able bastard?"

Wrestling, the two men rolled down to the very edge of the water. The two of them were rather evenly matched in size and build; they even looked alike, since neither had shaved for several days. Their style of fighting and the ungentlemanly tactics both of them used were very nearly identical; the struggle between them seemed to be a free for all, with no holds barred, fought between two brothers. In the end San Miniato's wrath and his paternal outrage won out; he sat himself down on Toffani's pot belly, and dealt him a rain of blows on the face that resounded noisily as they hit Toffani's wet cheeks.

"I give up, I give up," Toffani finally shouted, realizing that his opponent was ready to skin him alive; the tide was still coming in, and he was swallowing great mouthfuls of sea water.

"I'll tell you anything you want, but let me up: I'm drowning!"

San Miniato allowed him to sit up just far enough to get his head out of the water; Toffani coughed salty water.

"It's true. We kidnapped Paolo; we hoped that would keep you from bothering us. But I left instructions that they were to let him go—today, in fact—in the vicinity of Voi, and we haven't harmed a single hair on the kid's head. No one harmed him, and he probably hasn't even realized what happened; when they grabbed him, he was stoned out of his mind, and he kept smoking marijuana all day during the trip."

"My son stoned—what kind of bullshit are you trying to hand me, you bastard?" San Miniato screamed. "You're lying, you miserable shit!"

Alex Townsend-Reeves now took advantage of the distraction. He had crept up behind the two Italians unnoticed and, grabbing Toffani's double-barreled shotgun, aimed it at both the hunters.

"Brown, Allen," he said, with determination, "drop your guns, and you, San Miniato, leave that poor man alone. He's merely doing his duty, to a cause that neither of you, coming to hunt us like vermin, have any notion of. This shipment must arrive at its destination so that the liberation of this country, and of its people, who cry out for true independence, may come at last. I too have hidden my head in the sand like an ostrich; only now do I understand the need for a Second Emergence. These arms must get to Muriuki; he must liberate the country, take wing, and soar above a purified Africa like a phoenix." His eyes were gleaming with excitement, and his ivory-colored *kansus* stirred in the wind, like the tunic of a prophet.

Brown reacted first; he looked directly at Alex and began to walk toward him, very slowly.

"I don't know if Muriuki is going to take wing like a phoenix or like a vulture; what I am sure of is that you're out of your mind. You must be stoned on drugs or crazy drunk again. If this shipment was being sent to Muriuki, I must tell you that yesterday I heard on a broadcast from Britain that J. M. disappeared, and it's feared that the Government has liquidated him. The best thing you can do is drop that gun this minute if you don't want to get yourself in more trouble."

"That's not true. You're only saying that to confuse me," Alex roared, clutching the shotgun determinedly. "Muriuki is the prophet of liberation, and he can't have disappeared like that before the New Emergence has taken place. Furthermore," he added more reasonably, as though he were talking to himself, "this is the first time I've ever defended a just cause, and I can't miss this opportunity even though it costs me my life!"

"I swear by all that's holy I'll blow your brains out if you don't drop that gun this minute," Brown shouted, drawing closer to Alex and aiming his rifle at him. "Drop that gun, I said!"

"Get back or I'll shoot," Alex screamed, shouldering the shotgun. "You don't really know me, and this time I'm prepared to go all the way."

Brown realized they had reached a dangerous impasse, and lowered his voice.

"Come on, calm down, nothing's going to happen. Nobody's going to throw it up to you that you're abandoning a cause when the leader of it is dead or in prison. What's more," he added as he continued to approach Alex one slow step at a time, "you've never shot a gun, and the one you've got there is going to go off with a terrible explosion; at this distance, those slugs would slit my belly wide open as though you were cutting a big slice out of a watermelon, and all the beer I've drunk in my whole life would come pouring out, like a wineskin riddled with holes. You don't want to see a thing like that, right? You don't want to see all my shit come spilling out on this nice clean sand, or my blood spurting out over this beautiful transparent water. . . ."

Alex looked more and more horrified as Lawrence Brown spoke; at last he could bear no more and collapsed on the sand, clutching his belly as though he'd been hit.

"I can't, I can't," he sobbed, writhing on the sand. "I can't shoot a gun, I can't kill. I'm a no-good, impotent shit! Guni was right: I shouldn't have gotten involved in all this; I should have cut and run, the way I always have."

Brown had just picked up the gun that the poor wretch had dropped when Salim gave Tony, who was guarding him, a hard shove and began to run swiftly down the beach. Tony was just about to shoulder his gun and end Salim's sudden flight with one shot when Lawrence Brown stepped between him and the fleeing poacher.

"Leave him to me. I'll catch him. I'm going to teach him a good lesson!"

It seemed impossible that Brown, that mastodon, with his heavy muscle-bound shoulders and huge solid belly, could overtake that human antelope, whose feet barely touched the ground as he bounded across the sand. But Brown was driven by his pent-up, obsessive hatred of the vermin who had little by little stolen the game from his ranch; he took off in great long strides, his arms dangling like an orangutan's, and though his legs sank almost to his calves in the soft sand, he reached a long stretch of beach where the wet sand gave him a firmer foothold and began gaining on Salim. The seagulls pecking at small fish washed up on the beach took wing in great flocks.

Salim, who could already hear the hunter's heavy breathing close behind him, stumbled and fell face downward on the sand; Brown seized his chance and dived on top of him: The poacher reacted like a leopard that has been grabbed by the tail. With incredible agility, he slid out of the hunter's arms, sitting astride the huge body. The dagger in his hand, a precious *jembia* with a rhino-horn handle, flashed like lightning but Brown thrust his head to one side and the blade merely grazed his cheek. The hunter's fist shot upward like a pile driver and hit the poacher square in the jaw. Salim's body was flung half a foot upward by the violent impact and he collapsed unconscious on the sand, like a limp rag. The dagger was buried to the hilt in wet sand, its curved handle casting a long shadow across the white dune.

Brown rose to his feet and spat to one side in his characteristic fashion, then shook the sand off his clothes. He knelt down and tied Salim's hands behind his back, using his own belt and pressing his knee into the bandit's back, as though he were tying down a calf for branding.

At that moment the wind carried the sound of voices to them from the promontory, and they saw Judge McGredy coming down the path along the cliff, flanked by two Park rangers. The Judge was dressed in a safari outfit—a hunting jacket and shorts—and looked more stubby and bowlegged than ever. His police escort looked like a pair of gangling scarecrows; their uniforms hung on them like tents, and their stride could scarcely be described as martial.

"Well, well, what's been happening here? Whatever is all this?" McGredy said, reaching the stretch of beach where the boat lay offshore; he was panting slightly and his thick mane was badly rumpled by the wind.

Lawrence Brown explained the situation tersely. "These men have to be put in jail," he concluded, "they kidnapped my client's son and stole the guns in my car, and we've caught them red-handed bringing contraband into the country, which, from what I heard them say, must be an arms shipment. You can see if that's true by having a look at those bales they've unloaded."

The Judge stared at them with a gleam of malice. "It may well be that those goods aren't what you think," he said enigmatically. "But we had best get those bales unloaded and deposit them in a safe place. And then, if you'll be so kind, you'll accompany me to the police station in Malindi so that they can get a statement from you. And don't forget that you're to leave all your firearms there; the hunting ban decree also cancels all firearms permits."

He looked at the hunters and waited for their reaction. Lawrence Brown and Tony Allen looked as though one of those heavy bales had fallen on their heads.

"What's this hunting ban you're talking about?" said Brown. And Tony added: "And what's all this about turning in all our firearms, when I've just gotten back the rifle those criminals stole from me?"

324

With a deliberate gesture, the Judge reached into the inside pocket of his hunting jacket and took out a wrinkled, official-looking document.

"Here's the decree declaring a hunting ban. Dated yesterday. You can read it for yourselves. The second paragraph says quite clearly that all licenses for firearms are cancelled; and you will also note that the first paragraph cancels all hunting concessions as well—a provision that will no doubt affect the Galana Ranch."

With the blank expression of someone reading his own death sentence, Lawrence Brown took the paper and read aloud:

"One. The Government has decided to ban all hunting in Kenya with immediate effect. All hunting licenses are therefore cancelled forthwith. This applies to all individual hunters, professional hunters, and companies holding hunting concessions.

"Two. Nobody will be allowed to come into Kenya or enter any rural area of the country with firearms or any weapons for the purpose of hunting. All areas will now be converted for photographic safaris. The Firearms Bureau is instructed to cancel all licences for firearms related to hunting with immediate effect.

"Three. Officers of the Wildlife Conservation and Management Department, the Police, and all law-enforcement officers throughout the Republic, are instructed to implement this Government Order with immediate effect and stop all hunting activities from today."

Brown returned the document to McGredy without a word, and began to walk rigidly down the beach, like a robot. He strolled on the sand muttering words that would have made no sense to anyone unaware of his long obsession with the possibility of a total hunting ban.

"They've done it, the bastards have done it! They've wiped us out with one stroke of the pen and left the field wide open to poachers and dealers in contraband trophies; they'll leave this country as completely cleaned out of game as this beach. It's the end of wildlife!"

The others unloaded the boat, with McGredy supervising the operation from the shore; Brown continued to walk down the beach at the water's edge, until he very nearly stumbled over Salim, still lying tied up on the beach, the wash of the tide wetting the sand beneath his motionless body. He was half-conscious and curled up in a ball, like Friday at the feet of Robinson Crusoe when the latter rescued him from his pursuers. Brown bent down, and using Salim's

325

dagger, cut him loose. Salim shook his arms and his legs and his head, like a bird shaking its wet feathers and took off at a run; still stunned perhaps, he headed straight for the water. A little sailboat with wooden outriggers was passing by just then; the lone old fisherman aboard was guiding it with the sail rope knotted around his big toe. Salim plunged into the water and began to swim toward it, making signs to its occupant to pick him up. The fisherman spotted him, and coming in closer to shore, helped Salim aboard; the poacher hoisted himself up onto the prow and stood motionless as the craft again headed out to the open sea.

When Judge McGredy, who was supervising the unloading of the bales, realized what had happened, he walked down the beach to Lawrence Brown.

"Why did you do that?" the Judge asked. "That man's wanted by the authorities."

"That may be," Brown answered, unperturbed. "But putting Salim in jail would be like putting an antelope in a cage. Anyway, it's the end of the game."

As the last bale was shoved down the improvised ramp, it slipped off and fell into the water with a great splash. The heavy bale should have sunk straight to the bottom, though the water was only a few feet deep, but unexpectedly, it floated on the surface and the tide began to carry it away from the boat.

"Hey, look, it's floating away!" Lawrence Brown shouted, leaping into the water. "We'll lose the arms—come help me!"

Two men jumped into the water up to their waists and managed to rescue the bale and push it to shore. Judge McGredy had also jumped into the water after rolling up the bottom of his shorts, and before they could push the bale up onto the beach, he said: "Wait a minute, leave it there. I'm certain that packet doesn't contain arms, or anything like arms. You'll see—now!"

He took a jackknife from his pocket, cut through the cords of the netting protecting the bale, and slashed the plastic wrapping: A stream of sawdust poured out, and large chunks of bricks and stones cascaded out and fell into the sea. The water seeped into the plastic wrapping, soaking the sawdust, and in seconds the big bale deflated like a balloon and sank to the bottom, sending quantities of bubbles to the surface.

The Judge was delighted with his performance, just like a sleight-of-hand artist who has just pulled off a spectacular trick. The others watched, open-mouthed with astonishment.

326

"See? No arms or anything else; just a little sawdust and some rubble. I knew it all the time!"

"But didn't Alex just say it was an arms shipment?" Tony asked. "Would they have gone to all this trouble just to unload a few bales of rubbish on the beach?"

It was obvious that Bwana Maximum thoroughly enjoyed their confusion.

"Tell me one thing, Brown. If you had a top-secret, extremely tricky job you needed done, would you entrust it to characters like Toffani or Alex Townsend-Reeves so that the first time they got drunk or slept with a whore everybody would know? No, surely not. Muriuki *wanted* the authorities to find out, and that's why he turned the job over to these two. He even made sure that fake bills of lading for the shipment would fall into our hands, just in case it took us too long to swallow the bait."

"So there's no such shipment then?" Alex asked, appalled at having taken so great a risk to transport bales of worthless trash.

"Yes, of course the arms shipment existed, but Muriuki wasn't stupid enough to bring it into the country through Mombasa, knowing that the authorities were watching that area like hawks, especially after Murphy's accident. It entered the country via Uganda, and we just found it on a coffee plantation at Eldama Ravine."

"I still don't understand," Brown interrupted him. "Why organize the whole complicated business of sending a false shipment?"

"That sly fox Muriuki knew we were on his tail, and wanted to head us off in the wrong direction. As a hunter, you must know that if an animal is being hotly pursued by the hounds, he'll mingle his tracks with those of one of his fellows—one that's possibly younger and less clever—fooling the hounds and sending them off after the wrong quarry."

"Neat trick," said Brown. "It's called giving the change or putting the hounds on the wrong scent."

No one spoke. The wind had shifted, sending the fisherman's outrigger canoe over the water at a good clip; for a few seconds Salim's profile was still visible, sharply outlined against the red ball of the sun just coming up over the horizon.

Epilogue

THE MASERU HUNT CLUB was celebrating the opening of the season on the first Sunday in October, which coincided with the arrival of the first rains. It was a real spectacle, on a radiant morning such as this, to see all the horsemen wearing impeccable red and black riding costumes, in accordance with the British fox-hunting tradition, slowly canter across the broad plains of Langata, and the pack of joyous hounds following the clearly marked trail in the grass still damp from the night's downpour.

Fortunately, the hunting ban declared the day before in no way affected the activities of the club; the members had long since given up hunting real foxes, which had to be brought from England, at exorbitant prices, and contented themselves with following an artificial scent, "the drag," laid down beforehand by an African with good legs who ran in front of the dogs, with a big enough lead so that the pack wasn't able to catch up with him. On the other hand, the trail did not lack rough stretches, tall hedges, and steep cliffs, where the horsemen could give proof of their daring and skill, especially in the zone bordering the National Park where, very often, the track of an antelope crossed the artificial trail, or the hounds came upon a pride of lions hidden in the dense brush, who with a loud roar or two, sent the pack running in the opposite direction, momentarily giving rise to a thrilling mixture of fear and joy in the field.

That same morning, on arriving at the edge of a deep ravine, with a little *arroyo* swollen from the recent rains running through its bottom, the hounds left the artificial scent, crossed the brook, and entered a clump of trees with dense underbrush, barking wildly. Prince Jean-Humbert d'Alembert, who was an excellent equestrian and always rode at the head of the field, on seeing the pack stray off, dug in his spurs, obliging his mount to descend the steep slope and clear the raging stream in one clean leap. Once on the other side, the horseman had to hunch over in the saddle and part the branches with his riding crop to keep from getting his face scratched. In a little clearing in the underbrush, the hounds were milling about the trunk of a large thorny acacia. The rider noted that the horse was trembling beneath the saddle like a creature possessed, and had pricked up its ears.

The Prince's eyes were dazzled for a few seconds as he emerged from the shadow of the thicket into the clearing. But on looking up, he suddenly found himself confronting the mutilated body of J. Muriuki, which the vagabonds who had found it the night before had tied to the tallest fork of the acacia, out of the reach of hyenas. The horseman tried to cry out, but the only sound that emerged was a low moan, and he fell onto the wet grass in a dead faint as his spirited mount ran off across the plain at a full gallop.

That morning, Bob Fender woke up fairly late; perhaps because of his exhaustion from the day before, he had had a troubled night's sleep. The image of the ragged creatures he had seen from the window of his room, catching dragonflies in the rain, had haunted him in his dreams, with surrealist variations. The sun was already streaming through the curtains with the horrid orange diamonds, and even before he was fully awake, he had the acutely painful sensation that something was all wrong. Melissa, of course.

During the trip to Narumoro, he had managed to put that obsession out of his mind, but suddenly, on finding himself alone in his room, his anxiety and desire exploded inside him, making him feel nauseated. It was useless to think that it was only logical that such an intense and unexpected relationship should end in the same way that it had begun. The smell of the eucalyptuses of Rosslyn still lingered in his nostrils, and the dust of the trails through the Karura woods still seared his throat. He lay there staring at the telephone, which shined in the semidarkness with a beckoning gleam, but he managed to restrain the impulse to stretch out his hand and dial the Turners' number. It was hardly likely that they had come back this early from their weekend. Besides, having been left in the lurch the other day, he ought to let Melissa be the one to take the first step if he wanted to keep at least a minimum of dignity.

He finally flung the sheet back and leaped out of bed and into the shower, trying to banish those thoughts from his mind. But he was

329

still so tense that he nicked his face several times with the razor while shaving. The telephone rang in the bedroom, and Bob tripped on the rug and knocked over the breakfast tray as he came out of the bathroom. He answered in a deliberately distant tone of voice that he hoped sounded relaxed, in case it was Melissa. But it was Ambassador Poire, who needed to see him rather urgently and was inviting him to tea at his residence. As he spoke with him, Bob contemplated the little dish of marmalade lying upside down and the coffee spilled on the rug; he would come immediately, of course. He realized that the Ambassador's voice sounded unusually tense and concerned. What could be troubling him so much that he would call on a Sunday morning?

On stepping out into the street to get the car, Bob found the center of the city oddly deserted. What had happened to the hordes of beggars and mountebanks that usually hung around the hotel pestering tourists? It was as though the first rains had swept those vagabonds from the sidewalks, just as the swarms of dragonflies the night before had disappeared, leaving the streets carpeted with thousands of transparent wings. On certain corners, however, there were little knots of Africans, excitedly whispering to each other; but they fell silent and moved away as they saw him approach. Bob was reminded of what happened at Galana when the hunters downed an antelope: A few seconds later, from the most desolate wasteland, a number of human silhouettes inevitably emerged and gathered in clusters a certain distance away, in the shade of an acacia, waiting for the skinners to finish their work so as to fling themselves on the animal's remains. What could the victim of these little conspiratorial gatherings be this time?

As he went up to the parking lot, where Murphy's Toyota was, he was met by a great gust of fresh air that brought with it the smell of damp grass from the plains. In the empty space between two buildings he caught sight of the outline of the hills, so sharp in the clean air that it was as though he could reach out and touch them. When he put the key in the ignition, a strange sensation ran through his entire body, as though an umbilical cord connected the mechanical bowels of the car and his own insides. He could not get Melissa out of his mind: The leather of the seats still gave off her woman's scent and the red earth of the Karura trails was sticking to the tires still. And though he turned into Uhuru Avenue, heading toward the Muthaiga district, Bob sensed that a secret instinct to head back to a favorite haunt would sooner or later make the steering wheel turn toward the coffee plantations of Rosslyn, where the Turners lived.

On reaching the avenue that the Embassy was on, the jacaranda flowers blown off the trees by the storm crunched beneath the wheels of the Toyota, just as on the morning he had arrived in Nairobi, when the taxi driver had taken him by mistake to the Ambassador's residence. Bob remembered that then, too, it had rained the night before, and the garden had given off that particular smell of wet grass and dead leaves that had remained engraved in his memory as the characteristic smell of the country: the smell of Africa. The Ambassador received him in the same study, next to the dining room, where, as before, papers were scattered about. He was wearing the same bedroom slippers, and the red satin bathrobe that had been a gift from the boxer Castor Kingley. This time, however, as though to make his costume look even more realistic, the Ambassador had a big dark swelling around one eye and a little piece of adhesive tape on his nose; his bruises appeared to be very recent ones.

"A rather stupid mishap," W. D. Poire commented, noting that Bob was staring at him, without daring to ask the obvious question. "It so happens that the night guards here at the residence have gotten into the damnable habit of taking shelter underneath the balcony of my bedroom when it rains, and keep me awake all night long with their incessant jabbering and squabbling. I've never wanted to say anything to them, but last night I'd had quite enough and I went out to ask them to go somewhere else. What I didn't know was that to ward off the cold they're in the habit of bringing a bottle of that horrible brandy of theirs with them, and when they've been drinking, they don't listen to reason or obey their superiors. Instead of doing as I asked, they jeered and hooted and roughed me up; Martha, my wife, had to come out in the rain to defend me."

"What an unpleasant incident! I'm very sorry."

"What hurts me the most is being forced to recognize that these people only react when you deal with them with a heavy hand, the way their old colonial masters did. Not to mention the fact that in my case it irritates them, I think, that I'm black like them yet can't talk to them in Swahili."

Bob thought that it was rather sad that this man had crossed the ocean with open arms to meet his blood brothers, and they in turn had received him by manhandling him; but undoubtedly W. D. Poire unconsciously treated them with a paternalism that led them to rebel.

"In any event," the Ambassador went on, lightly scratching his bruised eyelid, "I didn't ask you to come here to tell you about my problems with the *askaris*. There are a number of things that are troubling me, matters that somehow are related to you. Have you seen the decree banning all hunting?"

Bob shook his head, and the Ambassador searched about among the papers that he had scattered about all over the rug, finally handing him one bearing the Presidential seal and dated the day before. Bob read it attentively before answering.

"Well, it would appear that the ecologists got their way. What they don't know is that if the Government doesn't try at the same time to stop the activities of the poachers and the illegal traffic in trophies, the measure may well be counterproductive. My stay at Galana has made me more realistic about the whole subject of conservation."

"What's suspicious is their having decided to declare the ban like that, from one day to the next, when they've been resisting doing so for so long; it's common knowledge that a number of members of the Government were involved up to their necks in the trophy racket."

"To what do you attribute this sudden change in attitude?"

"I think it's a grandstand play, to win prestige both at the international level, among the UNICORN delegates, and domestically. Many Africans see the world of safaris and "white hunters" as the last vestige of colonialism. You remember that Muriuki himself asked the Government to declare the hunting ban, in his speech to the Parliament."

The Ambassador paused for a moment before going on, lowering his voice slightly, as though he were afraid that they were being overheard.

"In reality, all this is only a smoke screen to hide a much more serious political event—something as serious as the kidnapping and possible murder of the leader of the opposition."

"Of J. Muriuki?"

"Himself. Yesterday afternoon, as Muriuki was returning from the races, he was detained by members of the Special Branch right outside the door of the Hilton, and since then nobody's seen him."

"Good heavens, I see now why the streets were so deserted when I came back to the hotel. They must have kidnapped him just minutes before I arrived from Mount Kenya. What do you think they're going to do with him?"

"Knowing the political habits of this country, and the unquestionable danger to the present Government that Muriuki represented, I wouldn't be at all surprised if they've decided to make him disappear for good."

"How awful! In other words, they're placing a ban on hunting animals and at the same time letting it be open season on the opposition?"

"Something like that. African politics are sometimes extremely tortuous. In any event, when Muriuki's supporters get wind of this maneuver, I don't think they're going to sit twiddling their thumbs. Now that the rains have come, we might very well see something besides grass start growing." He paused again, and leaned over closer to Bob. "Look, Fender, there are stormy days in the offing and— please don't take offense—I'd rest easier if you took the first plane out of here and went quietly back to the coast. I presume you'll still have time enough to complete your study on grass."

Bob was so taken aback he didn't answer for a few moments.

"After you called me away from Galana, leaving the project that I'd been preparing for months at a standstill, you're now asking me to go back there, right in the middle of the Conference?"

"There are days of turmoil ahead. This city may become the epicenter of a hurricane that's been building up for some time, and to be frank with you, I'm deeply concerned about your safety."

"Why should you be concerned about my safety, and not about that of any of the other delegates, or that of American residents in Nairobi?"

"Because of a series of circumstances, which would take me too long to explain, you happen to be in the very eye of the storm. You are undoubtedly not aware of it, but you're involved in the political intrigue that has cost J. Muriuki his life. At this point you might well arouse both the suspicions of the Special Branch, because they think you've poked your nose into matters that are their business to investigate, and desires for vengeance on the part of the opposition, who might think that you played a role in Muriuki's kidnapping."

"I'm tired of all this nonsense; you must be joking."

"I wish I were, but the truth of the matter is that, through a series of coincidences, you have come to be smack in the middle of a dangerous political intrigue, whose ramifications and consequences lie beyond my area of responsibility. If you don't leave Nairobi, I can do very little to guarantee your safety; as a delegate to UNICORN, you do not even have diplomatic immunity."

"I at least hope you're not one of those who think that I might be involved in some sort of absurd spy network or something like that. As Ambassador, you must know that that's not true!"

"What matters is not so much what I know, but what other people with fewer scruples think. Unfortunately, in Africa a person's life isn't worth much of anything."

"I think I've already heard something like that. You hold to the same theory as Bwana Maximum: What's most important is what the chicken thinks, right?"

"I don't have any idea what chicken you're talking about, but if that's what Judge McGredy told you, it's bound to be true. He's the person to whom the authorities here have given the task of protecting you; they were afraid the same thing might happen to you as happened to John Murphy."

"I don't know exactly what happened to John, but what I really don't understand is why they always connect him with me. The truth of the matter is that, since our college times, we'd completely lost contact with each other, and it was only because of my study of grass that we got in touch with each other again recently. Could you explain to me what John Murphy was really up to?"

The Ambassador gave him a long look before answering.

"As a matter of fact, Fender, I think you have the right to know certain things; we might perhaps have avoided certain problems if we'd been franker with you from the beginning. But if you don't mind, we'll go on talking in the garden. It's beginning to be too hot here in the study and . . ." he said, arching his eyebrows in the direction of the door to indicate to Bob that there might be someone eavesdropping. "If you'll wait for me for a moment, I'll go upstairs and change clothes."

While he waited for the Ambassador to come back, Bob went out onto the porch. The smell of vegetation was heightened by the dampness, and the only sound was the monotonous buzzing of the horse-flies above the flowerbeds. He remembered the first time he'd gone out to the Muthaiga Club, accompanied by Ralph Maguire, and the sensation of vertigo produced by the equatorial sun, the sounds of myriad insects, and the intense fragrance of the plants. Contrary to what Maguire had said that day, however, Bob knew now that the climate in Africa was not a figment of the European imagination but the very essence of the continent, the factor that determined all the rest. What mattered here was the color of the sky, the drifting of the clouds, the undulation of the horizon. In the midst of this grandeur, man was merely an accident of the landscape, with no particular importance or meaning. His entire stay in Kenya, Bob thought, had taken place between two tropical downpours—the heavy shower that had preceded him on the day he arrived, and the beginning of the short rains, also called the grass rains.

In a few moments, W. D. Poire reappeared, wearing tennis shoes and a red cotton sweat suit that was really a variation of his boxer costume, and they began walking down the avenue of trees that led to the outside gate of the grounds. As he strode along, Bob intentionally stepped on the fallen jacaranda flowers, which made a characteristic little *pop* as they exploded, like tiny burst balloons.

"You may perhaps remember the circumstances of your arrival in Nairobi," the Ambassador said, once he'd decided that they were far enough away from the house. "Scarcely two weeks after the accident that cost John Murphy his life."

"It would be extremely hard for me to forget that day. I heard the news right out there at the airport . . . and to top it all off, they'd lost my luggage."

"What you don't know is that around that very time we were expecting an agent from our intelligence service, who was coming to investigate the circumstances surrounding the accident. Ordinarily, I do my best to remain on the sidelines in such cases, since in my view the ambassador's task is not to mastermind the intelligence network, but since he was a colleague of mine, I couldn't allow him to disappear in thin air in the Tsavo desert under suspicious circumstances. I myself requested that an agent be sent, thus overriding Maguire, who was of the opinion that it was better to let sleeping dogs lie. And so, perhaps because I was still somewhat obsessed by Murphy's death, when you turned up at the Embassy I thought you were the man we were waiting for. When I gave you certain advice about your mission, I wasn't referring to your study on grass, but to the investigation of the accident on Mackinnon Road!"

"Don't you think that if you'd told me what had happened, I myself might have been able to clear up the mistake?" Bob said, after halting in his tracks for a moment. "I had in fact noticed something strange about our first conversation, but I was worn out from the trip and it would never have occurred to me that that was the reason."

"I immediately sent Maguire to talk to you and try to clear up the mistake, but at that moment we couldn't come right out and tell you either: That would have put the entire operation in jeopardy. And in the end they didn't even send the agent; I suppose Maguire's opinion prevailed over mine at the State Department; I'm not a career diplomat, after all!"

"What I still don't understand is why you people made me come back to Nairobi, thereby allowing the misunderstanding to go on."

"I did so in order to ensure your safety, since shortly after you left here, we found out that there were plans afoot to bring in a contraband arms shipment in the very area that you were in, and the persons who had thought that you were an agent might suspect that you were also involved in the arms smuggling operation. So I decided to get you out of trouble, using the Conference as the pretext. Although, as things have turned out, I'm afraid I didn't succeed," the Ambassador concluded, raising his two hands in a gesture of helplessness.

On leaving the residence, Bob drove along distractedly, thinking about all that, and when he looked around he saw that he had turned off the highway leading to Nairobi and was on the road to Limuru, a couple of miles from Rosslyn. A powerful instinct that—the one that makes you head back to a favorite haunt! Since he'd come this far, he decided that it was best to act as naturally as possible and present himself at the Turners' house as though nothing had happened.

On reaching the end of the little gravel road that wound in and out among the coffee plantations, he saw to his surprise that the wooden gate of the garden was standing wide open; and the watchmen were not at their posts. He also noted that the avenue of rolled earth beneath the trees, always so immaculately kept, was covered with a thick carpet of little branches and dead leaves blown off in the storm. Just one night's rain had caused a green fuzz to start growing along the edges of the sloping lawn, giving the entire grounds a rather abandoned look. Before getting out of the car and walking in through the door which stood ajar, Bob realized that the house was deserted: He did not even bother to knock, knowing that no one would answer. He walked through the rooms, listening to the echo of his own footsteps. Most of the furniture was still in its usual place, but here and there a little engraving or two, the carved ivory pieces in the living room, the silver ash trays, were missing: the sort of small objects of value that a person takes with him when he leaves a place for good.

All of a sudden Bob remembered the garret, and a spark of curiosity gleamed in his mind, mingled with an undeniable leap of hope: What might she have left in that attic full of ill-assorted objects, as witness to their first embraces? He went up the stairs two by two and crossed the terrace like a gust of wind, slipping on the puddles left by the rain. But when he pushed open the French door, protected by a little burlap curtain, he found the room completely empty. The whitewashed walls were bare and the floor, without a single rug or mat, turned out to be made of grimy, decaying planks—what had happened to all those antelope and leopard skins that had covered the floor, and the silky zebra skin that Melissa had stretched out on, with feline movements? Only the huge aquarium was still in its usual place, projecting its watery reflection on the bare walls, making the room look even more cold and desolate.

At that moment, he heard a little tapping on the glass and remembered the bird that used to come to peck at its reflection in the window. The noise, however, was not coming from there, but from the door. On turning around, Bob spied the silhouette of a man outlined on the glass and through the burlap curtain he recognized the squat figure and disproportionately large head of Judge McGredy. He was pressing his unruly mane against the wooden crossbars, like a caged lion, as he rapped impatiently with his kunckles on the glass panes.

"McGredy! What are you doing here?" Bob exclaimed as he opened the door, which had gotten stuck in its frame because of the humidity. "I thought you were down on the coast this weekend."

"As a matter of fact, that's where I was till noon today, but I took the plane from Mombasa because I wanted to talk to you."

"Well, well. I'm going to end up thinking I'm somebody important, because everybody wants to see me immediately. I'll tell you beforehand, though, that if it has something to do with my supposed double personality, the whole mystery has been cleared up. I've just talked with Ambassador Poire, who has explained the reason for the misunderstanding regarding my humble self that occurred on my arrival in Nairobi."

They sat down on a wooden bench in one corner of the terrace, from which there was a lovely panoramic view of the coffee plantations and the Karura forest in the background. Bob passed on to the Judge the explanation he had been given by W. D. Poire, though he noticed that as he was talking a hint of a sarcastic smile began to appear on the Judge's lips, and when he had finished his story, Mc-

Gredy sat there looking at him with that characteristic mocking expression of his.

"So that's what the American Ambassador told you, is it?" he asked Bob, not disguising his needling tone of voice.

"Yes, why do you ask? Don't you think he told me the truth?"

"No, what he told you is no doubt part of the truth, but not the whole truth. I don't believe the Ambassador is altogether aware of the activities of the intelligence agencies, in accordance with the well-known theory that it's better for the left hand not to know what the right hand is doing. Not to mention the fact that his own Deputy has been systematically keeping information from him. The only thing that Poire and I see eye to eye on is that you must leave Nairobi as quickly as possible if you don't want your bones to end up bleaching on the crest of the hills."

The Judge paused as he rummaged in the pocket of his safari jacket for one of his foul-smelling cigarettes; it refused for some time to catch the flame, but finally he got it lit.

"The packet is wet from sea water," the Judge said, inhaling deeply. "Just this morning, at the coast, I had an interesting encounter with a pack of scoundrels who were trying to unload—with the greatest secrecy—a mysterious shipment of bales of sawdust with rocks and stones inside. This was the famous arms shipment that the Ambassador was referring to, and that gave me a few headaches too. A false scent, naturally, to mislead the authorities as to the real route of the shipment, for the arms have been safe and sound all this time, hidden among sacks of coffee on a state in Eldama Ravine."

"Wait a minute! That's precisely where the Turners have their coffee state!" Bob interrupted him, very excited. "Don't tell me that they're involved in this whole business too?"

"We'll talk about that later, but don't interrupt me now if you want to know the true story. According to what I've been able to discover, the mistake about your identity came about not only through a series of unfortunate circumstances, but was also partly intentional. In reality, the Yankee intelligence services never intended to send an agent to investigate Murphy's death. But once you arrived, they used you as a lure to put the rival services on a false trail and make them believe the Americans were interested in finding out what had happened on Mackinnon Road."

"Of course they were interested. They would want to find out what happened to Murphy, wouldn't they?"

338

The Judge looked at him with a mischievous gleam in his eye that was almost childish.

"Didn't it ever enter your mind that the ones who set up the accident were the Americans themselves? No, don't look at me like that. What really happened is that the Yankee services had enlisted John to infiltrate opposition circles, and if possible become friends with Muriuki himself so as to wangle information out of him. But Murphy carried out his mission so well that he not only gained Muriuki's confidence but became a sympathizer of his movement and began to pass on to him certain information to which his job at the Embassy gave him access. As you can imagine, the intelligence agencies of the West couldn't stand by with their arms folded while one of their principal agents passed over to the enemy."

"It's hard to believe but at least he didn't do it for the money; that wasn't like him!"

"I'm of the same opinion. There's no question that that wretched Muriuki had a certain charisma, a very special magnetism. As I see it, Murphy was a little off his rocker too, and behind his cynical manner he had a sort of queer idealism. It could well be that when he went down to the coast that last time it was to get everything set up for the contraband arms shipment, at Muriuki's request; he knew every twist and turn of those back roads. So after his death, Ndume decided to change the route that the arms would arrive by, thinking that area would be too closely watched. He decided to send the contraband by way of the Uganda border, and looked around for someone who wouldn't arouse suspicion to handle the shipment."

"Philip Turner?"

"As a matter of fact, he knew that the Turners could be recruited quite easily because they were an ambitious couple who lived beyond their means and were already in a shaky position financially. Since Philip often made trips to Uganda, he could use him as the go-between, and the coffee plantation at Eldama Ravine was an ideal hiding place. Muriuki knew how to propose the deal in such a way that it wasn't easy to turn him down; his one error was to make Melissa Turner go out with you in order to find out how you figured in the whole picture. As we were having you watched, that's what put us on the trail connecting the Turners and Muriuki and finally led us to the arms cache."

"Well, I'm glad I was useful for something at least," Bob commented, not bothering to hide a slight trace of bitterness.

"I warned you, you'll remember, that a person ends up being what other people think he is. If you'd really come to investigate the Murphy affair and Muriuki's plot, you wouldn't have been able to fulfill your mssion any more successfully."

As they were talking, the great snow-covered peak of Mount Kenya had appeared behind the woods of Karura, at the very horizon line filled with roiling storm-clouds. It hung, far in the distance and perfectly inaccessible, against the smooth cellophane of newly washed air. When Bob and the Judge caught sight of that apparition, they fell silent for a moment, but immediately realized that in the face of that caprice of the African light and climate, it was better not to pay too much attention and go on talking as though it were nothing out of the ordinary. Perhaps if they turned around to look, the mountain would vanish, like the gazelle that makes its fleeting appearance in a clearing of the woods, ready to disappear in the bush at the slightest movement.